Strawberry Fields

Jess sighed and stood still for a moment, doubly burdened by the sleeping child and the food. What should she do for the best? Grace was a dear little soul but she'd never manage bread and cheese, not with the fever she'd had. Jess had given her the buttermilk, warmed, with bread crumbled into it and the kid had scarcely managed two mouthfuls before she fell asleep again. But Mollie must be very hungry, and Jess herself was as empty as a drum. If I don't get something inside me soon I'll be no good to the others, Jess thought, immediately practical. I'll go somewhere quiet, eat some bread and cheese and a bun, feed Mollie with the milk and some bread in it, and then go home with what's left.

But where to go? Jess looked around her. The snow was falling thickly but surely there must be a suitable place where she could make up some food for the baby and feed her, undisturbed?

Katie Flynn has lived in the Northwest for thirty-two years. A compulsive writer, she started with short stories and articles and many of her early stories were broadcast on Radio Mersey. She decided to write a series set entirely in Liverpool after a family get-together when the older people began to reminisce about the Liverpool of their childhood.

KATIE FLYNN
Strawberry Fields

ARROW

Reprinted in Arrow Books, 1998

3 5 7 9 10 8 6 4 2

First published in the United Kingdom in 1996
by William Heinemann Ltd

This edition first published in 1997 by Mandarin Paperbacks
and reprinted once

Arrow Books
The Random House Group Limited
20 Vauxhall Bridge Road, London, SW1V 2SA

Random House Australia (Pty) Limited
20 Alfred Street, Milsons Point, Sydney,
New South Wales 2061, Australia

Random House New Zealand Limited
18 Poland Road, Glenfield
Auckland 10, New Zealand

Random House (Pty) Limited
Endulini, 5a Jubilee Road, Parktown 2193, South Africa

The Random House Group Limited Reg. No. 954009

www.randomhouse.co.uk

A CIP catalogue record for this book is available from the British Library

Papers used by Random House are natural,
recyclable products made from wood grown in
sustainable forests. The manufacturing processes conform to
the environmental regulations of the country of origin

Printed and bound in Norway
by AIT Trondheim AS

ISBN 0 09 9416 03 4

For Sally Mimnagh,

who gives more than she takes . . .

and for the famous Mimnagh cats!

Acknowledgements

My thanks go first to Mrs Violet McKay for telling me about her childhood spent around Stanley Road and Snowdrop Street, and then to Ruth Baker, whose family were brought up in the Walton Road area and who, as a Salvationist, was able to set my feet firmly on the right path when it came to writing about the Army.

Still in Liverpool, I am very grateful to Captain Ray Collings of the Salvation Army for all the help unstintingly given, and in particular for taking me and my husband to meet Colonel Martha Osborne, who not only has an incredibly detailed and accurate memory, invaluable to anyone writing about the past, but whose sense of fun and wonderful narrative style have given me enough material for the next book as well as this one – many, many thanks, Martha! Thanks, also, to Tom Officer for lending me books on Ireland, and to Chris Billing for the loan of computer parts when I was desperate.

And moving over to Ireland, thanks to the staff of the Gilbert Library, who took endless trouble to find the books and information I needed. Then there was Billy Doren, whose knowledge of Dublin – and the books written about it – was second to none, and last but not least, my thanks to Sally Mimnagh, who told me more about the Irish in one evening than I could have learned from books in a dozen years.

Chapter One

December 1924

It was Christmas Day, 1924, and it was snowing. What was more, the snow was lying. Sefton Park was a wonderland, the grass smoothly blanketed, the trees outlined in white. All the way down Aigburth Road Sara Cordwainer, who was twelve years old, admired the magical scene. She sat between her mother and father in their big Rolls-Royce motor car, with the chauffeur, Robson, cut off from them by a glass panel, and stared with all her might, convinced that the snow had come because she had been good – and because it was Christmas, naturally.

Already, her day was planned. Church first, which was much more exciting on Christmas Day than on any other day of the year, then round to Snowdrop Street to pick up her old nanny, and home for all the wonders of Christmas dinner – roast turkey, crackers, a plum pudding to which Cook would set light just before she brought it into the room – and at tea time, presents round the Christmas tree in the white drawing room.

There would be a present at church today, too. The Reverend Atwell had started giving the young members of his congregation a present at the Christmas morning service six years earlier, and now it was expected. They were religious presents, of course, but nonetheless welcome, because they heralded the start of Christmas proper, Sara thought. She had kept every-thing the Reverend Atwell had given her, had them still. The first one had been quite simple; a beautiful picture of Jesus in his long white robe with a number of small children clustered at his knee. *Suffer the little children* . . . the text beneath the picture read.

Ever since then the small, gaily wrapped parcels had been handed out at the church door as the congregation were leaving. Nanny, who had retired when Sara started school, didn't approve. 'You get enough presents with-out the church handin' you more stuff,' Nanny had said, that first time. 'There's kids down Kirkdale and Bootle who don't get one present come Christmas, let alone half a dozen. Why don't the Reverend Atwell think of them, eh, stead of givin' hand-outs to folk what've got more than they know what to do with?'

'I don't know,' Sara said, puzzled. Surely there was no such thing as a child without presents on Christmas Day? Parents, uncles, cousins, friends, they all gave Christmas presents, so surely, unless a child was posi-tively steeped in sin, it would find something in its stocking on Christmas Day? 'If they came to our church they'd get a present though, Nanny. Why don't they come to our church?'

'Because they go to their own churches, that's what,' Nanny said with a snap in her voice. 'I'd like to see the reverend gentleman's face if the Carberys or the Sullivans turned up at 'is church!'

'Oh, well, if they go to their own churches, they'll get their presents there,' Sara said, very relieved. 'And if they don't go to church . . . but I expect they do, even the poor ones. Church is free, isn't it, Nanny? No one pays to go to church, it isn't like the tram.'

Nanny had explained to her that the small boys who hung on to the back of the trams did so because they had no pennies for a fare. 'They'd sooner ride inside, specially when it's cold an' snowy,' she said. 'But they need any pennies they get for other things ... food, coal ...'

But now, sitting snugly between her parents as the big car sailed smoothly churchwards, Sara was thinking more about the joys of Christmas than about Nanny's disapproval of the Reverend Atwell. At Christmas there was lovely food, nuts and chocolates on the sideboard, a big bowl of fruit which anyone could eat. Children were not usually encouraged to eat rich food, but Christmas was different. Why, this very morning schoolroom breakfast had included bacon and egg as well as the more usual groats and bread and butter. Sara was not particularly interested in food, but she was very conscious of atmosphere, and she loved the sparkle and excitement of Christmas, the fact that Nanny came to stay for two whole days, the festive air, even the groups of ragged children singing carols. The servants usually gave such singers mince pies and sometimes pennies, though Sara's parents did not approve.

'It encourages them to beg for money instead of working for it,' Sara's mother had said, and her father, equally against the practice, said that children were the responsibility of their own parents, not the parents of others.

But even so, Sara felt unusually content. She did not always enjoy school holidays, but this year she had spent a lot of time with Jane Carew, one of the maids. She and Jane had spent a happy afternoon threading peanuts on strings which they then hung outside the schoolroom window. Watching the blue tits, chaffinches and other little birds pecking contentedly at the nuts was a winter pleasure which never palled.

The car began to slow as it reached the street upon which the church was situated. There were people outside already, talking and laughing, and as the Cordwainers got out of the motor snow began to fall once more.

'More snow! I'll make a snowman in the park after luncheon,' Sara said, scarcely realising she had spoken aloud until her mother rounded on her.

'In the park, on Christmas Day? I don't think so, Sara, that wouldn't be at all suitable. Besides, you'll be busy entertaining Nanny.'

'Well, the garden, then,' Sara said equably. 'Nanny can watch; I'll make one in the garden.'

Her father turned and looked down at her. It struck Sara suddenly that he looked at her as though he didn't like her very much. So she smiled at him questioningly, though she had to tilt her head back to do so, for he was a tall, thin man. Disappointingly however, he did not smile back: he frowned. 'Not the garden,' he said sharply. 'Snow is only beautiful when it's untrodden. I won't have you churning up the snow in the garden. Get Nanny to show you a card game . . . or you could read to her.'

The chauffeur, about to close the car door behind them, gave Sara a most peculiar look. What a day it was turning out to be for looks, Sara thought, astonished. If she had not known what a very fortunate child she was she would have thought that Robson's was a pitying look. He cleared his throat and touched his cap deferentially, then spoke.

'If Miss would like to construct a snowman in the back yard, sir, I'd be happy to clear up after her. I meant to brush it clear of snow this afternoon, in any case.'

'Very well, Robson,' Mr Cordwainer said wearily.

'Sara, you may play in the back yard if you wish, after luncheon.'

'But only for half an hour,' Mrs Cordwainer broke in petulantly. 'Nanny has a snooze after luncheon, but I don't intend to find myself entertaining her when she awakes. Sara really must be indoors again by then.'

'All right, Mother, I'll come in as soon as Nanny wakes,' Sara said soothingly. 'There's Mrs Buckman, she's beckoning you.'

Mrs Cordwainer, who had seemed in a poor sort of mood for Christmas Day, brightened.

'Adolphus, I *must* have a word with Beatrice,' she purred, her voice, which had been lemony in the car when the subject of snow was raised, suddenly turning creamy. 'Wait, Sara.'

Sara waited. Her father moved off to talk to a couple of dark-coated, solemn-looking men, the car moved away with Robson at the wheel, and though she glanced round hopefully, no one she knew came into sight. Most of the congregation were already in the church, she supposed, and she edged nearer the grown-ups.

Then she saw the girl, standing against the church wall with a baby on her hip. She must have been thirteen or fourteen, older than Sara anyway, and she couldn't guess at the baby's age, not being knowledge-able about such things, but the girl didn't look old enough to be the child's mother. She's probably mind-ing her, Sara thought, moving a little closer. Martha, in my class at school, minds her little sister sometimes.

It was then that she noticed the baby's feet. They were bare, and a horrid purplish blue colour. And when Sara looked down, the big girl didn't have proper shoes either, only a pair of cracked and gaping boots, many sizes too large. And neither was warmly clad, though the baby did have a thin blanket half-wrapped round her, from which the blue, bruised-looking feet protruded.

The big girl saw her staring and moved closer herself. She smiled. She didn't have very many front teeth and those that she did have were broken and grey-looking. But there was something in her smile . . . it made Sara want to cry and also to hit something or someone very hard, though she could not have said why she felt either emotion.

'Hello, chuck,' the girl said. 'You goin' into church?'

'That's right. In a minute, when my mother's stopped talking to her friends.'

The girl smiled more broadly. 'Oh aye, I've gorra mam like that an' all. Talk the 'ind leg off of a donkey, mine.' She turned the baby so that it faced her. 'You know what I mean, don't you, our Moll? Our mam clacks from mornin' till night, don't she, queen?'

The baby gurgled and a thin little hand appeared above the blanket. The hand patted the girl's cheek, then withdrew quickly back into whatever warmth the blanket offered.

'Well, ain't you a one?' the girl marvelled. She turned back to Sara. 'Understands every word, she does . . . clever little bugger!'

'She's very pretty,' Sara said, more from politeness than anything, but when she looked into the baby's face, she saw she had spoken no more than the truth. The baby had skin like milk, big, blue eyes and soft little tendrils of red-gold hair which curled all over her small head. 'How old is she?'

'She'll be a year old in February,' the girl said, then added, in a very much quieter voice, 'If she lives, acourse.'

'If she . . . is she ill, then?' Sara asked, appalled by

the matter-of-factness of the remark. 'She's awfully cold, her feet are quite blue.'

'Nah, she's not ill; but she only 'as buttermilk, an' the clinic nurse says it ain't enough,' the girl explained. 'Me mam won't feed 'em for long, says it drags 'er down, and me da's out o' work, see – an' when 'e's workin' chances are 'e won't bring nothin' 'ome, 'cos 'e likes 'is bevvy, does our da, and that costs.' She sighed. 'You don't know what to want for the best, eh? If 'e's sober 'e beats us up, if 'e's drunk there's nothin' to eat. Why, me sister Grace – she's goin' on four – got a bang across the 'ead last night what knocked 'er cold, just about. Still, the ould feller went off drinkin' this mornin', so I left Grace lie. Me da won't go 'ome till the boozers close, now.' She jiggled the baby on her hip. 'We's glad of it, ain't we, our Moll? In fact it would be a good Christmas if we 'ad something other than buttermilk for the littl'un 'ere.'

'Doesn't the baby drink tea? Or orange juice?' Sara asked. Now that she was so close she could smell a rather nasty, sour sort of smell hovering round the couple. She had never heard of buttermilk, but it sounded all right. 'What does she eat? Bread and butter? Oh, but today it'll be roast turkey, I suppose, and plum pudding. Do babies eat things like that?'

The girl shrugged. 'I dunno. She ain't never 'ad the chanst. Nor me, neither.' She gestured towards the church porch, towards which the congregation were now drifting. 'You'd best gerrof, your mam'll give you stick, she's hollered you twice ... you are Sara, I s'pose?'

'Oh goodness ... thanks,' Sara said, turning away. As she turned the girl put a hand out, then hastily withdrew it and tucked it into the cloaklike garment which she wore round her shoulders. It was a man's

7

jacket with the sleeves cut off and the armholes roughly stitched closed, Sara realised. But the movement, suddenly, said all the things that the girl had never put into words. *I'm hungry*, it said. *I don't know where my next meal's coming from, nor the baby's, neither. And you're so warm in your pretty red coat and hat, your nice woolly gloves . . . don't go just yet, don't leave me out here in the cold!*

'Sara! Come here at once, please, your father and I are about to take our places.' Mrs Cordwainer's voice was that of someone used to being obeyed, which was probably why she turned straight round and went into the church, her hand tucked into her husband's elbow, enabling Sara to turn quickly to her new friend, stripping off her white woollen gloves as she did so. She thrust them at the older girl.

'Here, take these, put them on the baby's feet, they're ever so nice and warm. And . . .' her hand plunged into her pocket and came out again with a bright, shiny shilling. ' . . . Here's something for Christmas, just a little present. Buy some milk!'

The girl took the gloves wonderingly, turning them over and over, then she smiled brilliantly at Sara and took the shilling as well. This time, the smile turned her small, pale face into a thing of such beauty that Sara didn't even notice the state of her teeth.

'Thanks . . . you are good, I 'opes you don't gerrin trouble for 'elpin' me like this. Are you sure . . . But I sees you are . . . I'll get some milk right away, Moll shall 'ave a Christmas treat, a bottle of it, warmed all nice. Me an' 'er's ever so grateful, Sara.'

'What's your name?' Sara asked shyly, preparing to depart. 'I know the baby's Moll, but what are you called?'

'She's Mollie Carbery and I'm Jess,' the girl said.

'We're from Kirkdale, we ain't from these parts, we've walked a good ways to get 'ere, Moll an' me. Kept our minds off of our bellies, see? Now we'll walk 'ome, and we'll 'ave somethin' to look forward to, eh, Moll? Some milk for you, an' mebbe a loaf or a cake for me. Ta, Sara.'

'Bye,' Sara called softly. She ran into the church porch, then slowed to a decorous walk, glancing over her shoulder as she did so. The girl, with the baby hitched up on her hip once more, was making her way along the road, walking fast considering her burden.

Sara slid into the pew beside her mother and dropped to her knees. Her mother cast her an angry look but said nothing; there were people too close who might overhear. And presently the service began, with pomp and ceremony and some of the nicer carols. And during the third carol the sidesmen took the collection and Sara suddenly remembered where the shilling had come from. It had been her collection, and now it was being handed over a counter somewhere, in exchange for milk and food.

She watched the plate approaching. It was a huge affair and today it was well laden with money, notes even. I'll pretend to put something in, Sara thought, delving into her pocket. I'll have to, because church isn't a good place to explain something to a grown-up.

But she was saved by the collection itself as it turned out. Mrs Cordwainer saw the plate, heavily laden, making its way towards her, and obviously realised that her daughter's shilling would stand out as being the smallest contribution so far. She nudged her husband and said something to him in a low voice, there was a moment's scuffling, and then Sara felt something large and round being pressed into her palm.

'Put it in the plate, dear,' her mother hissed. 'I believe I gave you the wrong coin this morning.'

Sara did not argue. She put the heavy silver coin into the plate and passed it along to her mother, then her father, watching them contributing generously with a feeling of puzzlement. It was all wrong! They had ignored the shabby little girl with the baby in her arms even when they had seen their daughter talking to her. They refused to give money to carol singers, saying the children were begging, and even grudged them the mince pies and hot cocoa which the staff handed out. Yet they put generous amounts of money into the collection plate at church and saw to it that she, too, gave sufficient.

My parents are definitely Christians and therefore good people, Sara told herself. They go to church every Sunday, and Mother goes to sewing circle and makes clothes for the heathen in Africa. When the Liverpool Goodfellows came round collecting for Christmas parcels for the very poor, her parents always put money into the box. Yet they had not even seemed to notice Jess and the baby.

I'll ask Nanny why they don't give to Liverpool children, Sara decided as the congregation got to its collective feet to sing the last hymn. She'll know, and she'll explain it to me. Only I do wish that someone, either my parents or someone else's, had seen Jess and baby Mollie and given them some money, too. Perhaps as much as a whole half-crown . . . imagine what they could have bought with that!

And when the service finished the Cordwainer family made their way out of the church, pausing in the porch to wish everyone the compliments of the season, whilst Reverend Atwell handed Sara a small, flat parcel, gaily wrapped, and told her to be good and to enjoy her Christmas.

I never thought, I ought to have told Jess to come in and bring Mollie; probably the reverend would have given them both presents, Sara thought, assuring the clergyman that she would be good and would try to enjoy her Christmas. 'But there were two little girls outside . . .' she was beginning when the reverend switched away from her to the next child, behaving as though she had not spoken at all. More puzzled than ever, Sara turned away. How very odd grown-ups were, to be sure. They preached goodness, kindness, but they didn't appear to practise what they preached, not even clergymen.

Outside, the snow was still falling, but more gently now. Robson wasn't in the car but he came hurrying over to it when he saw them.

'Sorry, sir,' he said to Sara's father, opening the back door with a flourish. 'I never went out of sight of the car, but I had to keep movin', else I'd have frozen stiff in me seat.'

'You could have exercised in your seat, I suppose,' Mr Cordwainer said irritably. 'I do trust you've not been drinking?'

'No, indeed, sir, I never touch a drop,' Robson said and Sara, whose eyes seemed to have been opened today by her encounter with Jess, realised that Robson, a grown-up, was actually frightened of her father. Why? What could her father do to Robson, who seemed a sturdy, independent type of man? Nothing, surely! Except dismiss him.

Jess had said her father was out of work and had implied that this meant there was no money for milk. Sara frowned. Robson had no babies who needed milk, but if he lost his job he would also lose his room

11

over the garage and the meals he ate in the kitchen with the rest of the domestic staff.

'I'm glad to hear it,' Mr Cordwainer said, but he said it as if he did not believe a word and Sara saw the chauffeur's unease deepen. Quickly, without stopping to think, she burst into speech.

'Wasn't it a lovely service, Mother? I liked the last hymn . . . I wonder what my present is, this year?' She turned to the chauffeur. 'What did the other drivers do, Robson, whilst we were in church? What did Mr Hartley's chauffeur do?'

Robson turned to her eagerly. 'They walked, same as I did, Miss Sara. We must ha' covered a couple of miles, I'd say. Mr Hartley's man suggested the walk, an' he said we looked like a brigade of guards, so smart in our uniforms, all marchin' along the pavements swingin' our arms to keep warm.'

Mr Hartley was very rich; he had a house in the South of France and his wife wore mink, wonderful sables and Paris dresses. Their daughter was being educated in Switzerland and their son was at Eton. None of this meant much to Sara, but she knew her mother always talked about the Hartleys with a sort of awe, as though they were special people, like the King and Queen, or the handsome young Prince of Wales. So she imagined that her parents would be pleased that Robson had followed the Hartley chauffeur's lead.

Mr Cordwainer helped his wife into the vehicle, then pushed Sara in ahead of him. He said, through the glass panel once Robson had run round and jumped behind the wheel, 'Oh well, if Hartley's man went walking I suppose there can be no harm in it. Home, Robson.'

'No, Robson, *not* home,' Mrs Cordwainer interrupted pettishly. 'Dear me, Adolphus, it's Christmas Day!

Drive to number three Snowdrop Street, Robson. We are to pick up Mrs Prescott at that address.'

The chauffeur touched his peaked cap and put the car into gear. He had started it as soon as they appeared so that the engine was purring softly when they reached the vehicle and now it moved slowly away from the kerb as Mrs Cordwainer leaned back against the dark leather upholstery and heaved a sigh.

'I shall be glad when Christmas is over,' she said crossly. 'Well, Sara, aren't you going to open your parcel?'

'Yes, Mother, if I may,' Sara said. She was still feeling annoyed with Reverend Atwell but that was no reason for not opening a present. She untied the scarlet ribbon and unwrapped the paper, to reveal a cheaply bound copy of a book entitled *Bible Stories for the Little Ones*.

'Very nice,' Mrs Cordwainer said in a bored voice. 'How good of the Reverend Atwell.'

'I've already got a copy,' Sara said mutinously. 'Can I give it to someone else, Mother?'

'Certainly not. What would people think?' Mrs Cordwainer said at once. 'How very ungrateful you are, Sara.'

'I don't mean to be. But what good are two copies of the same book to me?' Sara said rather plaintively. Inside her head she added, *and it's a rotten book, too*, but she knew better than to say it aloud. 'I daresay there are lots of children who would love a copy of their own.' Her opinion of the Reverend Atwell had not been high since he had ignored her in the porch, but any lingering liking had just nose-dived. He had given her the same book two years running, which must mean that he didn't put any thought at all into those carefully wrapped little presents. 'It's greedy to have more than one needs of anything,' she added craftily. 'You've often said so, Mother.'

'Oh, very well, but don't say anything to Nanny,' her mother instructed. 'Goodness, it's started to snow again – I do trust we'll get Nanny home again when her stay is over without too much trouble.'

I wish she could stay for ever, Sara thought wistfully, but once again, knew better than to say it out loud. Mrs Prescott was a duty to her parents, not a pleasure.

The car was driving very slowly now through the whirling snow and Sara's attention left the passengers and went to the scene outside. Normally she would have been watching out for familiar landmarks but now, because of the snow, she scarcely recognised anything. But she knew where they were when they came on to Stanley Road, with the beautiful smell of railways and docks getting stronger the nearer they got to their destination.

Sara had asked Nanny once why all the streets in her area had such pretty names. Snowdrop, Crocus, Pansy, Daisy, Woodbine, Harebell and many more.

'It's much prettier than Aigburth Road, or the Boulevard,' she complained. 'I'd rather live somewhere called after a flower any day, Nanny.'

'Aye, the names are pretty enough, but that's about all you can say,' Nanny assured her. 'They're mean streets, narrow and noisy, and the folk what live on 'em don't have much. Still, what they have they share, and they stand by each other in times of trouble. You can't say fairer than that.'

The car crawled carefully down Stanley Street as far as the corner of Snowdrop. Robson slowed, peered into the side street, then stopped the car. You could see at a glance that there had been no attempt, here, to clear the snow and down the middle of the road was what looked suspiciously like a slide; at least four or five rough-looking boys were sailing along it with shouts of pleasure.

Robson turned and slid back the glass panel. 'I dussen't go no further, sir,' he announced. 'If I stop down there I doubt I'd get 'er goin' again. You stay here and I'll go and fetch Mrs Prescott out.'

'I'll go,' Sara said eagerly. She adored Nanny and didn't want to waste a moment of her company and also the thought of running down the street and past the sliding boys was fun, an adventure. But Mr Cordwainer nipped that in the bud at once.

'No you don't,' he said grimly. 'Young ladies don't go gadding about in this type of area without an escort. Besides, you'll get soaked and I don't want the upholstery to get wet.' He turned back to the chauffeur. 'Very well, Robson, go and get Mrs Prescott. We'll wait here.'

Robson cast a quick glance in the back of the car. 'What number did you say, sir? Not all the houses have their numbers displayed . . .'

'I know the house,' Sara said eagerly, recognising a cue when she heard one. 'I'll go with you, Robson, and show you the house.'

She was out of the car and walking along the pavement beside the chauffeur before either of her parents had opened their mouths to argue and indeed, as she closed the door behind her, her mother was talking to her father about Mrs Aubain, whose new hair-style had caused much comment in church that morning.

'Thanks, Robson,' Sara said, glancing up at the chauffeur as they walked.

'Thank *you*, Miss,' Robson said. He grinned at her and Sara grinned back, both entirely understanding the meaning behind the words. 'Mr Hartley was the magic word, eh? I must remember that. Your Gran's house is the last but one, isn't it?'

'My Nanny's house . . . yes, it's the one with the brass knocker,' Sara admitted. Her grandmother, a very fierce, correct old lady, lived in a large house in Crosby and enjoyed ill-health; it would have been lovely had Mrs Prescott been her grandmother, but you couldn't have everything, Sara reasoned. Grandmother could have been worse – she could have lived nearer, for instance. 'And it's the loveliest brass knocker, too, a dolphin it is. When I was little, I had to jump to reach it, but now, of course, I just go on tiptoe.'

The sliding boys stopped sliding to stare as they passed and one of them shouted, 'It's Mrs Prescott's Sara – wotcher, Sara! Ain't it great to 'ave snow, eh?'

'Hello, Jackie,' Sara said, delighted to recognise the speaker. He was a Callogan, his mother and father and a great many children lived just up the road from Nanny. 'Yes, the snow's good, isn't it? And how are you? How's Bet and Bert and the others? And your mam and da, of course.'

'We're awright, ta,' Jackie said. 'You awright, Sara?'

'Very well, thanks,' Sara said. 'It's Christmas, so Mrs Prescott's coming to stay. I love it when she comes.'

'When is you goin' to come to Snowdrop Street, then?' Jackie said at once, leaving the slide and his companions and falling into step beside Sara and Robson. 'You ain't been 'ere for a 'undred *years* just about. I 'pose your mam don't want you playin' wi' the likes of us.'

Sara felt her cheeks burn; once, she had come to Snowdrop Street whenever her parents felt like going away for a few days, and she had been in seventh heaven, but ever since discovering that Nanny let her play out her parents had refused all her desperate requests to stay with Nanny Prescott.

But it could have been worse. At least Nanny Prescott still visited them in Aigburth Road, so Sara had a good deal to be thankful for. Being denied even the solace of Nanny's down-to-earth, outspoken company would have been unbearable.

Now, she turned to Jackie. 'They say I'm too old to play out, it's for kids,' she said apologetically. 'But Mrs Prescott doesn't think that. Tell Bet I'm asking for her, and perhaps, one day, I'll come and stay again.'

Jackie dropped back as they drew level with number three. 'I'll tell 'er,' he said resignedly. 'Ta-ra, queen.'

'Ta-ra, Jackie,' Sara echoed, and saw the chauffeur's lips twitch, but then she was standing on tiptoe and reaching for the knocker, excitement flooding through her. She seized the brass dolphin and brought him down in a quick rat-tat, then stood back, but Mrs Prescott had obviously been watching for them for the door shot open to reveal her standing in the doorway, her round and rosy face breaking into a beaming smile.

'Sara, love! Give your old Nanny a big hug, then!'

'Oh, Nanny,' Sara gasped, hurling herself into the older woman's arms. 'Oh, Nanny, I do love you! Isn't it grand that it's snowing? Oh, Nanny, I wish you could stay for ever . . . where's your baggage? I'll carry it.'

'Baggage, child? But I'm only comin' to Aigburth Road for the day,' Mrs Prescott said. 'Your mam invited me; she said *for the day* when she wrote.'

Sara stared. 'But Nanny, you always come for Christmas, that's today and Boxing Day, sometimes the day after that, too. Oh, Mother was saying earlier that . . .' She remembered just what it was her mother had said and hesitated before completing the sentence. ' . . . That

I was to be sure to keep you entertained,' she said rather lamely.

Mrs Prescott was already in her brown coat with boots on her feet, furry mittens on her hands and a felt hat pulled down firmly over her greying hair. Now she put Sara gently to one side and walked through the doorway, then turned and carefully locked the front door behind her.

'We'll talk about it,' she said diplomatically. 'Mebbe there's a mistake. Now are you going to carry my handbag, dearie? Because there's a little present for you in there.'

'I will carry it, gladly, but the best present's you, Nanny,' Sara said rapturously. 'Oh, just knowing you were coming to stay makes it a good Christmas, and now the snow's just making it perfect! Say you'll stay the night, though, Nanny! I couldn't bear it if you were to go home and leave me all alone again.'

'Alone? And you with two good parents and a house full of servants?' Mrs Prescott said, but she looked pleased, nevertheless. 'Good morning, Mr Robson; nice to see you again.'

'Good morning, Mrs Prescott,' the chauffeur said politely, touching his peaked cap. 'No bag, today?'

'Not today. I'll have a word with Mrs Cordwainer when we reach the car but I'm certain her letter specified Christmas Day itself. Take my arm, Sara, it's really slippery and I don't fancy fallin' on me bum before all them boys.'

Sara, laughing, took the older woman's arm on one side and the chauffeur, after the slightest of hesitations, took her other arm. Walking carefully, for the icy pavement was treacherous, the three of them made their way back to the car.

'Madam,' Robson said, throwing open the passenger door. 'If you'll just climb inside . . .'

Mrs Prescott got in nimbly and settled back in her seat, then turned to address the Cordwainers, shooting back the glass panel in order to do so.

'A merry Christmas to you both! I've not packed a bag since your letter just said Christmas Day, Mrs Cordwainer.'

Mrs Cordwainer leaned forward. Sara, watching her, saw the colour rise beneath the powder on her mother's cheeks. 'Surely I said *for Christmas*, Nanny? In our book, that means for the Christmas holiday, which is both days. But since you've not packed a bag . . .'

Sara opened her mouth to protest but her father spoke before she could do so. 'Letty, my dear . . . it won't take Mrs Prescott a moment to pack a bag. Indeed, the child can help her.' He leaned forward. 'If Robson takes my wife and myself home now, and returns for you and Sara in an hour . . . would that be sufficient time for you to pack a bag?'

Sara could have jumped for joy but she knew better than to do such a thing. Instead, she smiled demurely at Nanny, though with pleading in her eyes. Oh, let Nanny say yes! She could go back into number three Snowdrop Street when Nanny did and check that her own little room upstairs, where she had stayed as a child, was still just as it ought to be! She could open the window and lean out and see that much-loved, much-remembered view of the railway, then the docks, then the gleam of the Mersey! Sometimes, on a clear day, the blue line of the Welsh hills could be seen against the sky . . . sometimes she was sure she could see New Brighton, almost hear the funfair!

'Nanny?' Sara's hand was on the door.

Nanny had been looking militant but suddenly she relented. She smiled and put her own hand on the doorhandle. 'An hour will be adequate,' she said firmly. 'Thank you, Mr Cordwainer, I'd be happy to stay for Boxing Day.'

It seemed odd to enter the well-loved little house to find the kettle not singing on the hearth and no fire in the grate, though it was neatly laid with sheets of the *Echo* scrumpled up and kindling sticks and small pieces of coal on top of them. Nanny had clearly not lit the fire that morning for the room struck chill and Sara shivered even as Nanny began to strip off her gloves, take off her coat, and carefully remove her black felt hat.

'Nanny, I know the fire's out, but . . . well, if you really thought you were coming back tonight, wouldn't you just have damped it down? And it's cold in here, you couldn't have had a nice breakfast or a cup of tea or anything! Did you really mean to come home here tonight?'

Nanny shook her head and tutted reproachfully, but Sara saw she was smiling. 'You're a knowing one, queen! Your mam invited me for Christmas Day, but I thought she'd probably stretch it to Boxing Day too, if I played me cards right. It's just that I don't like to be took for granted, chuck. Oh, I don't kid meself, I know I'm not exactly as welcome as the flowers in May, but I don't see much of you, nor you of me, eh? So I thought I'd call your mam's bluff.'

'She can be funny, sometimes,' Sara admitted. 'Where's your bag, then?'

'Behind the sofa,' Mrs Prescott said. 'Eh, now what's me pride done for us this time, Sara? We've gorran hour to kill in this freezin' cold house . . . what say we pop next door, have a warm by the Rushtons' fire? It's Christmas Day, we shan't get turned away.'

'We wouldn't on any day,' Sara said. 'I daresay we could go anywhere here and be made welcome, eh, Nanny?'

'Oh aye, what we have we share,' Mrs Prescott said. She headed for the front door. 'But I'd not trouble some of 'em . . . the Carberys, for one. Eh, wharra life they lead, them! A baby every year, himself out o' work this past six months, and scarce a mouthful of bread in the house most days, no matter how they try to mek ends meet.'

'I met someone called Carbery,' Sara said. 'It can't be the same family, though. They were outside church this morning.'

'No, it wouldn't be them; too far to walk on empty stomachs,' Mrs Prescott said. 'This is a poor neighbourhood, but the Carbs have touched bottom, I reckon. Still, maybe Stan'll get some work in the new year. And maybe he'll not drink all his money away this time, if he gets a job.' She glanced sharply down at Sara's hands. 'Where's your gloves, Miss?'

'I gave them to the girl I was telling you about outside the church,' Sara said rather diffidently. 'She had a baby in her arms, Nanny, and the baby's feet were *blue*. She was so pretty, but so very cold . . . I gave her my collection, too,' she added rather guiltily.

'You did? Good for you, chuck,' Mrs Prescott said decidedly. She opened the front door and ushered Sara out. 'Give a knock next door, and I'll explain what's happened. What did your mam say?'

'Oh, she'd given me a shilling, but when she saw the plate I think she realised that everyone else had given more, so she slipped me a whole half-crown. I put that in and she probably didn't realise I hadn't added the shilling as well,' Sara said. 'She's not noticed the gloves yet, though. I was lucky, because she hates it when I lose gloves.'

'You can say you left 'em at my house, and by the time Christmas is over she'll likely have forgot all about them,' Mrs Prescott said comfortably. 'Which gloves were they?'

'Oh, Nanny, I'm sorry, they were the pretty white angora ones you knitted me at the start of the autumn term,' Sara said guiltily. 'But the baby's feet were so cold . . .'

'You did right,' Mrs Prescott assured her. 'Them as have should give freely to them as haven't. I spent years tryin' to din that into my employers and their children, but it passed over most of their heads like water off a duck's arse. Seems you're kindly by nature, Sara.'

'Some people don't seem to care much about the people near them, Nanny . . .' Sara began, but at that point the door of number five flew open and a thin, angular woman with a huge smile and very few teeth shouted, 'Eh, if it ain't Annie Prescott and the little gal!' and pulled them both into the warm, overcrowded little room.

'Eh, Marj, we're frozen stiff an' we'd kill for a nice cuppa,' Mrs Prescott said, holding out her hands towards the blazing fire. 'I'm off to the Cordwainers' for a couple of days so me fire's out, no chance of anything 'ot. Believe it or not I'd forgot to pack me bag, so they've gone off 'ome whiles me and Sara here gets a few things together.'

'Kate, gi's a couple o' cups,' Mrs Rushton shouted and an indistinct voice replied that she'd not be a minute, she'd just gorra gerra brew on the go. 'Now,

Annie, what've you been up to, eh? You was sayin' only yesterday that you was packed an' ready.'

'Aye, well . . .' Mrs Prescott broke off as a spindly girl in her mid-teens came into the room, carefully holding two chipped white cups which steamed invitingly. 'Oh, Kate, luv, you're worth your weight in gold! We're that thirsty, Sara an' me, that our tongues are hanging down to our knees. And on Christmas Day, an' all!'

'Auntie Annie, you're always up to somethin',' the girl said jokingly, handing both females a cup. 'Sit yourselves down . . . I'll bring you t'rough a mince pie presently, or a piece of apple pasty if you'd rather.'

'Thanks, queen, but it 'ud only spoil our dinners, and the tea's a treat, jest what the doctor ordered,' Mrs Prescott said, sipping the scalding liquid. 'Eh, isn't a decent cuppa a treat, our Sara? Bet you never get better'n this at 'ome?'

'No, I never do,' Sara said, not quite truthfully, for she did not enjoy strong tea, much preferring milk or the delicious lemonade that Cook made for the schoolroom. 'It warms me up right down to my toes, Nanny.'

'Aye, that's right, a nice cuppa's a real winter warmer,' Mrs Prescott agreed. 'Eh, there's good smells comin' from your kitchen, Marj – can I smell a roast?'

'You can. With three of me boys in work, Kate here bringin' home an apron full of goodies from the Bellmans, and Alf workin' regular on the railway, we can afford a decent Christmas. I cooked the goose up at Sample's yesterday, now it's heatin' through whiles the spuds an' the cabbage boils. Aye, life's not so bad, this year.' She beamed at Mrs Prescott and Sara. 'I could give up the pub cleanin' tomorrer, if I'd a mind – we'd scarce miss the money.'

'Aye. But there's others not so lucky,' Mrs Prescott

said soberly. 'Them next door to you; things ain't so good when you've a dozen kids, none of 'em workin' yet, and your old man's not done a hand's turn for six months.'

'A dozen kids? In a house the same size as yours, Nanny?' Sara started to say, then stopped short. There were quite a lot of kids in this house and they all had to sleep somewhere. Either in the decent front, or the small back, or in the slip of a room which Sara thought of as her own. But . . . twelve kids and two grownups? How on earth did they manage? She looked interrogatively at her nanny, who was placidly drinking her tea from the cracked and handleless cup.

'I know, poor souls,' Mrs Rushton said. 'But there ain't many of us what haven't known the pain of an empty belly, so you do your best. Alf took 'em round a leg o' mutton yesterday and some veggies; they'll not sup on blind scouse this Christmas at any rate.'

'It won't go far between fourteen of 'em,' Kate said. She was a plain, cheerful girl with straggly hair and ears which stuck out, Sara thought, like a car with both doors open.

Mrs Prescott was about to reply when the door burst open and a crowd of kids surged into the room. They were all thin, with untidy hair, and they were all grinning from ear to ear.

'Is the dinner cooked?' shouted an urchin of about Sara's age. 'The smell's that good, Mam, I dunno as I can wait another second!'

'Well, try,' Mrs Rushton said grimly, 'because norra mouthful will any of yez get until your da's home. But if you're real starvin', there's a new loaf on the kitchen table and a packet o' margarine . . . there might be some jam an' all if you look behind the meat safe.'

The kids surged out of the room, shouting and laughing, and Kate turned to her visitor.

'Our Seth works at the jam factory; that's where I'll work when I leave school,' she said, sitting down beside Sara on the lumpy sofa. 'They give you jam cheap, sometimes, so we're better off'n some. Not bad, eh? Where'll you work when you're growed?'

'I'm only twelve,' Sara said. 'I haven't thought, not yet. I don't have any brothers or sisters, you see, so I can't work with them.'

'Only twelve? I'd ha' put you at thirteen, mebbe fourteen,' Kate said flatteringly. 'They grows 'em big up your way, queen. Have a mince pie!'

The pies looked good, but Sara was still uneasily conscious of what Jess had told her. Not everyone could eat, even when they were hungry. These people seemed happy and successful and talked cheerfully, but the mother hadn't offered the kids pies, it had been bread and margarine. She was being offered a pie because she was a visitor – but she would go home presently and have a very large luncheon, with plum pudding and fruit to follow. And there would be boxes of chocolates and heaps and heaps of nuts and at teatime more food, more treats.

'No, thanks, Kate,' she said, therefore, 'I don't want to spoil my lunch.'

And when they'd finished their tea Nanny said they'd best be getting back because she didn't want anyone thinking she'd not had a bag to pack . . . more laughter . . . and they had said their farewells and left, with Christmas wishes ringing in their ears.

One thing struck Sara as odd, though. As they were about to open Mrs Prescott's front door Mrs Rushton stuck her head out into the cold and shouted after them, a halo of steam rising from her open mouth.

'Ask your Letty if she ever thinks about the Sunday school treat, the year we was twelve,' she shouted. 'We 'ad some fun on New Brighton funfair! Our Sid remembers it an' all, he often asks after Letty.'

Sara, who knew that Nanny Prescott had once been her own mother's nanny, pricked up her ears. If Mrs Rushton was referring to her mother, she would have liked to hear a bit more! She glanced enquiringly at Nanny, but the older woman was inserting her key in the front door, turning it . . .

'That's nice. I'll tell her,' Mrs Prescott said vaguely, and then she had unlocked the door and they were inside the chilly little room once more, and Mrs Prescott sat at a chair in the window to watch for the chauffeur whilst Sara ran upstairs to take a look at the front bedroom.

It was lovely, running up the narrow, creaking stairs, turning on the tiny landing and going into the slip of a front room. Sara felt a warm glow envelope her; she had been so happy here! She had sometimes felt that the only times she was really alive were when she was with Mrs Prescott, sleeping in the little front room, kneeling on the floor on a summer's evening with her nose pressed to the glass, staring out at the railway, the docks, the river.

She had stared out at life, too, passing constantly in the street below. Kids at play, adults on their way to and from the public houses on Stanley Street, the occasional drunk lurching along, taking a short-cut from Commercial Road through into Stanley, a dog, sauntering along behind its owner, sniffing at walls and lamp posts, lifting a leg, breaking into a trot.

There wasn't a lot of life on Aigburth Road, or if there was she was unaware of it, because the grounds

of her home protected her from such doses of reality.
And the nursery with its barred window was high up,
and lonely, too, very different from the little bedroom
on Snowdrop Street. So now Sara knelt on the floor
and pressed her nose to the glass as, outside, the flakes
of snow continued to fall.

It wasn't easy, on such a day, to see her favourite
view, but it was just possible. There it was, outside the
window, her own particular, beloved slice of life. But
today there was little or no movement from the railway
– presumably no trains, or very few, ran on Christmas
Day – and even the Mersey, steel-grey against the
downward-swirling flakes, was quiet.

Still. Despite it being Christmas Day there was some
movement in the street. The sliding boys had scattered
and gone as the snowstorm increased but someone was
even now making her way along the pavement, head
shrugged down into shoulders, bundles firmly grasped
in skinny arms. It was a girl, skinny and underfed,
with something wrapped in a blanket on one arm and
a soggy paper bag from which large objects – they
looked like loaves – protruded. Sara had been breathing on the glass and fogging it up; now she rubbed
frantically, trying to make herself a proper peephole.
Yes, there was the figure, passing closer now, almost
directly beneath the window . . . frantically, Sara tried
to get the window open, she leapt to her feet and
wrestled with the little round latch that locked the top
half of the sash in place, got it back, shoved and pushed
at the bottom half . . . it was opening, icy air – and a
great deal of snow – was rushing into the room, Sara
was leaning out, head and shoulders into the storm,
her voice rising.

'Jess! Jess, it's me, Sara . . . oh, Jess, do look up!'

But Jess, if it was Jess, continued to slog along

through the snow, head down, her shopping clutched fiercely to her skinny breast. And the child, if it was the child, was now completely immersed in the thin blanket.

Reluctantly, Sara withdrew into the room once more. It couldn't have been Jess, it would have been too much of a coincidence and anyway, if it had been, she would surely have recognised her own name and looked up?

Struggling to pull the window down again, rather conscience-stricken by the great wet patches of melting snow on the linoleum, Sara glanced once more at the fast disappearing figure – and promptly tried to push the window up once more. But by the time she had got it a couple of inches from the sill, it was too late. Girl and burden had disappeared.

'But it *was* Jess,' Sara told herself miserably, making her way downstairs in answer to Mrs Prescott's shout. 'It was Jess, because the baby's feet were sticking out under the blanket – and I could see my white angora gloves!'

Chapter Two

Jess was as near freezing as a human being could be, she decided as she walked as fast as she could along Snowdrop Street. But beneath all the cold there was a warm little glow. That girl, Sara, had been a nice kid, and the money she'd handed over had bought not only some loaves of bread but two currant buns, a large piece of cheese and a bully beef tin full of milk.

She had been heading home, but now she paused in her onward rush. The trouble was, it was Grace and the baby who needed the food most and if the others saw it, it wouldn't last long. Wouldn't go round all that far, either. Mam always fed Da and herself first, then the boys, then the girls. Yesterday there had been a proper stew, made especially for Christmas – a neighbour had donated the meat. But somehow, it had all got ate, and neither Grace nor Mollie had had a sniff of it. Grace had been poorly, so hot you could have fried an egg on her, and Mollie was too little to fight her corner. Jess herself had only had a boiled potato and a smear of gravy and that hadn't gone far between her and Mollie.

Jess sighed and stood still for a moment, doubly burdened by the sleeping child and the food. What should she do for the best? Grace was a dear little soul but she'd never manage bread and cheese, not with the fever she'd had. Jess had given her the buttermilk, warmed, with bread crumbled into it and the kid had scarcely managed two mouthfuls before she fell asleep again. But Mollie must be very hungry, and Jess herself was empty as a drum. If I don't get something inside me soon I'll be no good to the others, Jess thought, immediately practical. I'll go somewhere quiet, eat some bread and cheese and a bun, feed Mollie the milk with some bread in it, and then go home later with what's left.

But where to go? Jess looked around her. The snow was falling thickly but surely there must be a suitable place where she could make up some food for the baby and feed her, undisturbed? Snowdrop Street was no good, someone might spot her and take the food off her, or her da might stagger down the road and try to bash her brains out just because she was the eldest. But there was always the marshalling yard.

Jess looked across Commercial Road, towards the railway lines. There were a great many buildings there, all different. Many a time, when she'd been younger, she'd played around in the sheds which the workmen used as shelters from the weather, somewhere to eat their carry-out. Surely she could find somewhere where she would be sufficiently sheltered to feed the child? Once Mollie's small belly was full and she'd had a bite herself she would take the rest of the food home, no problem. Grace might be persuaded to eat a currant bun soaked in milk, that was soft and easy enough. And I might have the second bun meself, Jess thought with watering mouth. Eldest children, she knew from bitter experience, make do with the leftovers, they don't often feast on currant buns. Accordingly, Jess hurried across Commercial Road, heading for the tiny cabins where the men working on the lines congregated at dinner-times. Someone would be about, but she might find one of the cabins empty.

In her arms, Mollie wriggled. She was such a pretty

baby, but she was usually hungry, same as all the kids were. Jess sighed and speeded up a bit.

'Not long now, Mollie-o,' she said comfortingly, giving the warm bundle which was her baby sister a hug. 'Jess's goin' to give you bread 'n' milk – what about that, eh?'

Mollie gurgled. 'Jess, Jess, Jess,' she chanted beneath the blanket. 'Milla-milla, Jess milla-milla.'

'That's it,' Jess said stoutly. She wriggled through a hole in the fence and began to cross the great swathe of wet and shining lines. 'Bread an' milk for you, my little love, bread and milk for Jess's best girl.'

The first hut she approached was full of men; she would have backed away but one of them hailed her.

'What are you doin' round here, alanna?' one of the navvies asked curiously, in a strong Irish accent. 'If you're after nickin' coal you're in the wrong place. What's that under your shawl, child?'

'It's not a shawl, it's a cut-down jacket, and it's me sister under it,' Jess said, her teeth chattering. 'I'm not tryin' to nick anything either, honest to God, I just want somewhere to feed the littl'un – I got food . . . see?'

She held up the soggy paper bag which contained the loaves, and lifted the bully beef tin to show that, too. Drawing closer to the cabin she saw that it was lit by a coke burner and that, Christmas Day or no Christmas Day, the men were all in their working clothes.

'Sure and she's speakin' no more than the trut',' another man put in. He gestured to an empty drum standing near the stove. 'Siddown, lass. You're welcome to a warm by the fire, you an' the babby.'

By now, Jess was so cold that warming up would be painful, she knew, yet she could not resist the lure of the coke stove. She crept nearer . . . oh, the warmth was bliss, sheer bliss. And it was so nice to see friendly faces around her, too!

'Thanks very much,' she muttered. 'I'll just break up some o' this bread into the milk . . . is it awright to put the littl'un down?'

'She's a real little beauty; a dote,' one of the men declared. 'Reminds me of my little Eilis, back home in County Cork.' He held out a huge, calloused hand to the baby. 'What do they call you, alanna?'

'She's Mollie,' Jess said. Her fingers were still so cold that she could not feel them and this was not helping her to break into the loaf of bread. The man who had spoken gave an exclamation and took the loaf from her. He produced a clasp knife from his pocket and began, very handily- Jess thought, to carve into the bread. As he cut he dropped the pieces into the milk, then stood the tin down by the stove.

'There! Leave it a minute to warm, then Mollie can have a good meal so she can.' He turned to Jess, giving her a rueful smile. 'You look as though you could do with a bite yourself, alanna. What's your name and where do you live? You should be in wit' your mammy and daddy on a day like this, what with the snow and the cold.'

'I'm Jess,' Jess admitted rather cautiously. These men – there were four of them – seemed well-intentioned enough but you could never tell. They might tell the scuffers that she was on railway property, send them round to the house, and then Mam would screech at her and Da would thump . . . no, you never told adults the whole truth, not if you were wise.

'And where do you live?' the questioner this time was younger than the rest, a young man with bright, dark eyes and soft dark hair under the navy cap which he pushed to the back of his head. 'We're from God's own country, which, mebbe, you've guessed.'

All the men laughed and Jess, encouraged, smiled too.

'Oh, I'm from nowhere in partic'lar,' she said, picking a sop out of the bully beef tin and popping it into the baby's eager mouth. 'We're keepin' out o' the way, baby an' me. Our da's 'ad no work for weeks, but when he's gorra bit o' money he'll be down the boozer, an' 'e were give five shillin' by a pal. Off 'e went, merry as Larry, but when 'e comes back 'e's likelier to kick than kiss.'

'Aye, I've known fellers like that,' the boy said. 'Best stay here for a while, then. No harm, not today.' He asked no more questions, to Jess's relief. These men were so kind, it would seem unfriendly to continue to deny them her name and address.

'We're none of us ourselves when we've drink aboard,' the first speaker said. He looked shamefacedly at Jess. 'But I've never hit woman nor child, no matter how much of the hard stuff has passed me lips.' He grinned round at his companions. 'Me old woman would kill me if I tried such a t'ing,' he added innocently. 'And she'd make two of me, would Deirdre.'

'Oh, Peader, your woman's soft as a lamb and you know it,' a big, ginger-haired man said, grinning. 'Sure an' she's built like a fairy so she is!'

The first speaker, who must be Peader, turned back to Jess, his eyes soft, sorry. 'So your old fella's fierce in drink, is 'e? Well, you give the littl'un a drap o' this, my treasure, that'll warm the cockles of her heart, and be the same token, have a drap yourself.'

He held out a bottle; it was black and smelt horrible. Jess put a hand out, touched it, then withdrew quickly, shaking her head.

'No thanks,' she said frankly. 'We don't like the smell, baby an' me.'

'It's good porter,' the dark-haired Peader said. 'Just a wee drop in the milk, alanna, and the baby'll smile for us. It isn't after gettin' you tiddly I am, but warmin' the pair of you.'

Warming! All of a sudden Jess wanted desperately to be warm, and to know that Mollie was warm, too. She let the man tip a small quantity of the rich, strong-smelling stuff into the milk and she continued to feed the baby, now and then taking a piece of the soaked bread for herself.

And he was right, it was warming! What with that, and the fire, and the good company, she had seldom felt better. The boy, who told her his name was Brogan, picked the baby up and began to play games with her, but presently Mollie, sated with bread and milk and soothed by the fire's warmth, simply lolled against his chest, eyelids drowsily closing.

'She's sound off,' Brogan said in a whisper to Jess. 'Do you want to take her from me now, get her home while she sleeps?'

Jess was warm herself now, and weary – so weary! 'I don't think I could walk home,' she murmured, for several of the men were snoozing, their faces ruddy from the fire's glow and the porter. 'Can I sleep here for a little while?'

'Course you can,' Brogan said. 'Course you can, girl. Sleep sound, sleep sound. And when you wake you can share my can o' tea, and have a bite o' bread an' cold mutton.'

Jess murmured her thanks and tried to raise her heavy eyelids, but the combination of a full stomach and warmth and the porter was too much for her. Very soon, she slept.

*

Brogan waited until both their visitors were fast asleep and then he, too, curled up on the floor. A couple of little girls had made his Christmas, for until they had walked into the cabin he had been suffering from such terrible homesickness that he had been afraid of breaking down in tears. Especially when Paddy began to sing in that light tenor voice of his. All the old songs, the ones Brogan's mammy had sung to him and his brothers when they were small.

He'd sat there in the faint firelight and remembered all the other Christmases. Never a penny piece to spare, never a great deal of food – but oh, the wonderful warmth of togetherness they had shared! A fire of turf or some hoarded coal, meat if they were lucky, but fish and potatoes almost always, little presents for the kids – a peg-man for Bevin, who was the youngest, a cracked pair of secondhand boots for another brother, a much-darned and patched jumper for a third, bought off the tuggers' carts as they made their way back to the Jewman who employed them in the heart of Dublin.

It wasn't a rich Christmas, Brogan knew that all right. But it was a good one. They went to mass, naturally, and somehow they always managed candle-money, and a bit over for to put in the box for the poor and needy.

'We're the poor and needy really, amn't we, Brogan?' the brother next to him in age, Martin, had said wistfully, once. 'When our daddy's out of work we don't have much.'

But it wasn't true, for didn't they have two whole rooms in their tenement block, the front first-floor pair as they called it? A whole room for sleeping in wasn't common by any means, no indeed, and they divided it, mornings, with hung sheets so that each could have his moment of privacy to wash and dress himself. And wasn't their living room neat as a new pin, and always clean water in the bucket by the fire and the Sacred Heart on the mantel kept dust-free, with a glass vase always sparkling before it, even if they could only rarely afford a flower or two to stand in it? So, 'There's many worse off than us, Mart,' he had told his brother. 'Oh, aye, many a one would envy us. But we aren't rich, nor even well-to-do, I grant you that.'

And when he and his daddy had realised that they would have to go over to England to work, how the family had wept and cried! Mammy tried hard to be brave, but she clung to Peader and to her son at the last moment.

'We've always managed,' she had said, her voice trembling and thick with unshed tears. 'Sure and we'll manage again. Don't go, don't leave us!'

But there was so little work in Dublin, that was the trouble! Peader had been a docker, but he'd rarely succeeded in catching the stevedore's eye and without doing that you'd scarce make enough money to buy bread let alone pay rent or keep the kids halfway decent. Brogan could still remember those awful mornings when his father had returned, silent, from the quays. Often he could not look at them, shamed by his inability to provide.

'I couldn't catch his eye,' he would mumble guiltily. 'Sure an' didn't I run like a greyhound along to the next read, and no more luck, me, that time? But there's other work beside labouring on the ships. I'll find something, sweet Deirdre, I'll not let you down.'

It wasn't really a matter of letting down, Brogan understood that. His mammy worked hard in her own right, trekking out into the countryside around Dublin, picking potatoes, then selling them in Moore Street,

Francis Street or anywhere else where she could find a pitch.

Brogan had worked too, of course. Selling the *Herald* and the *Mail* to the citizens of Dublin from the time he was ten, barefoot in the snow in winter or under the pitiless sun of high summer. He had jumped on and off trams to sell to folk on the top deck, hurled himself in front of jarveys crying his wares as they tried to start their handsome horses off at a fast trot, and finally taken home the unsold papers in wintertime to wedge against the old window frames in an attempt to keep out the wicked winds.

But even so, the money didn't keep them. Not quite. Always nearly, never completely. They would be doing well, eating regular, making ends meet as Mammy said, and then suddenly disaster would strike. Once, they put up the rent. Once, they increased the cost of the newsboy's licence, and you couldn't sell without a licence. Who 'they' were Brogan was never sure, just a part of that vast, throbbing over-class which seemed to spend all its time making sure that the poor remained poor.

Those small disasters had almost done for them. They'd had to go, cap in hand, to the St Vincent de Paul Society, who had sent round a tall, thin man with a long, cadaverous face and squinty little eyes. He had sat in their fine parlour and cross-questioned mammy until she had shed bitter, helpless tears. Why did they need the relief? What had changed? Could they not manage with one room less if the rent was too much for them? Others did it – if they could just cut their coat according to their cloth. . .

'I sold me winter coat, sir,' Mammy had said, not understanding. ''Twas that we ate last week, but now 'tis gone . . .'

The Vincents man pulled down his mouth and asked more questions. Who was in work? Why did not her husband find some other employment if he could not catch the stevedore's eye at the docks? There *was* other work, he had it on good authority that they were taking on labourers at such and such a place . . .

But now he and Peader, his father, were in decent work, and able to send almost all of their wages home. Rent in Liverpool was their biggest expense but they had found a lodging house which was cheap and relatively bug-free, and Peader said they must eat well – the work was too hard to stint themselves in that direction. Brogan knew that they were luckier than some, that they must put up with being far away in return for the benefits of regular work. And besides, his mammy was frugal and would save all she could and perhaps one day, perhaps when summer came, they could catch the ship home again and stand in the bows and watch as Ireland came into view through the land-haze. And until then at least they were earning, knowing that despite their homesickness, and the rough voices about them, they were taking some of the burden off Deirdre O'Brady.

Brogan sighed and felt the baby's warm weight in his lap with satisfaction. He had missed the kids, working with men all day and lodging with an old couple who cared nothing for the men in their home save to see that they didn't come indoors the worse for drink. So it was nice to have a baby in his arms again.

And presently, tired and satisfyingly full, with a mug of unaccustomed porter inside him, Brogan, too, slept.

He woke because the baby was wriggling against him, patting his face with one warm, starfished hand. He struggled into a sitting position – he had fallen over whilst he slept, to sag against the wall – and looked around him. The men had all gone, back to their work he supposed. The railway gangs did all sorts; some of them walked a stretch of line, they loaded and unloaded coal or great sides of meat for the cold storage depots, they cleared landslides and created cuttings. Sometimes they manhandled trucks on to whichever stretch of line needed extra freight, or replaced damaged sleepers with new ones . . . oh, they had a thousand and one jobs. But today being Christmas Day they could take it easy – or easier, at any rate. They had volunteered to come in today because they were far from home and could do with the money. And because of the dreadful weather and the sudden snowstorms, they could well find themselves desperately needed. Repairs had to be carried out at once when something went wrong in order that the engines could be ready and in the right place when they were needed next day.

So now, Brogan sat up and looked around him. The coke stove still burned brightly and there were signs that the men had left hurriedly – the tin mugs they drank from were laid on their sides, the newspaper-wrapped bread, cheese and cold mutton had been abandoned, but other than that he was alone with the sleeping girl and the baby.

The snow must have caused a problem, Brogan thought, getting to his feet, the baby still tucked in his arm. I'd best get out there now, or there'll be trouble – why did Peader leave me to sleep, I wonder? He sat the baby on the ground near the girl, who was slumbering still, well away.

'Stay there, Moll,' Brogan whispered to her. It would be a cryin' shame to wake the girl Jess so it would and her such a poor, skinny young thing! 'Wait wit' your sister until she wakes.'

The baby looked up at him, beaming, showing a tooth in her bottom jaw. Then she began to crawl towards the source of the warmth and light – the coke burner. Hastily Brogan turned her with his boot, edging her in the opposite direction, but it didn't last. The baby gurgled and set off once more for the stove, chuckling. Brogan, already turning towards the doorway, paused, uncertain. He could wake the girl, but it seemed awful hard – why should he not simply tuck the baby inside his donkey jacket and take her with him? It wasn't as though he would be outside for long, he would only go and find Peader, see if he was needed. If he was, he'd run back, wake the girl, leave the baby in her care, but if he wasn't, he would go back to the cabin and play with the baby himself, keep her occupied, until the girl woke naturally.

The thin blanket lay under the girl's head, but his coat was warm. He tucked the baby under his coat, buttoned it up, and set off into the early winter dusk. The baby was so light it made him want to cry all of a sudden, but he scolded himself. You're a man, Brogan O'Brady, he reminded himself, you work as a navvy, you can't shed tears because a baby's half-starved. And anyway, I'll tell the girl to bring her down again in our dinner-break. There's always something from me carry-out which she could have and welcome. We won't desert her, now we've found her.

When Jess awoke it was full dark and for several moments she had no idea where she was. She lay on a hard floor – well, there was nothing strange in *that* – but instead of darkness, with a lighter patch where the window should have been, there was a comforting red glow – and she was warm.

Luxuriating in this unusual awakening, she simply lay there for a moment, gazing round her. Warmth in winter! It so seldom happened to her, but it was true that right now she was warm and cosy from the top of her head to the tips of her toes. So Mollie must be warm too, and . . .

Mollie! In a flash, she remembered everything, the girl called Sara in the beautiful red coat and hat who had given her money and a pair of white woolly gloves, the baker's shop where they had let her have three fine loaves of bread and two currant buns, the dairy where she'd bought the cheese and they had poured a generous measure of milk into the old bully beef tin. Then there was the long walk through the freezing snow and wind . . . and the discovery of the cabin and the friendly Irish navvies.

But . . . where were they? She was alone, the baby had gone . . . had Mollie crawled out into the darkness? Jess scrambled to her feet and ran to the doorway. To eyes which had been gazing dreamily at the coke burner, the early evening outside seemed black indeed, but no baby cried against the shrilling of the wind. She could see no small, crawling figure amidst the gleaming rails.

But she could not see the men, either. Quickly, because she could not bear to lose her few possessions, Jess returned to the cabin and picked up what was left of the loaves, the little white gloves which must have fallen from the baby's feet, and the thin blanket. All the milk had gone, gobbled up as sops by herself and the child. It did not cross her mind that the men might have taken Mollie for her own protection, she simply knew that she must find her little sister. Mollie was an innocent child, Jess her only protector. She simply must find her!

Alone, with the blanket around her shoulders giving her what little protection it could, Jess set out into the storm.

Brogan slogged across the rails to where, dimly, he could see a lantern's light, and speedily found himself reunited with his father and the other men. They were standing by the side of the track, looking anxiously towards the engine sheds. Peader greeted him with relief.

'Ah, there you are, me boy! I was wonderin' whether I ought to run and get you, though you were sleepin' so sound, you and the little girls . . .'

'What's happened, Daddy?' Brogan asked. 'I woke and found you all gone so I guessed you'd been called away.'

'Landslide,' his father said briefly. 'Further up the line. They're sendin' us up on an engine to see if we can clear it. We could do wi' your muscle, Brog.'

'Right; but I'd best run back to the cabin . . .' Brogan was beginning, when he heard the thump and rattle of an approaching train.

'Too late, boyo,' Declan said. 'She's comin', and she won't wait for no man, let alone a bit of a boy.'

The engine drew up beside them. The driver, a Liverpudlian, leaned out, blinking against the falling flakes.

'Let's be 'avin' you, fellers,' he said cheerfully. 'No need to watch for signals today, we're the only train on this line. Gerrin the guard's van, then we can gerrup steam. It's ten mile out, by whar' I've been told; a tree's acrost the line an' the snow's caused a landslip. But you're big fellers, it won't take you a month of Sundays to clear it.'

'True,' Peader said. They waited until the guard's van was level with them, then they clambered aboard. Peader turned to heave his son up by one elbow, then stared at him. 'What's that you've got under your jacket, son?' he began to say, when the train started to move . . . with the men and the hidden child firmly ensconced in the guard's van.

Panic hit Jess as soon as she was out in the middle of the rails, trying to get across them to a light she could see burning, vaguely, through the fast-falling snow. Her bare feet, in their holey, battered boots, were constantly stubbed against a rail or a sleeper she could no longer see for the blanket of snow, and the lantern light seemed to move as she ran, and always further away.

But she knew she must keep going, must find Mollie. Her little sister was only a tender baby, and would not last long alone and blanketless under such conditions.

She heard a noise coming from the direction of the engine sheds but ignored it. She had lived near the railway long enough to know the sound of an engine being coaled up, getting up steam, but she knew it took a long time, too. Probably someone was preparing the engines for work the following day. So she simply hurried on, climbing on to a sleeper, then hurrying between the lines, sure that if she did not move fast when she did find Mollie, the child would be a tiny, frozen corpse.

She was actually standing on a rail when she felt it begin to vibrate. That's odd, Jess thought vaguely, and jumped down on to the hardcore between the rails, wincing as it penetrated the cardboard soles of her boots. There aren't any trains today, the fellers said so – wonder what that is, then?

She glanced to her right as she stepped on to the

next rail, which was vibrating worse than ever . . . and opened her mouth to scream.

But she never made a sound. The train struck her, carried her along, dropped her . . . devoured her into its great, clanking steel maw.

She never heard the squeal of the train's brakes nor the engine note change as the driver decided he had hit a slight obstruction on the line and speeded up once more. Like a rag doll she lay where she had been thrown, oblivious, at last, to rain, hail or snow, to wind and weather.

As soon as he could, Brogan showed Peader the child's small face beneath his coat and told him what had happened, but what with the rocking of the train and the warmth, Mollie was fast asleep again and Peader shrugged, chuckled, and said not to worry.

'The girl was sleepin' when you left her. Likely she'll sleep sound until we get back,' he said comfortably. 'She'd drunk porter, she was warm, she felt safe. Sure she'll sleep until the job's done.'

The other men grinned when they saw the baby, but agreed with Peader that no harm would be done by taking her with them.

'I never seen a child sleep sounder than young Jess,' Declan said. 'She'll not worry about the babe, not yet awhile.'

And then they arrived at the scene of the landslide and Brogan left the child wrapped warmly in his jacket in a corner of the guard's van whilst he and the other men struggled to clear the line. The tree, a huge one, had crashed down, bringing what looked like a mountain of earth with it. The men looked at the great tree, measured it with their eyes, spat on their hands and waded in. They got the tree off the line by sheer brute force, three a side, with Brogan doing his best and the fireman and the driver, who were 'big-wigs' and shouldn't have had to labour, willingly giving a hand. After all, it was Christmas Day!

Then the driver and the fireman climbed back into the cab and the labourers got out the huge, oddly shaped shovels which Brogan had found so hard to handle at first, and began to dig.

'Sure and I never t'ought I'd be movin' mountains almost on me own when I crossed the water,' Paddy panted, but the big shovel swung rhythmically as he spoke and he never missed a load. 'A good job they offered double pay today, for I'm sure as a man can be that this is double work.'

'You want to do it wit'out your donkey jacket,' Peader joked. 'Look at me son, now, an' him as skinny as a tinker's ass, but he's swingin' wit' the best of us, so he is.'

It took longer than they had guessed, however, and it was full dark before they climbed back into the guard's van, dog-weary.

'The girl's bound to have woke be now,' Brogan worried. 'Sure an' she'll want me guts for garters so she will when she sees I've got the baby.'

'She won't wake yet; she'll be deep in her first sleep,' Paddy protested. 'That wee girl hadn't had a warm sleep or a dacent meal for months be the look of her. Just you sit down an' rest, Brog. 'Twon't harm.'

So Brogan sat down in the draughty guard's van, and he was so tired, so muscle-weary, that soon he slept.

Brogan dreamed. He dreamed he was in a huge meadow, gay with flowers, and a soft breeze blew the scented air to him and the sun shone gold out of a clear blue sky overhead. The hedgerows were full of wild roses and honeysuckle, with the verge pink with foxgloves.

Brogan wandered in the meadow for a while, drowsily content, whilst the bees hummed and the birds sang and called and the sweet scents of summer charmed him. And then, coming across the grass, he saw a girl, and as she got closer, he saw that it was Jess, and he knew she had come for the baby.

He looked round wildly; there was no railway line, no embankment, no engine or train or anything of that nature anywhere near. And the girl was smiling at him, holding out her hands to him.

He turned away; how could he tell her he had taken the baby, and now he had lost her? But he could not run from her, so he stood his ground and presently he turned reluctantly towards her and he saw that she was very clean, and that her tangled hair had been washed and brushed. She looked pretty, he thought wonderingly, she was a really pretty girl, no longer a forlorn and ragged waif.

She smiled sweetly at him, then she spoke. 'Brogan? Where's me baby sister?'

He began to say he'd lost the child, and then something made him remember putting her inside his donkey jacket. He shoved a hand into the breast of it and there was the baby, cuddled up against his chest, warm and softly sleeping. He grinned at Jess and drew back the coat to show her the child nestling within.

'There she is, alanna,' he said softly, relief washing over him in waves. 'There she is, safe as houses and pretty as a picture. Will you be takin' her now, then?'

He went to hand the baby over, but Jess shook her head. To his horror, he realised that even as he watched she was growing fainter, until she was no more than a mist of a girl against the flower-filled meadow.

'No, I can't take 'er; it wouldn't be right. And I've gorra go. But you'll tek care of 'er for me, won't you, Brogan? You'll take care of me baby sister, me heart's darlin'? You wouldn't throw 'er on the world's mercy, Brogan, when it don't 'ave none?'

'Oh, but I'm a feller, fellers don't look after babies . . .' Brogan began, but it was too late. The girl Jess had faded like a wraith of mist in the morning sun, and even as he drew the baby out of his coat and held her imploringly towards her sister, the dream faded and he found himself awake and cold, whilst the guard's van continued to clatter along the tracks towards the city.

And presently, when the train came to a halt in the station yard and the men tumbled out, the dream had vanished and Brogan headed for the cabin with no premonition of what he was to find.

Brogan stared around the little cabin, scarcely able to believe his eyes. The girl Jess had gone! She was not curled up on the floor in front of the still-glowing coke burner, she was not sitting on the oil drum, nor taking the opportunity to have a bite from the food they had left for her. She was nowhere to be seen. Brogan stared around unbelievingly for a moment, then turned to his father, who had followed him in. The other men had taken the shovels and equipment back to the store.

'Daddy, she's gone! There's neither hide nor hair of her – she's even taken the little bit o' blanket so she has!'

'She'll have woken up and taken a little walk, per-haps,' Peader said doubtfully. 'Only . . . 'tis mortal cold out there for a skinny lass wit' nobbut rags to her back.'

'But she knew I had the baby,' Brogan said. 'When she fell asleep I was still playin' wit' the little one. Surely she'd have searched for us, not just – just gone?'

'She mebbe only woke up minutes ago,' Peader said reassuringly. 'She'll be out there now.' He turned back towards the doorway. 'Come on, wit' the pair of us callin', 'twill take us but a moment to find the lass.'

'I only took the baby out because she would crawl towards the stove,' Brogan muttered, turning up his coat collar and plunging into the darkness close on his father's heels. 'No baby-stealer, me, though she's a good little one, this one. Oh, Daddy, will she hear us against this storm?'

For now the wind was stronger, if anything, the flakes thicker.

'Never a peep will she hear if we don't shout,' his father called back, crossly. 'Let's be hearin' you, lad – Hey, Jess, JESS! Where are you hidin', alanna?'

But no sound came back to them out of the silent, snow-covered yard. In fact after covering most of the ground between the cabin and the engine sheds, Peader turned to his son and shook his head.

'She's took shelter somewhere, to wait out the storm,' he shouted. 'No use to search further, lad. We'd best get back to the cabin ourselves, see what . . .'

'There's someone over there, Daddy,' Brogan shouted back, gesturing to what looked like a thickening of the snow ahead of them. 'It's the fellers – have they found her?'

They hurried eagerly towards the other men; Declan walked along with a shovel over his shoulder but Paddy had taken off his working coat and was carrying something wrapped in it. The cold was so bitter that with one accord all the men turned back to the cabin; it was no weather for explanations. But once inside

Paddy laid his coat tenderly on the floor and opened it out so that a face just showed between the rough lapels. No one looking at that pale, still face could have thought her still alive.

Brogan gasped. 'Dear God, it's the girl Jess! Is she froze, Paddy? What in the name of all that's dreadful happened to her?'

'The train must ha' caught her crossin' the lines,' Paddy said heavily. 'Hours since, probably . . . eh, it must have been our engine, on the way to move that bloody tree. She must ha' died at once, Brogan, lad, she'd not have known a t'ing, I promise you that.'

'The train hit her? But what was she doin', Paddy, wanderin' around the yard in such weather? When I left her she was sleepin' sound, I swear it.'

Paddy shrugged and went to cover the face again, but Peader stayed his hand.

'No, Paddy, don't! Are you sure she's gone?'

'Aye. We found her across the lines, man – what was left of her.' Paddy drew the coat almost reverently across the ash-pale face. 'On Christmas Day! But He's taken her to be with His angels, no man can doubt that. I'll go for a priest.'

'And the police,' Declan said wearily. 'They'll have to stick their long noses in, no doubt.'

'Aye, no doubt.' Peader looked across at his son. ''Tis a sad and cruel way to go, son,' he said carefully. 'And we'd all have give our right hands to save the child's life, but it's happened. We've all seen death before, the death of an innocent. You must never blame yourself, for I know you, Brog. You'll start thinkin' that if you'd not taken the baby, if you'd left her here, the girl might be alive now. Well, I'm tellin' you, son, that first it was the will o' God and second that if you'd left the baby

49

it might have been that little one who died. She could have pulled the coke burner over . . .'

Brogan was staring at the dark bundle, which had once been a loving, caring girl. Now he leaned forward and pulled back the coat. He gazed at the girl's face and suddenly his dream came back to him in every detail, he could hear her voice, low, pleading, speaking to him from the heart.

You'll tek care of 'er for me, Brogan? You'll take care of me heart's darling? You won't throw her on the world's mercy, when it don't 'ave none?

'Brogan? She was a good girl she was, she'll not bear you any grudge, nor haunt you in any way.'

His father's voice was fairly throbbing with the intensity of his feelings, and he put a hand out to draw the coat back over the dead face, but Brogan stopped him.

'In a moment, Daddy,' he said gently. 'But Mollie must look her last on her sister.' He drew the baby, rosy and only just stirring, out of the breast of his coat. 'See, Mollie? That's your sister who loved you, who died for you. She wanted me to take care of you for her, and I'll not disappoint her.'

'Take care of her? But she's got parents . . . brothers and sisters . . .' Peader said doubtfully, only to have his son round on him.

'To be sure she has; a drunken father who beats his kids and a mother who has no time for them. Daddy, I should have known Jess was dead, because I dreamed of her, when we were coming home in the guard's van. She begged me to take care of the baby . . . she said Mollie was her heart's darling and she didn't want her thrown on the world's mercy, for it has none. What can I do but try to take care of Mollie for her?'

'But the parents will want her back; the police will be round here . . .'

Brogan knelt on the floor and put the baby down beside the dead girl and Mollie touched the cold, white face, then turned back to him. She scrambled back on to his knees and pushed her thumb into her mouth, then turned her face into him. Brogan tucked her back inside his coat and looked squarely at the ring of faces surrounding him. 'Well, fellers? What would you do?'

There was a long, long pause whilst each man consulted his own thoughts, his own conscience. Then Paddy spoke for them all.

'If I had a dream like that, sure an' I'd keep the littl'un as long as I was able. But it'll be a hard road for you, Brogan me boy. I must say, I don't hold wit' fathers who rule their kids wit' their belts nor mothers who give birth and then hand their babbies over to the older kids to bring up, but there's laws in England same as there are back home. It won't be easy.'

Peader looked thoughtfully around the cabin, at the faces in the glow from the coke burner, all serious, concerned.

'You must go home, boy,' he said after a moment. 'Right away, you must go home. We'll tell the authorities we found the lass on the line, it'll be a while before they know who she is or where she hails from, and we'll say nothing about the baby.' He smiled at his son. 'Ah, your mammy's wanted a girl all her life, aren't you the lucky fella to be bringin' her a little daughter!'

'Home!' Brogan could feel a smile starting. To go home – and with such a gift for his beloved mammy! 'Oh, but someone's bound to notice the baby on the ship, there'll be talk . . .'

'Go on the next boat out, and keep the babby quiet until then,' Paddy said. 'If you feed her well and keep her warm she'll not bawl out. Do as your daddy says, boy. Take her to your mammy.'

'More sprouts, Sara? How about you, Nanny? We've left most of the tureen untouched, don't distress Cook by sending such a quantity of vegetables back to the kitchens, I beg of you!'

Mr Cordwainer was trying to be jovial, to instil some Christmas spirit into the proceedings, but his best efforts were being thwarted by his wife, who was plainly sulking, and slightly by Sara, who had not got over the disappointment of losing Jess. This is turning out to be the oddest Christmas ever, Sara decided, as she allowed her father to spoon a few more sprouts on to her plate. Why on earth had Nanny passed on Mrs Rushton's message? It had only made mother angry.

But that had been no excuse for Mrs Cordwainer's behaviour ever since. She had criticised every single course, found fault with Sara's table manners and told her husband that he had chosen the wrong wine.

Sara realised that her mother's anger was partly directed against herself; she had undoubtedly invited Nanny for Christmas Day without realising that the older woman would assume she was not welcome for Boxing Day. This had made her look grudging in her husband's eyes. But to continue to make everyone feel uncomfortable seemed so unnecessary that Sara could not begin to account for it. Grown-ups, Sara decided – not for the first time – simply went their own way regardless and expected children to make the best of it.

And Nanny was too quiet; it worried Sara, who knew that Mrs Prescott liked to talk and laugh. In fact her Christmas Day was already in grave danger of being spoiled.

'Well, Sara? Have you quite finished? Sure? Then

since you're the last I'll tell Cook to bring in the pudding.'

Mr Cordwainer tinkled a little bell by his right hand and after a pause, the long door at the end of the dining room was flung open and Cook appeared, extremely red in the face, bearing the flaming pudding before her. Mr Cordwainer clapped rather self-consciously and Mrs Prescott followed suit so Sara, trying hard as well now, said, 'Hooray!' in a rather squeaky little voice and then clapped too.

'Really, Adolphus,' Mrs Cordwainer said as soon as the cook had left the room, 'you've not even tasted the pudding yet; the time for congratulating Cook is when we've tried the pudding, not before we've even cut into it. I daresay it will be nasty and we'll have to send it back untouched.'

Mr Cordwainer turned to his wife but before he could say a word Nanny was before him, and she was clearly furious – even more furious than either Cordwainer, Sara could see.

'Letty, you should be ashamed of yourself! I hope never to see a nastier exhibition of unrestrained temper . . . and from a child I brought up to the best of my ability, too! Now are you going to apologise and begin to behave prettily or shall I order the car to come round and take me straight home?'

There was an appalled silence. Sara, looking from face to face, thought she had never seen her parents so dumbstruck. And what on earth did it mean? Surely not that her beloved nanny was going to turn round and leave, after they had persuaded her to stay, too? She knew Mrs Prescott had been Mother's nanny, too, but she had never heard Mrs Prescott speak to her mother in any but the mildest terms, she had certainly never heard her so angry. But her father was nodding his head slowly, as though he agreed – oh, what on earth was going to happen?

And it had all started, she was sure, because Nanny had mentioned Mrs Rushton and Sid and a Sunday school outing, long ago. Sara supposed that there must have been a Sunday school trip both from the Snowdrop Street area and from wherever her mother had been brought up. But why Mrs Cordwainer should so dislike it being mentioned ... and then Mrs Rushton had seemed to know Mrs Cordwainer quite well, she'd said 'when we were twelve'. Actually, that gave Sara her first moment of doubt. Mrs Rushton was *old*, her hair was grey and her figure sagging. Oh, she was nice all right, but definitely old.

But a moment's thought cancelled that one out, too. Mrs Cordwainer had one child, not six or seven, and she had servants and a big house, a car, a chauffeur ... naturally she looked less strained than a woman who did all her own work, and cleaned public houses, as well. And Mother dyes her hair, too, Sara remembered. Its bright colour sometimes faded and then became bright once more, so Sara knew she dyed it. It was probably true, then, that Mrs Rushton and Sara's own mother were the same age and had gone on the same Sunday school trip. But that didn't explain Mrs Cordwainer's crossness, nor the martial sparkle in Nanny's eyes.

'Well, Letty?' That was Mrs Prescott. She's really brave, Sara thought, seeing the scarlet flame in her mother's cheeks. Suppose she's too brave – suppose Mother just tells her to go? But it was Christmas and Nanny, in some mysterious way, seemed to have the upper hand. Even as Sara stared, round-eyed, her mother heaved a sigh, glanced up towards the ceiling with an expression of pained long-suffering, and spoke.

'I'm sorry I've offended you, Nanny,' she muttered. 'Let's all have a helping of this delicious pudding ... Adolphus, will you serve?'

Nanny, passing her plate, gave Sara a small, secret smile, but Sara saw her mother watching her and did not add fuel to the fire by returning it. Instead, as she passed the plate, she gave Nanny's hand a discreet squeeze. And Nanny squeezed back, before turning the conversation neatly into safer, less inflammable subjects.

It's going to be all right, Sara thought thankfully, as conversation became general once more. And after we've had our meal, I'm going to show Nanny how to make a really huge snowman in the back yard!

Chapter Three

On the day after Boxing Day, Sara awoke to find that the snowstorm which had battered the city for two whole days and nights had ceased. Outside her window frail sunshine shone on trees and hedges heaped with snow, on a garden which might just as well have been a meadow so totally snow-blanketed was it, and on the hushed and wonderful world of deep winter.

'Miss Sara, it's time you were gettin' up. I'm now goin' down to fetch your breakfast.' Jane popped her head round the edge of Sara's door and beamed at her. 'The bloomin' snow's stopped, which is one blessing, an' the sun's shinin'. Your pa said we was to go to the park today, so that's just what we'll do, soon's I've finished me work.'

Sara sat up in bed and smiled back at Jane. 'Oh, lovely, I love the park,' she said enthusiastically. 'Poor Nanny, she loves it too, but we didn't get much chance to do anything, not with the storm. Just my luck, that it stops the very moment she goes home. But still, it'll be fun to go out of doors. You could help me make a snowman, Jane.'

'I could an' all,' Jane agreed. Jane was a nice girl, only six years Sara's senior, but she had a good many jobs around the house which she had to see to before she could think of amusing her young charge and Sara got thoroughly sick of hanging around whilst the maid helped with the laundry, ran errands or toiled around the place with a brush and dustpan. But today, Sara thought happily, standing before the schoolroom fire and buttoning her woollen stockings on to her liberty bodice, they were to spend at least some time out of doors. Mr Cordwainer, seeing her disconsolately hanging about the hall when he left the house the previous day, had announced that she looked pale and that it would do her good to visit the park daily, until school started once more in ten days' time.

'Your life in the school holidays lacks purpose, Sara,' he said severely, which Sara thought supremely unfair, since any purpose she had in mind was immediately squashed by either one or other of her parents. 'You need employment – the devil finds mischief for idle hands, you know.'

But though it was a shame that he had managed to turn a treat – which was visiting the park – into a duty, Sara was still grateful to him. He took very little notice of her as a rule, now he had twice done something which had, in its way, made things easier for her. She still remembered his approval of Nanny, his making it plain that he thought she was in the right rather than his wife.

And today is sunny; we'll have a really good time and Mother won't be able to stop us by saying Jane has work to do, because Father's orders are paramount, Sara thought gleefully, quoting, in her mind, the very words her mother used when it suited her to blame her husband for some irksome order or other. She fastened her back suspenders, not without difficulty, for they were small, fiddly things, straightened her skirt and was standing with one foot in a pom-pommed slipper and the other still clad only in a black woollen stocking, when the door opened and Jane came into the room. She was carrying a tray with Sara's breakfast egg, a plateful of bread and butter and a mug of milk on it, and whilst she transferred the contents of the tray to the schoolroom table, she announced in a mournful voice that she would have to go downstairs at once, to see the missus.

'Why, Jane?' Sara asked idly, picking up her teaspoon and tapping the brown egg thoughtfully upon its bald cranium. 'Does she want us to go shopping with her? Oh, don't let's! Father said I might play in the park, or – or go for walk by ourselves.'

'It ain't that, Miss Sara,' Jane said unhappily. 'My little brother Freddy just come to the back door. Mam's been took bad, she's in the Stanley 'ospital, they say it could be 'pendicitis. And if it is, someone's gorra look after the littl'uns.'

'Oh, I see,' Sara said rather blankly. She had been really looking forward to getting out of the house for a while, but now she felt ashamed that she had never thought to ask Jane about her family, but the girl had only recently been promoted to take care of her, Phyllis having left for a livelier household with more children – and more money, she had told her charge. 'Well, I'm awfully sorry your mother's ill, Jane, but of course your first duty is to her. You'd best go off, then.'

And Jane, having set Sara's breakfast down upon the table, promptly went, to return presently saying in a tone of hushed excitement: 'Madam says I may go home and see how things are. I'll not pack, since it may be a false alarm, but Madam says as how she'll see to you this morning, Miss.'

'That's kind of her,' Sara said glumly. She could imagine few worse fates than being 'seen to' by her mother on a snowy morning. 'I hope you find your mother much better, Jane.'

'Thank you, Miss,' Jane said buoyantly. 'Mind, a few

days at home's a bit of a treat ... in a way, acourse,' she added hastily, plainly feeling that she was being tactless in making such an admission. 'It's always nice to see me brothers and sisters.'

As she spoke she was taking her navy-blue coat and her matching hat with the pale green ribbon off the hook behind the nursery door and slipping them on. Sara could see that the maid was enjoying even the thought of going back to her home, and envied her. If only I had brothers and sisters, how pleasant being without Jane could be, she thought wistfully. There would be more than one, then, to plead with Mother and Father, or even to defy them! Perhaps a brother would always be able to get round Mother, like Christine Andrews says her brother can, or a sister could actually *enjoy* shopping, and do it instead of me. And then all the brothers and sisters could go to the park together, skate on the lake, make snowmen, have snow fights ... we could do lots and lots of things. None of us would have to depend on a servant, because we'd have each other for company, and for taking care.

But it was not to be. I'm sure there are advantages in being an only child, Sara thought, picking up her spoon as Jane left the room. She eyed the egg broodingly for a moment, and then decapitated it with unnecessary violence. Off with your head, off with your head! But it was no use railing against fate; she was an only child, and a terribly lucky one, who ate three good meals a day, wore warm clothing and never had to dread the snow and frost.

Because Sara knew she would never forget Jess and the baby and the way Jess's hand had stretched out and then tucked itself back into her jacket again. Mother said the poor begged for money instead of working for it. Sara knew, now, that in many cases that simply was not true. The poor would, for the most part, far rather work, but they didn't have the chance. And dimly, somewhere in her mind, she knew that there was another unfairness; that many of the women living in Snowdrop Street, even those who loved their families, did not actually want fourteen or fifteen children. It was yet another of the strange penalties of being poor, she supposed.

But it was not something she could ask about, of course. Jane would blush and giggle and say she didn't know she was sure, Nanny would tell her she'd understand when she was older, and Mother . . . well, she had no idea what Mother would say because Sara could never question her mother. Mother has no patience with children and precious little with grownups, Sara found herself thinking, and blushed. What a bad girl she was, to feel like that about her mother! I love her, of course I do, she told herself, sipping milk from her blue china mug. Only . . . she doesn't like me very much at all, she's never hugged me or given me a kiss and a cuddle in her life, which is why I'm more at home with Nanny than with her.

But being discontented with one's lot was a sin, so being discontented with one's mother must be even worse. When she comes up presently and tells me to put my nice coat and my best hat on, and my shiny black boots, so that she can take me off to Lewises and Blacklers and all the other big stores, I'll try to look pleasant, Sara planned. And once we're there we'll go round and round the millinery departments and the fashion departments and look at dresses and hats and hats and dresses . . . and she'll be horrified if I suggest that it might be fun to play in the snow for a little.

Sara finished her egg and had some marmalade on the bread and butter. Then she piled her dishes on the

60

tray and set off for the kitchens, three floors below. Normally, Jane would have taken the tray down but since she was away, Sara reasoned, there would be a good deal of disorganisation downstairs. The Cordwainers did not believe in employing more servants than were absolutely necessary, which meant that when a maid was sick or absent or even on a day off, everyone else in the servants' quarters had to work twice as hard.

She was on the ground floor and heading for the green baize door which led to the kitchens when her mother came out of the breakfast parlour, looking abstracted. 'Ah, Sara,' she said, peering at her daughter. 'What on earth are you doing?'

She rarely wore her spectacles but was extremely shortsighted, Sara knew.

'I'm taking my dishes down to the kitchen, Mother,' Sara said dutifully, however. 'Jane's mother is ill – didn't she tell you?'

'Oh . . . yes, of course, I was forgetting. And what are you going to do with yourself this morning?'

Sara's heart lifted. So it wasn't to be a dreaded shopping expedition, then!

'Well, Father said I was to go out, so I could go to the park with one of the maids, if one can be spared,' she said, therefore. 'Perhaps Ruby might enjoy a walk?'

But even the suggestion was enough to bring her mother's thin brows together in an impatient frown.

'Oh no, Sara. We pay the maids to work, not to enjoy walks,' she said tartly. 'Read a book, or – or do some sums.'

'But that isn't going out of doors, and Father said . . .' Sara began, indignation taking the place of caution. Her mother, who had begun to move on towards the stairs, stopped short.

'Oh, your father said so, did he? Well, I really can't spare a maid and the snow's far too thick anyway. You'll simply have to content yourself with the schoolroom.'

Her foot was on the bottom stair. Sara raised her voice in a last desperate plea for understanding, perhaps even sympathy.

'I *must* go out, Father said so! Oh, I wish Nanny was still here, she loves to walk in the park!'

Sara expected her mother to continue to climb the stairs, perhaps not even to answer her, so she was astonished when her mother whipped round, looking extremely cross.

'Well, she isn't. But if you're so keen to see her I'll get Robson to take you round there this afternoon. No, you can go this morning – why not? And I'll tell Adolphus that you can stay there until Jane comes back. And no playing out in the street, do you understand me?'

Sara would have promised anything, done anything, but she knew the value of a bombardment of words. If she played her cards right she need not actually make any specific promises at all.

'Oh, Mother, thank you,' she said fervently. 'I'll do everything Nanny tells me and I'll help her in the house, go shopping with her . . . I'll be very, very good.'

'I'll order the car for eleven o'clock,' her mother said, not bothering to reply. 'And I'll send for you as soon as Jane's back. And if it isn't convenient for Mrs Prescott she'll have to bring you home herself,' she added spitefully. 'And pay for a taxi – unless she brings you on the tram, of course.'

'Thank you, Mother,' Sara said again. She did not add that she knew Nanny would have walked home with her if necessary, nor that Nanny would be delighted to have her as a guest. Her mother, she knew, was quite capable of suddenly deciding that it had not been a good idea after all, and sharply retracting her promise.

But nothing of the sort happened. Her mother climbed the stairs and vanished around the corner and Sara continued on down to the basement.

In the kitchen, her news was greeted with some relief.

'It ain't that we don't want you, Miss Sara, but it's awkward, wi' Jane away,' Bessie explained. 'There's so much work, see, and cartin' your trays upstairs of a mornin', lightin' the schoolroom fire, makin' you a luncheon ... well, it's all extra, when Jane's off.'

'I don't mind at all, because I like being at Nanny's so much,' Sara said. 'We have a lovely time, Nanny and me. Can I give you a hand with the washing-up, Bessie?'

'It's good of you, Miss, but I'll do it in no time. You go up and pack yourself a bag,' Bessie said diplomatically, clattering dishes. 'And don't forget to wear your wellington boots, acos the snow's that thick you'll be soaked, else.'

Sara agreed to do so and hurried back up the three flights of stairs once more, to the schoolroom high up under the eaves. She had never packed for herself before but could see no difficulty; she would just pack her nicest things and some play-clothes and then go and wait for Robson to bring the car round.

'Where's all your knickers, queen? And I can only find odd stockings.'

Nanny had been absolutely delighted to find her charge on her doorstep, beaming and rosy, with the news that she was to stay with Mrs Prescott until the girl Jane returned to her duties. She had hugged Sara, and kissed her many times, thanked Robson for his care of her and carried her off to the neat front parlour, where she put a match to the fire and then brought in some ginger biscuits and a cup of hot milk.

Explanations had taken up the next twenty minutes, and Nanny had said she was sorry to hear about Jane's mother and would visit her at the Stanley, which was only just up the road. Then they had talked of all they could do over the next few days, and then they had examined Nanny's bowl of bulbs, which Sara had given her for Christmas and which they had examined only a couple of days before. There were four snub green noses showing above the soil; Sara was anxious about the fifth, for she had planted the bowl herself, with the assistance of Rogers, her father's gardener, and did not like to think that one of the bulbs might have been bad.

But now, unpacking in the chilly little front bedroom, for Nanny would not have dreamed of lighting a fire upstairs unless someone was sick, Nanny was showing some dismay over Sara's choice of clothing.

Sara looked at the garments spread out over the single bed. 'What's wrong, Nanny? I put in some knickers, didn't I? And some stockings. Only I wanted to bring my tartan kilt and my nice green cardigan . . . and then there were boots, and extra socks, and my pom-pom slippers – oh dear, and if I go back Mother will probably change her mind and make me stay.'

'Well, we won't risk that, but you need more than one spare pair of knickers, love,' Nanny said. 'And I can't find a single pair of stockings, they're all odd.'

'How can they be odd? They're all black, and woolly, aren't they all alike?' Sara asked. 'I can't see any difference. Besides, it doesn't matter, does it? Stockings are stockings.'

'And pairs are pairs. But I suppose we can manage with the stockings. And I'll take you on the tram to Paddy's market and we'll buy some knickers.' Mrs Prescott smiled grimly. 'That'll teach your mother to send you to me without the proper clothes!'

'Why? What's wrong with Paddy's market?' Sara asked, ferreting through the clothes in her bag. 'I've got my coral beads in here somewhere . . . oh yes, they're in my black strap shoes, I knew I'd put them somewhere safe.'

'There's nothing wrong with it, but your mother don't like it because Paddy's market sells secondhand clothing. Do you mind secondhand clothing, queen?'

'No, not at all,' Sara said unhesitatingly. 'So long as it's fairly clean, of course.'

Mrs Prescott laughed. 'Only fairly clean? You're a one and a half, young Sara! Come on then, I've done up here, we'll get ourselves a bite to eat and then we'll walk down the road, do some shopping. What do you fancy for your tea tonight?'

They were in Samples, choosing a cake, when a woman standing at the counter, a woman who Sara half-recognised as living in Snowdrop Street, spotted them. She was talking to the baker and jabbing a finger at a big yellow bowl covered with a washed-out piece of linen but as soon as she saw Sara's companion she turned to greet her.

'Afternoon, Annie. What're you givin' for the wake, tomorrer? I'm tekin' fruit buns – that's the mix, there. Mr S is goin' to cook it up for me. Our Ruth's gorra nice piece o' boilin' bacon an' Mrs Lamb's givin' a couple o' dozen eggs. You can't expect the Carbs to mek a contribution, with 'im bein' out o' work an' 'er 'avin' the young 'uns to see to.'

'Afternoon, Hannah. I'm doing sandwiches,' Mrs Prescott said. 'I saw your Ruth, so I'm doin' fish paste and cheese. It's a terrible thing . . . the poor feller who was drivin' the engine must be half out of his mind!'

'You're right there,' the other woman agreed. 'Eh, I've allus worried about the rails bein' so near, but who'd ha' thought it could come to this?'

Sara pricked up her ears. What had happened? Had there been a train crash? She loved to look across at the big engines getting up steam, and at the lines and lines of goods trucks, but she knew there were accidents; trains collided, or left the rails, or crashed too hard into the buffers.

'Tragic,' Mrs Prescott said. 'Though that poor kid had a mis'rable life if you ask me. Stan hit the kids more'n he praised 'em . . . and there was never enough to eat. Nesta isn't so bad, though she's no patience with kids, but her old fella . . . well, you know how it is.'

'Aye; none better. My Ben drank once, but 'e's give it up now, thank the good Lord. Now tell me, Annie, 'ave they 'eard owt of the baby?' Hannah Evans was small and round with brown, birdlike eyes and a set of very white false teeth which looked as though they had been made for someone a good deal larger. Now she looked hungrily at her companion, as though gossip was edible, Sara thought, vaguely disturbed by the idea.

'Baby? What's this all about, Hannah?'

'Well, it seems young Jess took the baby out walkin' with her, an' when they found her, they didn't find no baby.' Hannah Evans paused discreetly, glancing down at Sara and then, quickly, away. 'Only from wharr I've been told the train went right over 'er . . . I thought mebbe there weren't no way to tell . . .'

'I've not heard any more than you have,' Mrs Prescott said quickly. 'I'll see you tomorrow, then, Hannah.'

'Right, Annie. I'll be off then. If you hear anything more, let me know.'

Mrs Prescott agreed and presently she and Sara left the shop with a large fruit cake in the wickerwork basket Sara carried.

'Nanny, what happened to Jess? I met a girl called Jess outside the church, on Christmas Day. I told you.'

'Yes, so you did, queen, but there's a mortal lot o' gels called Jess, and I doubt Jess Carbery would walk all the way to . . .' Sara's exclamation cut her off short. She looked down at the child. 'Oh, love, don't say it were *that* Jess?'

'Yes, it was, Nanny! What happened to her?' Sara asked, in anguish. It was something bad, she just knew it was, as much by the older women's tone as by their actual words.

'She – she was killed, love. By a train. Hit by a train. They say she died instantly, there weren't no sufferin'.'

Sara stared down at her boots and saw them wobble as tears brimmed in her eyes. Poor, poor Jess! She'd had so very little, now she had lost even that. But what about the baby? Jess had adored that baby – how would it manage, without her?

'And Mollie? The baby? I told you, Nanny, I gave Jess my angora gloves to keep the baby's toes warm. Did she have Mollie with her?'

There was another pause before Mrs Prescott answered her, and then Sara could tell that she was thinking hard.

'Yes, her mam says she had the baby with her, but folk are that ungenerous . . . they wonder, you see, if

67

Nesta . . . well, if she got rid of the baby, somehow. There are women what want babies . . . or she might've handed the child over to an orphan-home, once she knew about Jess. Jess took care o' the baby, see? But no one knows, rightly. Mollie's disappeared.'

'You told Mrs Evans you didn't know what had happened to the baby,' Sara said, fighting to keep her voice steady for her eyes were still brimming. She remembered them so well, it seemed impossible, and impossibly cruel, that Jess was dead and Mollie bereft of her only friend and protector. She remembered Jess saying *if she lives*, remembered her own shock at the words. Now it was Jess who had died and from the sound of it, Mollie had either died too or simply disappeared. She turned her face up to her nanny's, the tears still unshed. 'You did say you didn't know, Nanny.'

'Well, Mrs Evans is a good woman but a rare one to gossip,' Nanny explained. 'I didn't want to see bad made worse, queen. There's plenty what think wherever the baby is, she's better off than wi' the Carbs, which makes you wonder. A sweet, pretty thing she was, Mollie Carbery, but there's no doubtin' it, livin' wi' that family she couldn't be neither sweet nor pretty long. Not without Jess, that is,' she added.

'And when did it happen?' Sara said as soon as she had command of her voice again. 'I saw her at noon on Christmas Day I suppose, or thereabouts.'

'It was later on that same day,' Mrs Prescott said. 'Jess had bought bread and some milk and when she left the baker thought she meant to go straight home, but my guess is that she realised her father would take the food off her – or her mother, for that matter – and went into the goods yard. She'd lived near the lines for long enough to know that they only run a Sunday service on Christmas Day, but there had been a landslip because of all the snow, I suppose, and a train was taking a gang of men to the spot to clear the line for traffic next day. Neither the driver nor the fireman saw Jess, and probably, what with the driving snow and the wind and the darkness, she didn't see them, either.' Mrs Prescott touched Sara's cheek with a gentle hand, smoothing her bright hair back from her face. 'She didn't feel a thing, queen; it were too sudden, too quick.'

'She said she'd buy bread and milk with the money I gave her,' Sara said in a small, choked voice. 'She must have done just that. Oh, Nanny, Mother would say I should never have given her the money . . . and how I wish I hadn't! You could say the money was stolen, only it was me who stole it, not Jess. Could God have got muddled and punished her because the money should have been in the collection?'

Mrs Prescott stopped short and caught Sara's shoulder, turning her so that they faced one another across the snowy pavement.

'Don't you dare even think such a thing, queen,' she said fiercely. 'Remember the picture in your room? Suffer the little children to come unto Me, He said, and that's just what He meant. Our Lord would never punish a child in such a way, why you'll be up there with a gold crown on your 'ead and a pair o' wings on your shoulders 'cos you give that poor little kid a bit of 'ope. No one, not even your mam, would criticise you for givin' to the poor, at Christmas or any other time.'

'Oh. Good,' Sara said faintly. 'Will they find the baby, Nanny? Will they find little Mollie?'

'Oh, bound to,' Mrs Prescott said comfortably, turning her face towards home once more. 'And if they don't it'll be because someone took pity on 'er, and took 'er away from them Carbs. Now best foot forward, queen, or I won't have a potato peeled by teatime!'

Brogan got off the ferry when she berthed and stood for a moment on the quay, fighting the tears that brimmed his eyes. He had wept, and others with him, as the ship drew near to the land and they knew they were almost home at last. But now they were ashore the air was thick with fog, the streetlights could barely be seen through it. Smells which he associated with his home and nowhere else assailed his nostrils; fish, seaweed, mud, and the scent of boiled potatoes coming from the tenements behind the docks where the women were cooking the evening meal.

It was cold, but nowhere near as cold as Liverpool; a mildness in the air, which he thought was reflected in the manners of the people, was as much a part of Dublin as the Liffey, flowing brown to the left of him, or the domed Custom House, or Ha'penny Bridge, which he would presently cross in order to reach the maze of little streets known as the Liberties, where the O'Bradys had lived as long as any of them could remember. And God knew why those streets should be called the Liberties, Brogan thought bitterly now, glancing down the front of his coat at the slumbering child which he held to his breast. Liberty wasn't something which came naturally to those who struggled to survive there: he only hoped he was doing the right thing for this defenceless scrap.

In fact Brogan knew very well how the Liberties had been given their name. All Dublin children were taught in school that, long ago, the Liberties had been a straggle of mean huts and the people there had not been taxed, because they were outside the city walls and had none of the good things which the citizens of Dublin had. So they nicknamed the area 'the liberties' because of not paying tax and there you were, a misnomer if ever he heard one.

But now, all he could think of was his own place, his mammy cooking a meal for the family, his brothers clustering round, one boy telling about his day, another interrupting, all laughing, getting as near the fire as they could, happy to have exchanged the chilly, fogbound streets for the little oasis of comfort and warmth that was the O'Brady living parlour. Brogan, striding on, smiled to himself. He would get such a welcome! His mammy would undoubtedly weep all over him . . . oh, but when she saw the baby! He'd had seven brothers, four of whom survived, but there had never been a girl, never a sister for them. It had grieved his mammy, who had always dreamed of a girl-child, but she'd made the best of it.

'Sure and aren't I the lucky one, with fellas all around me?' she teased them. 'Oh, who wants old girls when they can have fine, strong sons?'

When he had first come ashore he had thought it milder than Liverpool but as he walked through the quiet quays the wind began to creep inside his collar, up his sleeves, and it was cold. He turned his coat-collar up and peered down at the baby once more. She was rosy-cheeked, sleeping soundly. Eh, but she'd been good! Not a peep out of her had there been, neither on the journey across the Irish Sea – Brogan had clutched her fiercely as the small ship crashed into the trough of a wave and staggered up to the crest – and everyone had thought he was fighting seasickness. Good job I wasn't, he told himself now with grim humour. How would I have managed if I'd wanted to lean over the side? I'd have lost Moll for sure!

But he hadn't, so all was well. And very soon now she could come out from her hiding place and reap the admiration which, Brogan thought, was her due. Besides, she was soaking wet. The men had clubbed together and bought a pile of towelling for him to use but he had no means of washing it aboard so had simply jettisoned each piece and moved on to the next – and the last had been the last, so he should hurry himself, get back to his mammy, who was someone who understood a good deal more than he did about babies.

He crossed O'Connell Street, admired the brightly lit shop windows, the figures of one or two smart couples strolling along it. He reached the Ha'penny Bridge, and climbed the steps, then set off across it. It was really called the Metal Bridge or the Wellington Bridge, but everyone knew it as the Ha'penny Bridge, from the days when they'd charged you a halfpenny toll to cross. It was a beautiful bridge and even with the fog swirling and hiding the waters of the Liffey, dazzling in haloes round the gas-lights, it was a lovely sight with its delicate wrought-iron railings and the arches which spanned the walkers beneath.

He could have taken several ways from here to get home and the fog seemed thicker by the river but nevertheless he decided to stick to the Quays. He walked swiftly, his scarf up round his mouth now in the fog and deepening dusk. Where Merchants Quay met Low Bridge Street he turned left, then began to weave his way up towards Thomas Street. He turned right into Cornmarket and then he was on Thomas Street, crossing it, diving down Francis Street and then into Swift's Alley, his breathing quickening, a smile tilting his mouth. Home! Swift's Alley might not be everyone's idea of gracious living, but . . . it was home!

He dived into the narrow entry, turned right, and there it was. A tall tenement block with the washing lines which looped the house-fronts hung with limp, unmoving linen, the lines themselves beaded with moisture. He guessed that the womenfolk would have left their sheets and towels hanging out rather than bring them into the rooms still soaked through. He hurried in through the doorway, feeling the child stir sleepily against him. The lobby was damp with all the footsteps of folk passing through but it was clean; a good deal cleaner, he thought protectively, than some of the big public buildings he had known. It smelt of carbolic soap, fish and potatoes, with the faint rivery smell which seemed to hang over the whole city – and of course the smell of the fog. A smell of coal fires, and salt-sea, and wet wood and stone.

He climbed the stairs quite slowly, able to wait now that he was so close. The baby woke properly; it was time for her to be fed, he supposed. She began to struggle but he soothed her, cooed to her, kept his coat round her. She was his reason for coming home, his special surprise, she must not put in an appearance too soon!

The door to the O'Brady room was closed. He turned the handle carefully, then pushed the door open cautiously, bit by bit, so that he could see inside without being seen. The door opened straight into their main room, naturally, with the second room leading off from the first, with no door on to the communal landing.

'It's a fire hazard, that inner room,' a priest had said once, when he was visiting them. 'How would you get the children out safe, Mrs O'Brady, if there was a fire ragin' in your nice parlour?'

'Sure an' I'd t'row 'em t'rough the window,' his

mother had said, smiling. 'My kids are full o' spirit, Father – they'd bounce, every last one of 'em.'

The priest had smiled, too.

'But best keep a bucket of water in the bedroom, even so,' he had advised mildly. 'Bouncin' fireballs is no joke, Mrs O'Brady.'

But now, Brogan looked into the room, and it was as if he had the second sight; everything was just as he'd imagined it. Mammy, stirring a pot, the steam making the little black curls round her face curlier than ever. The boys with their tin plates at the ready, watching for the moment when Mammy said it was done and dipped into the stew with her big ladle. The firelight turning the faces to rose and gold, the lantern on the table casting a cool primrose light, hissing softly away to itself.

Someone gasped; Mammy turned. She stared for a moment, then the ladle flew into the fire and Mammy flew across the room seizing Brogan so hard, squeezing him so fiercely, that he feared for the baby.

'Mammy! Ah, Mammy, I've missed you sore! But don't squeeze me to death, I've a present for you under me coat!'

They were all round him, hugging, exclaiming, asking where Peader was, why Brogan had come home alone – and after Christmas too, when all the fun and frolic was over and done for another year!

'Did you have a good Christmas, my dearest?' his mother asked, still hanging on to his coat sleeve as though she dared not let him go in case he disappeared. 'We had a good time, or as good a time as we could have, wit'out you and me darlin' Peader. I sold oranges on O'Connell Street on Christmas Eve, and I had a line waitin', honest to God I did!'

His mother was delighted with her fruit-selling, she

wanted everyone to know that it wasn't only potatoes she could sell, no indeed, selling was something at which she excelled, her shining eyes said. And wasn't she the prettiest woman ever, Brogan thought fondly. Her eyes were blue as summer skies, her hair black as a raven's wing, and she had dimples and the sweetest smile. No wonder Dubliners had queued up to buy her oranges on Christmas Eve!

'I made five bob in an hour,' his mother was saying. 'Where's me present then, Brogan? Did your daddy send it? Oh, why didn't he come home wit' you, son? He's sadly missed; isn't it dull and flat without your daddy, then?'

The boys agreed that it was and stared at Brogan's coat, which was now heaving gently as the baby tried to escape from its folds.

'It's a puppy!' yelled Martin. He had always wanted a puppy but Mammy said it wasn't fair with them living on the first floor and no way a puppy could run out to do his business.

'A puppy!' Donal echoed. He was a sturdy six-year-old and toothless until the second ones came through. He grinned gummily at his eldest brother. 'Jeez, Brog, you've brought our mammy a puppy!'

Hastily, before hearts were broken – and Mollie was seen as second-best – Brogan undid his coat and lifted the baby from her warm little nest. Peader had formed a sling from an old scarf which had held her secure all through their journey but now she stared at the faces around her as though she could not believe her eyes.

'It's a girl,' Brogan said, but he felt there could be no doubt. Mollie was so pink-cheeked, so bright-eyed, the picture of feminine charm and innocence from the top of her curly head to the tip of her rosy toes, and Brogan heard the admiring gasps, the cries of 'Oh, Brog, what a little dote! Where did you get her, the darlin'? Is she yours, boyo?' with real pleasure. They liked her – and Mammy was gazing at Mollie as though . . . oh, as though all her dearest wishes had come true!

'Brogan? Where . . . How . . . Who . . .?'

''Tis a long story,' Brogan said, taking off his coat and hanging it on the hook behind the door. 'Serve up the meal, Mammy, whiles I tell you how I come by her.'

'You're a good, kind fella, and 'twas no fault of yours that the child's sister was killed,' Deirdre said when his story – and the plate of stew and potatoes – was finished. 'Sure and I'll look after her as though she were me own flesh and blood, and won't I love her as I love me own, too?'

'I never doubted it,' Brogan assured her. 'Daddy's the same, he didn't want her to go back to a man who beats his kids. She's no trouble,' he added hastily. 'And I'll send all me wages home, same as before. I'll work harder, Mammy, so you aren't burdened by the kid.'

'She's no burden,' his mammy insisted. She had taken Mollie on her knee and had spooned bread and milk into her eager mouth. 'But, Brog, I've just had a t'ought. What'll we tell the neighbours?'

'Tell 'em she's an orphan from the country, left wit' us by a cousin,' Niall said after a moment's silence. 'Do you remember your cousin Fidelma? Doesn't she seem a likely one to do somethin' strange, now?'

Everyone laughed except for Bevin, who was too little to remember the strange cousin who had come a-visiting two years since, and driven them all mad with her odd ways and her demands to be taken here and there, to see the sights of the city.

'Ye-es, but not concernin' a baby,' Mammy said at

length. 'It 'ud be better if we picked a cousin called Mairenn, who did wrong and dared not take her child home to the farm with her. Can you remember that? You're the baby, Bevin, you tell me the story.'

'I'm not the baby now, am I though?' Bevin said proudly, pointing at the child on his mother's lap. 'She's the baby – Mollie's the baby. Oh, isn't she a pretty one, Mammy? Isn't she tarrible sweet now?'

'She is. Now tell me where she come from, me little jewel.'

Bevin frowned.

'From – from heaven, Mammy? From God, to us, for bein' good?'

The bigger boys began to laugh and jeer, but Mammy stopped them short with a frown and a shake of the head.

'That's very true, Bevin, and aren't you a broth of a boy now, for knowin' it? But what'll we tell folk who ask how we come to have such a lovely wee girl, now?'

Bevin had been scowling angrily at his brothers but now his brow cleared. 'Oh, that's aisy, so it is,' he said scornfully. 'Mairenn from the farm done wrong, and dussen't take the baby back with her, so we took her, the darlin'.'

Mammy clapped, Brogan cheered, the boys all laughed and followed suit. Even the baby, enthroned upon Mammy's lap, smiled and gurgled.

'There we are, then,' Mammy said triumphantly. 'She'll be Polly O'Brady from now on . . . my dear little Irish Liverpool baby!' She turned to Brogan. 'You'll be stayin' now, won't you?' she coaxed. 'You wouldn't want to go back to that old Liverpool, they'll mebbe ask you questions you can't answer, son.'

The child recently re-christened Polly had finished her bread and milk so Brogan took the dish and carried it over to the basin standing on the table against the wall. He put it in the basin and then refilled the kettle from the bucket and stood it on the metal trivet which poked it into the red heart of the fire.

'Mammy, I wish I could stay,' he said from the heart. 'But there's no job in Dublin that 'ud pay me like the navvyin' job in Liverpool. And though Mollie – I mean Polly – is small now, she'll eat her share, need clothin', go to school when she's big enough. It all costs, Mammy.'

'We'll manage, but I daresay you're right and you should be with your daddy,' his mother said contentedly. 'Can she crawl, the little cherub?'

'Put her down on the rag rug and you'll see for yourself,' Brogan said, smiling. His mother, who had borne so many children, was like a child with a lovely new dolly. She could scarcely wait to take it out, show it to the neighbours. 'Where'll she sleep, Mammy?'

'Where but in me bed, the dote,' Deirdre said fondly. 'And later, in a nice orange box. For I have to work, no matter what. But the rest of you came on the streets with me when you were small, well-wrapped up in a nice fruit box, she'll be no different.'

'She's too big for a fruit box, Mammy,' Brogan said anxiously. 'She'd be out of it and crawlin' amongst the traffic in no time. See?'

And sure enough, Polly was off, crawling briskly across the linoleum, heading for the fire's glow. But she was re-directed by several small, grubby hands, and when she reached a chair she tried to pull herself into a standing position by it and was much praised by the onlookers.

And presently, Brogan went into the second room with his brothers whilst his mammy pulled out her bed, which was a good straw mattress, a pillow and a couple of blankets. She cuddled Polly, already sleeping soundly, down, and then bade her sons goodnight.

'I'll not wake Brogan, he deserves a lie-in, but the rest of you had best be up betimes,' she said as she stood in the doorway between the two rooms with her hair brushed out so that it was like a dark halo around her head. 'There'll be oatmeal for breakfast and some bread and jam. We've still got some left over from me Christmas store.'

'I'll get up when me brothers do,' Brogan said. 'I don't mind, Mammy, honest. I'd as soon be up, because tomorrow I must get me a ticket for the return trip on the ferry boat. Daddy and the other fellers are covering for me – they've told the boss that I was called back to Ireland on Christmas Day to see a sick relative. But I don't want to lose me job, and Daddy's hopin' for advancement quite soon. He's steady, is our daddy, and the bosses know it. Sure and it wouldn't do him a good turn if I stayed away any longer than I need, so I'll be off when I can.'

His mother sighed but she knew better than to argue. Brogan knew that the harder his daddy worked and the more money he earned, the sooner he would be able to come home here for a good holiday if not for ever, and his mammy realised it too.

'Right, Brog,' she said. 'See you in the mornin', then, me laddo. And it's sleep you're in there for, boys, d'you hear me? No chatterin' half the night and keepin' your brother from the rest he needs.'

But nothing could have prevented Brogan from sleeping that night, not the narrowness of the straw mattress he shared with Martin and Donal, not the whisperings of the older boys, not even the terrible throttling snores of Niall, who suffered with catarrh. And once he was asleep he did not stir until morning, though he dreamed, and twitched, and cried out a couple of times.

He longed to dream of Jess again so that he could ask her forgiveness, but all he dreamed of was that the baby ran away from him on the ferry, and climbed the rail and fell over the side, and when he dived in after her it was straight into thick yellow fog, in which not even the brown waters of the Liffey could be seen or felt.

Chapter Four

When Brogan got back to Liverpool it was to find the snow melting in a fierce, almost springlike wind, and the whole city in an uproar over the missing baby.

'There's been a piece in the paper,' Peader hissed to him when they were in bed that night in their lodgings. 'Mollie's mammy says as how she's been stolen away by gypsies . . . but one of the fellers says she's tryin' to make capital out of it so she is . . . hopin' someone will pay her money for her loss. Sure and would you believe a woman could be so wicked?'

'Jeez, I hope they never find out where the littl'un's gone; and we've decided to call her Polly, by the way, for safety's sake,' Brogan whispered. 'Because if they try to take Polly away me mammy will kill me and anyway, that woman, that Mrs Carbery, she never had no time for the kid, Jess said so. Oh, Daddy, I don't want to be throwed in gaol – specially not an English gaol.'

'Devil a bit will they throw you in gaol; for what can they prove, eh?' his father whispered back. 'A nine-days' wonder, so it is, and that's the end of it. Give it another week at the most and no one will know who you mean if you say "Mollie Carbery".'

'I hope you're right,' Brogan said devoutly. 'Best say nothing then, eh, Daddy?'

'Far best,' his father said shortly. 'I'm goin' before a board to see whether they think I could do safety man;

there's a dacent pay rise goes wit' the position. We don't want to risk losin' that, do we?'

So Brogan decided to pretend that he, too, had never heard the name Mollie Carbery. He would think of the child always, now, as Polly O'Brady. And on that comforting thought he slept at last.

Sara thoroughly enjoyed her stay with Mrs Prescott, though she was sorry when the snow began to melt so that Snowdrop Street no longer looked white and enticing but grey and drab and wet, instead.

Despite Mrs Prescott making sandwiches for the wake, neither she nor her young charge attended Jess's funeral.

'They're an unpleasant family, or the parents are,' Nanny told Sara. 'Neither her nor him would raise a finger to do anything for the child whiles she was alive, and they'll do precious little now she's dead. Nesta – that's the mother – talked to the *Echo* because she hoped to make capital out of her loss, but whatever money they paid her for her story went on drink.'

'But Nanny, women don't drink, do they?' Sara said doubtfully. 'I know men drink, but I thought women stayed at home.'

'Well, you were wrong. Nesta Carbery drinks whenever she's got the means to go down to the Jug and Bottle and buy the stuff,' Nanny said distastefully. 'It'll not be long before they're turned out, anyway. People like them never pay the rent.'

Sara would have liked to have paid her respects to Jess, particularly as she still felt deeply guilty over having given Jess stolen money. Despite her Nanny's comforting words she still felt uneasily that the money might have been unlucky in some way. But the days passed, and once or twice she saw members of the family passing by, grey-skinned, apathetic, miserable, and had to echo Mrs Prescott's words – that perhaps poor Jess was the lucky one.

And the neighbours didn't like them, didn't extend to them the same tolerance they extended to others, though they were quick to offer food, clothing, even odds and ends of bedding, to help the family after their loss. She saw that good women, like her nanny and her neighbours, would exchange a word or two with Stan or Nesta Carbery and then quickly move away, as though they did not want to remain in their company. It seemed strange to Sara.

Finally, however, she managed to put her finger on what was wrong. The neighbours felt let down that such a family could exist in their very street, and that they could do nothing about it. A good many people in the street had large families and struggled to keep their kids and themselves fed and clothed, but no one simply gave up on the kids and concentrated solely on themselves. No one but the Carbs, that was. He bragged and bullied, she whined and whinged, but it was easy to see that anything which went into their home would end up on the backs or in the bellies of Nesta and Stan. The kids, from the moment they were born if Mollie was anything to go by, would have to fight their own battles, make their own way in life.

'Sara, my dear, Jess and Mollie were very unfortunate little girls, but they've gone to a better place,' Mrs Prescott said to her the day after the funeral, when she saw Sara moping around the house. 'Have you seen Grace Carbery? She's like a little ghost, wanting something that those wretched parents of hers can't, or won't, give. As for Mollie, I don't, myself, believe she's dead. I think someone saw her and pitied her and took her away to another, better home. But in any event, you must stop blaming yourself or even thinking about them now. It's downright morbid and unhealthy, and if you continue to do it, then I'll have no choice but to send you back to Aigburth Road and your mother and father.'

'Nanny, you wouldn't,' Sara gasped, unable to believe that her nanny could possibly sink so low, but Mrs Prescott nodded firmly.

'I would, queen. Once you were home you'd stop thinking about them, so if you can't do it here, you'd best go home.'

'I'll stop blaming myself if I possibly can,' Sara promised unhappily. 'I know it's silly, or a part of me does, but there's another part which says I took money which didn't belong to me, and I know that's bad. The Reverend Atwell is awfully strong against theft, I'm sure he'd say at once that money intended for the church must go there, no matter what.'

There was a short silence, and then Mrs Prescott went out of the room – the two of them had been sitting by the fire in her parlour – and rummaged around in the back kitchen, to return presently with something in her hand. She held it out.

'There you are; a shilling. It's for your collection next Sunday,' she said briskly. 'You are to put it in the plate together with whatever money your parents may give you. So that's easily settled.'

And oddly enough, it was. A great wave of relief washed over Sara as she took the money and put it into the pocket of her best coat.

'Oh, Nanny, thank you,' she breathed, reaching up and kissing Mrs Prescott's soft cheek. 'You don't know how much better I feel!'

And it was true. Knowing that she would presently be paying the money back to the church from which she felt she had taken it removed the burden of guilt from Sara and made her feel very much better.

And the very next day she met the boy.

'Oh, Sara, me head's splittin',' Mrs Prescott said next day, when she and Sara met over breakfast. 'I don't even fancy the porridge, and it's usually me favourite way to start the day. Can you be a good girl, queen, and amuse yourself today? You'll have to do some shopping for me – can you go along to the chemist, and ask Mr Hanson for some of his headache cure? It's better than aspirin, most of us swear by it. And then I need some scrag end to make a stew – I'll have about a pound in weight – and tell Mr Lowey I'll have a nice lean piece of pork for the weekend; I'll call in Saturday. Oh, and can you get me half a dozen eggs, and then you can play out, if you like. Only don't stray too far, and if you can bear it, come in around noon and see how I feel. If this headache keeps on, though, all I'll want will be a cuppa and some more aspirin tablets. Now can you manage all that or shall I get Mrs Rushton or Kate to give a hand?'

'Of course I can manage, Nanny,' Sara said rather hotly. 'I love shopping, and I won't let anyone cheat me. Not that they'll try, because they know I'm staying with you.'

'Right. You could call round for young Cammy – you and she get on well, I've noticed that.'

'We do,' Sara owned. 'She's taught me ever so many games, Nanny. Some of them are real good ones. But she's the best skipper in the world, I should think – she can do all the fancy steps and when we race I keep missing jumps but she turns the rope as smooth and even as – as a wheel. Yes, I'll give her a call when I go past.'

But when she got round to number five Snowdrop Street, she was in for a disappointment. Cammy had really bad toothache. She came to the door, her face swollen and lopsided, with a hot rag held against the offending cheek, to tell Sara that she was being dragged off to the dental hospital in Pembroke Place.

'I don't want to go,' she confided in a breathy whisper. 'But me mam'll 'ave me guts for garters if I don't gerron on the tram with 'er and go up there. And right now I woun't care if they pulled me bleeding 'ead off, so long as the pain stopped an' all.'

'You would; it would hurt like fun I bet,' Sara said. 'I am sorry, though, Cammy. I'd come with you, but Nanny's not well and I'm going to do her marketing and take care of her. She's got one of her heads.'

'You mek it sound as though she keeps spare 'eads in a cupboard,' Cammy said, then winced and put a hand to her cheek. 'Oh, gawd, don't mek me laugh, it's too bleedin' painful! See you later, then, queen. Be good.'

It was easy enough to be good when you were doing the shopping, though Sara still found it exciting to go by herself along Stanley Road. She didn't hurry, either, in fact you could have said that she dawdled. Past the tobacconist with its little tins of pipe tobacco, boxes of rich-looking cigars and packets of cigarettes with a handsome, if elderly, sailor on the packet, and on to the Misses Irving's confectionery shop. A lovely window this, you could almost smell the sweets, though the toffees, liquorice walking sticks and sherbert dips looked rather dusty and neglected. But through the door you could see the big jars of sweeties, and the smell which came out was enough to set a child's mouth watering.

King's grocery shop came next. Quite interesting,

with lots of advertisements stuck to the window glass so you could hardly see inside, and sacks of flour, oatmeal, haricot beans and lentils piled up against the wooden counter. Nanny shopped at King's, so in Sara popped and bought six fine-looking eggs.

After that there was only the chemist, Mr Hanson, on the corner of Fountains Road, and because she needed to go in she scarcely glanced in his window, though the big jars of coloured water caught the light as she passed them and looked, for a moment, like enormous rubies and emeralds. Inside the shop she explained about Mrs Prescott's headache and was given a tiny pink bag with some tablets in.

'Two, three times a day, with a nice hot cup of tea,' Mr Hanson said. 'She'll be right as a trivet by tomorrow morning.'

And once over the road, which she crossed cautiously, conscious that she was unaccompanied by an adult, there was a good walk past the Stanley Hospital – she ran most of it – to cross Easby Road and reach her favourite shop.

It was a pawnshop – Williams was the name above the door – and his window was a delight. Clothes, curtains, shoes, ornaments, bits of furniture, toys. It was a treat just to look, though Nanny would never even pause a moment by the window of the pawn.

'Why not, Nanny? There's some very pretty things,' Sara had said, tugging at Mrs Prescott's sleeve. 'Do come and look!'

But Mrs Prescott had been firm. 'They're unredeemed stock,' she said. 'That means the folk put 'em in pawn and then couldn't find the five bob or whatever to get 'em out again. It's a sad window if you ask me.'

But Sara, though she acknowledged that it was sad

when people didn't have the money to buy their things back – she was hazy as to the actual business conducted by pawn-brokers – still enjoyed looking in the window and was able, this morning, to have an uninterrupted stare, though she was jostled somewhat by passers-by, for the street was busy with people shopping after the holiday.

Despite the fact that she knew herself to possess many more of the world's goods than most people, Sara still yearned after one or two things in the window. A pair of china kittens with blue eyes and grey fur, their little heads tilted to one side, for instance. They would look lovely on the schoolroom mantel, or even in her bedroom. And then there were the ice skates. Fancy, a pair of ice skates in Stanley Road! Whoever had put them in pawn must have either nicked 'em or been rich, she and Cammy had decided when they discussed it, because ordinary folk did not own ice skates.

But wouldn't I love a pair, Sara thought now, nose pressed to the glass like any other wistful but penniless urchin. I bet I could skate ever so well, if only I had some skates to put on. But then it'll be spring soon, and the ice will all go away, so there's not much point in wanting *them*. How about a nice tennis racquet? Only I've no one to play with. Well then, how about a skipping rope?

But gazing into the pawn was not what Mrs Prescott had meant by 'amuse yourself', so Sara gave the objects of her desire one last, long look and then trotted past Miss Gourley's hairdressing establishment and Mrs Lang's florist shop with scarcely more than a glance. The florist was exhibiting a display of rather weary-looking holly today and the stiff wax heads wearing unattractive and over-curled wigs in Miss Gourley's window were too like dead people to Sara's way of thinking. So she hurried along until she reached the butcher's for which she was bound.

Mr Lowey's shop was not full, but there were women waiting to be served so Sara took her place at the end of the line, scuffing her feet in the sawdust and trying to breathe shallow because the smell of blood and bones was not pleasant. However, the line moved quickly and presently she was standing at the top of the long wooden counter, with Mr Lowey's boy, a spotty-faced individual called Bert, facing her.

'Yes, Miss? Can I get you somethin'?'

'Mrs Prescott said to ask you for some scrag end for a stew and a nice lean piece of pork for roasting, she'll pick the pork up Saturday,' Sara recited. 'About a pound of scrag, she said.'

'And how is Mrs Prescott?' Mr Lowey called from further down the counter. 'Not poorly, I 'ope?'

'She's got a headache,' Sara admitted. 'It's really bad, that's why I'm doing her shopping. But after I've done I can play out.'

'Well, at least the sun's shining,' Mr Lowey observed. 'You'll 'ave to run about to keep warm though, chuck. It don't do to 'ang about when the wind's cutting like this one is.'

Sara hadn't noticed that the wind was particularly cold but walking home with her now laden shopping basket she did think that perhaps, since Cammy was busy at the clinic, wherever that might be, she might stay indoors, do a jigsaw, or write another story in her homework book. She had begun one only the previous day in which a brigand with a big black beard, a heroine who looked very similar to Sara and a friendly orange cat figured large. It might be fun to go on with it . . . at least until Cammy returned from the clinic, hopefully minus both the toothache and the tooth.

Accordingly she returned to number three and made a cup of tea, then carried it carefully up the stairs, for Mrs Prescott had succumbed and gone back to bed.

'Oh, bless you, queen . . . you've got the pills an' all,' Mrs Prescott said huskily, as soon as Sara appeared round the bedroom door. 'Once they're down the little red lane I'll feel heaps better. And nice hot tea – oh, I am being spoiled today.'

'What about some bread and butter, or a piece of the fruit cake you got back from Samples yesterday?' Sara said softly. She felt like a nurse, and very virtuous into the bargain.

'No thanks, queen, nothing to eat. But you make yourself something before you go out to play,' Mrs Prescott said. She had taken the little pink pills and now she lay back on her pillows, smiling faintly. 'When you come in for tea, I'll probably be up and scrubbin' the kitchen floor for something to do!'

'I don't think you should, Nanny; I'll come in before it gets dark and see how you are again,' Sara said. She guessed that Mrs Prescott would feel a good deal more comfortable if she knew her charge was safely playing out and not fiddling around in the kitchen below, where there were so many things which could do her harm. Sharp knives, hot fire, even an attempt at cooking could be dangerous if you spilled boiling water over yourself. 'Well, if you're sure you're all right I'll be off, Nanny. I'll buy myself a pastie from the shop for my lunch. I've got some change.'

'That's grand, queen,' the woman in the bed said feebly. 'I don't fancy you tryin' to cook and that's a fact, though I know you've a sensible head on your shoulders. And now I think I'll have a bit of a nap.'

She lay down on the pillow again and, Sara suspected, was asleep before her guest had left the room.

True to her word, Sara walked down to the nearest canny house and went in. It was only someone's front room on Stanley Street, but the lady of the house, Bessie Arthurs, stood behind the counter which her sons had made for her, dispensing soup for 2d, stew for 4d – more if you wanted bread and butter with it – and a meat and potato pastie for 6d. Sara, whose mouth had watered at the sight of those hot meat and potato pasties, produced her money, seized her pastie, thanked Mrs Arthurs for her kindness and made for the door once more. It was a *huge* pastie, it could have fed three or four . . . but she would manage most of it without too much trouble. She would just take it home and . . .

Her thoughts stopped short. If she went home Mrs Prescott would worry, she just knew it. No, she would take the pastie somewhere quiet . . .

Somewhere quiet? On Stanley Road? In the school holidays nowhere was quiet, even down the jiggers you'd find kids playing. I'd best go over to Kirkdale recreation ground, Sara thought rather desperately. It's too snowy for the kids to bother to go there, and the Free Library is only a stone's throw away; when I've finished my food I can nip over to the library and take a look at the books.

It was a cause of some grievance that Mrs Prescott didn't like her to borrow books from the Free Library. 'You could catch anything, queen,' she said disapprovingly. 'There's all sorts handle them books, you could get scarlet fever, brain disease . . . oh aye, you may widen your eyes at me, but books carry disease, I'm tellin' you.'

But Cammy borrowed books from there, and most

of the women in Snowdrop Street, and they didn't drop dead from brain disease. I'll risk it, Sara decided as she plodded up towards Orwell Road. It's a shame though, the pastie will be cold long before I get to the reccy.

However, she tucked it inside her warm coat and ran quite a lot of the way and turned into Sessions Road rather hot and breathless but still with the pastie nicely warm against her chest.

Down past the side of the Free Library she went and into the recreation ground. The bowling green was still snow-covered, but most of the flower-beds and lawns were clear, now, and Sara quickly found a seat which was quite dry. There were no kids about, either, which was nice; usually the place swarmed with boys illegally playing football and girls skipping, but it was dinner-time. No doubt the kids were all indoors, having their meal.

Sara unwrapped the pastie; the smell curled up, delicious, warming, promising. She took a big bite and chewed vigorously. It was absolutely prime, as good as any food she had ever eaten, and she was really hungry, it was ages since breakfast.

Then she saw the girl. She was a tiny creature of about four or five, skinny and big-eyed, and dressed in a ragged cardigan over a patched dress. The dress was too short, so that it did not hide her bare legs, blue with cold. She was staring at Sara's pastie and as she turned her head she reminded Sara sharply of someone.

''Ello, Miss,' the little girl said. 'Vat smells good!'

Sara smiled at the child's wistful expression. 'Hello! Yes, it does smell nice, but it's far too big for one person. Are you hungry? I can break it in half easily, then we can both enjoy it.'

'I'm turble 'ungry, I am that,' the girl said. 'The fing

is, I 'aven't 'ad no time for no dinner. I'm huntin' for me baby sister.'

Sara stared at the little girl and suddenly she remembered Jess saying that she had another sister, a sister who had been poorly on Christmas Day. Could this be that sister? She did look rather like Jess with her pale, draggly hair, and thin white face.

Sara stood up. 'What's your name?' she said, carefully. She did not want to frighten the child off. 'I wonder if – if I might have known your sister, you see.'

The child stared at her briefly, then her eyes returned to the pastie in Sara's hand. 'I do 'ave a sister; she's called Addy,' she said. 'Who's you?'

'I'm Sara. Just let me divide the pastie and then perhaps we can have a proper talk.' Sara smiled at the little girl, divided the pastie into two pieces, and then held one piece out enticingly. 'You said you were hunting for your baby sister; would that be . . .'

One minute the child was taking the pastie, the next she had glanced over her shoulder, eyes widening. Sara followed her gaze but all she could see was a man in a navy cap and jacket walking unconcernedly across the grass, so she turned her attention back to the child once more, only to find that the little girl had vanished.

Startled, Sara glanced around her. There was no one nearby but, over to her right, she saw a small, shabby figure, running as hard as it could along the gravelled path. She reached the end of the path and swerved to her right, disappearing into a bed of snow-laden shrubs.

Sara jumped to her feet and set off in pursuit. It was, in a way, my fault that Jess got killed, and I still don't know what happened to baby Mollie, she told herself as she ran. But if I go straight across the grass I won't be far behind the kid and perhaps if I reached her we could talk, I could explain . . . help her. That might make up for what happened to Jess. And the kid did say she was searching for her baby sister – oh I do want to catch her and tell her it's all right, I'm her friend!

But the skinny little scrap could really run and Sara was still a long way behind when she herself ran full tilt into someone. A sturdy someone, who caught hold of her shoulders and said, in a rich Irish accent, 'And where d'you t'ink you're goin', alanna? Dear God in heaven, you nearly had me flat on me back and me twice your size and weight!'

'Nowhere . . . anywhere . . . I'm trying to catch up with a – a friend,' Sara panted, trying to wrench herself out of the man's grip without any success at all. 'I don't know why she ran away, unless she thought I was going to ask for the piece of pastie back! Do let me go, sir, because I did an awful thing . . . someone was killed . . . and that little girl . . . oh, now she really *has* disappeared – might have been the sister . . . Jess and Mollie's sister, the one who got left behind on Christmas Day! If I could find her, talk to her, then between us we might find Mollie!'

'If the kid's disappeared . . . *Jess*, did you say?' The man held her away from him, holding her by the shoulders now. 'And *Mollie*? Not – not Jess and Mollie Carbery?'

'Yes, that's right,' Sara said. She realised that her eyes were tear-filled and scrubbed crossly at them with both fists. 'It was a Carbery, I'm sure it was. She – she told me she was looking for her baby sister, she said she was hungry but she hadn't time . . .'

'Look, alanna, I knew Jess too, and the baby as well . . . but there's no point in standing out in this

94

cold. Come over to the shelter. At least we'll be out of the rain.'

Sara had not even noticed that it had started raining but now she looked about her and saw the raindrops pitting the remaining snow, falling quite hard on the gravel paths and the empty, winter flower-beds.

'Are you comin'? Devil a bit do you know me, but take a good look; I'm sixteen, me name's Brogan O'Brady, and I've never harmed chick nor child in me life, I promise you that.'

Sara stared. He looked dependable, she thought, and nice. He had very dark hair beneath a navy cap, eyes so dark a brown that they were almost black, and a square chin. He was wearing a navy jacket and trousers and big boots and despite the cold, or perhaps because of it, his face was flushed. But Nanny had said not to talk to strange men ever, under any circumstances. Did he count as a man, though, at sixteen? It was a knotty problem. Surely it would be all right – she would be sixteen herself in four more years! She stared very hard at him and decided to trust him.

'Yes, all right, I'll come with you,' Sara said, making up her mind. Nanny also said you had to judge people as you found them, and she found this young man worthy of her confidence. 'My name's Sara – Sara Cordwainer. What did you say you were called?'

'Brogan. 'Tis Irish,' her companion said. 'This way; we aren't supposed to cross the grass but I daresay there's no one to notice, and it's the quickest way to the shelter.' He pointed as he spoke and Sara saw, on the opposite side of the grass, a rustic shelter with a seat in it.

In rather less than a minute the two of them reached it and sat down, turning to face one another as they did so. Then they both smiled, Sara rather diffidently.

She had made a fool of herself, talking about Jess and Mollie like that: what must he have thought? But she found out soon enough.

'Now, Sara. When did you meet Jess, or have you known her a while, maybe?'

'No, I met her the day she died, on Christmas Day. They were outside our church when we went for morning service. Jess had Mollie in her arms, you see. I feel awfully bad about them both, because . . . but tell me how you knew her.'

'I met her on Christmas Day too, but late on, in the afternoon.' Brogan paused, frowned, then continued. But he looked down at his hands now as he spoke and did not meet Sara's eyes. 'Oh Jeez, now I come to think I reckon I was mebbe the last person to see her alive. You say you saw her outside your church?'

'I did. She was outside my church with the baby,' Sara said. 'They were dressed in – well, in rags and they were cold and hungry so – so I gave Jess my collection and my white angora gloves. She put them on the baby's feet. Then they went, and I read in the paper that she bought bread and some milk and wanted somewhere to go and eat and must have wandered on to the rails . . .'

She stopped short, giving an involuntary shudder as she did so. 'I thought it was my fault that she died – she bought the food with my shilling, you see. If I hadn't given it to her she could have been alive today. So I'd love to find Mollie, or the other sister, to – well, to try to make up, I suppose.'

Brogan patted her arm. 'Aye, I can see that you would think that. But Sara, if it hadn't been for me Jess maybe really might have been alive. I'll tell you about it.'

*

Brogan was careful what he said, of course, because the secret concerning the baby was no longer his to reveal. But he liked this serious young girl with the deep blue eyes and the gentle, sensitive countenance; her guilt was absurd, but he could understand it. He, too, had suffered from guilt over Jess's death until his parents had convinced him that the poor little girls were both of them better off, now.

So he told Sara how he and the rest of his gang of navvies had met the young girl carrying the baby, how they had fed her, taken her in, warmed her . . . and left her sleeping when the landslip occurred.

'And when we came back, they'd gone,' he said heavily, at last. 'We looked for 'em all over, without any luck. Until we met one of the other men, carrying Jess's body wrapped in his coat. Now you thought yourself guilty, alanna, but as you can see, my guilt was the greater. If I'd woken her, instead of leavin' her sleepin' . . . well, who can say what might have happened?'

'And Mollie? The baby?'

'We looked all over the marshalling yards but we saw no child,' Brogan said truthfully. 'She couldn't have been wit' her sister, that's for sure, and she was too little to get very far on her own. 'Tis my honest belief that some good person must have found her, and taken her away to be loved and cherished, as babies should be. And from what poor Jess told us, it was the best thing to do so it was, for her father was an awful feller by what she said, and her mammy little better.'

'So there really was no blame on you,' Sara said thoughtfully. She looked up at him and smiled, a very sweet smile. ''Twasn't your fault, Brogan.'

'No? When if I'd woke her, instead of leavin' her there, sleepin', her life might have been saved? What worries me most is that Mollie was crawling, you know, and she might easily have crawled out of the cabin. Then Jess would have woken up and gone in search of her sister, and got killed.'

'It could have happened, of course,' Sara said after a moment's thought. 'But you can't ever know, Brogan. If things had been different, if you'd woken Jess, she might have picked up Mollie and gone out with her and they might both have been killed instead of only one. Don't you think that's even likelier?'

'I think you're right,' Brogan said. 'The hand of God is over us all, alanna, and we should neither of us take on guilt. Shall we have a bargain? We'll stop blaming ourselves for what we couldn't help. How about that, eh? Will you shake hands on it?'

'Yes, of course,' Sara said. She put her small paw into Brogan's large one and they shook hands solemnly. 'Oh . . . that little girl! I'd forgotten her. Do you think she might have been a Carbery, Brogan?'

'Nothing likelier,' Brogan said. 'But she'll turn up again, Sara, and when she does, either you or meself will try to give her a bit of somethin' to eat and a few coppers.' He smiled down into the small face lifted to his. 'But this city's full of kids in rags wit' no food in their bellies. Times are hard . . . Dublin's the same.'

'Do you mean that we should help anyone we can help?' Sara asked. 'I will then . . . and when I do, I'll think of Jess. And I'll say my prayers for Mollie, and hope that wherever she is, she's well and happy.'

'That's the ticket,' Brogan said. He sighed and stood up, stretching. 'Now no more blamin' yourself for what you can't help, eh, young wan? I'm on a night-shift this week; better get back to me lodgings or I'll be good for nothin' be eight in the mornin'.' He paused, looking down at Sara. 'I'll let you into a secret, Sara. I've lived in England for a whole twelve months now, but sadly do I miss my mammy, my brothers and my little sister. There's fine men work on the railways, but very few young ladies, such as yourself. I'd like to meet you again, have a bit of a crack. I'd like to tell you all about us O'Bradys, from mammy right down to Polly, who's the youngest of the family so far.'

'I'd like that ever so much,' Sara said eagerly. She stood up too, and dusted down the front of the little red coat she wore. 'I don't have a lot of friends of my own, apart from school chums, when I'm in Aigburth Road. Where do you live though, Brogan?'

'We lodge in Beckett Street, me daddy an' meself. It's not too far from here.'

'Well, I'm staying in Snowdrop Street; that's off Stanley Road,' Sara told her new friend. 'I've a friend called Cammy who lives a bit further along the road but I would like to see you again.'

'Snowdrop runs between Commercial Road and Stanley, doesn't it? We walk through there, sometimes, when we're comin' home after a day's work. Will you an' me be meetin' somewhere round there, now and then, to have a bit of a talk?' Brogan turned up his coat collar and stepped out of the shelter into the rain. 'Best get goin', young Sara!'

'That would be very nice,' Sara said. 'Only . . . where could we meet? Once I'm at home I only get to go to school and back, but when I'm with Nanny it's easier.'

'Then you must visit Nanny more often,' Brogan said. 'I miss the young chisellers more than you'd imagine. There's no kids workin' on the railways.'

He laughed and Sara laughed too.

'No, I suppose not, but I'm not a kid, you know. I'm twelve. What's a chiseller, though? If you don't go too fast I'll walk along with you – you can tell me what it's like, working on the railways.'

Companionably, they fell into step and began to cross the park. The rain was light but Sara was glad of her thick coat and pulled out the scarf she wore round her neck, tying it over her head.

'A chiseller's just a way of sayin' a young boy, a young blood. As for working on the railways, 'tis hard work, but not unpleasant most of the time. We're out of doors in all weathers, of course, and soaked to the skin or froze now an' then. Me daddy's up for the job of safety man and a grand job that is, so I'm hopin' he'll get it. But I've other ideas so I have. I go to the Gordon Institute 'cos in March I'm hopin' to start work as a fireman, which is the first step to bein' an engine driver meself so it is.'

'I know the Institute; it's opposite Crocus Street, isn't it?' Sara said. She giggled. 'I've seen young men going in and out so I thought it was a public house.'

Brogan laughed with her. She's a dote, he found himself thinking. A pretty, lively young wan who's kept too close, from the sound of it. 'No, 'tis for the learnin' and betterin' of the working man,' he told her. 'Sure an' they treat you like a school kid, but 'tis worth it to get the learnin'.'

They were on Orwell Road now, Sara having to walk fast to keep up with his longer strides, though Brogan conscientiously kept slowing down. And on the corner of Rickman Street, alongside the fried fish shop, Brogan drew his companion to a halt. He pointed.

'I'm after gettin' some fish an' chips for me dinner, before I go indoors. Want some?'

'Oh, Brogan, I bought a pastie for my dinner and I never ate it . . . but whatever did I do with it? I halved it with the little girl who ran away . . .'

'Sure, you left it on the seat, where you'd been sittin' when the child approached you,' he assured her. 'It'll be in some creature's stomach be now . . . I'll get you some fish and chips; wait here.'

'I'm glad someone's got it, then, but I've got some money . . .' Sara began, but he shook his head at her.

'No, no, I'm buyin', don't shame me by refusin'. And since you know the Gordon Institute, I'm after goin' there three evenin's a week, save when I'm on a shift which stops me, so you can find me there, five to seven or five past nine. You'll come? You won't forget?'

'I'll come whenever I'm staying with Nanny,' Sara promised. 'And I'm going to be staying with Nanny regularly, from now on. Otherwise there'll be trouble!'

'I can tell you've a sharp tongue and a determined nature,' Brogan said solemnly, making her laugh again. 'But I can't tell whether you prefer cod or haddock – you'll have to let me know which to buy!'

'I like both, and besides, I don't know which is which,' Sara assured him. 'Are you sure you've got time though, Brogan? You said you wanted to get some sleep before your night-shift.'

Brogan assured her he had plenty of time and went into the fried fish shop. She was a good kid. Talking to her had cheered him up, made his day. It would have been lovely to tell her that the baby was safe with his mother in Dublin, but sure and such knowledge would be far too heavy a burden for a child of twelve to bear. He'd keep in touch with her, however, talk about his family to her, and maybe one day, when Polly was a woman grown, he would be able to share the secret with young Sara Cordwainer.

Little Grace Carbery had hoped the girl would share the big pastie with her; she looked a friendly sort of girl, but just as Grace had taken the proffered piece she had seen the park keeper coming and had made herself scarce. She had been in bad odour with him ever since she and Jess had sat themselves down on the bowling green to eat a melon they'd prigged from a nearby greengrocer's shop.

'We don't want your sort here,' the park keeper had shouted, and he had hit at their bare legs with the long twig broom with which he'd been sweeping the gravel paths. 'Gerrout, you iggerant slummies.'

So naturally, when she saw the man approaching, she had run as fast as she could to the other side of the park and then made her way back through the bushes, quick and skinny as a snake, until she was behind the seat which backed on to the bowling green. With Jess beside her she might have faced the man out, she thought wistfully, together they might even have cheeked him, but by herself all she could do was run and hide.

But after a few frightening moments she had peered through the prickly, evergreen hedge, and seen that the park keeper wasn't a park keeper at all, but simply a feller in a navy donkey coat – and he and the pretty girl seemed to know one another, since she had run slap bang into his arms and there they were, chattering away, heading for the opposite side of the rec.

Grace looked carefully round her; no one was near. She squatted on the ground and took the first bite from her half of the pastie, closing her eyes the better to savour it. It was delicious, one of the nicest things she had ever tasted! I'll save it, she thought, eat it slowly . . . just one more bite . . .

The half pastie disappeared into Grace's tummy and she stood up and went hesitantly towards the seat. She had noticed something lying on the wet wood . . .

The rest of the meat pastie was there! There was one bite taken out of it but it wasn't even a particularly big piece . . . oh, had the girl left it for her? If so . . .

Grace sat down timidly on the extreme end of the seat, looking nervously around her like an animal which fears a trap. Was it a trick? Would the girl come back presently and pick up the pastie and walk off with it? But nothing happened. When she looked across the couple had disappeared into the falling rain and the pastie was getting soaked. If she didn't do something it would be ruined, worthless.

Hesitantly, Grace reached out both hands and picked the half-pastie up. Seconds later, she was savouring, for the second time that morning, the most delicious meat and potato pie she had ever tasted. Oh, the flavour of it, the richness of the gravy, the warm and lovely taste of the onions! I really oughter save a bit, she told herself, but somehow it all got eaten up there and then, on the seat, in the rain.

And presently, when she got up and made her way back to the road once more, she felt full and comfortable for the first time for ages. And very grateful to the pretty girl who had given her half the pastie and then left the rest of it too, sitting on that wet wooden bench.

But she did wonder why she had told the girl she was searching for her sister, when she knew very well, really, that wherever Mollie was, she was better off, because she wasn't with the Carberys. Without Jess, Mollie's life wouldn't have been much, Grace thought now, heading for home. She was soaked and needed to get out of the weather before her father came back from wherever it was he went during the afternoons. Pubs, clubs, she had no idea, she just knew he was usually out of the house until very much later in the evening.

She had been heartbroken by Jess's death, because Jess had been the only member of the family who cared about her. When she, Grace, had been the baby of the family Jess had carted her around on her hip until she got too heavy, as Jess had been carting Mollie right up to her death. And though the new baby was, naturally, her first responsibility, she still cherished Grace as much as she could.

But you can't be a baby once you're four years old; you're a proper, big girl, once you're four, Jess said so. And poor Grace, trying to be a proper, big girl, had still envied Mollie because she had Jess, and had envied Jess because she had Mollie. Indeed, her first thought, after the appalling shock of Jess's horrible death, had been that now Mollie could sleep beside *her*, keep *her* warm of a night. But even if Mollie hadn't disappeared it wouldn't have worked because Grace knew she didn't have Jess's strength. She was only four, going on five. It took her all her time and energy to keep herself alive, she could never have taken on the responsibility for another soul, not even that of a baby like Mollie.

Chapter Five

Summer 1931

'Polly O'Brady, will you put that kitten down this minute and do as I tell ye! Your big brother and your daddy are comin' home tomorrow and no end to arrange. I'm after wantin' a heap o' things and you've done nothin' today but play.'

Polly was sitting on the living-room windowsill with a book beside her and the ginger kitten in her lap. She could scarcely remember the time when the O'Bradys had lived in two rooms, for now they had four, all on the first floor which meant having it to themselves, apart from the stairs, which were common property.

With the money she made from street selling plus what Peader and Brogan sent home, Deirdre had gradually taken on two more rooms, so the old bedroom was now a proper kitchen and the two back rooms were bedrooms, one for the big boys and one for the small boys, Polly and her mammy.

Now, however, Polly glanced across the room at the kitchen door; me mammy's got eyes that see round corners so she has, she thought, awed, for there was no way that she could be seen from the kitchen sink so far as she could make out and she'd only picked the kitten up minutes ago.

'I'm not playin' now, Mammy, I'm doin' my eckers,' she said untruthfully, picking up the blue exercise book and waving it vaguely in the direction of the kitchen door. Her homework had been done a week or more ago since this was summertime and schools were out, but she had been looking it over just now, which was the same as doing it, more or less. 'You know you said to do it now, so's it wasn't a bother to me later, when Brogan and Daddy come home.'

'Sure and I know you're bound to do your eckers, but you've got all the holidays to tackle it, alanna, so don't give me that! Brogan's more important to all of us than any old schoolwork, so leave the kitten, come away from them books, and get after those messages.'

Polly pouted and gave the ginger kitten a cuddle. She had named it Lionel and stuck to the name though her brothers codded her about it and told her that it was no name for a kitten, particularly a ginger one.

'It's no dafter than her calling the dog Delilah,' Niall had pointed out. He was a man grown, and very rarely teased. 'Particularly since Delilah's a girl's name and the dog's a feller. Samson, now, that's a good name for a dog. You could have called him Samson, alanna.'

But Polly had preferred Delilah, so the dog, a large, odd-looking creature of indeterminate parentage, was known as Delly by everyone except her and did not seem to mind what he was called so long as he was with the O'Bradys most of the time, particularly Polly.

'Polly, do as I tell you now; I'm warnin' ye!'

Polly knew when her mother was serious. She set the kitten down on the floor, jumped off the windowsill and dusted the fur off her short pleated skirt.

'All right, Mammy, I'm goin',' she said placatingly. 'I'll just give a bit of a wash to me hands and brush me hair, then I'll be off. Is it a list you've been writin' in there?'

'Yes, I've written a list,' her mother called back. 'You'll want to go to the market on Francis Street because you'll get good stuff there. Or Iveagh market, of course. And Tad will go wit' you, if you ask him nicely. There's a lot to carry for a little girl.'

'Tad's a monster, so he is, and he won't go anywhere wit' me, not if I know it,' Polly said indignantly. Last week Tad had been her best friend, but he had codded her once too often. 'Worse than a brother he is to me . . . much worse. I'll never speak to him again . . . not politely I won't.'

The door between the living room and the kitchen was open and now Deirdre poked her head round it. She was smiling.

'Oh, you, Polly O'Brady, you're always full of what you'll do to poor Tad every time you argue, but you're rare fond of the lad, are you not? Who gave you your very first kitten? And that wretched mongrel dog of yours? And the mice?'

'It was Tad, though the cat ate the mice,' Polly admitted. 'But Mammy, last week Tad took me all the way over to O'Connell Street to see the fine shops and then he wouldn't let me ride home on the tram, he said weren't me legs made for walkin' like the legs on him were. And yesterday I wanted to swim in the Basin and he said it was for boys, not girls. He said to swim in the bleedin' canal if I wanted . . . he said bleedin', so don't shout, I'm only repeatin' what he said! So you see he's mean to me, Mammy.'

'You're spoilt, that's the trouble. We all give you your own way too much,' Deirdre said with mock severity. 'Will you take Ivan with you, in the pram, then you won't need help wit' the carryin'?'

Ivan was the youngest O'Brady now. Polly had somehow assumed that she herself would always be the youngest and had been astonished and hurt when Mammy had told her that she was going to have a little brother or sister. She had chosen a sister and had been offended as well as surprised when the baby turned out to be a brother after all, but she had grown quite fond of Ivan in her way, though she kept a close watch on Mammy and the brothers to make sure they didn't favour the baby above her.

'Oh, Mammy, I can't take Ivan, he keeps wantin' to walk so he does, and doesn't that hold me up more'n anythin' else?' Polly asked. 'I'll ask Tad if he'll come, then, if there's more than I can carry alone. Honest to God I'll ask him, Mammy.'

'I believe you; t'ousands wouldn't,' Deirdre said, handing over a long list written on the margin of the *Herald* newspaper. 'Just think, Polly, tomorrow and the day after and the day after that Brogan and Daddy will be here, takin' us out for a day, jokin' you, playin' wit' Ivan . . . it'll be the first time Daddy's set eyes on Ivan, d'you realise that?'

Since Ivan, who had been napping in the kitchen, curled up on the old wooden rocker, chose that moment to wake with a roar of 'Mammy! Ivy wanna d'ink so he do!', Polly could only envy her father his happy ignorance. Ivan had not been a placid baby and he was not a placid toddler and since it is the fate of the older children in a family to keep an eye on the younger ones, Polly knew better than most what a trial Ivan could be.

'When I was a baby I was put to the Poor Crèche, on Meath Street, I wasn't landed on me brothers day and night,' Polly scolded Ivan when he whined for something. 'The ould wans there didn't give me no peggy's leg to keep me quiet, nor take me for walks through the markets to keep me amused. They smacked us if we cried and gave us yesterday's bread and watered buttermilk so they did. And that's what'll happen to you, me fine feller, if you don't do as I say.'

But of course Ivan was unimpressed. 'Wan' kitty,' he whined. 'Wanna cuggle kitty.'

So now, faced with taking Ivan or approaching Tad Donoghue, it was no contest. Polly and Tad had parted on bad terms, but she would have to go round to his room and speak softly to him, or suffer the various outrages which a healthy, spoilt two-year-old can put on an elder sister.

'Here's the money, then,' Deirdre said, handing Polly the worn little red purse which Peader had sent for a Christmas gift several years since. 'And there's a few pence extra – you can treat yourself and Tad, or you can pay him for carryin', see which he'd rather.'

'If I could take the pram without Ivan . . .' Polly ventured, but Deirdre shook her head.

'Oh no, you bold madam, I've heard tales like that before so I have! Just you run off now, and don't be all day about it, either. I've got the sheets on the line but I'll want a hand to fold 'em, later.'

With four whole windows to call their own, sheets were not the insurmountable problem they had once been, but even so, sunny days were a blessing to thank the good God for, Mammy often said. She hauled in her rope, hung out her wet linen, then prayed, and with a bit of luck, with wind and sun, they would be dry before darkness fell. Little clothes could be hung on the wooden clothes horse before the fire, but in winter sheets were more of a curse than a blessing. Living in Swift's Alley, you had to keep washing all the time, and sweeping, cleaning, burning. The women did their best but there were four families in each of the four rooms on the next storey up and they suffered from fleas, bed-bugs, all sorts. It wasn't their fault,

Mammy said. They had so little money coming in they couldn't afford the carbolic, the Keatings powder, the time to scrub, even. But the O'Bradys were lucky because they'd got Niall, who was working as a clerk in an office and bringing almost all his wages home, and Martin, who was working hard at senior school and helping his Aunt Bridie to sell fish, door to door, at weekends and Donal, who sold the *Mail* and the *Herald* after school and all day during the holidays, the way Brogan, Niall and even Martin had once done. And best of all so far as wages went, they had Daddy and Brogan, working across the sea in Liverpool and earning better money than they could ever have brought home for labouring jobs in Dublin.

Not that Brogan was a labourer; not any more. He was fireman on an engine, and working like a black slave, he told them, at evening classes, for to better himself.

'What could be better than a fireman? Or an engine driver?' his younger brothers wondered aloud, but Mammy said engine driving was cold, dirty work.

'One day, all my sons will wear smart suits and white shirts and work in offices, and we'll have a nice little house on Dominick Place, right near the park, or we could move out of the city, go down to Booterstown, or Black Rock,' Mammy would say dreamily. 'Fancy, livin' at the seaside, with the sands to play on whenever you wanted.'

So because they had earners, now, and not so many babies – it never crossed Polly's mind to wonder why their mammy no longer produced a baby each year, as she apparently had before their daddy went off over the water to Liverpool – Mammy no longer had to drag herself and her wicker cart out of the city before day broke, to pick potatoes when they were ready, nor did she squat on the pavement all the rest of the day, selling those same potatoes to anyone who would buy.

'I'm a lady now,' she would tease, as she got them ready for school or cooked hot porridge for the workers and made a huge pot of tea. 'I work a little, now and then, for extrys, but I'm not a wage slave, thanks to me boys and me dear Peader.'

Things were different in the Donoghue household. There were a grush of kids, as the boys said, ranging from Tad, who was nine, to the newest baby, a girl named Aileen, and though the boys tried, and Mr Donoghue was a docker and often in work, he never took a penny of his money home for his family, regarding it as his own property.

'If me ould feller dropped dead tomorrer we'd be no worse off,' Tad often said. 'We'd be *better* off, because we wouldn't get bate till we was black an' blue, and nor would me mammy.'

Polly hated Mr Donoghue and was afraid of him, too. He would swagger out of the tenement building, having eaten the lion's share of any food that was going, with his tall ash stick, the mark of his trade, and his wide leather belt with the brass buckle. Down to the nearest pub he would go and when he wasn't drinking he was out at the brickfields, playing pitch and toss with the school which the men had formed there. If he won, he drank heavier than ever. If he lost he came home and belted his wife or beat his kids.

So in a way you could understand why Tad could be tricky, at times. Which made it easier to bear. And though he didn't have anything to speak of, he was generous. Polly guessed that the kitten he'd given her had been stolen from a litter, that he'd found the dog Delilah wandering the street and nicked the mice and the smart cage from one of the expensive shops on

O'Connell or Parnell Streets. But he'd given them to her freely, when he could easily have sold them – you couldn't say fairer than that, could you?

So having made up her mind that Tad was at least the lesser of two evils, Polly left her own block and headed for Gardiners Lane and the Donoghues'. They lived on the top floor, in an attic room with a sloping ceiling – a dozen of them, more or less. Mrs Donoghue was a nice woman, but her ould feller blacked her eye most days and sometimes she walked funny, sort of bent up, and other times her face was swollen out to the side, or one arm she kept clutched to her body.

'The ould feller found a clock in 'is carry-out,' Tad had said on one occasion when she'd mentioned Mrs Donoghue's swollen face. 'So he belted her. God love her, she doesn't deserve it. When I'm a man I'll kill that bugger stone dead so I will.'

'What's a clock?' Polly had asked Niall that night. 'Not the sort that you hang on the wall, the sort you find in your carry-out.'

Niall looked puzzled but Martin gave a roar of laughter.

'It's a cockroach, Poll,' he said at once. 'Who found one in their carry-out? Not your friend Tad?'

'No. He doesn't get a carry-out. It was his daddy, and his daddy belted his mammy and Tad said one day he'll kill the bugger stone dead so he will.'

'So he ought,' Mammy's voice said from the fireside where she was mending socks. 'So he bloody ought. That feller's bad or mad or a bit of both. I thank God fasting that Peader's not that kind o' man.'

But now, hovering by Tad's tenement, Polly wondered whether to go straight up and knock, or whether to hang about hopefully. But it was past ten in the morning, surely Tad's ould feller would be down at the docks, or at the pub, or even out at the Brick-fields, by this time? There was one good thing about tenement life, though; everyone knew everyone else's business. So Polly hadn't been hovering more than a few seconds when a woman came out. She had an armful of wet linen and a fancy peg-bag. It was Mrs Wilson, a hard ticket as the boys called her. Mammy called her a stuffy-nose, but Polly quite liked her. Mrs Wilson might look down on her neighbours and talk of her days as the priest's housekeeper before she'd caught Mr Wilson, and him only a tram-driver when all was said and done, but she approved of the O'Bradys.

'You keep the children nice,' she had said to Polly's mother once. 'I've only the one, but it's hard enough keepin' him decent, let alone half a dozen of 'em.'

Mrs Wilson was beginning to peg her clothes on the line, but she turned and smiled down at Polly as she did so.

'Mornin', Polly – is it the eldest Donoghue chiseller you're after wantin', then? He passed me on the stairs just now so he can't be far away.'

'Thanks, Mrs Wilson. I'll go and take a look in Thomas Street, see if he's out there.'

She hurried out into the road, well aware that Tad could be miles away by now, and probably was. What a nuisance, and she'd got a list a mile long, she could have done with Tad's muscles for to carry her messages home!

She found him eventually on Thomas Street staring into the window of Byrne's the poulterer. Polly knew from past experience that there would be a nasty smell from the chickens, ducks and pigeons hanging on either side of the doorway so although, like Tad, she coveted the feathers, she rarely lingered outside Byrne's. She hurried over to Tad though and reached him just as he bent forward, grabbed a handful of particularly fine feathers from a cock's tail, and pulled.

The whole string veered sideways alarmingly of course, and Mr Byrne, from behind his counter, roared a threat, but Tad, with a handful of feathers, was away, running down the street at a pace which had Polly panting in seconds. But she caught him up at last and gave him a thump with her shopping basket.

'Tad! What did you want to do that for, and me wit' me mouth open, about to ask if you'd help wit' me messages? I had to run like the wind to catch you,' she added aggrievedly. 'And me basket's heavy even wit' nothing inside!'

Tad was small for his age but very strong – he needed to be as Polly well knew. He had dark hair which curled when it was given the chance – but Mrs Donoghue made the barber shave her boys' heads so they didn't need a haircut more than once in a couple of months – and blue eyes fringed with thick, black lashes. He had a nice grin, a soft voice, and a fund of hair-raising and probably untrue stories which made him popular in the lobbies and stairways when the kids congregated to scare themselves with talk of ghosts, banshees and other such things.

'I thought you wasn't never goin' to speak to me again, because of not takin' you swimmin' in the Liffey,' Tad said, but he grinned as he said it. 'I thought you hoped you'd never see me again in this life – wasn't that what you shouted?'

Polly dismissed this with a wave of the hand not engaged with the basket. 'I may have said a thing or two, in me temper,' she admitted airily. 'But well you know, Tad Donoghue, that I was never after meanin' any of 'em. You busy?'

'Busy doin' nothin', yes sure I am,' said the irrepressible Tad. 'But I don't mind doin' nothin' with you, if you're in a better mood than you were yesterday. Where's Delly?'

'Donal's took him on the fish round,' Polly said. 'I said he could; if there's one thing Delilah does love, 'tis a nice piece of fish. Or even quite a nasty, smelly one,' she added conscientiously, remembering Delilah's unfortunate predilection for ancient herrings. 'I was nursin' dear Lionel, sittin' in the window mindin' me own business and thinkin' about the summer, and then Mammy said she wanted messages doing and here I am. Only I've got a list as long as the bloody Liffey,' she added pathetically. 'And how I'm to carry me basket back once 'tis loaded wit' stuff God above knows.'

'Oh, give it here,' Tad said with all his usual good nature. 'I'll lend you a hand. Where's first?'

'Thanks, Tad,' Polly said, handing over her basket. 'Me mammy said I could treat you if you give a hand. What 'ud you rather, ice cream, cake or tuppence?'

Tad shrugged. 'Dunno as I mind, Poll. Let's get the messages done, then we'll t'ink about it. Where's we to go first?'

Polly consulted her list and sighed. It was indeed long and would mean quite a lot of walking.

'Mammy wants us to go to the Iveagh market, and then to Moore Street because she says they've the freshest fruit in Dublin. She's sent the big boys for the spuds, thanks be to God,' she added piously. 'Spuds weigh heavy so they do.'

'There's no need to traipse to Moore Street wit' everything half the price on the Francis Street stalls,' Tad said firmly. 'Or did she want to send you over the Liffey for a reason, d'you think? If your daddy's comin' home today was she after sendin' you for something he really likes?'

Polly consulted her list again, then shook her head. 'No, it can't be that, for there's not even tobacco on me list – I don't know that me daddy smokes, come to that. We'll start in Francis Street then, Tad.'

'Sure,' Tad said, hefting the basket. 'Will we be buyin' ribs, from Durney's?'

'That's right,' Polly said. 'Why?'

'We might ask Mr D for some bones for your Delly,' Tad said. 'Then I could take 'em home for me mammy to make us a broth. Pork bones make good broth, wit' an onion or two and mebbe a carrot.'

'All right, we'll do that,' Polly told him. 'I'm wantin' a good shirt to fit our Donal from the Iveagh, too. Mammy says he's growed out of his old one and she won't have me daddy shamed on Sunday, at Mass.'

'Oh, the old priests don't notice, 'tis the other old women who point, if you're raggedy,' Tad said knowingly. He was usually raggedy. 'Mind, me daddy's always smart. Mammy puts his suit, shirt and shoes in the pawn on Monday morning, early, an' takes it out again on Saturday, late. Wish I had a dacent suit to pawn,' he added wistfully. 'I could do wit' the money.'

'Well, mebbe,' Polly said vaguely. As they talked they had made their way through the crowds of shoppers on Thomas Street and turned right, into Francis Street. 'What'll we do when we've got our messages, Tad? It's a beautiful day, wouldn't you say? Too nice for hangin' round the alley.'

'We could do all sorts if we had pennies for the tram,' Tad said. 'We could go all over.'

Polly smiled. 'Right you are, let's go to Phoenix Park, shall us? It's nice there, Niall said so.'

Tad pulled a face. 'It's real hot today; I'd sooner go

to the canal, then we could swim,' he said longingly. 'I can swim – almost. We can go to a quiet bit, where the fellers don't go. Would you like that?'

It was definitely an olive branch but even so, Polly looked doubtful. 'Last time we was there we saw that dead dog, remember? The poor feller, wit' his legs in the air and his poor eyes clamped shut. I don't want to swim wit' no dead dog.'

'Aw, janey, that won't happen again,' Tad protested at once. 'Anyway, I'll look after you, alanna. You'll be safe wit' me.'

Brogan couldn't stop smiling. Making his way across Liverpool, down Beckett Street, along Fountains Road, he smiled like an idiot whether anyone was looking at him or not. And when he and Peader got on the tram just outside the Stanley Hospital, even the conductor, taking their fares, noticed it.

'Where's you off to, then?' he enquired blandly. ''Cos you've gorra grin on your gob like a bleedin' Cheshire cat.'

'I'm goin' home,' Brogan said simply. 'First time for five years. I've been livin' in Crewe for eighteen months because the work took me there, so I've been away from all me family, even me daddy here. It's good to be seein' them all again.'

The conductor whistled sympathetically. 'No wonder you're grinnin', pal! And don't tell me, you're from God's own country – right?'

'That's right. Dublin. Swift's Lane, off Francis Street.'

The conductor heaved a sigh. 'I come from there meself, or rather me mam did,' he said reminiscently. 'She were just a child when her mam and da crossed the water – her family live there still, in Enniskerry. O'Mara, the name is. We've never been back, ourselves, but me mam talks about Enniskerry as though it were paradise – always 'as.'

'Dublin isn't paradise, and Swift's Alley's a bit rough, mebbe,' Brogan said. 'But there's something about it . . . I dunno.' He turned to his father. 'What do you say, Daddy?'

Peader shrugged. He had told Brogan that life in Liverpool wasn't the same without him, that he was seriously considering trying to get a bit of a decent job in Dublin when they got home, but Brogan doubted if he would really do such a thing. He was the safety man for a large gang now, on good money with a lot of responsibility. Of course he missed his family, anyone would, but his conscience would not let him take the easy way out. Returning to Dublin and no job, letting his wife and kids keep him, was not Peader's style. He had always looked down on the men of the tenements who took it for granted that their wives would support them and the large families they gave them. He'd disapproved of a baby every year, too, and told his sons frankly that they should learn self-discipline before they married. Brogan had not been at all sure what his father meant at the time, though he knew now. A woman should be loved, honoured and cherished, his father had told him when Brogan took his first young lady to the cinema. You young fellers think women are only good for one thing – taking to bed. Well, that's selfish, wicked and wrong. If you give a girl a baby then you have to support the pair of 'em, and if you want your wife to stay healthy and sweet then you must deny yourself from time to time.

Brogan had said he understood and promised to be careful; it hadn't been difficult. The girls he took out were nice girls, but they hadn't lit any particular flame within him. It had been easy simply to say goodnight to them after a few kisses, easy to part. But now there was a girl he thought he cared about, only she'd been sent away. And anyway, he was a man and Sara Cordwainer was a child – but bidding fair to become a very lovely young woman.

But now Peader, who had been looking out of the tram window, turned to face the conductor.

'Sure and isn't everyone's home special?' he said. 'The air's softer, over there,' I guess, and the water's sweeter. The girls are prettier, the people kinder. Otherwise perhaps we'd not want to go back so bad.'

The conductor laughed and patted his shoulder.

'Aye, the Irish are a lovely people and there's Irish in most of us scousers,' he said in his heavy Liverpool accent. 'Good luck to you, fellers, and good sailing.'

When they reached the dock the sky overhead was blue, the sun shining.

'We're goin' to have a good voyage, Daddy,' Brogan remarked as they hefted their bags up the gangplank, jostled by a great many other would-be travellers. 'Not like the last time – janey, how the waves heaved! Still, even that weren't as bad as when I took the wee one over under me jacket.'

He had lowered his voice but even so Peader glanced anxiously about him.

'Don't speak too loud, lad,' he muttered. 'I'm always careful. Your mammy would kill the pair of us if we had to take Polly from her. Deirdre's a kind and lovin' woman, but who'd have thought she'd take to the child the way she has? She dotes on her, dotes.'

'So do we all,' Brogan said. He had last seen Polly when she was only two years old, but under his mother's care she had grown prettier and more self-confident than ever. She was talking well, walking, playing nursery games . . . he had been as proud of her as though she had been his own get. But now she was a really big girl, seven years old, and doing well at school. Mammy wrote regularly and Polly often added a little letter of her own and Brogan was always astonished at her cleverness. He couldn't wait to see her now, the child that he had stolen, or rescued, depending on your viewpoint, he supposed.

'The nuns all t'ink she's a little wonder, so they do,' Peader said now, as they settled themselves in the bows, eyes front. Everyone wanted to be the first to spot Ireland through the heat-haze which hung over the land, and here in the bows they would be shouting 'land ho!' long before the rest of the passengers. 'She's always bringin' home holy pictures and medals for good work.'

'I know,' Brogan said. 'I often wonder about the other kids, you know, the other Carberys. I used to catch a glimpse of one or two of them, but I suppose they changed as they grew up. Anyway, I've not seen one for ages.'

'Do you still see that girl you told me about?' Peader asked presently. 'What was her name, now? I disremember it.'

'You mean Sara. Sara Cordwainer. No, we've not met for years, Sara and meself. There was trouble more than a year before I left the Pool – did I not tell you? Her father discovered that she and I had met once or twice whilst she was staying with her old nurse. There was nothin' in it bar friendship, she was only fifteen or so, but he's an awful toffee-nosed feller, real high in the instep. She wrote to me once and told me they were sendin' her away to school and she didn't know the address, so I couldn't write back. She said they'd stopped her visitin' in Snowdrop Street. I went and visited her gran, but she said there was nothin' she could do.' Brogan sighed. 'Poor kid, and we was only good friends when all's said an' done. Still, there you are. It's all over, not that there was anything ... but she's a young lady now, not a child, I doubt I'd recognise her if we met face to face in the street.'

He knew he would know her again, though, thought he'd know her anywhere. He'd felt awful sorry for her the last time he'd seen her, being treated like a criminal just for walkin' alongside a feller in workin' clothes. He had spotted her walking along Stanley Road with a basket swinging from one hand and when he'd called she had rushed across the pavement and hugged him, clearly very pleased to see him once more.

Brogan was equally pleased to see young Sara. They had met several times over the years and had enjoyed one another's company on each occasion, the age-gap becoming less and less important as she grew up. She was bright, intelligent, understood the work he did in evening classes, discussed it with him, encouraged him. On previous occasions they had been to the Walker Art Gallery together, and to the Museum, too. Once, they'd gone to a cinema show – Brogan had given her a cuddle when the film was frightening – and once to the pantomime. He had enjoyed her enjoyment of the show more, by and large, than the show itself. But it had been twelve months since they had met, for it was only possible to do so when Sara was staying with her grandmother in Snowdrop Street. So of course he'd been delighted to see her again, delighted at her unselfconscious dart into his arms, as well.

'Brogan!' she had said, her eyes shining, her mouth curving into a smile. 'Oh, how nice it is to see you! It must be almost a year since we met – my mother's been poorly so it hasn't been possible for me to stay in Snowdrop Street. But you're on your way home, you don't want to stand gossiping here. Can we meet later?'

'Sure we can,' he had said, delighted. She was turning into a beautiful young creature, with rich dark curls tumbling on to her shoulders and a perfect, heart-shaped face lit by big, dark-blue eyes. 'I've so many t'ings to tell you – I've passed all me exams so far and me family are well – I've a letter from me mammy tellin' me all Polly's latest tricks. Shall we walk along the road now and have a cuppa, and you can read me letter? Then we might go along to the Commodore, there's a cowboy film on, you've always liked a good cowboy film.'

He knew she loved the cinema and was fascinated by his family, particularly Polly. She often gave him small presents to pass on to the child, which he faithfully did – a length of velvet ribbon, a silver locket, a tiny enamelled box for trinkets, a warm woollen scarf. Now he beamed down at her, reflecting that she must have cheered other passersby too, with her bright, animated little face and the way she swung her basket.

'Look, I'll walk you back to Snowdrop Street so you can explain to your gran that you're with me,' Brogan said. 'Then we can go to Cunningham's Dining Rooms so that we can have tay and a fancy cake while we talk.'

'That would be lovely,' Sara said. 'Oh, Brogan, you look so happy and well! Come on then, you'll have to lead the way. Nanny and I don't go to posh places like Dining Rooms!'

He had laughed, taken her arm to swing her round . . . and the car had drawn up beside them. A man got out. He was tall and cruel-looking with slicked-back black hair and a thin, high-bridged nose.

He looked at Brogan as though he were a dog-turd he'd just trodden in, then he turned to Sara.

'Get in the car,' he said, and his voice was like a whiplash. 'How dare you walk the streets like a common tart and consort with filth from the gutters?'

Brogan stared, almost unable to believe his ears, but Sara turned to him at once, tears brimming in her big eyes.

'Brogan, I'm sorry! It's my father . . . I have to go.'

The last words were cried rather than spoken as the tall man jerked her across the pavement and almost threw her into the car. He tapped on the glass panel which divided them from the driver, and the car shot off. The last Brogan saw of Sara was her tearful young face turned beseechingly towards him, a hand raised in farewell.

He'd taken his courage in both hands after that and gone round to number three, Snowdrop Street. The lady who answered the door said that she was Mrs Prescott and listened when he tried to explain what had happened, how mistaken Mr Cordwainer had been. Then she had smiled at him and held out a plump, work-roughened hand.

'You'll be Brogan; Sara often spoke of you,' she said. 'I'm Mrs Prescott, I was once Sara's nanny, and her mother's, too. But I don't think I can help you, because I know Sara's father to be an arrogant and unbending man. He's said he won't allow his daughter to stay in my house again and I'm afraid he means it. But one of these days, when she's older, she'll come back to me. I can do nothing until then.'

'What if I write?' Brogan said desperately. 'I'd like to write to her fine, so I would. There can be no harm in a letter, surely?'

'She'll never receive it,' Mrs Prescott assured him.

'They're sending her away, to a school somewhere, and all her letters will be opened. Mr Cordwainer told me to my face that he'll tell the school authorities she's not to receive any letters, including mine. Oh, she'll write to me, I've no doubt of that, and perhaps we'll manage to arrange something, but for now there's nothing I can do.'

And she had been right. Not a word had he heard from Sara from that day to this, though he thought of her often. She was already special to him. He had hoped they would meet again, one day, but he supposed, now, that it might never happen. He was a fireman, soon, he believed, to be an engine driver, but to go higher he might have to leave the LMS, maybe even leave the English railway systems. And he intended to go higher. One day he would have a wife and family to keep and he did not want to do it by taking a job in a foreign land and scarcely ever setting eyes on his dear ones. He admired his father for doing what he did, but it was not for him. When he married – if he married – he would not want to leave his wife for years at a time. And the only way to be sure of being able to support a family was through a well-paid job.

'Well, a shame it is that your friendship with the little girl was cut short. But you're goin' back to the land of beautiful colleens, so you'd best forget your Sara and whatever trouble there was,' his father said comfortably, now. 'Besides, there's no reason for you to marry just yet. Marriage changes a feller – and a woman, for the matter of that. Too many youngsters jump into marriage and into bed and discover their mistake too late, that's what I always say.'

'But you and Mammy are well-suited, wouldn't you say?' Brogan said slyly. He knew how desperately his daddy loved his mammy – and missed her, too. 'Why shouldn't we think of that, us O'Bradys?'

'Ah, well now, your mammy's one in a thousand,' Peader said. 'And I'll be settin' eyes on her in a few hours . . . ah, glory be to God, I'm a lucky feller!'

'Is that it, Daddy? Or is it a cloud?' Brogan's knuckles were white from gripping the rail, his eyes stung from the strain of peering ahead. On the horizon he could see a line, darker than the line of the ocean, with a faint haze hovering over it.

His father slung an arm about his shoulders. That's it, son,' he said softly. 'That's Ireland – God's own country. Oh, God love you, we'll be ashore in no time . . . see the lighthouse? We'll be seein' Dun Laoghaire plain as plain in a moment. And then Dublin, son – home!'

Side by side they stood by the rail, eyes straining ahead, taking note of every landmark on the coastline of Ireland, in imagination already disembarking, making their way through the familiar streets, turning into the Alley, mounting the stairs . . .

'See it? See it? That's Ireland so it is! We're comin' home!'

Brogan saw the land shimmer and twist and saw his father duck his head, cross himself, begin to thank God for the smooth crossing, for the coming landfall. Heard the murmur around him . . . *We're home; that's Ireland that is . . . and we'll be dockin' in the heart of Dublin within the hour.*

He turned away from the rail for a moment to look at the people straining towards the land. Mostly men, who had been away for years, working to feed their families. Good men, reliable men. Loving men. Men not ashamed of the tears in their eyes. Like his father; like Peader.

Sara stepped down off the train at Lime Street station and looked curiously about her. Someone would be meeting her, that was for sure, but she had no idea who it would be. Father? Mother? Possibly even the chauffeur, though whether the family still employed Robson she had no means of knowing.

She had been away from home for three whole years now, and she was a young lady of eighteen, not a girl any more. And she had not missed either her parents or her home one bit. But she had missed her nanny and Snowdrop Street and had been absolutely furious when she had discovered her father's ban – as though she had been some flighty little piece intent on an assignation, instead of merely loving her old nanny and wanting to meet a friend who happened to be a young man.

'A labourer,' her father had sneered as he bundled her into the car. 'Have you no pride in yourself Sara? No pride in your family, your station? Even if you had merely been passing the time of day, as you say, you don't behave like that! Smiling, letting the creature take your arm . . .'

'He didn't take my arm,' Sara had shouted, embarrassed and angry all at once. 'He turned me round – I was going in the wrong direction, only I didn't know it. Father, I've met Brogan perhaps a dozen times over the past three years, we talk about a friend from Snowdrop Street, someone we both knew, who died –'

She got no further. She had no *friends* in Snowdrop Street but only acquaintances, and she could not possibly share a *friend* with someone who looked like a – a dirty chimney sweep anyhow.

Sara had said no more. Her father ranted and she sat silent. But at home, her mother had started as well and between them, they had made her life so miserable that when the day of departure dawned, it seemed that she was not heading for a punishment, but an escape.

And so, in a way, it proved. The school was in Switzerland, on the edge of Lake Como. There were mountains, the lake itself, wonderful countryside where grapes ripened on the hillsides in autumn and the meadows were ablaze with wild flowers in summer. She found she could learn languages with ease and could soon make herself understood in French, German and Italian. What was more, she made many friends, for the girls at the school were intelligent and interesting.

They thought it a little strange that she did not go home at holiday times, but not very strange. England was a long way off. There were seven other girls from England out of a total of a hundred and fifty pupils and only one of them went home as a matter of course for the long summer vacation.

Sara had realised long ago that she was an unloved child and it had made her very unhappy, since it seemed obvious that a child who cannot arouse affection in her own parents must be repulsive indeed. But school put things in perspective. Mother love did not come naturally to all parents, she learned, and English parents, apparently, particularly upper-class English parents, were often deficient in maternal and paternal love. As she got to know the other girls she realised that they, too, suffered, particularly her friend Anita, whose parents also treated their offspring with hurtful indifference.

'But I started at boarding school in Bournemouth when I was seven, and I soon realised that lots and lots of parents don't really care for their children,' she assured Sara. 'Some of them were really cruel and the children were awfully unhappy, but I had a wonderful nanny who took great care of me, and a big sister who is just perfect . . . so I stopped worrying that Mummy and Daddy scarcely ever visited the nursery when I was home in the holidays. I mean they didn't seem to think much of Veronica, either, and there isn't a nicer person in the world, truly there isn't.'

So Sara took comfort from this and wrote dutiful letters home and tried not to care that her parents' rare replies were always more like lectures than letters. And in due course she sat the necessary examinations and passed them, and prepared to rejoin the real world, which meant to leave school, and Switzerland, behind her.

Thanks to the school she now spoke French, German and Italian fluently, and Madame Audierne, who was headmistress of the school, had made sure she was taught a good many social graces and a good deal of commonsense. Sara understood a great deal about fashion, about the importance of always looking one's best, and about being a gracious hostess. Mme Audierne boasted that her girls left school able, if necessary, to entertain and amuse the highest in the land, and though Sara acknowledged that this was a flight of fancy, she still realised that she was now the possessor of considerable poise and self-possession.

Standing on Lime Street station however, watching the hustle and bustle of passersby, it did occur to her that she was also singularly ill-equipped to reach her home on foot. Despite the heat she was wearing a fashionable Robin Hood hat, an equally fashionable dark-green suit with curved white lapels, silk stockings and high-heeled strap shoes. Not the sort of clothes in which one set out on a long walk. Coming up in the train she had been studying a copy of *Woman* magazine, and thought wistfully that life would have been pleasanter had she been clad in a pair of the extremely fashionable beach pyjamas and a huge straw hat – and think of her father's rage should he see her in such an outfit!

There was a taxi-cab, of course. She could go outside, hail a cab, and then demand that either her parents or a servant pay him when they reached Aigburth Road. But before she could do anything so desperate, a voice hailed her.

'Sara? Sara! Over here!'

It was Mother, exquisitely turned out as usual and with a hat very similar to the one Sara wore perched rakishly on her tinted head. Sara found herself smiling, glad to see her mother, though she reminded herself sharply not to get carried away. She had managed very well without parents for three years and they had clearly managed very well without her. She must never become dependent upon them again, either for love or for any sort of moral guidance. So long as she remembered that, she thought, they might rub along quite comfortably.

So she went forward and laid her cheek carefully against her mother's powder and paint, and then pointed out her trunks and got a porter to carry them out to the car, which was waiting, her mother assured her, outside.

'Father couldn't come, he's at the office, of course, but I thought I'd better meet you myself in case Robson didn't recognise you. It's been a long time,' Mrs Cordwainer said coolly and Sara said sharply, 'I'm surprised you recognised me yourself, Mother, for I'm sure you saw very little more of me than Robson did, one way and another.'

For a moment she wondered if she had gone too far, but she need not have worried. Her mother was looking thoughtfully at Sara's outfit, and nodding approvingly. She had probably not even heard Sara's words.

'That is a very pretty hat,' Mrs Cordwainer said. 'Pearls would look well in the neck of that coat – do you have some pearls?'

'Not so far as I know,' Sara said. 'And I don't know that I want any, thank you. I think that pearls would look dull against the white of the lapels.'

This time her mother really did look surprised, then she shrugged and took Sara's arm.

'You're quite the fashionable young lady,' she said lightly. 'I shall enjoy having you at home now you're grown up. Come along, I want to see what other clothes you're hiding in your trunks. And in a few days we must talk about having a coming-out party for you. You are eighteen, after all.'

Sara said nothing, but she smiled to herself as she followed her mother's elegant back out of the station. If she really thinks that I'm going to turn into a paper pattern of herself she's got another think coming, Sara told herself grimly. Wait till she hears I want a job! Wait till I say I'm off to see Nanny for a weekend – and just let them try to stop me now!

Brogan and Peader had a marvellous welcome when they reached the house in Swift's Alley. Mammy wept and hugged them, the boys cheered and shouted and asked if there were presents in the bags, and Polly beamed and jumped up and down until her curls danced and kept gabbling away in her sweet, breath-

130

less voice until Mammy laughed and told her to stop or she'd be sent off to bed so she would!

'But there's roast ribs and a huge pan of new spuds and butter for our tea – I got the butter from the dairy on Francis Street, Mammy sent me there wit' me friend Tad from the next block,' Polly informed Brogan. She could not remember him too clearly – she had been two when he'd last been home – but Peader had been back more recently and she almost throttled him with hugs.

'Colleen, colleen, don't strangle me dead before I've so much as walked in the door,' he begged, and then his wife cast herself on his chest and he hugged her close whilst tears ran down his cheeks and dripped on to her black curls. 'Ah, Deirdre, Deirdre, me darlin' girl, never has a feller missed a woman more, I've been heartsick for you every day these t'ree years.'

Brogan turned away, catching hold of Polly's small hand. They deserved a moment to themselves, those two, who had worked so hard and longed for each other so much and who were reunited at last.

'Come on, Polly, you show me the new rooms, and then you can take me a walk around the city,' he said encouragingly. 'Donal, Bevin, you come too ... now where's that fine boy I've heard so much about – me baby brother, Ivan?'

'He's there, the bad spalpeen,' Polly grumbled, hooking the baby out of the corner where he was beating a pile of building blocks with a small wooden hammer. 'Aw, come on, you tarble boy, Brogan's goin' to take us a walk.'

'Where would you like to go?' Brogan said when they had descended the stairs and were crossing the courtyard. 'Go on, you choose.'

There was a babble of suggestions. Donal pulled at

his sleeve, Polly clung to his hand, Bevin, who was twelve now, nudging thirteen, ran ahead, shouting the news to the neighbourhood that 'Me brother's come home so he has!'

This was home, Brogan thought contentedly, suggesting that they should do one thing at a time now, and not to forget he was home for a whole two weeks. Home was kids bawling at you, the pram which Polly and he were pushing between them bouncing over the cobbles, the sky soft and blue overhead.

'I don't care where we go, then,' Polly said, capitulating as suddenly as she had begun the argument. 'Go on, Donal, you choose.'

'Sure an' anywhere'll be fun,' Donal said, promptly following suit. 'We could go to the Basin, Brog. That's what Bevin 'ud like.'

'Then the Basin it is,' Brogan said. 'I'll just pop into John's Lane on me way past, though. Light a candle that I'm home safe.'

'Mammy'll do that an' all,' Polly observed, whilst Donal, who was fourteen and a practical person, remarked that most of the men he knew would have wanted to pop into Deegan's pub on their way past rather than the church.

'I'll do that later,' Brogan said, not wanting to appear a cissy in his brother's eyes. 'Come on, 'tis a long walk to the Basin from Swift's Alley!

Chapter Six

Brogan and his father had returned home on a Saturday. In true Irish fashion there was a downpour of rain on the Sunday, wetting the faithful, Mammy said gloomily, as they made their way both to and from Mass. Monday, too, dawned overcast – not that the O'Bradys cared! You could sell newspapers in any weather bar rain, the boys always said, and it was the same with fish, which never sold well on a Monday anyway. Folk wanted fish for Wednesdays and Fridays, that was obvious, so unless they fancied it specially, they would not buy the rest of the week.

So when Tuesday proved to be a brilliant day, the family decided that everyone would take the day off. The boys deputed others, cousins, friends, to do their jobs and everyone put on their oldest, most practical clothing, for today they were going to Booterstown on the train, to pick cockles on the long, sandy strand.

It was the height of a child's ambition, Brogan thought, as he watched his mammy cutting a carry-out for each of them. His mother's famous soda bread, a lump of real butter which Polly had run down and bought from the shop on Francis Street earlier, wrapped in cabbage leaves to keep it cool, and a screw of salt in a piece of blue paper. They would pick enough cockles for to make a meal, and lastly Mammy had got a big, scarlet tomato each from one of the market stalls. Riches! And Peader carried a covered bucket with tea in it – they would make a fire of sticks to heat it up, if they could find enough dry ones, that was. If not they'd drink it cold. 'And why not? Sure and I have me bottle of cold tay every day of me workin' life,' Peader reminded them.

They walked to the Tara Street station in a noisy, laughing crowd, Mammy and Daddy arm in arm, Mammy holding Ivan on her hip. Only he was a heavy, wriggling burden and since they couldn't get the pram on the train Brogan took charge of him, letting him walk a wee way, then picking him up and running with him to catch up with the others.

'I'm your horsie, amn't I, big feller?' Brogan said when Ivan screamed to get down again. 'Give your horsie a cut – a little one, mind – and he'll gallop right round the corner wit' you.'

Ivan liked that. He liked sitting on Brogan's shoulders, too, and hanging on to Brogan's ears and yelling to every passerby to 'Look at me! I'm onna norsie, so I am!'

The family piled into a carriage as soon as the train drew in, only Mammy and Peader managing to get a seat. But no one minded. Brogan piled their carry-outs and their jackets on the long string hammock of a rack which hung above the seated passengers' heads whilst his father sat himself carefully down next to his wife, the bucket of tea stood on the floor between his boots.

The train started with a jerk and Peader steadied the bucket whilst Donal hung out of the window despite many warnings from Mammy that it was dangerous and he'd get a blast from the engine in his eye and then he'd be sorry. He was still shouting against the wind that he wasn't the sort of donkey to go gettin' things in his eyes when he squawked and withdrew his head, one hand to his face.

'Oh, 'tis the size of a housebrick, I'll die for sure,'

Donal roared, and Niall told him he was a donkey indeed whilst Mammy scolded and Daddy said he'd done the same himself, many a time, and advice came both from family and other passengers. Pull your eyelid down over your eye now, feller. Blow your nose real hard, that'll do it. Screw up your eyes to make the water come, then blow your nose. But Bevin, probably imagining a trip to the hospital instead of a day at the seaside, turned and gave his brother a hearty clout. The blow made Donal shout again but his eye watered so much that the blast ran out with the tears and he was cured, though he glared at his brother resentfully.

When the fuss was over Brogan hung on to the luggage rack and gazed at the gardens and houses rushing past the window and Polly and Bevin hung on to him. Polly kept talking, though he could not hear much above the racket of the train. She kept pointing to the pictures which hung below the luggage rack and eventually Brogan realised she was asking which of them was Booterstown.

He examined the brown photographs, then leaned forward and ran his finger along the titles beneath each.

'None of 'em's where we's going,' he told Polly. 'Well, not today. Booterstown's a good place, you'll like it right well. But we'll go to those other places one day, alanna . . . we'll go to Killarney, and the beautiful Wicklow Mountains, and to Ballybunion. When you're a bit older.'

Polly just nodded. She did not even look surprised at such optimism and Brogan realised that to Polly all things were still possible. She had been in Dublin most of her short life and this would be her first visit to Booterstown, but she didn't waste time wondering why they'd not been before or when they'd go again, she just enjoyed the present . . . or would, once they got there.

Presently, Polly stood on tiptoe and shouted something else at him.

'What was that?' Brogan bawled, but at that moment the train slowed and stopped and there was a stampede for the platform. Brogan picked the baby off his mammy's lap and slung him round his neck, the child's fat little legs on either side of his face. Then he jumped down, turned and lifted the little ones down, finally offering his hand first to his mammy and then to an old lady who thanked him in a very regal manner, though she then wiped her nose on her sleeve, which didn't look quite so good.

Mammy came down on to the platform like a queen, with only the lightest touch of her fingers in his . . . she was a wonderful woman, Brogan thought with delight. How many women did he know who'd borne nine children, raised six of them, and taken on another child, yet still managed to smile and laugh more than she sighed, to seem carefree when burdened with a thousand worries – and had skin like new milk still, and hair without one strand of white? Not many, that was for sure. Not any, now he came to think.

'Mammy, you're a wonderful woman so you are,' he said to her, bowing and making Mammy laugh and flick his nose with her finger and the baby scream with pretended fear and cling like a limpet to Brogan's long-suffering ears. 'I hope I may meet a woman like you one of these days, else I'll not marry, I promise you. You leave every other woman I've met in the ha'penny place, so you do.'

'Your mammy's one in a t'ousand; when the good Lord made her he threw away the mould,' Peader said, jumping down and then reaching back for the bucket.

136

'Praise be to God, we'll get there wit' our tea-bucket unspilt at this rate!'

Polly waited patiently until they reached the beach, and then, sitting on the sand beside Brogan and taking off her plimsolls, she asked the question that she'd been trying to get out for ages, only the train clattered so, and the boys kept talking.

'Brogan, I wish we could have brought me friend Tad wit' us, so I do. Tad's never seen the sea, it's too far to walk to Booterstown and the Donoghues don't have pennies for the tram or the train.'

Brogan had undone his boots and was pulling off a pair of wonderful thick socks. Polly thought his feet must be stinkin' hot and said so, but Brogan said the woollen socks kept his feet cool because they sucked up the sweat and stopped his feet from scraping on the boot-leather.

'And as for your friend Tad, why didn't you call for him? Mammy and Daddy would have brought him, sure they would,' he added, wriggling his freed toes which were white as Polly's own. 'We wouldn't have grudged the lad a train ticket.'

'I didn't think,' Polly said sadly. 'It's selfish I am, Brogan, for he's a good friend to me. But he doesn't live in Swift's Alley now.'

Brogan raised a brow, then stood up, bent down and pulled her to her feet. 'Why not? Tell me whilst we paddle.'

They ran over the sand and down to the water, which creamed soft and easy against the shore. They both paused at the edge, then went in solemnly, slowly, and Polly's feet felt the salt sea water for the first time and she squeaked, and kicked foam, and decided that it was the best thing in the world so it was, and she'd

137

come here again so she would. Kids could earn money, she and Tad would earn money for the train ticket and come here and spend days and days on the beautiful golden beach!

But Brogan wanted to hear about Tad, so she marshalled her thoughts, took his hand, and spoke as they waded deeper.

'Well, the Donoghues aren't a very nice family – that is, the mammy and daddy aren't very nice. Well, that isn't right either, Brogan, because the mammy's nice, all right, but she can't stop the daddy taking all the food and beating the kids up and blacking her eye every Sat'day night, just about. He's a wicked great man, Mr Donoghue, he beats Tad's ould wan wit' his fists an' the kids wit' his big ash stick . . . he's a docker . . . and he drinks all the money away, even the money Mrs Donoghue makes from her work. Well, it's not so bad when he is working, but when he doesn't get a job then he goes home and searches for the money . . . she hides it, of course. And when he finds it he takes it though she cries and cries. So that was what happened to the rent money, it was so. He took it, an' when Mrs Donoghue couldn't pay sure an' the landlord turned 'em out. So now they live in Gardiners Lane, and it's all the fault of Tad's ould feller.'

'The wicked bugger,' Brogan said between his teeth. He said it low, and vicious, but Polly heard it clear as clear. He had sworn, this wonderful big brother of hers, who was a fireman on a real train like the one she'd just travelled on, and who was studying each night at a big school for fellers, to better himself! But she did not say she'd heard; she guessed she'd not been meant to do so. 'But, Polly, why do you call Mrs Donoghue "the ould wan"? You don't speak so about your own mammy.'

'It's what Tad calls her,' Polly said, unrepentant. 'So anyway, last Christmas Tad's ould feller drank the rent money for three whole weeks, and they couldn't stop him. And the landlord turned them out – God love them, they all stood around crying, with their things at their feet, whiles Mr Donoghue tried to kill the landlord's men and got locked up by the polis and bound over to keep the peace.'

'And what happened to the rest of 'em?' Brogan asked. 'Ah, see that swirl in the sand there, alanna, by your right foot? That's a cockle, diggin' himself down deeper.' He rolled up his sleeve and plunged a hand into the water, producing a round, fat cockle shell. 'Now I'll put it in me pocket . . . go on wit' the story.'

'I will, so,' Polly said. 'So everyone was sorry for them, and then someone told Mrs Donoghue there was a house wit' rooms going begging in Gardiners Lane. It's a good place to play, because of the ruins, but the house there is awful. The walls run wit' wet and the windows don't fit properly and there's cracked glass in 'em anyway. They can get water from a tap at the bottom of the road but it's a long way to lug it, and though Tad's awright, the younger kids always have coughs and colds, boils on their necks, flea bites and bug bites . . . it's an awful place, honest to God it is.'

'Well, next time we go out we'll take your friend,' Brogan said soothingly. 'And all the cockles you pick you can take round to him. And a nice loaf, to eat wit' the cockles . . . mebbe even a lump of butter, eh?'

'Oh, yes *please*, Brogan,' Polly said eagerly. 'You are kind; Mammy's kind, too. When I was cross with Tad a few days ago she told me to go and make up wit' him, she even gave me some money for to treat him wit'. Only . . . Mammy said we would pick cockles for our carry-out; will there be enough for Tad's whole family? There are a real lot of them.'

'You and me'll pick like machinery,' Brogan said promptly. 'I'll show you where the cockles hide, how they look when they're buryin' themselves, and you'll soon get the knack. Come on, we'll have a contest, you and me.'

It's quite definitely been the best day of me life so far, Polly thought dreamily, as, sandy, damp and satisfied, they made their way to the station to catch the train back into Dublin. She had burned the tops of her feet because they'd caught the sun even through the water, but hadn't she picked a grand bag of cockles, indeed? Brogan had helped and had explained to Mammy and Daddy that he and Polly wanted to take them home for the Donoghues, and the family had done so well at the picking that there was plenty for everyone at dinner-time.

'You break 'em open by putting the lip of one cockle between the shell of another and twisting,' Daddy told them. 'At home, we'd boil 'em and they'd open themselves, but here on the beach it's open the shells the hard way and suck 'em out one at a time. Aren't they the best t'ing out, now? Fresh and sweet – Molly Malone herself didn't sell better!'

The train was late, but that didn't matter, not to Polly, at any rate. Daddy, Brogan and Niall were going down to Deegan's pub when they got home again, and they would bring a jug of porter back to drink with the rest of the cockles and lemonade or ginger beer for the kids.

'It's been a real holiday, hasn't it, Bev?' Polly said when at last the train chugged in and they scrambled for seats. She sank back on to the hard wood, glad that the train was almost empty going this way, feeling sleepy, sun-kissed, satisfied . . . and knowing that the blue cloth bag of cockles would be divided fairly and half of it given to the Donoghues. 'Oh, Brogan, will you come wit' me when I take the cockles round? Only I'm that scared of Tad's ould feller, and you're big, he won't want to knock you about.'

'He'd better not try,' Mammy said, overhearing. 'Or I'll go round there meself and knock his ugly head off his ugly shoulders, so I will. And you'll come wit' me, won't you?' she added, nudging Peader, who was half-asleep already.

Peader sat up and gave her a mock salute. 'Certainly, certainly,' he said groggily. 'What was it you said, me little flower?'

Laughter, codding, full stomachs, damp feet in hot plimsolls, sand between the toes . . . what's best, Polly thought dreamily, sagging against Brogan. Oh, but the memories I'll keep in me head for the rest of me life, that's the best. I'll see it in me head whenever anyone says 'cockles' or 'Booterstown'. What could be better than that?

Tad lay on his back on the straw mattress which he shared with his two younger brothers and his sister Meg, who was eighteen months old. The other boys were already snoring, replete after the best meal they'd had for weeks – cockles, three whole loaves of fresh bread and sufficient butter for all to have a share.

Polly and that Brogan feller had brought the food round. Tad hadn't met Brogan before, or not that he could recall, but he had liked him. Not just because of the food, either, but because Brogan had been real nice to Mrs Donoghue, and had told Tad they were real sorry they'd not thought to invite him to go along, but that next time they wouldn't make the same mistake.

So Brogan was all *right*. And Polly was a fine lass, though there was times when he wondered about her. She said some strange things, so she did. She said she could remember being *born*, of all things – said she'd been pulled out of warm darkness, which must be the doctor's bag, into a room full of dancing firelight and friendly faces. And she said Brogan had pulled her out, and sat her on her mammy's knee, and her mammy had hugged her and cried.

Only it couldn't be so, because Tad didn't know anyone who remembered being born.

Then there was her name. All the other kids in her family had decent Irish names; Polly was an English name. And all the O'Brady chisellers were dark-haired, but Polly had lovely red-gold curls.

She's a changeling; the fairies brought her and swopped a little O'Brady child for her, and one of these days she'll simply disappear, Tad told himself. But he didn't believe it, because sure and didn't everyone know that changelings were spiteful creatures, who'd trick you soon as look at you? Polly wasn't like that at all at all, she was gentle and kind – though she could take your feet off at the ankles so she could when she played hurley with a bundle of rags and a piece of plank.

She was only a kid, though. And a girl – girls weren't supposed to want to play with boys at all, let alone play hurley. But Polly would do anything. She might have curls and big blue eyes, but she could take the football off a bigger and better player, tricksy as a cat on her small feet, and she could run like the wind, hang on to a moving tram by the post on the rear, climb a wall like that same cat, though God knew where she found the footholds ... she was all right, was Polly O'Brady.

Tad sighed and opened his eyes. They had a nice home, did the O'Bradys. And they talked nice to their mammy, and hardly anyone hit anyone else. All kids fight, everyone knows that, but apart from giving one another a smack from time to time, the O'Bradys never seemed to want to scrap. And Mrs O'Brady was pretty, like a young girl, and she never had black eyes, or too many babies, or a swollen cheek, such as his own mammy tried to hide from time to time.

But there were several earners in the O'Brady family, and he, at ten, was the eldest Donoghue. He did his best to make a living, carrying all the money straight home to his mammy, but it was hard because he was small for his age and there were days when the Donoghues didn't eat and then he wasn't much good at any work he happened to pick up.

But Polly liked him. He knew she did.

Above Tad's head there was a huge yellow-brown fungus growing out of the blackened wall; he quite liked that fungus. It came and went according to the season but right now it was in full fig, with a wavy edge and an odd, rather exciting sort of smell. He lay in the darkness gazing up at it and thinking about Polly, and about the cockles, and the seaside she had talked about with such enthusiasm.

There were scutterings in the dark corners. Black clocks, with their many legs going and their hard-shelled bodies clattering. It took a blow with a hammer to kill them, they were so big and strong. Or you could tread on them with a booted foot, only Tad didn't have boots – wouldn't have, until he started work. Unless a miracle happened, of course. Unless his daddy dropped dead and stopped stealing his mammy's small savings whenever he was out of work.

Tad had rather liked living in Swift's Alley, and in a way he liked living in Gardiners Lane, too. There weren't many houses in Gardiners Lane, but there were lots of ruins. The ruins had been houses and shops once, he knew, but they'd simply crumbled away and fallen down, and now they made good play places, if you were careful. And in summer, the wild flowers grew here, the tall pink spires of flowers which Polly said were called rosebay willowherb, the yellow piss-the-beds, the bright, golden-eyed daisies. A lot of kids played in Gardiners Lane but not a lot lived there. The tall, skinny house, leaning sideways, in which the Donoghues lived had been condemned years ago, but that only meant the landlord charged less rent. And filled the house to overflowing when he could.

Still. We've got two rooms here, Tad told himself drowsily, as sleep at last began to steal over him. We'd never have run to two rooms in Swift's Alley, but here there was no one to stop us taking over this room . . . and not many fellers in Dublin can say they've got big yellow funguses and trees growing in their bedrooms!

The tree had seeded in the fireplace and sprung up, growing amazingly strongly all things considered. It reached for the sky, ignoring the narrow little window which, in any case, had no glass in it, and Tad knew, because he'd gone out and stood well back and looked as hard as he could, that already a bunch of hopeful leaves had appeared out of the chimney top.

The only time Tad could remember the landlord coming round Mammy had been warned by little Liam. Liam had rushed into the room and grabbed her skirt.

There's a man, Mammy, lookin' in the downstairs

front,' he had gabbled. 'Mrs Donovan said to tell you he'll be up in five minutes.'

Mammy had said not a word. She had gathered the bigger children round her with a gesture and they had stormed into the second room. It was tiny, cold, damp, and it had not taken them more than two minutes to clear all signs of occupation. They had piled the mattresses up, higgledy piggledy, in the living room, then assembled rather self-consciously, round the fire. Mammy had started to cut the loaf, Biddy had hauled the baby on to her lap and begun to sing to him, and the other boys had bustled round getting dishes out and pretending to lay the table for a meal.

The landlord knocked, but came straight in after, never giving them a chance to go to the door.

'I've come to have a look at me property,' the man said gruffly. 'You've just the two rooms?'

'Just the one,' Mammy said. 'As you very well know.'

He stared very hard at her, then gestured around him at the children clustered near the small, sullenly burning fire.

'And where do all them children sleep? Answer me that!'

'Here,' Mammy said. 'Where else?'

He said nothing but stalked over to the door and flung it wide, then went across the narrow hallway and flung open the door opposite, too.

He looked around the damp little room with the tree growing up in the grate and the big, wavy fungus on the wall. He looked at the pigeon droppings on the floor – pigeons roosted on the roof and the broken tiles let their droppings in – and at the boards to the right of the door which had rotted clear away from the weather in the winter. Then he turned and stared at his audience of Donoghues.

'You could have this room as well for another bob a week,' he said in quite a different tone. 'Not big enough for another family, you see . . . if you don't take it, I can't let it.'

Mammy said nothing. She just stared at him, then let her eyes slide past him. To the damp, the rotted boards, the tree, the pigeon droppings, the glassless window.

'Should we say sixpence?' The landlord was almost whining now, almost appealing to their better natures! 'I'm not a rich man, I can't afford to have a room stand empty.'

'Mend the roof, and put glass in the window.' Tad was astonished at the sound of his own voice, he almost looked round to see who had spoken. 'It might be worth sixpence a week then.'

The landlord stared at him. A long, thin face, set with mean little eyes, a thin nose, a thin, tight mouth turned down at the corners. 'But you don't spend money on a house that's been condemned!'

'Sure and a decent body wouldn't ask rent for it, either,' Tad pointed out. His mammy smiled, but to herself, as though at her own thoughts. 'Two bob a week me mammy pays for our room, and the kids is always sick 'cos it's so damp. It even smells of damp.'

The landlord stared, then turned to Mammy.

'You'll have trouble with that chiseller one o' these days so you will,' he said angrily. 'Fellers like that get carried home on a door.'

'For speakin' the truth?' Mammy said, suddenly making up her mind to be equally bold. 'For tellin' you what you should have knowed – that the place isn't fit for anyone to live in as it stands?'

The landlord frowned, then turned away. He began to descend the stairs, calling back to them over his

146

shoulder. 'Very well, I take it that you don't want the second room. And I like the rent on time, don't forget that, either.'

'You'll get it,' Tad called after him. 'For the one room.'

So now Tad lay in the darkness in the miserable, smelly, damp little room with his brothers and sisters sleeping all around him and mused on his lot. Why did his mammy let his daddy hit her? Why did she let Daddy hit his kids? Why didn't she make him give her money, if only a little, towards the rent, the food? Why did Daddy get the lion's share at mealtimes? And above all, why, in God's name, did Mammy keep on having babies, year after year after year, when she couldn't feed them, when for three years now, the babies had died?

Polly's mammy didn't keep having babies. Sure, she'd had Ivan, but she hadn't had any since. Women who kept having babies weren't all that strong, and they had to pay money to the women who brought the babies, or to the doctor who brought them. Then they were very weak for a while after, and they had to feed the baby which sometimes meant they couldn't work.

I'll ask at school, Tad decided finally. And I'll ask the father why are people made so different and why do men hit their ould wans? Or perhaps not the father; I'll ask Mr Roberts, at school. He's a grand man so he is, he'll tell me if he knows.

Beside him, Dougal kicked out, then turned over, making their straw pallet rustle and squeak. Meg was lying on her back and snoring fit to bust, her arm flung out, her fingers curled as though in her dreams she grasped at something. Tad sat up on his elbow and very gently turned Meg over so that she was lying on her side. He couldn't bear the thought that a clock might crawl across her face and fall into the open cavern of her mouth. She might be choked to death and she was only little. Also, it stopped her snoring.

He glanced around the room. All the others appeared to be asleep and Liam was whimpering; full stomachs could give you nightmares when you weren't used to it, or keep you awake half the night. Because it was summer the air coming through the window was flower-scented, almost pleasant. It made Tad think of the Brickfields, and the canal bank, and the green countryside which he had never yet set eyes on. It sounded nice, did the countryside. Polly had told him that when times had been hard her mammy had gone out into the countryside and picked spuds to sell in the Moore Street market. And even now, if they needed something extra, she would go and pick gooseberries or black currants and sell them, too. Polly had gone picking gooseberries with her mammy earlier in the year; she said it was lovely, really lovely, away from the city.

Tad had thought himself well on the way to dreamland, but suddenly he sat up. A thought was coming clear in his head and it was a good one, he didn't want it to escape him, he wanted to remember it, to bring it out and look at it lovingly in the days to come.

Everyone starts somewhere, that was the thought. All men, his own daddy, Polly's daddy, had once been a boy, as he was. And not only them but Mr Roberts the schoolteacher and the landlord, the lamplighter who walked up and down the street with his long pole and made the gaslights flare, the fishmonger in his striped apron and straw hat, the tram conductor who took pennies from the grown-ups and shouted at the chisellers who stole free rides and jumped off his vehicle before he could demand payment.

The Lord Mayor of Dublin, even, with his gold chain and his fancy medals, he had been just a boy once. And the film stars at the picture palaces, and the soldiers who stamped up and down the streets in their smart uniforms . . . they had all been just boys, once.

So it stood to reason, Tad told himself, that a boy could be anything. He didn't have to be like his daddy, whether that daddy was a cruel, drunken docker, or – or the Lord Mayor of Dublin himself. He could put his mind to it, and he could be anything! Tad looked around him, at the dirty little room, the crowded mattresses, the moonlight streaming in through the window and falling, silver-striped with the black of shadows, across the beds. I'll be Somebody, he told himself, slowly lying down again. I'll work and scheme and try my hardest, and I'll be Somebody, so I will. I'll go down to that place Polly went and I'll pick cockles and sell 'em, or I'll dip a big net in the sea and find fishes and sell them, too. Or I'll pick potatoes and knock the dirt off and stand in Moore Street market and sell them. But whatever happens, I'm not going to end up beating some poor woman in a crowded, dirty little tenement room in Gardiners Lane.

And on that thought, Tad fell happily asleep.

They hated leaving, hated going back.

'But sure and I'd hate bein' home and out of work,' Peader said resignedly as he and Brogan stood at the rail and watched Ireland getting smaller and smaller behind them. 'And wasn't it a grand holiday, Brogan? Ah, we couldn't have had a better time if we'd been millionaires.'

'That's true so it is,' Brogan agreed. 'And it won't be too long, Daddy, before you're home for good. After all, Mammy's got a good deal of money put by and now Niall's got a good job and Martin's looking for one . . . well, you'll be able to go home to stay. Then you'll find a job, even if it doesn't pay like being the safety man for the gang does.'

'I've thought of applyin' for a job with the Irish railways,' Peader admitted. 'But we're doing well so we are. I'm half afraid to make changes, in case it turns out they're for the worse. But I do hate to leave, indeed I do.'

'True. But I don't know that I'd want to go on living in Swift's Alley,' Brogan said, surprising himself. Wasn't it home to him and hadn't he been brought up there when all was said and done? But back in Crewe he lodged with an elderly couple and they had a fine, clean little house and a wonderful garden. The front was a picture, all flowering trees, shrubs and flower borders with a circular lawn and an ornamental pond, but the back garden, which was very long and large, was laid down to vegetables and when they found out that Brogan was fascinated by the thought of growing things the Simpsons gave him a sizeable plot for himself.

'Grow what you like, lad,' Mr Simpson said. 'If you do the work I'll buy the seed and Mrs Simpson will cook what you produce for our meals. Anything that's over you can sell, because I'm too old to tackle a great garden like this alone. What d'you think?'

'I think it would be grand,' Brogan said honestly. 'Sure and there's nothin' I'd like better than to try me hand at growin' things.'

He had worked hard in the garden and it had taught him a lot. When he came home after a day of heaving coal in the heat of a small cab he simply wanted to rest, but very soon he found that digging, planting and weeding in the open air was a most relaxing and rewarding pastime.

'You've got green fingers,' Mrs Simpson said when she came down the garden and saw his rows of peas, broad beans, summer cabbage and carrots all coming on apace. 'Not everyone can grow things, you know.'

'They look more like black to me,' Brogan said ruefully, examining his hands, but Mrs Simpson just laughed and said it was a way of saying he'd the magic touch, that he could grow things where others failed.

'When winter comes, get Mr Simpson to show you how to enrich the land with manure from the farms,' she advised. 'We all need food to make us grow and the good earth is no exception.'

They were not Catholics, yet they seemed to be good people. They attended church every Sunday and gave to various good causes and had decided to take in a lodger not simply for the extra money to augment the pension, but because both Mr and Mrs Simpson liked young people about the place.

'We were never blessed with children,' Mr Simpson told him one evening as they worked in the garden, for they shared the work now since Brogan wanted to try his hand with flowers as well as vegetables. 'And since neither the wife nor myself have brothers or sisters we have only remote relatives left now, no close family. But we've a great many friends, a nice home . . . and now you, Brogan, to bring a bit of life into the place!'

'What's wrong with Swift's Alley?' Peader said now, dragging Brogan back to the present, to the ship's rail, the heaving sea beneath the ship, the sight of their homeland vanishing into the mist. 'You never found fault wit' it before, lad.'

'Oh, Daddy, it's not finding fault that I am, it's just

that I'd like to see Mammy and the kids in the country, with a bit of space round them. You've not seen the Simpsons' place, not far from Crewe, but it's made me realise that there are other ways of life which are ... kind of slower, softer, I suppose.'

'I thought the same meself, in fact,' Peader said slowly. 'I asked your mammy if she'd like to live somewhere else, somewhere wit' a garden, perhaps, and she said she would indeed, but not yet. Not until we're safe, whatever that may mean.'

Brogan nodded slowly. He knew what his mother meant and so did his father, but the truth was they scarcely knew what it was to be safe, with landlords always liable to put up the rent, the council to increase the fees you paid at school, or an employer deciding to give you the boot. Safety, if it meant security, he concluded, was not for the likes of them.

But that didn't mean that they could never be safe. I'm still working at me books, he reminded himself fiercely, and soon now I'll be driving an engine, or perhaps I'll learn about motor-car engines so I can put them right when they go wrong, for it's a practical turn of mind I have, or so my teachers at the Gordon Institute told me. And once I've got a good enough job, then I can make Mammy safe, see that she's secure, so that she isn't worried where the money's coming from.

Peader, standing beside him, sighed. 'Women! But one of these days we'll whisk her away to live somewhere decent, eh, Brog? Ah, Ireland's gone into the mist now; let's go below and have a glass of porter!'

Sara didn't wake on Sunday morning until the maid swished her curtains back and let the mild September sunshine flood into the room. Then she sat up in bed, stretched, yawned, and blinked across at the maid.

'Morning, Bessy! It looks a nice day.'

'Morning, Miss Sara. Did you enjoy yourself, last night?'

'It was very nice, thanks,' Sara said politely. 'I danced every dance and had supper with Captain Franklyn. He'd be a lot nicer if he didn't keep feeling his moustache in that horrid, sly sort of way, as if it was a false one and he was afraid it had fallen off.'

Bessy snorted, then tried to turn it into a cough. She came over to the bed and took the cosy off a small teapot. 'Tea, Miss Sara?'

'Oh, please, Bessy. I want to go round to Mrs Prescott's this morning. After all, I've been back in Liverpool three whole weeks, it's about time I went to Kirkdale, whatever anyone thinks. And it's the harvest supper at church this evening; I wonder what I should wear? I do have rather a lot of new clothes . . . Mother and I seem to spend all our time shopping.' She did not add, *It's the only thing we have in common*, because that would have been unkind, but she knew it was true, nevertheless. In the three weeks since she returned her mother had taken her out every morning, sometimes to meet friends, sometimes to go round the picture gallery or the museum, but mostly to visit the shops, particularly the big stores.

Sara sat up on her elbow and sipped her tea. 'Now the harvest supper – that takes some thinking about because not only will the Reverend Atwell be there, Mr Alan Hepworth will attend, too. So that means best bib and tucker, eh, Bessy?'

'You shouldn't joke about Mr Hepworth, Miss Sara He's always calling round, asking after you,' Bessy said, her hand on the door knob. 'Besides, Mrs Cordwainer approves, so I suppose that means he's gorra bob or two,' she finished, dropping her 'smart' accent and grinning at her employer.

Sara grinned back. 'You're right there, except that he's gorra bob or *three*,' she said. 'Actually, he really is rather nice and all the girls are after him, so reeling him in would be quite a catch.'

'Then do it,' Bessy advised. 'Has he asked you yet, Miss?'

'Twice. But he expects to have to dance to my tune for a bit longer, he's made that clear,' Sara said cheerfully. 'Oh, I shouldn't tease him, but I'm not at all sure I want to marry anyone, yet.'

'Don't blame you,' Bessy said. 'I ain't goin' to marry anyone till I'm good and ready, and when I do I'm goin' to make the feller sign a contract to say he'll hand over his pay packet without openin' it first, that he'll give me everything I want that he can afford, and that I can go dancin' twice a week without him.'

'Bessy, you are truly disgraceful, you shame womanhood,' Sara said, giggling. 'I'll remember that the next time Mr Hepworth proposes; I'll say would he like to glance at the contract I've got in mind and see whether he approves and would like to sign on the dotted line.'

Both girls laughed, then Bessy sobered, and opened the door.

'If you want anything, Miss, just ring the bell,' she said, and let herself out on to the landing.

Sara finished her cup of tea, then she swung her legs out and stood up. My life is hollow and full of vanity, she told herself. When I was a child I wanted desperately to help girls like Jess Carbery, but there was so little I could do. But now I ought to be able to do my bit. Yet when I talked about getting a job Mother and Father said I should wait until I'd settled down in Liverpool again and when I wanted to offer my services to one of the charitable institutes I was told I would be doing someone else out of a job. And at the back of my mind there's this skinny young girl who didn't have enough to eat, who spent all her time and energy trying to keep her little sisters alive – and whose life was brought to a terrible close because no one cared enough. I'm sure if she could do so Jess would say to me now, 'Find Mollie! Look after Grace! And all I do is what everyone else does – I go to parties, attend church services, and tell myself that one day I'll find out what had happened to the Carbery family and perhaps do my bit towards helping them. But life's never that simple – I'm still a child so far as my parents, and authority, are concerned.

But before she considered her future, she would go and see Mrs Prescott. She had announced her intention of going over to Snowdrop Street as soon as she reached home, but somehow it had never been convenient for her to go visiting, and because she wanted her homecoming to be as trouble-free as possible, she had postponed undertaking the journey. She could not believe that her mother and father would continue to disapprove of her visiting her old nurse but in any event, she did not intend to put it to the test. She would go first and talk about it later, she decided.

Accordingly she got up, dressed in a bronze blouse, grey suit and black court shoes, then went down to the breakfast parlour.

Mrs Cordwainer was sitting at the table, nibbling toast. She looked up and smiled as her daughter entered the room.

'Ah, Sara dear – good morning! I thought we'd go out to Crosby later to visit my friend Fanny.'

Sara smiled and took her seat at the table. She reached across for the toast, then changed her mind; it would be cold by now, she was late. Instead, she poured herself a cup of coffee from the tall silver pot.

'Good morning, Mother, isn't it a lovely day? But I'm afraid I can't come out to Crosby with you, I've a previous engagement.'

'Oh? With whom, dear?'

'I'm going to see an old friend, someone I've known for years,' Sara said truthfully. 'But I've not seen her since I left the city, though we did write from time to time.'

'Ah, a school friend. And will you be back for luncheon? You won't forget the harvest supper tonight, dear? It helps to raise funds for the poor of the Indian subcontinent, I believe. I've bought half a dozen tickets, several of our friends and relatives will be coming.'

'How nice,' Sara said vaguely. 'I'll be back in good time, Mother.'

'Good. You're calling a cab, I presume?'

It was a discreet way of finding out just where she was going, Sara guessed. She smiled, looking down at her plate. 'No, indeed. It's not far at all, only a few steps in fact.'

Her mother relaxed. She really doesn't want me to see Nanny, Sara realised. It's absolutely ridiculous, but I'm going to have to be very careful. If Mother was jealous of my affection for Nanny I could understand it, but she doesn't love me herself, I've always known that. She *likes* me now I'm a grown-up, a young woman, and she is beginning to enjoy my company, but loving . . . well, that's a very different kettle of fish.

'Oh, then if you really can't come with me, my dear, I'll get a cab to Crosby as soon as I'm properly dressed. Your father has the car. I wonder if Mrs Spry would care to accompany me? She's thinking of buying a little property outside the city. I believe I'll send Fletcher round to ask if she'd like to come with me.'

How extraordinary! She doesn't like to be alone, that's why she's been clinging to me, Sara thought, astonished. Well, I never would have thought it – and when I was a child she was always so eager to get rid of me!

Presently she went up to her room and got her handbag, settled her new hat at a becoming angle on her dark curls, and set off. She found herself more excited than she had been since her homecoming, for once in the streets, by herself and on foot, a good deal of her past came flooding back. Going off to school in the city with her satchel on her back and her hockey stick in one hand and one of the maids, impatient to return to her work, hurrying her along. The tram ride with other girls also wearing the navy and scarlet school uniform, everyone chattering, exchanging gossip, writing in each other's autograph books. A craze for fortune-telling, another craze for cigarette cards, a time, earlier, when she never trod on a crack in the paving stones for fear that it would open up and swallow her. Then there had been the piano lessons, to which Jane had accompanied her whilst Robson drove them to the teacher's home and came back for them an hour later. That had meant going through the city at night, with the lamps lit, the gas flaring softly, white, primrose, deep yellow. And the great buildings towering above the small girl and her companion – St George's Hall, the Picton Library, the Walker Art Gallery – as much a part of her past as were the stairs which led up to the nursery, the long, echoing corridors of her school and the smell of cabbage and boiled socks which heralded a school dinner.

But nostalgia attacked her hardest on the tram, when

she climbed aboard it on Croxteth Road and it began to rattle along towards the city centre. They passed her old school and she saw that it wasn't a huge or imposing place but quite small compared with the Swiss school, and they passed a friend's house and she craned her neck, hoping to see Eliza, but all she saw was a black cat, sunning itself in the front garden.

She had to change trams on Old Haymarket and stood for a moment, tapping her foot impatiently on the big, fudge-coloured paving stones. But then her tram came along with 'Stanley Road' written on its board and she hopped aboard and went and sat on one of the hard slatted wooden seats. Well she remembered *them*; her bottom had been striped by them many a time!

And presently, the excitement began to build as the tram rattled along, sounding its bell warningly as the crowds on the streets, trying to dodge amongst the traffic, grew thicker and less willing to give way. The tram roared along the Vauxhall Road and Sara saw familiar, much-loved sights and the smells which went with them; the great bulk of Tate & Lyle's sugar refinery, scenting the air with sweetness, further along the smells from the distillery, further yet the scent of freshly cut wood from the saw mills . . . and a glimpse, always longed-for when she was on the tram with her nanny, of the Leeds & Liverpool canal, the water gleaming dully, like unpolished pewter, under a cloudy sky.

And then they were on Stanley Road and she was so excited that she could not stop smiling. When she was first in Switzerland she had thought about Brogan a lot, remembering him with great affection, but gradually, as the years passed, she began to see that they had scarcely known one another, really. But she had liked him so much, even being on Stanley Road again made her see a picture of him in her head. His dark hair and eyes, the height of him, the easy strength . . . her tummy gave a most peculiar lurch when she remembered him hugging her in the cinema once, when she'd been scared by the film. She must find him again, tell him she was back, renew their friendship.

Through the window she saw the long procession of milliners and hairdressing establishments, picture palaces and pawn-shops, passing in front of her eyes. And then she saw her stop approaching and she jumped to her feet and the conductor tinged his bell, the tram driver applied his brakes . . . and she was getting down . . . she was there!

Chapter Seven

In three years, very little had changed. There were still a great many people thronging the pavement, many carrying small attaché bags or worn suitcases. They were women, Sara knew, going to the pawn to collect their decent stuff for Sunday. Soon they would be reclaiming blankets as the weather grew colder but for now it was mainly Sunday suits, the respectable shoes, the ornaments for the mantel if you were having a bit of a hooley round your place, Saturday night.

Several people glanced at her, then looked away again. The differences between a child not yet fifteen and a young woman of eighteen are considerable, Sara realised, and besides, though she had been respectably dressed as a child, she had not been smart or fashionable. Now she was both, and suddenly she began to feel a little uncomfortable, even a little ashamed.

Who was she to walk down this busy, happy road in a suit and hat which had cost more than a good many of these people earned in a year? She had done nothing for it, after all. She despised her parents for being greedy and uncaring, but what had she actually done for those less fortunate? Once, long ago, she had given a child a pair of gloves and a shilling and because of it, the child had died. Oh, she knew it hadn't been her fault, she could not possibly have known that a spontaneous, generous act would have such terrible consequences. But what had she done since?

Sara sighed and turned the corner into Snowdrop

Street. It was no use feeling sorry for herself, because that was just what she was doing, really. A child has very little real power; she had done what she could without arousing adult wrath and if it hadn't been enough she was sorry, but the past is the past. Now, however, she was eighteen years old and had real earning power, if only she could find someone to employ her. And then she would use her money properly and wisely, and she would make those enquiries about the Carbery girls which she had always intended to make once she grew up. Or she hoped she would. Human nature being what it is, she reflected gloomily, she would probably marry some suitable young man, leave her job, and start a family. That was what most girls did and Sara knew it was what her parents expected her to do. Whether she would or not remained to be seen, for though she thought Mr Hepworth very pleasant, she was not at all sure that she actually wanted to marry him.

She reached number three and took the brass dolphin in her hand. She no longer had to stand on the step to reach it. She lifted the knocker, let it fall, then stood back and waited.

She heard the footsteps at once and smiled to herself. Good old Nanny, the years hadn't changed her light step! In fact she sounded younger than ever, as though not seeing Sara for three whole years had brought about a magical shedding of the burden of age. But before Sara had done more than think this the door opened and a woman appeared in the doorway. She was probably in her middle thirties, Sara thought, with a plain but kindly face, dark hair pulled back into a bun and very bright dark eyes.

'Good mornin', queen,' she said cheerfully. 'And what can I do for you this fine mornin'?'

'Oh!' Sara stammered, totally taken aback. 'I've come to see my nanny . . . Mrs Prescott, I mean. Don't say she's ill!'

'Oh no, she's not really ill, but she's not been too good . . .' The woman peered at her, then light seemed to dawn for she smiled suddenly. 'You wouldn't be young Sara, would you? Sara Cordwainer?'

'That's right,' Sara said. 'What's been the matter with Nanny? I've been away from home for three years, you see, so I've not seen her all that time, but we've been exchanging letters and she never said anything about her health failing. Only she's not one to grumble about herself, so I suppose she wouldn't have said? Er . . . are you a neighbour? A friend?' Another thought struck her. 'Mrs Prescott is here, isn't she? She's not in hospital or anything?'

'No, she's here,' the woman said. 'I'm sorry, chuck, wharrever am I thinkin' of?' she stood aside, gesturing Sara to enter the narrow hallway. 'I'm Mrs Prescott's lodger, my name's Boote – Clarrie Boote.' She held out a square, capable hand. 'How d'you do, Miss Cordwainer! Your gran's much better now, out of hospital, on her feet, but she's having a sit down and a cuppa, wi' a biscuit or two to dunk in it.'

'How do you do, Miss Boote,' Sara said, feeling quite weak with relief. Thank goodness Nanny was all right now – but what had ailed her?

She put the question to Miss Boote, who sighed.

'Well, I could say anno domini, Miss Cordwainer, but I suppose it's a combination of things, really. She got a nasty old infection which swelled all her joints and gave her a high fever so they whipped her into the Stanley. They did a good job, cured the fever, but ever since she's found it hard to move about much. It's chronic rheumatism, if you ask me, brought about by the 'flu, or whatever it was.'

'How awful,' Sara breathed. She could not imagine her nanny ill. But Miss Boote said she was better, which was something to hold on to. If Nanny wasn't here I don't know what I'd do, she thought. She's like a rock, always steady, always understanding – always there.

'Yes, Mrs Prescott has a good deal to contend with,' Miss Boote agreed. 'But I give a hand when I can.'

'I'm glad you're here,' Sara said, though she wondered why Nanny had suddenly decided to let one of her rooms. 'She isn't getting any younger and the company will do her good.'

'And me rent helps,' Miss Boote said frankly. 'I gather there was a rift in the family and she don't get much help from *that* quarter.'

'I don't think she's got any family, or not anyone really close,' Sara said cautiously. 'But Nanny's always been very independent.'

Miss Boote, who had been about to open the parlour door, turned and stared at her.

'No family?' she said slowly. 'Then what do you call yourself?'

'Mrs Prescott was my old nanny,' Sara explained. 'She is no relation. I call her nanny because ... well, because she was my nanny until I started school.'

Miss Boote snorted. 'Your nanny? She's your grand-mother, child – didn't you know? Oh aye, her daughter Letty married your dad and she's had no time for her mam since the day she was wed. She let your gran move into the house and take care of you when you was small ... d'you mean to say she never let on that you was all related?'

Sara leaned against the wall, with its pattern of brown roses on a cream ground. 'Related?' she said

163

faintly. 'My grandmother? But she can't be – Mother's mother lives in Devonshire, she's an eccentric and doesn't care for children. And I know Father's mother quite well, though to be honest, we don't like each other much.'

'Devonshire! When your gran told me she'd let her daughter tell you fairytales rather than lose you altogether I couldn't believe me ears,' Miss Boote said scornfully. 'Didn't anyone ever let on? They must ha' known, surely?'

'If they did they never said,' Sara assured her. 'I must see Nanny – I must ask her why she didn't tell me herself.'

'Well, go slowly, like,' Miss Boote advised. She put her hand across the door, preventing Sara from simply rushing in. 'Remember she's been poorly, so just take it slow, don't get her all excited and aerated.'

'I won't,' Sara said at once. 'But I have to ask! It isn't that I disbelieve you, in fact I'm certain you're speaking the truth, but – well, you know how it is.'

'Aye, I do. You must be fair astonished,' Miss Boote agreed. 'Just remember to go gently, though, queen. I don't suppose it's been easy for your gran all these years. There must have been times when she longed to tell you, and I aren't sure what stopped her, either . . . some threat, I daresay, knowin' your mam as I do. Or did, rather,' she added conscientiously. 'Because we've not set eyes on each other since her marriage. We don't move in the same circles, like,' she finished.

'Wait a moment, Miss Boote,' Sara said urgently, as Miss Boote went to open the door. Another question had come to the forefront of her mind. 'You say you knew my mother – did you know her from when she lived with her mother?'

'Aye, though she were a good bit older than me. My

mam and your gran was neighbours, chuck. We lived quite near here in them days, just round the corner in Commercial Road. Me dad were landlord of the Great Mersey public house for a while, then the drink made him bad so he took a job as a warehouseman and we moved into a little house in Commercial Road. We stayed on until Dad retired . . . in fact we didn't move out till they found a house in Formby, ten year back. So you see, I knew Letty quite well, she used to take me to school if me mam was busy. She were a right tartar,' she added reminiscently. 'Very sure of herself, and very pretty. You have a look of her, only you've a sweeter expression.'

Sara was about to ask the next question when a voice came faintly through the heavy wooden door.

'Clarrie? Who is it? It sounds . . . it sounds . . .'

Sara waited no longer. She flung open the door and ran across the room to where Mrs Prescott sat in a chair by the fire. She looked a little greyer, and possibly a trifle more frail, but otherwise she was just Sara's dear nanny, the person she loved most in the world.

'Oh, Nanny, it's me, I'm home! Switzerland was wonderful, but it wasn't home and I'm just so glad to be back at last. But how are you? Miss Boote said you'd been poorly, but were better now.' She kissed the older woman lovingly, then stood back. 'You look very well,' she said bracingly. 'But you've not much colour in your cheeks – what a pity it's autumn . . . but the weather's fine enough for some outings to bring back your rosy glow, Nanny! I'll tell Mother I want the car in a day or so, when we have another sunny morning, and we'll go out on the spree. Oh Nanny, it's so *very* good to see you again after all this time!'

Mrs Prescott was smiling, her cheeks pink, her eyes very bright. 'Oh Sara, my dear girl, I was beginnin' to wonder whether they'd ever let you come back!' She heaved a huge sigh. 'There's somethin' I've got to tell you, and I aren't lookin' forward to it one bit for I can't help feelin' I'm breakin' my word. But . . .'

'You don't have to tell me a thing, *Gran*,' Sara said, emphasising the word. 'Because I know, and I couldn't be more delighted than if I'd been told my gran was Queen of England. It's the best news in the world, it's made me so happy I want to sing, and if you don't want to go into details I'll quite understand.'

'Clarrie, you're a very dear girl,' Mrs Prescott called, but all she got from Miss Boote, halfway up the stairs, was a chuckle, so she turned back to Sara. 'Well, I can't pretend I'm sorry that all the lies and evasions are over, Sara my dear, but when you were born Letty made me swear on the Bible that I'd never breathe a word of our relationship and I were so besotted with you, queen – you were the loveliest baby – that I'd ha' done anything, promised anything, just to be allowed to help bring you up. For it were clear from the first that your mam wasn't goin' to take an interest, and intended to turn you over to servants,' she finished.

'Why wouldn't my mother admit you were her mother, though?' Sara said thoughtfully. I don't mean to upset you, Gran, but it seems very odd. Father must have known, for instance.'

But Mrs Prescott was shaking her head.

'No, he didn't know the whole truth, because Letty told him a fairytale, too. She said she was adopted, that I'd always wanted a child of me own so I'd adopted her from a respectable couple when the father died.' Mrs Prescott sighed. 'Eh, havin' Letty was me one mistake, and didn't I pay dear for it! You see, queen, I never had a husband. The truth is my mam put me in service with a rich family out at Bootle, but

I was a flighty piece and I got into trouble. The baby's da was me employer, and he was married, of course, so when they realised what had happened I was sacked, in disgrace. I had a hard time of it because me own parents cast me off – they were strict chapel – so I had to earn enough money to rear me child and keep meself, but somehow, I did it. Yet Letty despised me from the moment she discovered that her father had been a married man, and rich. She despised me first because I were weak enough to get in the family way and then because I'd not made use of her father. As soon as she could she left home, and invented a past for herself that satisfied her. When I said it were lies she got very angry, and said if I wanted to see her ever again I'd go along with it.

'Well, for a long time I let her go her own way. She married, but she didn't invite me to the wedding, and I understood when she told me the story she'd told Adolphus. A rich, reclusive mother living in Devonshire was all right for outsiders, but Adolphus had to know a bit more than that, so she became an adopted child.

'But that, of course, gave me certain rights and to do your father justice, queen, he insisted that I be treated as part of the family, even though his wife refused to acknowledge me even as an adoptive parent. So he invited me to stay when Letty's time was near, and when you were born the nurse brought you through . . . and I knew I'd do just about anything, queen, to be near you.' She patted her granddaughter's hand. 'The rest you know, just about.'

'Yes, thanks to Miss Boote,' Sara said. 'I'll go and put the kettle on, Gran. Well, what a story! And you kept it to yourself all those years!'

'Aye, because Letty said so long as I kept me mouth

shut and never told you I were your grandmother she'd see I saw you regular. Which she did, until she shipped you off to Switzerland.' She paused, to turn in her chair as Sara walked behind her, heading for the kitchen. 'She said she'd not broken her side of the bargain because no one could see you whilst you were abroad, but I didn't see it like that. Other kids come home, holiday time, I told her. Why not our Sara? But she wouldn't give in, said it was fair enough, so I talked it over with meself and decided when you came home, I'd tell you everything. And now I'm going to close my eyes for ten minutes whilst you mash the tea; I'm wore out . . . isn't that odd?'

Sara said that it wasn't odd at all, then went into the kitchen and began to prepare a tray. No wonder I never liked my mother; she's a liar and a cheat, she thought. She cheated Father by making him believe she was adopted, not illegitimate, and she lied to me and forced Nanny – I mean my grandmother – to lie to me, too.

Presently she carried the tray, laden with teapot, cups, milk and sugar as well as a prettily painted plate piled with crumpets, through into the living room and put it down on the low table in front of the fire. Her grandmother, who had been lying back in the chair with her eyes closed, looking very weary, opened her eyes and smiled.

'Sara, that does look nice! Now I've told you the truth, and I want you to promise me something. Don't hold it against your mam, queen! She lied herself into a position where she simply had to tell more lies, you see. If your father had been a gentler, more understanding feller, she could have owned up, told him – and you – the truth, but he's a cold fish, is Adolphus. I used to comfort meself with the thought that they were well suited, and I reckon you're a throw-back, queen, because you aren't at all like either of them. But having it out with Letty wouldn't do anyone any good, so . . . will you promise me?'

And oddly enough, it was easy to make the promise, knowing very well that Gran was right. What is done cannot be undone and nothing would change even if she did confront her mother with her past misdeeds. Forcing Mrs Cordwainer to face up to what she had done would help no one, least of all Gran.

'Old history, old history,' Gran said, when Sara tried to put her thoughts into words. 'You're right, queen. It's best buried and forgot.'

Sara speared a crumpet and sat forward in her chair, holding the fork out to the fire and toasting both her face and fingers as well as the crumpets. And looking round the firelit room, and hearing the clock in the corner strike four, Sara thought she had seldom been happier.

'Are you ready, Sara?' Mrs Cordwainer was standing in the circular hallway of the big house on Aigburth Road, pulling on her pale leather gloves. She was wearing a cream and gold dress with a mink jacket over it and her hair had been curled and piled up on top of her head. Mrs Cordwainer noticed Sara and posed for a moment in front of the big cheval glass to the right of the front door, then turned to her daughter. 'I don't like to be late, even for a harvest supper, which is scarcely the same thing as a service. But the Reverend Atwell will want to say a few words, and your father has been told he may be asked to say grace, so it wouldn't do to be late.'

'I'm ready,' Sara said coolly. 'You look very smart, Mother.'

'Thank you, Sara. You do me credit – that silk coat

is very pretty and goes well with your dress. Green suits you, and the shoes are delightful . . . yes, really elegant. I always wore very high heels when I was younger but now I find them difficult to walk in. Ah well, there are compensations in growing a little older . . . we mature ladies can wear fur with aplomb; fur tends to make young girls look older than their years, I always think. Your father's gone to bring the car round; he isn't finding it easy to cope with so we'd best go outside and wait for him there.'

'Where's Robson? Or is it his day off?' Sara asked idly as the two of them left the house and stood outside on the gravel sweep waiting for the car to come round. 'I haven't seen him since I've been back. I know Father does drive himself quite often now, but not to social events, does he?'

'Oh, Robson left last week,' Mrs Cordwainer said coolly. 'I'm not sure of the details, but the government took us off the Gold Standard, whatever that may mean, and the pound slumped, or your father's shares fell – something of that nature, anyway. So your father decided he would have to make some economies.'

'But Robson's been with us since I was a kid; what'll he do? Where will he go?' Sara asked. 'What about his flat? Surely Father won't need it? Can't Robson stay there?'

'No, indeed. We could let that flat for a nice little sum, if the need ever arose. As for where he is now, I'm sure I can't say.'

'But what will Robson *do*?' Sara repeated helplessly. 'Without a roof over his head, even? What will happen to his wife?'

'She'll go wherever he goes, of course,' Mrs Cordwainer said impatiently. 'No doubt he'll get another job somewhere and move into whatever accommodation the new job offers. It's not as if they had children.'

'They did have a child,' Sara said in a low voice. 'They had a little boy, but he died when he was three. Don't say you didn't know, Mother, you must have!'

'I most certainly did not; I know nothing about any of the staff, other than that which it was my duty to know,' her mother replied immediately. 'Robson's private life was none of my business – nor yours, I might add. Ah, here comes Adolphus.'

There was a note of relief in her voice. Her mother did not like being cross-questioned about the sudden disappearance of Robson; she obviously considered it a matter of such little importance that discussing it seemed absurd.

She is the most selfish woman alive, Sara told herself as she and her mother waited on the drive for the Rolls. I'll have to go down to the kitchen tomorrow, see if I can find out what's happened to the poor chap.

Despite her father's many driving lessons with Robson, it seemed that he was not a natural behind the wheel. The car, when it finally came round the corner, was spitting and coughing, with a red-faced Adolphus behind the wheel. He stopped to let them get aboard but would not switch off the engine or linger a moment longer than necessary.

'The bloody thing is as temperamental as a woman,' Sara heard him say furiously as he wrestled with the gear lever. 'I'm not at all sure getting rid of Robson was a good thing; I'm of the opinion that two of the maids, or the cook, could have been dispensed with more easily.'

'Nonsense, Adolphus,' her mother said immediately. 'You're an intelligent man, it's only an *engine*, for goodness' sake, you'll soon learn to master it. And do go a little faster or we'll be last, and I hate arriving anywhere last.'

But when they reached the big marquee set out in the square in front of the church it was already full and the Reverend Atwell was impatiently consulting his watch. When he saw the Cordwainers his brow cleared, and he waved to them and hurried over.

'Ah, my dear Mr Cordwainer ... Mrs Cordwainer, Miss ... I was almost giving you up,' he said with somewhat strained joviality. 'You have been deputed to say grace, Mr Cordwainer, I was beginning to become a little anxious.'

'Well, we're here now,' Mr Cordwainer said shortly. Sara saw that he had oil on his hands and a smear of it across his forehead. 'It's that cursed motor car – I don't seem to be able to handle it like Robson could.'

Mr Atwell clicked his tongue, whether in sympathy or in reproof for the swear word Sara could not say, then he took her mother by the elbow and began to lead them into the marquee.

'This way, Mrs Cordwainer ... I've written out a grace for you to say, Mr Cordwainer, I hope you can read my writing ... if you could walk this way ...'

He was ushering the family into the marquee when there was a concerted gasp from behind them. Sara glanced back. A trio of small and dirty boys were hovering just outside, peering within, and for a moment Sara saw the scene through their eyes and was impressed.

The long tables were covered with stiff white damask cloths and were laden with food and fruit of every conceivable sort. The cutlery shone silver by the light of hissing oil lamps, and waiters in black and white hovered solicitously behind the guests. There were flowers, too – pink, crimson and yellow roses, long-

stemmed carnations, and the blue and silver-grey cultivated thistles so beloved of flower-arrangers. The
scene, glowing with colour, must seem like another
world to the urchins who were gazing, wide-eyed and
open-mouthed, at the scene.

The Reverend Atwell glanced back too, gave an
exclamation of annoyance, then smiled sweetly at the
Cordwainers and pointed to three chairs just inside
the entrance, at the very end of the long table.

'There you are, I hope you won't find the seating
draughty but of course those who arrived early took
the better places ... do sit yourselves down ... the
grace is written out on that sheet of cream vellum, if
you'd be so good as to run through it in your head,
Mr Cordwainer, whilst I deal ... excuse me a moment.'

He had spoken in his usual hushed, rather syrupy
tones, but as he turned away from them and hurried
back to the marquee entrance his voice changed completely, becoming sharp and shrewish, with overtones
of bullying.

'You! You boys! What d'you think you're doing, eh?'

'We're jest lookin', your rev'rince,' a boy replied in a
clear, piping treble. 'It's so grand, your rev'rince, so we
was jest tekin' a look.'

'Well, you can clear off,' the Reverend Atwell said
menacingly. 'Go on, clear off, we don't want your sort
here!'

'Very true,' muttered Mr Cordwainer, on Sara's right.
'Abominable urchins; they'll probably chatter whilst
I'm trying to read this confounded piece of paper and
that would finish me – finish me!'

'They're only kids,' Sara began, and then heard the
boy's treble raised once more.

'Oh, but your rev'rince, there's a deal o' grub there –

you can't eat all that grub, surely? There might be some of them bread rolls over, per'aps . . . or an apple?'

'This food isn't for the likes of you, it's for the ladies and gentlemen who come to my church,' the Reverend Atwell said furiously. 'Go on, get out! You'll get nothing but a thick ear if you remain anywhere near this marquee.'

Sara turned in her seat. She could feel her face growing hot but she had to speak, she could not let such remarks go unchallenged. She cleared her throat and spoke. 'Mr Atwell, the children are doing no harm – surely if you were to give them some fruit . . .'

Her voice was lost in the huge marquee, but her father heard. 'That's enough, Sara,' he said crossly. 'Just let me concentrate on this abominable writing, for God's sake, or I'll muff it, I know I will.'

'But, Father, to deny those little boys even a piece of fruit . . .'

A gentleman sitting opposite her, wearing a dark suit and pince-nez, nodded approvingly, but before either of them could speak the Reverend Atwell was again in full flood.

'Did you hear what I said? You're upsetting my parishioners with your begging,' he hissed. 'Out, out, OUT!'

Afterwards, Sara supposed that it had happened so quickly that only one or two people were aware of it. A subdued voice said, 'Shame!' – it came from the gentleman opposite – but elsewhere, the subdued hum of private conversation continued. Beside her, Mr Cordwainer muttered over the grace and her mother murmured gossip to the lady on her further side. Reverend Atwell beckoned to a waiter and several of them approached the marquee entrance whereupon the boys fled precipitately into the darkness.

Sara sat very still, shame and self-disgust flooding over her. Why had she not stood up to Reverend Atwell properly, refused to be hushed? Because she was a coward, that was why – because she didn't want to make a fool of herself in public.

The vicar returned to the table and took his place. The waiters began to hand bread rolls, to pour wine, to bring out from some hidden kitchen heated plates. Sara took a deep breath. She could at least do something to show how she felt!

The waiter leaned over her shoulder with a round basket full of small bread rolls, a saucer of butter in the middle. 'A bread roll, Miss? And some butter?'

'Thank you,' Sara said. She took the basket firmly out of his surprised hand, then stood up, pushing back her chair as she did so. 'I shan't be a moment.'

She carried the bread rolls and the butter out of the marquee and into the darkness of the city square. The boys had not gone far; she could see them sitting in a row along someone's low house-wall, every face turned towards her, like hungry sparrows watching for a householder to throw them crumbs.

'Boys, there's some bread and butter here,' Sara called, her voice much stronger out here than it had been in the marquee. 'Would you like some?'

Would they! There was a stampede! The bread was taken, divided, rubbed in the little curls of butter, devoured before her eyes. And they'd not begged, and they did thank, Sara thought triumphantly, as the basket was returned, empty, in an incredibly short space of time, to a chorus of 'Fanks, Miss, that were great . . . you are good.'

'Glad you enjoyed it,' Sara said. 'Don't go away.'

She returned to the marquee, and her place at the long table.

'I was never so ashamed in my life! Taking great plate-fuls of food out to those . . . those slum kids, simply marching out with it as though you had a right to it! The Reverend Atwell didn't know where to look . . . his wife was hissing to her neighbours . . . I'll never be able to hold my head up again.'

Sara's mother's voice was shaking with rage and embarrassment and what was worse, the car wouldn't start so here they sat for all to see whilst Mr Cord-wainer, hot, grease-smeared, cross, tried again and again to turn the engine over with the starting handle – and failed.

'I simply gave some boys some food,' Sara said patiently, for the umpteenth time. 'They weren't beg-ging, they asked very politely if there might be some over, and Reverend Atwell was abominably rude to them. So I took them a few bits and pieces.'

'A few bits and pieces! You were offered potatoes and you took the entire tureen – the same with the green peas and the baby carrots! The waiters were sniggering, everyone was staring . . . and then you took them out a whole strawberry flan – do you know what Scottish strawberries cost, Sara?'

'No, and I don't suppose you do, either,' Sara said. 'Do stop nagging, Mother. We have so much, who are we to deny others a share?'

'You're nothing but a prig, a nasty little prig,' her mother said suddenly. 'If this is your nanny's influence . . .'

'Nanny Prescott has scarcely seen me for the past three years, so I don't really see how she can be blamed,' Sara said quietly. 'But you are right over one thing; Nanny always tried to teach me to be generous to those less fortunate than myself.' She paused, but reflected that so far as she could see, her mother couldn't be angrier, so she might as well get it out of her system all at once. 'You talk a lot about heathen in Africa and being generous to others, Mother, but neither you nor my father have ever raised a finger to help those who need help most. You give money sometimes, you sew cotton vests and gossip with your friends, but you don't attempt to do anything to alleviate the terrible poverty on our own doorstep. Why, it wouldn't have hurt you to keep Robson on and cut down on the money you spent on clothes and shoes, but it never crossed your mind, did it? It would have been too great a sacrifice.'

There was a moment of shocked silence and then Mrs Cordwainer began to cry. Between wails, she asked God what she had done to deserve such a child, one who actually dared to criticise her own mother, one who made trouble for her parents, made them look ridiculous, wore on her back sufficient clothes to pay a chauffeur for six months, yet blamed an entire congregation for not letting slum children take the food they had paid for from the harvest supper . . .

'Letty, if you don't stop I'll go mad,' Mr Cordwainer said. He pulled open the door of the car, walked round to the passenger side, and almost dragged his wife on to the pavement. 'It won't start and I, for one, have had enough. I'm getting a taxi. Are you coming, or do you prefer to walk?'

'Adolphus, speak to Sara! She's done our reputation more harm in the last hour than I would ever have believed possible! We shall be laughing stocks . . . and what is more, I'll never dare show my face in church again, not until she's apologised to Reverend Atwell and promised on her word of honour never to do such a thing again.'

Mr Cordwainer turned wearily to Sara. For the first

time it struck Sara that he looked rather ill as well as bad-tempered.

'Well? Are you going to do as your mother says?'

'No,' Sara said firmly, though with fast-beating heart. 'I don't think I did wrong to give the children some of the food, so I can't say I'll never do such a thing again. And I thought Mr Atwell behaved extremely badly – he made a laughing stock of himself, I didn't have to do a thing.'

A taxicab, cruising past, was hailed and came over to the kerb. The driver leaned out.

'Yessir?'

'The Towers, Aigburth Road, my man,' Mr Cordwainer said briskly. 'Come along, Letty, in you get. We'll sort it all out under our own roof.'

Mrs Cordwainer, still protesting but with increasing feebleness, got into the taxi but when Sara would have followed her, her father held out a restraining hand.

'No, Sara. Will you apologise to Reverend Atwell and promise never to behave in so common and blatant a way again?'

'No, I won't,' Sara said immediately. 'I told you, Father, that I thought . . .'

But she was talking to thin air. Her father jumped into the cab and banged on the glass and the cab drove off, leaving Sara standing on the kerb staring foolishly after it. The last she saw was her mother's face, spiteful, triumphant, as the vehicle rounded the corner of the square and disappeared into the night.

It was late, and because the car had been so difficult the Cordwainers had been the last to leave – or to attempt to do so, at any rate. The Reverend Atwell had taken himself off very much earlier, without so much as a glance in Sara's direction, and the rest of the congregation, though they had called goodnight and appeared at least not hostile, had gone long since. Now, Sara stood hugging herself in her thin silk coat and wondering what on earth she should do. It was miles to walk home and besides, she guessed by her father's attitude and that last glimpse of her mother that if she did walk home she would find the house barred against her. But what to do? She had no money, of course, so she could not hail a taxi even if there was one passing, nor could she catch a tram. Her beautiful black patent leather shoes with the thin little ankle straps were not practical for walking anyway and ... she glanced upwards ... it was going to be a very cold night. The sky was clear, the stars twinkled and a moon lurked behind a chimney pot. She would have to keep moving or she'd freeze.

Accordingly, she took a few steps along the pavement, and stopped again. The paving stones were very uneven; perhaps she had better walk in the road? But cobblestones, she soon discovered, were worse to walk on than the most uneven paving, so she returned to the side walk and then went over and sat on the wall where the children had sat earlier in the evening. She had best orientate herself. She would go to Kirkdale, of course, and knock her grandmother up, but previously she had always either caught the tram or been taken to Snowdrop Street by car. Which way should she begin to walk?

After some thought she turned her steps towards the direction in which she seemed to remember St George's Hall lay. If she could find that, she could make her way home quite easily.

She had been walking for no more than ten minutes when she realised that she had thought of Snowdrop Street quite naturally as her home. Well, so it is, she thought defiantly, plodding along with increasing difficulty and clutching the silk coat close to her throat. It was more like home than the house on Aigburth Road, even though she had been brought up there. Number three Snowdrop Street was home to her because her grandmother loved her, had looked after her with tender care. Under no circumstances could she imagine Gran simply deserting her in the street at dead of night!

However, she had been deserted, which meant, so far as Sara could see, that she need never go back to the Aigburth Road house again. I'll live with Gran for ever now, and make something of my life, she told herself. I don't want Father's money or Mother's lifestyle, I just want to live with Gran and lead a useful sort of life. I'll get a job, and catch a tram to work each day and Gran and I will have holidays by the seaside sometimes, and sit and talk by the fire . . .

But she had forgotten; Gran had Miss Boote, now. For a second she just stood stock still whilst dismay and misery washed over her. Gran had a lodger! Miss Boote was very nice, a sensible, down-to-earth sort of woman, Gran was very fond of her, but it had not hitherto struck Sara that Miss Boote must be sleeping in the little front room, the room that Sara had, quite unconsciously, always considered her very own!

So what to do? For tonight, in an emergency, she could sleep on the sofa, she supposed. And perhaps there was some way . . . she could not share Gran's bed, that would not be fair, but there must be someone, somewhere, who wanted a lodger, as Gran had? Someone who would give her a room?

She had no money, of course. This would mean she could not afford to become a lodger until she got work of some sort, and she doubted she would get work without an address. But this was no time for such sombre thoughts, such foolish apprehension. She would make her way to Snowdrop Street and ask Gran to let her sleep on the sofa just for a night or two, and then, together, they would work out some plan for Sara's future which did not include a return to Aigburth Road.

Satisfied that she was doing the best thing, Sara began doggedly to walk once more.

Peader had been on a late shift. He trudged home rather than walked, because he was tired and because he no longer lived right on top of his work.

When he was given the job of safety man and began to earn better money he decided to change his lodgings and now he had a slip of a room all to himself in the home of an elderly couple in Salop Street, just off the Walton Road.

Peader liked it very much. Walton Road was lively; a positive hive of activity in fact, so that he felt he was at the centre of things once more as he had been in Dublin. And he liked the situation of his new home, too. Behind the jigger which ran along the back of all the small houses in Salop Street was the Co-op bakery and the smell of fresh bread which permeated the area was a lot nicer, to Peader's way of thinking, than the smell of railway engines, oil and soot, which he lived with all day long. Then there was the Queen's Arms public house on the very corner of Salop Street. It was lively, too, but in a good-natured sort of way and Peader, who had never been a heavy drinker, soon took to going there for half an hour of an evening. Sometimes he played dominoes, or pitch and toss, but usually he just sat in a corner and yarned with one or two other quiet men, like himself.

After the pub came a building contractor's yard,

then a couple of houses, and then the Salvation Army Barracks, which amused Peader because next to that was the Queen's Cinema ... everything you wanted, he told Deirdre in his letters home. Mammon, which was the pub, God, which was the Barracks, and entertainment, which was the cinema. Of course for him, God wasn't really represented by the Barracks; his faith needed the warmth of the Catholic Church, but he knew Deirdre would appreciate the joke.

And after Mass on a Sunday, Peader had taken to cinema-going, joining the long queue which stretched right across the front of the Barracks sometimes, and was glad that the government had not yet succeeded in stopping 'Sunday flicks'.

He missed Brogan, though, and had been very pleased when, shortly after their return from their Irish holiday, Brogan wrote to say he was coming to Liverpool to sit an examination and could his daddy possibly let him share his room for a couple of nights? Naturally Peader wrote back at once saying 'yes', so Brogan would be along in a day or two, to sit this exam at the Gordon Institute, where he had studied when he first came to England.

Now, Peader was crossing Stanley Street though, still a long way from home, and it was midnight and past and a frosty one, at that. Still, it was better than fog – anything was better than fog.

As a safety man he dreaded fog because his gangs couldn't work – it was far too dangerous – and without the safety man the trains couldn't run, either. And Liverpool is a foggy city, what with the Mersey, and the coal fires and the industry. So when it was foggy Peader was sent off up the line with a supply of detonators, to warn approaching trains that they were near a station and must begin to apply their brakes.

'What's a safety man, Daddy?' Polly had asked when he had last been home, sitting on his knee and stroking what she called his 'rustly' chin, because he'd not shaved for a day or so. 'What does a safety man do?'

She was delighted when he told her that he watched out for his gang, warning them of approaching trains and thus preventing accidents, and mystified her when he said that when it was foggy he did it by putting detonators on the lines, because detonators were explosives, and she thought that it was very wrong to lay explosives on a railway line, someone had said it was wrong ... people did it in the Troubles, and it was a naughty thing so it was.

But Peader had explained; the detonators were put on the rails and when the train ran over them they exploded, making a lot of noise and creating quite a display of sparks but doing no damage whatsoever.

'Then what's the use of them?' Polly the practical asked. 'I thought you meant they stopped the train dead, blew it up, *pow, pow,* like that!'

'You're a horror so you are,' Peader told her, laughing. 'The bangs tell the engine driver that he's getting near a station and must begin to apply his brakes, for it takes a big engine quite a distance to get to stopping.'

'Oh, I see,' Polly had said, scrambling off his knee. 'I'll be a safety man when I grow up – I like bangs so I do.'

But tonight Peader and his gang had just been doing their usual job, checking that their length of line was safe, that the points were in the right position for the next train, that there were no little landslips, that the troughs were full of water so the moving train could extend its scoop and replenish its water tank as it passed ... and having done their duty, they had dispersed to their several homes where they would stay until their next shift in two days' time.

What made Peader pause when he saw the girl he could not imagine, except that it was so very late, so very cold, and she looked so very forlorn. But she didn't look like a street girl. Peader steered clear of the Liverpool street girls. They weren't like the unfortunates of the Dublin slums, they were pert, sleazy, foul-mouthed girls, who swore and shrieked and laughed and sold their favours to anyone who could pay their price. And they didn't just hang about the streets looking pathetic, either. They accosted, teased, accused. No, Peader would not have paused had he thought the girl a Liverpool whore.

The girl didn't see him. She was wearing a thin, shiny-looking coat which she hugged about herself, and a long skirt which swished against the paving stones as she walked . . . and she wasn't walking either, not really, she was more stumbling along, as though every step was a pain to her.

Peader turned towards her, uncertain. Suppose he scared her? But she had stopped and was leaning against a shop-front, her hand to her heart. She looked pale and sickly, but that was probably the gaslight.

Making up his mind, he walked over to her, stopping when he was well short of her. It would be too bad if she shrieked out when all he intended was to ask her if she was all right, needed help.

'Are you all right, ma'am?' he said, therefore. 'It's awful cold and late for a young lady like yourself to be on the street. And not too safe, either,' he added, remembering tales he had heard of men taking to burglary, robbery, all sorts, when they were out of work and down on their luck.

'Oh . . . hello. Thank you for asking . . . it's these

shoes,' the girl said. 'They're no good for walking, I can assure you. But I've not got far to go, now, – I'm heading for Snowdrop Street.'

'Oh aye? I know it; I used to lodge near there. But I'm on Walton Road now so I've quite a step still.' He looked at her thoughtfully. 'Will you reach Snowdrop Street though, ma'am? You look wore out. I could give you me arm for the rest of the way if it 'ud help. It's no distance, really.'

'Well, I am tired . . . and I'm cold, too,' the girl admitted. 'But it's not fair to take you out of your way. I'll manage, but thanks, anyway.'

Peader looked at her more closely still. She was even younger than he had thought, probably in her mid to late teens, and very much a little lady. And now that he was so close he could see she was wearing evening dress, and the thinnest coat imaginable, as well as downright silly shoes. One heel was already turning over – they weren't up to walking, that was plain.

'It's no bother,' he said, therefore. 'I'll walk you to Snowdrop Street, for I've a daughter of me own and I'd not like her to be out on the street so late at night and in such flimsy clothing. Take my arm.'

After a moment's hesitation the girl sighed, pulled herself away from the wall and took his proffered arm.

'Well, I will, and thank you very much indeed,' she said. 'It's really awfully good of you, because I've been very frightened as well as very tired, and I'm so cold I can't even feel my hands or feet. And now I'm beginning to wonder what on earth I'll do if I can't make my granny hear when I knock the door. She isn't expecting me, you see, and she sleeps in the back, not the front.'

'She isn't expecting you?' Peader said gently. 'You've not run away from home, alanna? Because if so, perhaps you should t'ink again. Your mammy is probably half mad wit' worry.'

The girl laughed rather bitterly. 'Half mad with worry? I think not. And anyway, I haven't run away from home, I've been turned out. Or rather, I've been abandoned, left.'

'In that dress?' Peader said. 'You'd best tell me the whole tale – my name's Peader O'Brady, by the way. I'm safety man for a gang of navvies on the railway there.' Her jerked his head, indicating the distant yards. 'What's your name, alanna, or would you rather not say?'

He half expected this pretty girl to deny him her name but the girl stopped walking for a moment to stare at him incredulously and then she began to laugh, softly but with real mirth.

'My goodness, this is so incredible, Mr O'Brady, that it's almost like a theatrical farce. My name is Sara Cordwainer, and I believe I know your son, Brogan.'

After that, of course, he had to hear the whole story. Sara poured it out, keeping nothing back. The harvest supper, the rage of her parents, the abandoning of her in the dark square. She told Peader how she had discovered that the woman she had been told was her old nanny was really her grandmother, how her parents had tried to keep her from that same grandmother, and how desperate she had felt when she had recently realised that there was now no spare room at number three Snowdrop Street.

'But your ould one has a whole house to herself, bar one room for the lodger,' Peader pointed out. 'Sure and she'll find a spot for a granddaughter, so she will. Can you doubt it, alanna, if she loves you?'

'Oh, you're right, she'll try to fit me in, but it won't

be fair to disturb her and upset Miss Boote,' Sara said, distressed at the mere thought of causing more trouble, more unhappiness. She acknowledged to herself that her parents would be unhappy, if only because they felt she had made fools of them. 'It's a tiny house, truly, Mr O'Brady.'

'Well, I don't think you should worry, because I'm sure you'll be all right,' Peader said. 'As for your gran not hearing you knock – have you ever heard an Irishman shout?'

It made Sara laugh, and that was good for her. She was even beginning to feel warmer, with Peader at her side. And presently, when they reached Snowdrop Street, he proved his point. When polite knocking with the dolphin knocker produced no response he took her elbow and steered her to the jigger.

'The back way's often the best,' he whispered. 'Come on, I can unlock the gate – if it's locked, which I doubt.'

There were no street lamps in the jigger but the moon was still bright enough to guide them to the right back yard. Peader stood under Mrs Prescott's bedroom window and threw a handful of gravel at it. It sounded like pistol shots in the dark of the night, but when Sara called 'Gran? Are you there? It's me, Sara!' it was only a moment before the curtains were drawn back, the window slid up, and Gran's face appeared in the gap.

'Sara? My dear child, what on earth . . . wait, I'll come down.'

'I'll leave you now,' Peader said diplomatically. 'You'll have a lot to tell your gran so you will and I've a way to walk.' He took her hand and shook it. 'When me boy comes over here to take his exams in a day or so, maybe we'll walk round, pay you a visit.'

'Oh, I *wish* you would,' Sara said eagerly. 'I've not seen or spoken to Brogan for three years. And in a way it was his fault that I was shipped off to Switzerland . . . oh, I can hear Gran at the door, do come in for a moment, you've been so kind!'

But this Peader refused to do and in fact by the time Mrs Prescott had unlocked and unbolted her back door and creaked it open, he was probably already on Stanley Road and heading, fast, for home.

'What's happened, love?' Mrs Prescott said as soon as she got Sara indoors and in front of the dead but still warm parlour fire. 'That evening gown will never be the same again and as for your shoes . . . well, girls will be girls, I suppose.'

'We went to the harvest supper and I disagreed with the Reverend Atwell's attitude and said so. Afterwards my father said if I wouldn't apologise he wouldn't take me home and I was in the middle of explaining why I wouldn't apologise when he told the taxi driver to drive on and they left me,' she said briefly. 'Gran, I forgot about Miss Boote, but can I sleep on your sofa tonight? I'm just absolutely exhausted and so cold that if I don't cuddle down soon I'll probably fall over.'

'The sofa? No, indeed, we'll share my nice double bed,' Mrs Prescott said decidedly. 'Come along, I've a hot-water bottle in already and plenty of blankets. Remember when you were small and used to stay with me? I'd put you to bed in the little front room and by midnight you'd be in bed with me, cuddled up all warm and close, because you said you were frightened, alone in the other room.' She chuckled. 'Not that you were frightened, you little monkey, you just liked to share my bed, and wake me up at the crack of dawn in the morning, and play old harry with my lie-ins.'

'Yes, I remember. Oh, Gran, I was awful then and I'm awful now,' Sara said. 'I'll try not to put my cold feet on you, and I'll try not to wake you too early, as well. Not that I will, I'm far too tired myself.'

And presently she climbed between the sheets, clad in a vast cotton nightdress belonging to her grandmother, and cuddled down blissfully into the warm bed.

'I'll bring you a cup of hot milk with a drop of rum in it,' Mrs Prescott promised, but by the time she came up the stairs again, with the hot milk and a plate of marie biscuits, Sara was fast asleep.

Grace came out of the front door at the fastest pace she could manage and shot across the pavement, turning right around the side of the house and making for the roadway beyond the court. Her father had recently come home from the pub, and he was in a wicked rage. He had smashed in through the door, she had heard his onslaught, heard the door slam back into the wall, and he had started to scream and curse, shouting that his wife was a slut, his home a filthy hole fit only for rats, his kids bastards who wouldn't piss on a man if he was afire.

Grace had been asleep in the bundle of rags which was the best they could manage for a bed, with assorted young Carberys beside her, but she woke pretty fast when her father began to shout. She sat up, every nerve quivering, her heart thumping so hard it could actually be seen when she glanced down at her thin chest. Bang, bang, BANG it went . . . he's coming, he's coming, HE'S COMING!

The Carberys had long since been turned out of Snowdrop Street for non-payment of rent and now had the basement flat in this tall, ugly block. The kids slept in the back room and the family lived in the front, which meant that if you wanted to leave the back room you had to go through the front. And that meant risking a confrontation with Stan Carbery, and a drunken Stan Carbery was terrifying. But if he came through . . . Grace wondered whether she might burrow so deep into the rags that he would not find her, then abandoned even the thought. She dared not risk it. She simply had to escape . . . she would make a run for it the moment he wasn't looking.

She slid out of the rags and padded over to the door which separated the two rooms. It wasn't closed – well, it wouldn't close, her da had broken the hinges years back – so she was able to see through the crack into the dim, candlelit room beyond. Her mother was backed into a corner, swinging what looked like a black bottle full of something, and she was shouting almost as loudly, now, as her husband.

'Gerrout of 'ere, you swine,' she screamed. 'I'll break this bottle over your bleedin' 'ead if you comes one step closer!'

Mam must be very drunk, Grace reflected. Usually she fled the moment her husband entered the house if he was in a violent mood. She never even woke her kids, so that they could defend themselves, but let them bear the brunt of her husband's wrath. But tonight she was fighting back, it seemed.

'The wicked bugger ma' me leave 'is bloody rotten pub,' Stan Carbery roared. Grace caught a glimpse of his face – scarlet, bug-eyed – as he lunged at his wife, but she waved the bottle and he pretended to change his mind, beginning to shout again. 'He shaid I were the worshe for booze, the wicked bugger!'

'So you bloody are,' his wife shrieked. 'Gerrout, go on, gerrout of me 'ouse this instant, Stan Carb!'

'Whose bloody 'ouse? *Whose* bloody 'ouse?'

The trouble was, the door opened the wrong way.

Grace would have to run round it once it was open in order to get out of the outer door, and then she would have to climb the area steps ... she shuddered at the thought of her father clawing her back down again by the legs, falling on her, crashing his fist into her skinny, vulnerable frame. He'd near killed her a couple of times ... oh, if only Jess were still alive, Grace thought, whilst the sweat of terror beaded her brow and made her breathe short. If Jess were still alive she'd think of something, do something!

But in the further room, her father had suddenly begun to see things. Grace knew the signs and thanked her stars. He was hitting out at nothing now, wiping the air with both fists in a desperate, ugly paroxysm of fear. Whatever he imagined was attacking him was doing a good job, Grace surmised, as he suddenly dodged and began to retreat, shouting all the while.

'No ... no, you don't, you buggers ... gerroff, will you? Leave me be, I ain't done nothin' ... leave me be!'

It was the moment. Grace slid round the door and set off at a fast pace across the room. She was out of the living-room door and tugging at the outer one when her mother said: 'Wharra you doin', you little bitch? Don't you run off an' leave me to tackle this bastard by meself! Stan, she's ...'

It acted like a spur. Grace tore the door open, shot through it and ascended the area steps so fast that she could not afterwards remember her feet so much as touching them. And at the top, she simply ran, though she had no stamina and knew she would speedily have to stop to regain her breath.

But there was no pursuit. Panting, sobbing, she made for the one place where her father would not pursue her – the graveyard of the nearest church. And once there, safely ensconced in the shed where the sexton kept his gardening tools, she had leisure to think.

Why had Mam given her away to her da like that, knowing him to be capable of killing when the drink was on him? And why was it always her who was the object of his greatest fury, his most violent wrath? Addy, her only remaining sister, who had run away eight months before, said it was because Grace had been Jess's favourite, and their father had always hated Jess.

'Why, Addy?' Grace had asked helplessly. 'Why did he hate Jess? She was good, was Jess, real kind an' all.'

'She weren't 'is get,' Addy had explained kindly. 'Our da always said our mam played 'im false when she got our Jess.'

'I don't understand,' Grace had said. 'What d'you mean?'

Addy had sighed and cast her eyes at the sky, but at least she had answered.

'Mam was 'avin' a baby, see? She weren't wed, not then. She told our da it were 'is baby, that 'e was the dad, see? So then they got wed. Only our da reckoned she'd gone wi' another feller, an' the baby – Jess – were the other feller's. See?'

'I think I do,' Grace had said. 'I wish . . . I wish our da di'n't 'ate me so much, Addy.'

Addy had shrugged. 'Our da 'ates the 'ole lot of us,' she said cynically. ''E 'ates me 'cos I'm the eldest gal, an' you 'cos you're the next, an' Reggie 'cos 'e's a little lad, an' . . .'

Grace had got the message though and from that moment on had accepted, albeit sadly, that her father hated her. She had not known, until this minute, that her mother hated her too.

But at least I'm safe now, for a bit, she told herself,

curling up on a pile of old newspapers. She checked the pocket of her ragged cardigan and the possession she most prized was still there, so that was all right. And the sexton didn't hate her. He left the door of his shed unlocked and the newspapers handy . . . she thought he must pity her and pity was better than either hatred or indifference.

But she still wished Jess was alive, wished she'd been able to find baby Mollie and take care of her as, once, Jess had taken care of the young Grace.

In her worn-out, confused mind, she told herself that the next best thing to being loved was loving.

And then she slept.

Chapter Eight

Sara slept like a log and didn't even stir when Mrs Prescott got out of bed next morning and crept down the stairs to get breakfast for Miss Boote – not that this was in any way necessary, for she and her lodger had long ago come to an understanding. Miss Boote made the breakfast if she was downstairs first, cooking a pan of porridge and cutting bread, making a pot of tea and so on. But if Mrs Prescott was about early they sometimes had an egg, or even fried bread and a piece of bacon, for Miss Boote was secretary to the manager of the County Bank on Walton Road and bicycled to work which meant, Mrs Prescott insisted, that she needed a good breakfast to keep her strength up.

But when Mrs Prescott came quietly into the bedroom, having waved Miss Boote off on her trusty steed, Sara was sitting up in bed and stretching and declaring that she hadn't had such a good night's sleep for ages and ages, and did Gran think that they might find her a job today?

'Goodness, Sara, whatever next?' Her grandmother said, thoroughly startled, for though Sara had mentioned getting a job before she had not taken her seriously. 'I can't imagine your father lettin' you work for your living – not if he didn't like it when he saw you speakin' to a young railway worker, and objected because you gave children some spare food. He would undoubtedly think you were letting him down.'

She was half-joking, but soon realised that her granddaughter had thought the whole thing through very thoroughly.

'Yes, Gran, I know what you mean, but they've washed their hands of me, you see. They simply drove away from me – I could have been robbed or murdered or anything. You'll say they'll guess that I've come to you, but if so, why haven't they been in touch, to find out? They haven't, have they?' she added with a transparent hopefulness which went to the older woman's heart.

'No, they haven't,' Mrs Prescott admitted. 'But I'm sure they would have been terribly worried if they'd realised you had no money, no means of gettin' either here or back to your home . . .'

She was interrupted. 'I have no home,' Sara said firmly. 'Apart from here, I mean, and I can't stay with you, Gran. It wouldn't be fair.'

'It would be the best thing that ever happened to me,' her grandmother told her. 'Miss Boote and I are very good friends, but it's through circumstance, you see. You are my flesh and blood, chuck, and I've loved you from the day you were born. Don't go off and leave me alone again!'

'Oh, Gran . . . but you'll want your bed to yourself . . . and you need Miss Boote's money, I know you do . . . and I can't pay you anything until I get a job,' Sara said, her brow creasing with worry. 'If I could have a little bed in the parlour . . .'

'You shall have a little bed in my room; we'll sell the double bed and buy two singles at Paddy's market,' Mrs Prescott said. 'I saw respectable, clean secondhand beds for sale the last time I was there. How snug we'll be, queen! I like to read before I nod off – how about you, eh? I 'member you always used to read in bed as a child.'

'I still like to read, but Gran . . .'

'No nonsense, no argufying,' Mrs Prescott said briskly. 'It's agreed, then. I'll sell my double bed and buy two singles this very day – you can come with me if you don't mind walkin' slow – and then you may take a look around for likely employment. We might do worse than ask Miss Boote, in fact, now I come to think, because she works in a big bank, they might easily need another young lady to do whatever it is they do in banks.'

Two days after Sara arrived at her grandmother's house, Brogan came knocking on the door. Sara, delighted to see him and wanting to know what had been happening to him in the three years since they last met, asked him in, but the visit was not a success.

Brogan, who had seemed self-confident, breezy, amusing, when they'd met before was not at all at ease in Mrs Prescott's neat front parlour, or with the young lady Sara had become, she could not tell which it was, she could just sense the unease. And he seemed shy of talking about his family, which had previously been a favourite topic of conversation. In fact he sat on the small sofa, dwarfing it with his size, and played with his cap on his knee and avoided her eyes. So in the end Sara asked him what on earth was the matter.

'Nothin',' Brogan growled, staring at his cap. 'Nothin' at all at all.'

'Then why won't you look at me when we're talking?' Sara asked, frustrated and disappointed that this meeting, which had meant so much to her, was going so badly. 'Your cap can't be that much nicer to look at than my face!'

He laughed, but reluctantly. 'If there's somethin' the matter, then that's it,' he muttered. 'You're a young lady now, and a smart one. You don't want nothin' to do wit' the likes of me. I was a fireman on an engine, now I'm drivin' goods trains on branch lines; if I'm lucky I'll move to passenger trains next. If I spend the rest of me life workin', then I'll mebbe end up ownin' a little house, ridin' a decent bike, respected by me workmates. Nothin' in this world could mek me gentry.'

'Who cares?' Sara said scornfully. 'I like you as you are, Brogan. Now do stop being so silly and tell me all about Crewe, and your lodgings.'

He tried, that was the worst part. She could see him trying. He looked steadily at her as he spoke and he described his lodgings, his garden, even his work on the great engines chuffing all over the country, taking the LMS passengers to their various destinations. But Sara saw his eyes were full of misery and in the end she just couldn't stand it. She interrupted a laborious description of one of the stations he visited as seen by a railwayman needing a bite to eat by jumping to her feet.

'Brogan, I'm sorry, but you know I'm job-hunting – I told you, didn't I? I've an interview with a Mr Esmond at the Ocean Accident Insurance this afternoon and it's in Exchange Buildings, wherever that may be. So I'll want to be getting something to eat before I leave and . . .'

Brogan got to his feet, too.

'It's all right, it's all right,' he said quickly. 'Just goin' I was . . . I want to do some revisin' for this examination. It's mathematics – you need to know mathematics if you're goin' to get on. Say goodbye to your gran for me, and t'anks for the cup of tea.'

And whilst Sara, appalled at herself, was beginning

to stammer that she hadn't meant . . . there was still time . . . he had left the room.

'Brogan, don't . . .' she began, running after him, but he was halfway down the road, cap pulled low, coat collar pulled up, before she had got further than the step.

It put a damper on the rest of the day, of course. Sara changed into the grey flannel suit she and Gran had bought from a dealer in the market – it was a bit on the large side, but a piece taken out of the waistband soon cured that – and cleaned the shoes she had picked up at the same time. It was the first time Sara had ever worn a garment which had first been worn by someone else and she hated it, but needs must, she told herself resolutely. It had been washed and ironed, what more did she want? One thing was certain, she did not intend to go, cap in hand, back to Aigburth Road for the rest of her clothes – not after the things that had been said.

For the day after she moved in with Mrs Prescott, the Cordwainers had come visiting. They had sat side by side on the small sofa and tried to lay down rules for Sara's return and future conduct. And when Sara and Mrs Prescott had made it clear they were not interested, both parties had lost their tempers.

'If you don't come with us right now, today, you'll never darken my doors again,' Mr Cordwainer had shouted, just like the papa in a Victorian melodrama. 'You're spoiled and selfish, you never gave a thought to your mother and myself when you stormed off after the harvest supper.'

'Stormed off? Father, how can you say such a thing? I was still speaking when you just jumped into the taxi cab and told the driver to take you home! You left me, without a penny piece, to make my own way home!

And what's more I was in evening dress, with an icy wind blowing . . .'

'Rubbish,' her father blustered, his cheeks reddening slightly. 'We implored you to accompany us, your mother and I, and you refused to do so. What choice had we?'

'You're a liar, like Mother,' Sara shouted, shaking with fury. She had always thought herself a meek soul but now she discovered that this was not so. 'She lied to me and to you too, for all I know. Mrs Prescott's my grandmother, Father – did you know that? Yes, and that means she's your wife's mother . . . and look how your wife treats her! Believe me, I'm happier here than I could possibly be living in Aigburth Road surrounded by lies and evasions. You can tell your smart friends any story you like, maybe they'll even believe you, but here people are judged on what they do, not what they say. And I'm staying here!'

'Then we've much to be grateful for,' Mrs Cordwainer shrieked, her voice rising to unladylike heights. 'How dare you call your own mother a liar – your own mother, Sara! As for lying to you, I did no such thing! I simply kept the truth from you because . . . oh, because it didn't suit me to have people, my sort of people, knowing about my background. I'd risen above it and I didn't intend to be haunted by the – the spectre of Snowdrop Street! It was for your sake I did it, you detestable little prig – for your sake! Oh, what a serpent we've nourished in our bosoms, your father and I! You've had the best of everything, a marvellous education, beautiful clothes . . .'

'But no love,' Sara said softly, almost to herself. 'Never, never that.'

It hadn't ended there, of course, there had been more. But they'd left at last, handing out another ultimatum on the doorstep. Either Sara repented, apologised and came home at once . . .

'Goodbye Mother, Father,' Sara said politely at the end of the tirade. 'I shan't be seeing you for a while I don't suppose, so take care of each other.'

It took the wind out of their sails. They stared at her, then her father gave a strangled snort and marched round to the driver's side of the car, leaving her mother to fumble with the handle of the passenger door and sob into her handkerchief.

But at least I know where I stand, now, Sara said to herself as she walked to the tram stop in the grey flannel suit and the sensible black walking shoes with a small cream-coloured felt hat pulled down over her hair. I've got to earn my living, so I'll accept the first job I'm offered, and I'll give Gran most of my salary and keep myself decent with the rest. I've had eighteen years of being given whatever I wanted in the way of material things, now I'll try to see how I manage on my own.

Two hours later however, sitting disconsolately on the tram as it roared and rattled up Vauxhall Road, it wasn't nearly so easy to be optimistic. Mr Esmond was very kind, he said her languages were undoubtedly useful and she certainly seemed fluent – not that he could tell, since he knew only a modicum of schoolboy French – but the fact was, it was necessary to use a typewriter, and he could not afford to pay her a wage whilst she learned something which every other young lady he was interviewing had been doing for a number of years.

'But they don't all speak French, German and Italian, do they?' Sara had said hopefully, giving him her very best smile. He had smiled too, but wearily, even as his eyes had flickered approvingly over the grey suit, the flat shoes. I believe Gran really was right; I'll stand a better chance of a job in respectable, rather worn clothing than I would in something smart and new, Sara realised.

'No, you're the only one with any sort of command of foreign languages,' Mr Esmond admitted. 'But there's a lady who runs a small translations bureau a few streets away from here. We use her if we have an emergency. And she can type.'

'I see. Well, it's been nice meeting you,' Sara said, getting to her feet and holding out a hand. Mr Esmond shook it, looking stunned. How odd – did he expect me to snarl at him, or burst into tears? Sara wondered. But apparently it was the right thing to do because having shaken her hand he went over to the door and held it open for her, speaking as he did so.

'I'm sorry to have to disappoint you, Miss Cordwainer, because I know jobs are difficult to find these days. But will you take a bit of advice? There are a number of establishments in the city which teach young girls all the essentials of office work, including typing. Or there are evening classes at which the same skills can be acquired. I believe it would be sensible to acquire such skills before applying for other jobs.'

'But some people don't want typing, do they?' Sara asked hopefully. 'Employers must know not everyone can type.'

'That's true, but most girls who are trying to find a job straight from school are fourteen or fifteen, considerably younger than yourself. I doubt you would be taken on as an office girl, not at eighteen years of age.' His eyes flickered over her again, assessingly. 'Look, your parents chose to continue your schooling so surely they wouldn't balk at a secretarial course? It's not costly and you'd find it easy work after all those foreign languages!'

'And without secretarial skills you don't think I'll get work?' Sara said slowly.

'Oh yes, you might get shop work. But an employer is going to expect an eighteen-year-old to have had experience, you see.' He gave her an encouraging smile. 'It's a bitter pill, more schooling, but it's for the best. Good luck, Miss Cordwainer.'

It was not until she was actually on the tram that Sara began to feel, for the first time in her life, that she was a failure. She had been rejected because her skills were inadequate, because every other girl Mr Esmond interviewed could, at a pinch, have done the job.

So as the tram rattled down Vauxhall Road Sara scanned the copy of the *Echo* which she had bought from a street vendor, replayed Mr Esmond's advice over in her head, and faced facts. She spoke several languages and she had passed several examinations, but she could not type, nor could she keep books. The paper did not have thousands of job advertisements, but every single one for office staff specified either book-keeping or typing. There were one or two office juniors wanted but she was sure that Mr Esmond had hit the nail on the head; she would not get offered such a job because she was too old, and anyway, the salary for such a position was so tiny that it would scarcely do more than pay her tram fare from Kirkdale to the city centre each morning.

Still, it was no use sitting here fighting silly tears and letting despair drown her. She must be practical. As soon as Miss Boote arrived home this evening, she would take her to one side and explain her predicament. She had seen very little of the lodger apart from their first meeting and Gran said that Miss Boote did good works, evenings and weekends. Perhaps I could help her, Sara thought hopefully. Then, if I had to get just a little, tiny, badly paid job, at least I'd be doing some good, somewhere – and I wouldn't feel so guilty, either.

When her stop came she got off the tram and headed for Snowdrop Street and as luck would have it just as she reached the front door and was about to tap and open it, Miss Boote came cycling down the road. She usually came straight past the front door, on to Commercial Road, and down the jigger on Pansy Street, because she left her bicycle in the back yard overnight, but today, seeing Sara, she dismounted and wheeled her bike on to the pavement.

'Hello, Miss Cordwainer,' she said. 'Any luck with the interview? Mrs Preston told me you were seeing an insurance company this afternoon.'

Sara shook her head. 'No, they needed a typist,' she said rather bitterly. 'It didn't say that in the advertisement or I wouldn't have bothered to apply. Still, the man was very nice. He gave me some good advice, or I imagine it was good advice. Miss Boote, I wonder whether I might beg a few moments of your time when you've had your evening meal? Only I do need to talk to someone about jobs!'

'Certainly,' Miss Boote said cheerfully. 'Tell you what, I'm working in the soup kitchen on Westminster Road tonight; care to come along, give a hand? We can talk as we work, and no one will interfere with us.'

'I'd like that very much,' Sara said promptly. 'But . . . won't they expect me to – to bring something with me, like bread, or vegetables? Only I don't have any money at all, apart from what Gran gives me for the tram.'

Miss Boote laughed. 'No one will want anything but your labour, Miss Cordwainer,' she said cheerfully. 'But you'll see, this evening. Can you be ready by seven? Only we serve from seven to ten, and after that it's just preparing for the next day, so I get there around seven if I possibly can.'

'Yes, of course. Only I don't have a bicycle and I don't know where Westminster Road is,' Sara told her new friend. 'And I can't ask Gran for any more tram fares.'

'A tram fare wouldn't do you much good, anyway,' Miss Boote assured her. 'Trams don't go across the city, through the small streets, you'd have to go into the centre and out again, which would make you later than if you'd *crawled*, I daresay. What about a seater?'

'A seater?' Sara stared. 'What's that?'

'You sit on the bike seat and I stand up and pedal like fun,' Miss Boote explained. 'Or you could sit on the carrier,' she slapped it, 'which might be a bit safer, come to think. Only I daresay you wouldn't want to be seen two to a bike, eh?'

'I don't mind at all,' Sara said stoutly, though inwardly her heart failed her a little. If anyone she knew saw her they'd think she'd run mad or returned to her second childhood. Kids rode two to a bike, not adult ladies! But still, she didn't have a tram fare, she didn't fancy walking . . . 'It will be fun,' she added defiantly. 'Seven o'clock it is, then. Shall I wear my grey suit?'

Miss Boote laughed heartily and ran her bicycle down the pavement again and on to the road. 'To serve soup? No, no, Miss Cordwainer, you should wear your oldest rags – everyone else will!'

'Ready, Miss Cordwainer? Hop aboard, then.'

Feeling really silly, Sara sat herself astride the narrow little carrier which was just above the rear mudguard.

She clutched the bicycle seat and smiled a wobbly smile at Gran, who was watching them and laughing – it was enough to make a cat laugh, Sara thought ruefully as Miss Boote shouted to her to hold tight and launched herself, and the bicycle, into a wobble away from the kerb.

'We're off!' Miss Boote called back over her shoulder. 'Not much traffic about, fortunately, but we'll push across Stanley Road, I think. You slide off when I stop, Miss Cordwainer.'

Presently, Sara 'slid off' and they pushed the bicycle across the busy road, then remounted to turn into Fountains Road, which was wide and, to Sara's relief, relatively traffic-free.

'I try not to breathe along this stretch, 'cos of the Stanley Mortuary,' Miss Boote announced breathlessly over her shoulder. 'Been down here before, have you, Miss Cordwainer?'

'No, I don't think so,' Sara said. 'Are you sure you wouldn't rather I walked, Miss Boote?'

But Miss Boote assured her passenger that it was 'a piece of cake, honest', and continued to pedal on and to shout over her shoulder as she did so.

'We're just passin' St Athanasius' Church,' she announced presently. 'Big, ain't it? And St John's Presbytery's there . . .' the bike wobbled perilously as she pointed. 'And a bit further along yet, between the Saddle Inn – that's a nice pub, very quiet – and the Kendal Castle – that's a bit livelier – there's the Jewish synagogue. If it were Saturday you'd see 'em all comin' out wi' their little caps on and their long beards. All we need is a mosque, I tell them at the Barracks, and everyone's represented round here.' She laughed heartily at her own joke.

How odd, she seems to know the public houses as

well as she knows the churches, and she obviously takes a great interest in both, Sara thought. Now I wonder why that is?

She was soon to know. They turned into Westminster Road, wobbled along for a few hundred yards, and stopped beside a hall with big doors which opened out on to the pavement. Several shabby-looking men were making their way towards it and Miss Boote hailed them as she passed.

'Evenin', Mr O'Hare! How's your rheumatiz? Evenin', Mr Ross, come to give us a hand gerrin' rid o' that broth you like? Evenin', Mr Fellowes, I've brung you me copy of yesterday's *Echo*, I know you like a read before bed.'

The man thus addressed turned and laughed. 'I thought that 'ud be you – you're a caution you are, Miss! 'Alf the time that newspaper *is* me bed! Still an' all, I'm grateful for it.'

Miss Boote brought the bicycle to a halt outside the hall and waited whilst Sara disentangled herself from the carrier, then stood the machine in the small wooden porch.

'Come along in, Miss Cordwainer, and I'll introduce you,' she said. 'When we've finished wi' the soup though, I'll have to leave you for a few minutes. I'm goin' round the pubs tonight, so I'll need me uniform or God above knows what the customers will think.'

'Uniform?' Sara said, thoroughly bewildered. 'What uniform?' It was news to her that it was necessary to wear a uniform to go into a public house, but then so far as she knew women never went past the doors of the pubs. Oh, round the back, perhaps, to get a jug of ale which they would drink at home, but never up to the bar!

Miss Boote took her elbow. 'Ah, there's Mrs Puddifoot – you'll like her, she's a good sort. And Miss Edrich, and Mrs Callowe . . . they'll show you what to do, but by the time I leave – and I won't be long away, not above an hour – you'll have picked it up.'

'But the uniform,' Sara persisted. 'Why the uniform, Miss Boote?'

'Because if you go into a pub without the uniform they might think . . .' Miss Boote broke off, staring incredulously at Sara. 'Don't tell me your gran hasn't said anything to you? I'm a Salvationist, Miss Cordwainer, a member of God's Army!'

At first, Sara worked in a daze, scarcely able to believe what she was doing. Her parents had despised the Salvation Army and had brought her up, she now realised, to do the same. She had put money in their collecting tins behind her mother's back from time to time, and once or twice she had listened, with tapping foot, as they sang carols in the streets at Christmas, but other than that she had seldom thought about them, save as people in rather old-fashioned clothing who appeared in the city centre, armed with shiny brass instruments, and played bouncy hymns and the better known carols.

'They sing in the streets; for *money*,' her mother had said, as though it was a crime so dastardly that she hardly dare put it into words. 'They wear *uniform*, the women as well. The bonnets are all right, but those heavy coats and skirts!' She had shuddered expressively. I wouldn't been seen dead in them, and the shoes are really frumpy – dreadful things.'

'I'm told they do a lot of good,' her father had said. 'For the lower classes, of course. But then so do the Goodfellows.'

Damning by faint praise, Sara had thought it, and

now, as she worked beside Miss Boote, Miss Callowe, Mrs Puddifoot and Miss Edrich, she realised that her father had been way, way out. The Goodfellows collected money for the poor, they didn't work for them. They didn't put huge aprons round their middles and clean and prepare great mountains of vegetables, chop bones with a hatchet to make stock, beg butcher's scraps to enrich their soup. They didn't serve the soup, either, unlike her fellow workers, none of whom was too proud to take it over to an old woman who sat dribbling down her stained coat, only just able to lift the bowl to her lips.

'Where do you get the vegetables?' she asked Miss Boote at one stage, when a skinny boy came in, staggering under the weight of a sack of cabbages. 'They can't all be presents!'

'Yes, they are, the shopkeepers are always generous,' Miss Boote told her. 'The joke of it is, we have a lot of kiddies and women during the daytime, though it's mainly men at night. And if we have to buy anything – crockery, utensils – it is paid for by the ould fellers of the wives and kids we feed!'

'Then they contribute willingly? But why don't they give their wives the money, then their wives could make soup for them,' Sara, ever practical, said. Miss Boote laughed and ladled more soup into more tin pannikins.

'It don't occur to them that they're contributin', for the most part,' she admitted. 'We go into the pubs with the *War Cry* and tell them we need the money desperately, for to feed the poor. They've had a few, they're merry, very likely, so they put their hands into their pockets – it's only a few pence, and they think it'll keep us quiet, off their backs. Yet that money goes to help to feed their wives and children, more often than not.'

'You mean they'll give you a few pence, but they won't give it to their wives?' Sara asked, shocked. 'That doesn't make sense.'

'It makes very good sense. You see, we're in the pubs and the fellers what drink their money away love the pubs. They're amongst their mates, it's warm and cheerful in there with no crying kids, no hungry, weeping wife. So they'll put on a bit of a show, boast a bit, chuck their money about. Sometimes they offer to buy us a bevvy, as they call it, and we smile ever so sweetly and tell them to pop the money into the collectin' tin, we'll have our bevvies later.'

'Well, I don't understand it, but it's good,' Sara said after a moment's thought. 'What else do you do for the poor, Miss Boote?'

'We run hostels for the homeless, places where wives can stay when their husbands beat them up, soup kitchens – this is one – and cheap canny houses where those with a few pence can get a good, hot meal. And we try, very gently, to show them that God cares. That's if they want to come to the citadel, that is.'

'I see. And – and could I come to the citadel? I don't mean to be one of you, exactly, I just mean to see what happens there.'

''Course you could,' Miss Boote said briskly. 'Well, I'm off to do me stint in the pubs down the Walton Road. God knows, there are plenty of pubs there, yet it's a poor area. The women have large families and a lot of the men are unemployed.'

'Don't they get this assistance they talk about?' Sara asked cautiously. She had heard others besides her father being contemptuous of anyone who could not manage, saying that the person should ask for public assistance.

'It's means tested,' Miss Boote said briefly. 'Can't stop now, queen, got to be off. But I'll be back in an hour and we'll tootle off home on me old bike, eh?'

She disappeared into the night and Miss Callowe, who had been standing beside Sara cutting the long brown loaves and handing over a slice as each diner approached, poked her in the ribs. She was a girl of about Sara's own age, with lovely smooth, light-brown hair, but she had gaps in her teeth and those that remained were grey and unhealthy-looking.

'Hey, Miss Cordwainer ... Lord love you, what a mouthful! D'you have another name?'

'Yes, I'm Sara,' Sara said happily. 'What's your first name, Miss Callowe?'

'Margaret, but everyone calls me Maggie,' the girl said. 'Are you goin' to join us? The uniform's lovely, honest. I got a new one a few months ago 'cos my old 'un was too tight and very worn, so Captain Edwards helped to pay for it, because I work in Sykes the baker on Walton Road, and it ain't a job what pays much.'

'The uniform is pretty, but I don't know about joining you,' Sara said guardedly. 'Actually, I haven't got a job at all at present so I can't afford so much as a new hanky.'

Maggie laughed. 'You'll gerra job, you're ever so pretty and your teef's good.' She indicated her own mouth. 'Mine are awful poor – the dentist up at the centre says it's 'cos I weren't fed right, as a child.'

'Goodness – what did your mother say when he said that?'

There was a pause before Maggie spoke.

'I ain't got no mother, nor no father, norrany more,' she said quietly. 'They dumped me in a children's 'ome when I were five. I 'spec' they're dead, now. So you see, the Army's more'n just a friend, it's me family an' all.'

'I see,' Sara said inadequately. 'I'm sorry, Maggie.'

'Don't be sorry; likely it were the best thing that could 'ave 'appened to me,' Maggie said, suddenly cheerful. 'I gorra lorra friends, the Army 'ostel's a nice place, an' one day I'll marry some feller an' gerra place o' me own.'

'I'm sure you will,' Sara said gently. 'Oh, the soup's running low; what happens now?'

'You shout someone . . . Mrs Puddifoot will do . . . an' they'll bring a fresh pan through,' Maggie told her. 'What's left's a bit thin an' all . . . ask Mrs P for more veggies in the next lot.'

On her way home that night, sitting on the back of Miss Boote's bicycle, Sara thought about her evening. She had enjoyed it tremendously, even though what she had secretly hoped for had not come to pass. She had not found herself serving either the missing Carbery or the other one, Grace, the older girl that Jess had mentioned. Well, if she had served them they had both changed, which, Sara thought ruefully, would not be out of the question – she herself had changed.

But she had looked very hard at every child aged around seven or around eleven; that was how old Mollie and Grace would be, by now, she had calculated, and none of them had had either Mollie's wonderful red-gold curls or Grace's extraordinary likeness to her elder sister.

But even if I've not actually helped either of those children, I've helped others whose plight may be similar, Sara told herself robustly, as Miss Boote dismounted from the bicycle and she slid off the back. It would have been an *unbelievable* coincidence had I met either of them on my very first foray into trying to help the poor.

And presently, over a hot cup of cocoa, she told Miss Boote that she had been looking for the Carbery children, just in case her friend knew of them.

'I've not heard of 'em,' Miss Boote said when Sara finished the story. 'But has it occurred to you, queen, that they might have bettered theirselves by now? They might be doin' all right, Mr Carbery could've finished wi' the booze and the kids might be properly fed an' that. You never know. It does happen, with God's help.'

It was a cheering thought to go to bed on, and Sara fell asleep happily, hoping against hope that Miss Boote was right. But though the dream hadn't troubled her for years, that night she dreamed of Jess, and the tragedy, and it seemed to her that Jess was trying to tell her something, trying to tell her that she must keep on looking, because there was something she could do for Jess's little sister. And in the dream Jess came right up to Sara and whispered in her ear and Sara suddenly knew what it was Jess wanted and what she herself must do.

But when she woke in the early hours she could remember only the unhappiness on Jess's small, pale face, and a sense of loss.

Next morning Sara was late up, but despite this she was extremely cheerful. She sang as she washed and dressed and, in the kitchen, ate a hearty breakfast of porridge and toast.

'Who's left you a hundred quid?' her grandmother asked, cocking her head on one side. 'You sound happy this mornin', our Sara!'

'I am. Until last night, Gran, I felt so sorry for myself

you wouldn't believe. I told myself I was an unloved child, that my parents hadn't prepared me for real life, that I was a failure. I – I don't mind telling *you*, Gran, but I've set my heart on finding that Carbery baby and making sure she's all right, so the soup kitchen seemed a good place to start. I didn't see any sign of her, but somehow I'm sure I will, one of these days. And last night I met someone much worse off than myself, and she was cheerful, sensible . . . she counted blessings she didn't have, and was happy. So who am I to moan and grumble just because my parents didn't care for me much, and I don't have a job or any visible means of support?'

'I'm glad you feel like that, queen,' Mrs Prescott said rather drily, 'because I had bad news this mornin'. Your mother wrote. To be blunt, she's stopped my allowance.'

'Allowance? I didn't know she made you one, Gran. But why on earth has she stopped it? Not because I'm here, surely?'

'Oh no, she doesn't mention you. She says that Adolphus has lost a good deal of money from this coming off the Gold Standard, whatever that may mean, and can no longer afford some of his charities.'

Sara, who had been cutting herself another slice of bread, stopped short, the knife halfway through the loaf. 'She said *what*?'

'She said your father can no longer afford . . .'

'I heard what you said, I just couldn't believe . . . Gran, how dared she say such a thing! You, a charity, indeed! Oh, I'd like to make her eat her words!'

'Aye. A cold thing, charity can be, when what's given is given grudgingly. But after a few minutes' thought I realised your mam didn't mean nothing by it. She was simply saying to me what she had been saying to a good few others, I'd guess. I remember you said they'd dismissed the chauffeur . . .'

'Yes. Without a thought for him or his wife,' Sara said, bitterness returning at the thought of poor Robson on the street. 'The flat went with the job of course, but they wouldn't let them stay even though it's empty, now.'

'Well then, losing the little pension your father paid me won't put us on the streets, because so long as I can pay the rent we've a roof over our heads, and Miss Boote's money means we can pay that without too much effort,' Gran said reassuringly. 'But I won't lie to you, queen. We'll be in Queer Street if you don't get work quite soon. I'm very thankful you're here with me, though, for I doubt I could manage without some help.'

'Oh, Gran! Do you mind telling me what Father paid you?'

'Well, he used to pay me ten shillings, the same as my other pension, but he put it up to a guinea a week about four years ago. I was having a bit of a struggle so one day I put on me best things and got on a tram and visited your father in his offices. I said I didn't want to upset his apple cart, but me rent had gone up and I wasn't findin' it easy to manage. He doubled the money he gave me immediately and I thought he was very generous, but afterwards, I wondered if he thought I was about to blackmail him! Because I'd never called at his office before, and he seemed very anxious to get me out in good order, so to speak.'

'Oh, Gran, as if he could have thought such a thing! Then for the past four years you've had a total of thirty-one shillings; and you've been paying all your bills, your rent, your food, with that?' Sara said wonderingly. 'How on earth do you manage?'

'Very nicely, queen, up to now. The rent's eighteen and six a week, Miss Boote pays me eighteen shillings, I put a bit aside for Christmas, birthdays and so on, and that left me with well over a pound a week for food, coal, lamp oil, and all the other small household expenses. Oh, I managed very well, in fact. But losing a whole guinea . . . well, it's going to make things hard, very hard.'

'I don't think you can manage,' Sara said after some thought. 'Thanks to Miss Boote the rent's paid, but you have to feed her, and yourself, on rather less than ten bob a week. And what with coal, and lamp oil, and tram fares, you'll never do it. Oh, if only I'd got that job with the Ocean Accident! The money was very good – twenty-two bob a week, and luncheon vouchers!'

'Oh, I'll learn to manage on less, once I get used to it,' Gran said bracingly. 'After all, before Miss Boote came along I managed. Only I have to feed me lodger decent, and that *is* goin' to present a problem.'

'I'll get a job,' Sara said between gritted teeth. 'I'll get a job if it kills me, Gran!'

'Sshh! If you bounce about an' keep gigglin' we'll never see her.' Tad grabbed Polly's hand and squeezed it warningly. 'And I'm tellin' you, if she looks in our direction, just you duck down, Poll, or run like the divil . . . 'cos if it comes to gettin' out of here fast I'll leave you in the ha'penny place so I will!'

It was Christmas Eve and Tad and Polly were ghost-hunting in the ruins in Gardiners Lane.

No one went there, not after dark. Not even lovers, Tad had said authoritatively, and he should know, living next door to it as he did.

'In ten years' time our tenement will be a ruin just

like next door,' Tad was apt to boast. 'Sure and aren't the walls fallin' down already, and there's a tree growin' up through me bedroom, leaves an' all in summer, an' if you don't believe me I can show you so I can.'

Polly believed him. She had seen the tree, and the fungus, and admired both, but when she went back to her neat home and sat down to her tea – pink shrimps and bread and butter with apple pancakes for afters – she had burst inexplicably into tears.

'What's the matter, alanna?' Mammy had asked, concern in every line of her body as she bent over her daughter. 'Don't you like the nice pink shrimps? And there was me, thinkin' they were your favourites!'

'They are, they are,' Polly had wailed between sobs. 'And I don't have a tree growin' in me bedroom, nor a fungus the size of a nellyphant above me bed! Nor I don't go to bed hungry five nights out of six!'

And her mammy had crooned and cuddled her – and marched out of the house and round to Gardiners Lane and when she marched back she had Tad with her. Polly had got the impression that she had Tad by the metaphorical ear, and had probably fought a battle to get him at all.

'Here's Tad come to have tea wit' you, Polly me love,' she had said cheerfully, pushing Tad into a chair. 'He's never tasted pink shrimps you say, so I thought it would be nice if you shared 'em.'

But that had been ages ago; last summer. Now it was Christmas Eve and Polly and Tad were out to find the banshee.

Mrs Crumplin had heard the banshee time out of mind, she had told the children a couple of days before. She had heard her a-wailin' and a-shriekin' in the ruined houses and she'd told the father so she had and what had he done? Nothin', nothin' whatsoever, because he knew full well that if he came and sprinkled the holy water and exorcised her – if you could exorcise a banshee – then six months later, sure as sure, down he'd drop, stone dead!

'I don't believe in the banshee,' Polly had said stoutly, clutching Tad's hand. 'She's not a ghost, not really. My brother Niall says she's just superstitious nonsense.'

'Oh, aye? And since when's your brother Niall an expert?' Tad had said hotly. Polly suspected that he was quite proud of the banshee in the ruins next door and did not want cold water poured on the story. 'And if it wasn't the banshee we heard as I were walkin' you home last night, Polly O'Brady, what was it?'

'It was a cat,' Polly said accusingly. 'You *know* it was a cat, Tad, you *said* it was a cat. Or a dog, you said.'

'I didn't want to scare you,' Tad said rather unconvincingly. 'I didn't want you clutchin' me and squawkin' before me pals.'

So of course she had called him a big liar – and wasn't it God's truth? – and he'd denied it and told her that if she really didn't believe in the banshee, then how about a hunt through the ruins on Christmas Eve?

'It's one of the best nights in the year for ghosts,' he had said. 'So if you really don't fear such t'ings . . .'

And now here they were, on Christmas Eve, within a foot of the ruins, with a clear sky above them and a big moon shining and a frost making Polly's toes tingle.

'We'd best hide in where the front room was,' Tad said, taking her hand firmly in his. He pulled her in under the wobbly wooden door arch and ducked sideways. 'Here, crouch down, where the fireplace was, and wait . . . and don't you dare giggle!'

'I won't,' Polly assured him in a low voice. Truth to

tell, she had no desire to giggle. It was spooky in here, pitch dark but for the silver wash of the moonlight coming through the empty doorway. Indeed, when she glanced up at the house wall, which ended a dozen feet in the air, she half-expected to see the banshee, outlined against the moon, sitting on the wall and combing her long, draggly grey hair. But all she saw was the moon, the jagged outline of the wall, and a thin, bare tree-branch held supplicatingly out towards the moon's disc.

'You'd better not giggle, I'm tellin' ye,' Tod said. 'Are you scared?'

It would have been nice to have said that of course she was not scared since she knew the banshee didn't exist, but Polly felt she was in the wrong place for a whopping lie like that. Even if the banshee didn't exist the devil did, the father said so in church on a Sunday, and she had no desire for a creature such as that to suddenly manifest itself beside her and drag her off to hell for telling big lies.

'I am, so,' she admitted therefore. 'It's dark as the divil in here, Tad ... will we go out again? We'll see the banshee just as well outside.'

Tad put an arm round her and hugged her to him. He smelt faintly of dirt, of boiled potatoes and of young boy, but his hug was comforting. Polly, cuddling gratefully close, decided it was a nice smell so it was. It made her feel brave.

'There; is that better? Are you still afraid?'

'It's better, but I'm a bit afraid still,' Polly admitted. She did not want Tad to take his arm away and leave her cold and alone again. 'How long'll we have to wait before ...'

Even as she spoke they heard it. An unearthly moan, rising, rising, until it was a full and terrible caterwaul of grief and woe, uttered, Polly was sure, by no mortal mouth.

'Oh, God have mercy on us,' she squeaked, clutching Tad and trying to burrow into his ragged jacket. 'I want to go home, I want me mammy!'

'In a minute,' Tad hissed. 'We don't want to walk right into her, that's for sure. I don't want her throwin' her comb at me so's I die inside six months, indeed I don't.'

'Where is she, then?' Polly quavered. 'Oh, Tad, it's gettin' closer so it is – let's run home to your house!'

The wailing was indeed getting closer. Tad was beginning to answer her, to tell her that she was safe with him and they'd hang on where they were until the banshee had given up for the night and gone elsewhere, when there was the lightest of light thumps on the wall above them. Looking up, Polly very nearly screamed aloud, for she saw a pair of burning lights, an outline . . . and then she realised what it was. It was a big old cat, that was all – he must have been as scared by the banshee as Polly herself had been and was looking for human comfort.

'Oh, Tad, the poor cat . . . pussy, pussy, come here,' Polly coaxed, almost forgetting her own fright at the cat's abrupt arrival. 'Does the banshee like cats? Only if not, we'd better . . .'

The cat was outlined against the moon now, so that Polly saw the subsequent events quite clearly. The cat threw back its head and opened its mouth, and from its throat came the long, wailing note, the sobbing crescendo, the final, awful, yowl which Tad had so convincingly blamed on the banshee!

He must have known she'd guessed, though, for his embrace became imprisoning and Polly could feel him laughing right down through both the arms that held her. Furious, she bit and thumped until he let her go, then jumped to her feet.

'Tad Donoghue, you're a liar and a cheat! You *knew* that cat came here to make that noise, I bet you've watched it many a time from your bedroom, haven't you? Oh, you just wanted to scare me . . . I hate you, you're wicked, I – I hope you have a rotten Christmas, so I do, and a thin old New Year!'

She would have run out, left him, but he jumped to his feet and grabbed her arm, though he was still shaking with laughter.

'Polly, Polly, Polly! Sure an' I was only jokin' wit' you! I did know the cat yowled on the wall there, but we could've seen the old banshee, because Mrs Crumplin's heard her many a time, she says, an' there's no sayin' that she wouldn't have come anyway, tonight bein' Christmas Eve and all.'

Polly paused. He did have a point, she supposed. 'But you knew about the cat, you just wanted to scare me,' she said accusingly. 'That was a mean trick, Tad Donoghue.'

'It was,' Tad said, pretending to hang his head. 'And it's sorry I am, alanna, but I couldn't resist. Aw, come on, let's wait a bit longer.'

But Polly wouldn't. She was cold and though the terror had warmed her through very nicely, she could still hardly feel her feet.

'No, I'm headin' for home,' she said firmly, turning towards the gaping doorway.

'You're scared,' Tad said. 'You know she could be in one of the other ruins so you do, but you won't look, not little Miss Polly!'

'I will so,' Polly said at once. 'But I don't believe a word of it – remember that, Tad Donoghue!'

'Right, right. Let's have a look at the rest of the ruins,

then, and go home after that,' Tad said. 'Take my hand, then if either of us sees anything, we can drag the other one away.'

'If we see anything, we shan't need dragging,' Polly observed as they set off along Gardiners Lane, heading for the next ruined building. 'We'd be off like shot from a cannon. Though ghosts don't hurt you, do they – apart from the banshee, I mean?'

'Dunno. There's one down your way chucks things about,' Tad said. 'Polter-something. They move furniture and throw vases. And the banshee doesn't hurt you, exactly. It's only if she t'rows her comb at you . . .'

'You'll die within six months; I know,' Polly sighed. 'And why the old terror's got a comb, when everyone goes on about her draggly grey hair, all knots, is more than I can make out.'

'She's a woman, that's why. Women like to think they're beautiful even when they're not,' Tad said. 'I 'spec' the old banshee thinks all the fellers admire her, draggly hair an' all.'

They were laughing and kidding now, quite loudly, all thoughts of banshees and ghosts forgotten for the moment, at least. The second house was, furthermore, even more a ruin than the first. It was little more than half-walls, and in summer the grass and wild flowers ran riot over its fallen bricks. Now, the two children went over to it, climbed the lowest of the walls, and stared critically around them.

'Nothin' here. Nor anyone, either,' Tad said after a brief inspection. 'Oh, I've had enough of this, Poll. Let's go to your place. Your mammy might be roastin' chestnuts.'

'All right,' Polly agreed. She, too, was tired of the tricky moonlight and the cold. 'Which way'll we go?'

It was possible for two agile – and wicked – children

intent on taking a short cut between Gardiners Lane and Swift's Alley to scramble their way over walls and between tenement blocks, but tonight Polly decided she would rather go the long way round. Climbing a wall silvered by moonlight and jumping into the thick ink-black dark the other side meant one could end up with broken knees or worse.

'Let's go along Francis Street,' she said therefore. 'The stalls will be open till midnight – we might get a bargain.'

'With what?' Tad asked. 'Have you got any money, then?'

'Not a farden,' Polly assured him. 'I forgot. But someone might *give* us something they didn't want or couldn't sell. You never know. Besides, it'll be nice to have the gaslights; sort of warming.'

Tad agreed, so the two of them set off along the dark, deserted length of Gardiners Lane and presently emerged into the hustle and bustle of Francis Street, with the gaslights hissing and dispensing their strong white light on the vivid scene and the stallholders shouting their wares, wishing customers a merry Christmas and heckling passersby to buy their holly, mistletoe, oranges, wooden engines, rosy apples.

But the two children weren't on Francis Street long for they took the first left turn they reached and were soon in the lobby of the O'Bradys' tenement block.

'Come on up,' Polly urged Tad, groping across to the stairs, for the place was unlit and windowless, save for a tiny cracked glass pane in the door. 'If Mammy isn't roastin' nuts I'll get some pennies and we'll go and buy some.'

'Oh well, awright then,' Tad said with a reluctance which Polly knew very well was assumed. Poor Tad seldom had luxuries such as roasted chestnuts! 'Only I'd best not be long – me mammy may need me.'

Up the stairs they went but halfway up them someone opened a door on the landing above and light flooded out, golden lamplight, looking warm and inviting.

Polly paused, for someone was coming down the stairs towards them. She was a young girl of thirteen or fourteen with light-coloured hair, and she was smiling at them. It was a rather sweet smile, Polly thought, returning it.

'Your mammy must have heard us comin' up,' Tad said in Polly's ear. He passed her, then turned to grab her hand. 'Come on – you're tired, I'll give you a heave.'

'Mammy didn't hear us comin',' Polly observed scornfully. 'Don't you use your intelligence, Tad Donoghue? 'Tis the lady here . . . Mammy opened up to let her out.'

Tad looked up the stairs, then down them. 'Which lady?'

'Why, the one . . .' Polly stopped short. 'Sure and she passed us, Tad, and went on down. Don't say you didn't see her?'

'I did not. And nor did you, Polly O'Brady,' Tad said roundly. 'Because there was no lady, that's why, and we'd best hurry or your mammy will close the door and we'll be in the dark again.'

'But I *did* see her, truly I did, Tad,' Polly panted, hurrying up the stairs in her friend's wake. 'She was lookin' right at us. She had light-brown hair an' a raggedy shawl thing, and bare feet . . . and a lovely, friendly sort of smile.'

They reached the landing and Tad pushed Polly ahead of him into the O'Brady living room.

'Hello, Mrs O'Brady,' he said. 'It's a cold evening, out . . . you've had a visitor, have you?'

Mrs O'Brady had a big shovel in her hand; she had just withdrawn it from under the hot coals and the nuts smoked black and sweet on it. She turned to smile at the two of them, but shook her head in answer to Tad's question.

'Visitor? No, we've had no visitor. I heard you two talkin' as you came into the lobby, so I opened the door to give you some light on the stairs.' She turned to her sons, squatting on the hearthrug with hopeful eyes fixed on the chestnuts. 'Go and get some salt, Bevin,' she ordered. 'Salt is great wit' hot chestnuts.'

'Told you so,' Tad said triumphantly. 'There wasn't no woman, Polly, you imagined it.'

'Oh! Well, perhaps she came from one of the upper floors,' Polly suggested. 'She was only a girl, Mammy, thirteen or fourteen I suppose, and she had a raggedy shawl on, and bare feet. Or it may not have been a shawl.'

'Was it one of the poor unfortunates?' Mammy said, lifting nuts off the shovel and gasping as they burned her finger-ends. She handed them round to the boys, then loaded the shovel afresh and pushed it back into the coals. The girls she alluded to were country girls who had come to Dublin to work in the houses of the rich and become pregnant, usually by the master of the house. When they were turned out they had to sell their favours or starve, for they had no means of returning from whence they came and in any event, knew their parents would not have them back in such a condition. The people of the Dublin tenements felt great pity for such unfortunates, and helped them when they could and never blamed them for plying the only trade they knew. 'If one of those girls . . .' she paused delicately. 'If one of them had business in the block they might come in for a while, I suppose. It might have been one of them.'

'No, it wasn't an unfortunate,' Polly said at once. 'Sure an' don't I know most of 'em by sight? But this girl wasn't like that. I could tell. She wasn't old enough, I don't think.' Polly paused, uncertain how to convince. Could she say that the unfortunate girls were rarely that shabby, that dirty? And they didn't have calm, serene smiles. 'She was more like a sort of angel,' she said apologetically. 'I know she wasn't an angel of course, but she had that sort of look.'

Tad guffawed, but Polly's mammy gave her a curious glance. 'And you say she was thin and dirty, with a shawl round her shoulders and bare feet? Yet she had the face of an angel?'

Tad guffawed again and Polly's mammy gave him a handful of nuts so hot that he spilt them and had to scrabble about on the rug to pick them up. Polly gave the nuts a kick, scattering them still further. 'Hold your noise, you!' she said rudely. 'He told me the banshee was shoutin', Mammy, and it was just on old tom-cat.'

Her mother smiled. 'Want some nuts, alanna? Well, I can't answer your question because I don't know who the girl was, the poor darlin'. Eh, bare feet on such a night – Christmas Eve, too!'

'She wasn't cold,' Polly said, then looked surprised. Why was she so certain? No one person could ever judge the coldness or misery of another, surely she must know that?

'She was a ghost!' Tad shouted suddenly, then crackled the burnt shell off a nut and pushed it into Polly's indignantly opening mouth. 'G'wan, Poll, you wanted to see a ghost an' now you've seen one!'

Polly started to shake her head, quite prepared to

give Tad a thump for his mockery, but her mother put a hand on her, quieting her.

'Not a ghost; an angel,' she said quietly. 'A Christmas angel, who can't be seen the rest of the year, but becomes visible for a few moments on the eve of the Christ child's birth.' She dropped a kiss on her daughter's smooth brow. 'You're a very lucky girl, alanna,' she said lightly, but with an underlying seriousness which Polly could hear even if Tad could not. 'To see such a one. Good will come of it.'

'I've seen me guardian angel,' Polly said, awed. She knew it was true, too, truer than Tad's old banshee. 'She had a sweet face, Mammy.'

'Well, there you are then,' Mammy said, jiffling the shovel to make the nuts turn themselves over. 'More nuts, boys.'

And then, before Tad could scoff or Polly question, she turned the conversation to Christmas presents, to the goose which the baker on Francis Street was cooking for them, to the Mass which they would attend next morning. And she gave each child hot milk with a drop of spirit in it and told Tad he could sleep on the sofa if he wanted to stay the night. But he said he'd best be getting back since his mammy might need him, and made his escape.

Polly went off to bed glowing with expectation and happiness. She had seen her guardian angel, not many people could say that, and it was nearly Christmas Day!

Chapter Nine

The first Christmas that Sara spent at Snowdrop Street was like no other Christmas she had ever known. Despite her efforts she was not in a permanent job – not a proper one, that was. But at least she was earning money.

She had talked to Miss Boote as soon as she could about her chances of getting a job – any sort of job, because once the tiny allowance from the Cordwainers had been cut off, it was pointless trying to take Mr Esmond's advice about training. There was simply no money available for such a thing.

'I could pawn something, I suppose,' her grandmother had said, looking undecidedly around her neat living room. 'I've never done it before, but then I've never been desperate. Oh, queen, I feel so helpless! I'm too old to earn and that's a fact, and yet for you to take some dreadful little job with no prospects seems so wrong! There must be some way of getting enough money to see you through secretarial school – I wonder whether I might sell some bits and bobs?'

'You're pawning nothing and you're selling nothing,' Sara assured her grandmother firmly. 'There must be a way round it; I'm going to talk to Miss Boote as soon as she comes in tonight.'

Miss Boote, practical as ever, had a solution, of sorts.

'Evening classes,' she said firmly. 'Anyone can better theirselves at evening classes. And in the meantime, what's wrong wi' shop work?'

'It doesn't pay as well, does it?' Sara asked rather cautiously. She did not fancy standing behind a counter all day, but told herself that needs must. If it was all she could get then she would have to try shop work.

'It doesn't pay badly, not if you go for a saleslady in one of the big stores,' Miss Boote had assured her. 'And you've got the right accent, the right looks ... and they'll give you a sort of uniform – black dress and shoes, that sort of thing. I'm not sayin' it's ideal, but I am sayin' it's worth considering.'

She was right and Sara knew it, so she set about lowering her sights a little and six weeks before Christmas was taken on by Barringtons department store, in their glove and accessory department.

'It's sixteen shillings, which is very good for a beginner,' Sara told her grandmother excitedly as she came into the living room and stripped off her washleather gloves. 'I'll be handling some awfully pretty stuff, too ... and the other girl, Miss Warrender, seems really nice.'

Miss Warrender was nice, and so was the floor walker, Mr Bratby. He took Sara to lunch one day and told her she had the makings of a first-rate saleslady, and Miss Warrender and she giggled all afternoon about it.

'He'll be sneakin' up to you in the staff room and pinchin' your bum next,' Miss Warrender said. 'He's sweet on you, I can tell.'

'Oh, Miss Warrender, you're crazy. He's forty if he's a day and married with three kids,' Sara said. She felt so *young*, chattering to Miss Warrender, running to and fro at the customers' behest, being sent on errands by the senior staff. It was like being back at school again, with prefects and teachers telling you what to do and your friends to giggle with.

But it was too good to last. She had been minding her own business one icy morning in early December, cleaning the glass top and sides of the big display case, when she heard a young man addressing her fellow assistant. Men didn't frequent the glove department as a rule, so being only human, Sara turned round and looked.

Miss Warrender was serving a tall young man with dark hair, wearing a light-brown mackintosh and a darker brown trilby hat. From where she was standing it was difficult to see his face so Sara moved round as unobtrusively as she could and got behind the main counter once more. She was beginning to polish the glove-drawers whilst still concentrating on the customer, when a voice said, 'It's a pair of dark-brown gloves I'm searching for, Miss. Size . . . oh, I'm not too sure about size. My mama's hands are very slender, similar to . . .'

He glanced at Miss Warrender's hands, which could have been described as chunky, and then, helplessly, across at Sara, polishing away. He brightened. 'Similar to that young lady's, I suppose.'

It was Alan Hepworth – and he was looking at her hands, completely ignoring the rest of her. Sara bridled, then sighed and returned to her work. She should have expected it – she was a shop assistant, not a woman at all, now. But Mr Hepworth was talking.

' . . . If she wouldn't mind trying them on,' he was saying. 'Only my mama will be so disappointed if I get the wrong size – normally, she would come in herself but she's got a slight cold in the head . . .'

Later, Miss Warrender would say to Sara: 'Cold in the bleedin' 'ead my foot; 'e were buyin' them for 'is fancy woman!', but that was just her way. You had to have a laugh, she would have said, or you might as well cock your toes up.

Now, however, she was on duty. She turned to Sara. 'Miss Cordwainer, there's a gentleman here . . .'

Sara moved forward even as Mr Hepworth raised startled eyes to her face; the name had done it, of course.

'Sara? I can't believe it! Your mother told me you'd returned to Switzerland . . . oh, I suppose you're home for the holiday, but what on earth are you doing behind that counter?'

'Selling gloves,' Sara said rather tartly. Trust her mother to think up some fairy story that couldn't possibly hold water for long! She turned to her colleague. 'Yes, I'll try the gloves on for the gentleman, Miss Warrender.'

'Thanks, Miss Cordwainer.' Another customer loomed, a fat, peroxided lady with long scarlet nails and a discontented expression. 'I'd best attend to this lady, then, if you'll take over here.'

With no real choice, Sara picked up the dark-brown gloves lying in a welter of others on the counter.

'Are these the ones, sir? The colour is called dark chocolate . . . they're top of our range, very superior, soft leather.'

'Yes, I daresay,' Mr Hepworth said distractedly. He lowered his voice. 'What's going on, Sara?'

'I don't live at home any more,' Sara said patiently. 'I'm working for my living, as you can see, Mr Hepworth.' She slid the gloves on to her hands; they fitted beautifully and felt wonderfully warm and comfortable, too. She held out her gloved hands. 'See?'

'No, I don't,' Mr Hepworth said. 'Your parents must be distraught! You can't like being a shop girl for goodness' sake!'

'It's rather nice, actually,' Sara said, taking the gloves off with great care – she remembered the times at home that she had peeled her gloves off inside out and cast them on the nearest chair; but she hadn't known then that they cost a week's wages and more, and could split if handled roughly. 'It's a living, anyway. Shall I try these ones on now, sir?'

'Yes, yes, why not? Well, I don't understand it. Your mother definitely gave me to understand that you were in Switzerland. I asked when you'd be coming home and she said she didn't know. My mama said . . .' he paused and looked cautiously at Sara and it occurred to her that she didn't know Alan Hepworth at all, nor he her, despite the fact that they had kissed in the comfortable darkness of a taxi, and she had once spent a couple of hours in the cinema, fighting off his rather tentative advances.

'What did she say?' Sara said, however, suddenly curious. It might be interesting to find out whether her mother managed to fool women of her own age and station in life.

'Well, I don't know whether I ought to say this . . .'

'If you don't get on with it, I'll have to serve someone else,' Sara said impatiently, seeing a skinny, fashionable young woman approaching the counter. 'I can't turn down sales, Mr Hepworth, because I'm paid on a bonus system.'

'Oh! Look, I'll have the dark-brown ones, and would you try the lighter ones again, please?'

Sara pulled them on and Mr Hepworth leaned a little closer. 'My mama said that your mama was unnatural, and had no affection for you. She said it stuck out a mile, though I can't say I'd ever noticed.'

'Your mother was right,' Sara said. 'My mother doesn't like me very much. The chocolate-coloured

231

gloves are thirty shillings, sir, and the lighter ones twenty-eight and eleven.'

'I'll have both,' Mr Hepworth said recklessly, pulling out a fat wallet. 'Wait till my mother hears that I've found you – and where!'

Sara sold him the gloves, sending his bill and his bank note off in the little jar thing which whizzed it along to the cash desk where Miss Addington abstracted it and sent back his change and the receipted bill. Then she turned to the next customer and began serving her, for the department was getting busy.

Two days later, her mother turned up. She said nothing to Sara, she just went to the counter and began to try on gloves, ordering Miss Warrender to fetch the appropriate scarves and handbags to match her choice in an impatient, unpleasant way. She's heard I'm here and she's come to make sure, Sara thought. Good! Now she can see I'm not afraid of hard work and I'm coping without them!

An hour later, when her mother had placed an enormous order and gone on to gowns, the floor walker came over, rather diffidently, and told Sara she was wanted in the office.

'Wharrever for?' Miss Warrender asked. 'Lord, when we're so busy, too!'

Sara, whose feet were aching, thought that a trip to the office would be quite restful compared to running backwards and forwards, fetching gloves, scarves and leather handbags for impatient ladies who no sooner set eyes on them than they wanted something different. So she went at a walking pace through her own department, across lingerie, through gowns and up the stairs which led to Ye Olde Oake Restaurant and the offices.

The girl behind the big desk looked up at her, brows arching.

'Yes? Can I help you?'

'I'm Miss Cordwainer, from gloves,' Sara said. 'I've been told to come up to the offices.'

An expression of pity crossed the girl's face, but she said, 'Oh yes, Miss Cordwainer, it was Miss Whyte wanted to see you. Go straight through.'

Sara went to Miss Whyte's door, knocked and entered. Miss Whyte was a fat, elderly lady with grey hair piled up on her head and an anxious expression. She looked up when Sara entered the room but did not smile. She indicated a chair, however, then began rearranging some artificial red roses in a green glass vase, fiddling with them as though she did not want to meet her employee's eyes.

'Sit down, Miss Cordwainer. I'm afraid we've had a complaint.'

'A complaint?' Sara was completely bewildered. 'I'm sorry, Miss Whyte, I don't understand. We're awfully busy but I don't think I've left anyone waiting and I didn't take my lunch-hour today because of Miss Elgar from gowns being off . . .'

'It isn't that. Well, not precisely, anyway.' Miss Whyte cleared her throat uncomfortably. 'A – a customer said you'd been pert, Miss Cordwainer. She – she said that she wasn't prepared to shop at a place which employed pert young girls. And she's a very good customer.'

Sara sighed. Suddenly, she understood.

'It was my mother, wasn't it, Miss Whyte? Mrs Cordwainer. I imagine she told you she wouldn't shop here whilst you continued to employ me. Is that a good guess?'

Miss Whyte was as red as the artificial roses. Sara could see her trying to make sense of what had happened and failing; only seeing a good customer whistled down the wind because of some young girl she scarcely knew.

'No, it's not that at all . . . a customer said you'd been pert and we really can't have that sort of thing, as you realise. I'm sorry you take the attitude that the store is somehow to blame . . .'

'I don't!' Sara said, shocked at such a blatant twisting of the facts. 'I never said that, I just said that it was my mother who had complained. And it was, wasn't it, Miss Whyte?'

There was a moment's silence whilst Miss Whyte struggled with her conscience, and then she heaved a deep sigh.

'It was Mrs Cordwainer, yes. She told me she wanted you to return home, said you'd left after a quarrel . . .'

'It wasn't true, Miss Whyte. My mother turned me out.'

'Yes. I did wonder . . . but there's no doubt that your mother won't shop here whilst we employ you.'

'It's probably just an idle threat, Miss Whyte,' Sara said, even as her heart descended into her neat black court shoes. 'She's shopped here all her life, I can't see her changing to another store just because I work here.'

'Miss Cordwainer, have you any idea how much money your mother spends in this store each year?'

'A – a hundred pounds? Fifty?' Sara was guessing, but she had to say something. 'But no matter what she spends . . .'

'Last year she spent three hundred and fifty pounds fifteen shillings and sixpence. This year she has already spent four hundred and seventy-two pounds, nine shillings and elevenpence. These are vast sums, Miss Cordwainer, so it means that at a time when by and large customers are spending less and less, your mother is not someone we can afford to lose.'

'I see that,' Sara said, with increasing despair. 'But I have no money except for what I earn, I can't afford to lose my job!'

'Mrs Cordwainer spends many times your annual salary in our store, Miss Cordwainer,' Miss Whyte said gently. 'I'm sure, if you will just go home and tell her you're sorry for whatever took place, you will have no need either of your salary or your job with us. I shall be sorry to lose you – and so will gloves – but your mother's ultimatum has left us no choice.' She held out the pieces of paper she had been fiddling with. 'Your cards, Miss Cordwainer.'

Sara could not believe this was happening, yet she knew it was, knew that what her mother had done she had done quite deliberately, after some considerable thought. She had – she thought – cut the ground from under Sara's feet; now Sara would have to go home!

Sara turned towards the door; at least she now had some experience to talk about when applying for another job. Provided her mother could not run her to earth she might be safe at some other store. She had got the door half open when something occurred to her. She turned.

'One of these days, Miss Whyte, I shall probably be a married woman with a reasonable income at my command. If you think that I shall shop at the store which turned me away at a customer's spiteful whim, then you are very much mistaken.'

Miss Whyte sighed too; she looked very sorry, but Sara could tell that the older woman's resolve had not been shaken.

'I've no doubt you're right, my dear, but that, as you say, is in the future. The present is hard and getting harder. No one ever thought the Wall Street slump would continue to affect trade the way it has, and going off the Gold Standard does not seem to have helped at all. In fact, unless business looks up, there may not *be* a Barringtons of Liverpool by the time you're a married woman.'

'Well, I tried,' Sara said ruefully. 'Is it any use asking you if you'll give me a reference? Only I've worked hard for you, and I've learned a lot. It may be possible, if I have a good reference, to get another position.'

'Certainly. I'll write one myself and give it to you before you leave tonight,' Miss Whyte said. 'But for your own sake, Miss Cordwainer, I think you'd be well-advised to look for work outside the centre of the city.'

'You're probably right,' Sara said, not pretending to misunderstand the warning. 'I'm sorry about the threat, but I had to try. It's not only me, it's my grand-mother I have to think about. I'm living with her and she only has a tiny pension.'

Miss Whyte stood up and came round the desk. She patted Sara's shoulder, then shook her hand.

'I feel very bad, very bad,' she said heavily. 'It would not be true to say I had no choice, but your mother does have influence, Miss Cordwainer. She told me so. She said she would put it about that I'd encouraged you to flee from home, she'd see that I lost customers from all walks of life, but particularly those in more affluent circumstances. And she could do it, you know. Would do it, if I . . .'

'It's all right,' Sara said. 'You'll pay my wages at the end of the week, when I leave, I hope?'

'I'll see you're paid the full week, but you must leave tonight,' Miss Whyte said. 'Come to accounts with me and I'll see to it right away. No need to go back to gloves, except for your coat and bag, of course.'

When Sara got home and told her grandmother and

Miss Boote there had been a good deal of recrimination, but then Sara said that she would not be beaten, Miss Boote gave her three cheers, and Mrs Prescott went out to the kitchen and came back into the living room carrying a bottle of sherry.

'It's for medicinal purposes, usually, but I think we need cheering up before we begin to plan our campaign,' she announced. 'Miss Boote, you've been a good friend to my girl; what do you suggest?'

Miss Boote looked embarrassed.

'Well, there is one thing . . .' she began. 'But I scarcely like to suggest it.'

'Fire ahead,' Sara told her. 'Any idea has to be better than mine, because my head is quite empty.'

'All right, I will. You know I work in a bank on Walton Road, quite near the Salvation Army Barracks?'

'Yes, I know. Not that you talk about it much,' Sara said. 'Oh, Miss Boote, don't say there's a vacancy in your bank?'

'No; wish there were,' Miss Boote said gruffly. They were sitting round the fire and she stared steadfastly into the flames. Oh Lord, her idea must be so dreadful that she dare not face us whilst she talks about it, Sara told herself. Never mind, any job is a job, with Christmas coming up.

'The Co-op have got a big bakery just past the Barracks,' Miss Boote said at last. 'They're gettin' ready for the Christmas rush and lookin' for temporary staff. It pays well, because it's temporary,' she added. 'You'd get eighteen bob a week, mebbe more.'

'But I don't know anything about baking,' Sara said doubtfully. 'What good would I be to them?'

'Go along and find out,' her grandmother said decisively. 'Sara, my dear, if you can just get work for a few weeks it will tide you over until something more suitable comes up. I'm afraid you won't get anything but temporary work this near Christmas; for the most part firms are suited.'

So Sara went along to the Co-op bakery and got a job, though not the one she had imagined at all. She rushed into the house at six that evening, with her hat on the back of her head and one shoelace undone, to announce the moment she got through the doorway, 'I got it!'

'Wonderful,' her grandmother said, giving her a hug. 'What're you doin', flower?'

'You'll never guess! I'm delivering, on a big old bicycle with a huge metal carrier at the back and another at the front. Each carrier has a big basket on it . . . they asked if I could ride a bicycle so I said I could . . .'

'But you can't,' her grandmother observed, aghast. 'Oh, queen, you'll get killed! The roads are so danger-ous, all that traffic, horses, cabs, motor cars, trams . . .'

'I shan't get killed because I'll be careful, and the job starts on Monday, so I've time to learn on Miss Boote's machine,' Sara said. 'And you'll never guess – it's twenty-two and sixpence a week and they'll want me until mid-January – a whole lovely month!'

And then Christmas arrived, and when Miss Boote announced that she would be serving Christmas dinner to the poor, and Sara said she would like to go along, Mrs Prescott said that she might as well go too.

'I'm not a Salvationist, but I believe in giving practi-cal help where it's possible,' she said. 'And what's more practical than serving a Christmas dinner? Besides, it would be no pleasure for me, to eat alone.'

'We wouldn't let you do that, Gran,' Sara said at once. 'We'll be back mid-afternoon, won't we, Clarrie? We thought we'd eat our main meal in the evening.'

'Nevertheless, that would mean I'd be alone all day and I'm not standing for it,' Mrs Prescott said firmly. 'How I'm to get there I don't know, since the trams run a Sunday service on Christmas Day and I'm afraid me walkin' days are over, but I'll get there somehow. I might get a taxi; I don't think I could walk.'

'I'll give you a seater on my delivery bike, Gran,' Sara teased. She had learned to ride the machine just in time to start the job, and though she admitted privately to Gran that she and her loaves, cakes and puddings had several times met the hard ground, she had managed to dust both herself and her bakery goods off so that no one knew what had happened.

'And since they're going to sack me halfway through January I don't suppose it matters whether someone tells on me or not,' she had told her grandmother when describing her experiences on the bike. 'Besides, I haven't fallen off nearly so often lately. I'm getting quite good at it.'

The problem of getting about was becoming a very real worry for Mrs Prescott however, and though of course Sara knew a taxi was possible, fares would be a problem.

'It won't be long before she can't manage to step up to the tram,' Sara told Clarrie Boote, when her grandmother had gone early to bed one night. 'I suppose we could run to a taxi on Christmas Day, but what about other events?'

Miss Boote said little, but that evening she turned up with a wheelchair. It wasn't new and it wasn't smart, but it worked.

'There you are, Mrs P, your chariot,' Clarrie said proudly, bringing it round to the front door. 'All you need is someone to push you, and you're away!'

'Where did you get it?' Sara marvelled. 'You are so clever, Clarrie!'

'I asked Major Brett what happened to his old mother's chair, and he said we could have it. She died twelve months back,' Clarrie explained. 'They're ever so handy if your legs aren't so good.'

So Christmas Day dawned and the three women set off. Clarrie and Sara took it in turns to push the wheelchair, not bothering to bring the bicycle because Clarrie was in uniform and Sara wore her only decent garment, the grey flannel suit.

They had left early. Sara woke before seven and went downstairs to make tea for them all. After that she helped her grandmother to dress and then made breakfast. It was still only seven-thirty in the morning as they wended their way through the empty, echoing streets, talking softly so that they woke no one who still slumbered. The air was crisp, with a nip in it, the pavements and hedges rimed with frost, and as the darkness gradually gave way to dawn they drew gradually nearer their destination.

'Well, I never thought I'd be goin' off to work on Christmas Day,' Mrs Prescott said over her shoulder as her two companions swung along the pavements in the first pale dawn light. 'Apart from the years when your parents asked me over, Sara, I've had quiet Christmas Days, by and large. And aren't I looking forward to this one, with lots of people to talk to and lots of laughter!'

'You can be sure of that,' Clarrie said. 'We laugh a lot, in the Army.'

'It's funny,' Sara said, jumping the cracks in the paving stones as she walked along as though she was still eight years old and not eighteen. 'I seem to laugh much more now than I ever did at home – or at school, either, for that matter. I go to back doors and bakeries and retail outlets as they call them, and everyone's jolly, they all have a laugh with me, tease me about the bike, the way I ride it, even the way I talk. All sorts of things make them laugh – the way I pull my skirt over my knees, how I wobble all over the road when I glance over my shoulder, how I look in the rain when I'm as wet as a herring . . . It's amazing, really it is. Why, even when I worked in Barringtons, Miss Warrender and I would have a good old giggle.'

'Aye. They say religion's the opiate of the poor, but I think laughter is, meself,' Clarrie said. 'Belief in God is good, it gives you a glow and satisfaction, too. But laughter takes you right out of yourself, like.'

'In that case, I'm surprised the rich haven't taken out a patent on it and refused to allow others to indulge,' Gran said from her wheelchair. 'Still, let's be thankful that we can still laugh all we like. I'm sure I still do . . . especially now I've got you two young'uns using your legs for me!'

'They don't think much o' laughter, the rich,' Clarrie observed. 'Nor the powerful, for that matter. When did a teacher ever encourage her class to laugh? When a maid giggles, chances are she'll get give the order of the boot. And do you know why? Laughter puts folk down, that's why. It makes the pompous look foolish and the proud trip and fall.' She grinned at them. 'That's why I'm in favour of it,' she declared, 'and why you'll always hear laughter in the Army ranks. How are you feelin', Mrs Prescott? I never realised before how bumpy the pavements are!'

'It's the kerbs that are worst, I think, and cobbles, of course,' Sara said. 'Never mind, Gran, you're nearly there – just think of the Christmas dinner we're going to be preparing, and serving . . .'

'And eating,' Clarrie put in. 'There'll be plenty, there always is.'

'All right then, and eating. Just put up with the bumps for another few hundred yards and you'll be in sight of the Barracks!'

Grace and the black and white kitten had found each other on Christmas Eve, when the pubs were spilling their customers out on to the pavement with shouts of 'A merry Christmas!' and much laughter.

Grace had been hanging about outside the Mile End pub on Scotland Road, partly because she knew from experience that landlords – and customers – would sometimes feed starvelings such as herself and also because when the bakers in Scott's, which was next door to the pub, finished their night-shift they were generous with left-overs – buns that hadn't risen right, the 'corners' of the big, square fruit cakes they made and sold by the piece, farl which had gone stale and so on.

She was managing quite well, was Grace, mainly because she did her best, now, to keep away from her home. Nights were dangerous there, unless you worked it so Da was asleep before you went in, so Grace usually slept rough except when it was so bitterly cold that she was afraid to be out. But though her father was bad tempered in the morning quite often, he was rarely violent. Violence went with the drink, or with the frustration of having no money and therefore being unable to drink.

So there was Grace, bundled up in any number of old, torn rags, sitting in the corner of the pub doorway waiting for closing time. And here by the pub she stood a good chance of food. Men with a bellyful of beer would hand over the remains of their carry-out, or a few coppers, to a child such as herself provided she was around at the right time.

And the kitten, tiny, milky-eyed, clearly must have got the message, for it came round the corner, huge ears pricked, tiny, thin body poised for flight . . . and walked almost into Grace's arms.

'Hey, little feller,' Grace said. He was so soft and fluffy, so wide-eyed and wondering! 'Come an' see what I've got!'

He came. He purred astonishingly loudly, his whole body vibrating with the sound. He rubbed against her skinny ankles, then jumped on to her knee. He accepted a share of a nice, soft currant bun, then he stood on his hind legs, reached up . . . and licked her chin.

Grace had forgotten what it was like to know a flood of total, complete love. She kissed the kitten between its ears, on the end of its tiny pink nose, and then she tucked it up warm, against her body, protected from the wintry chill.

'You an' me, we's both strays, kitty,' she told it as it settled, purring, close to her heart. 'We'll be give some nice food presently, an' then we'll find somewhere snug to sleep, jest you an' me. An' tomorrer's Christmas Day – we'll go to the soup kitchen down the Scottie an' 'ave somethin' to eat . . . we'll 'ave a real good Christmas will us two.'

The kitten purred on and when the pubs were empty and Grace had pennies in her pocket and her collecting bag full of bits and bobs of food, the landlady, cleaning through, put her head out of the door.

'Here, chuck – you goin' home, now?'

Grace, wordless, shook her head, ready to run. But there was no need, on this occasion, at least.

'You're one of the Carbery kids, ain't you?' the landlady said. 'Eh, we've 'ad your ould feller in 'ere once or twice. Well, tomorrer's Christmas . . . no, by 'eck, it's today already! Come on, then, you can sleep in the bar. Just this once, mind.'

Grace needed no second invitation. She was over the threshold and curling up on one of the brass-studded leather benches before you could have said 'knife'.

'Thanks, missus,' she said, as the landlady closed the outer door and went through the room to return to her own quarters. 'We're ever so grateful.'

'We?' the landlady said, raising her brows. ''Oo's we when you're at 'ome?'

'Me an' me kitten; he's asleep in me jacket,' Grace said.

The landlady laughed.

'You're both welcome,' she said. 'I'll get you a breakfast tomorrer, set you up for the day, like.'

Grace thanked her again as the older woman left the room, closing the door gently behind her. Then she snuggled down. What a Christmas this would be – breakfast, a kitten . . . what more could she ask?

Brogan arrived in Liverpool from Crewe on just about the last train to run on Christmas Eve and went out for a drink with his father before settling down for the night. They went to the Queen's Arms on the corner of Salop Street and Walton Road and had an enjoyable time, for Brogan knew a number of the regulars there and they all wanted to know how he was going on.

He enjoyed telling his former workmates that he was now an engine driver, and he enjoyed the conviviality, the bright bunches of red-berried holly, the mistletoe bough nailed to the central beam, but all the while he talked, sang, listened to singing, his mind was elsewhere.

If Sara's still in Liverpool with her gran I'm going to

go round, tell her how I feel about her, ask if we can exchange letters, be friends again, he kept telling himself. This time I'll not sit like a tongue-tied fool in her gran's front parlour whilst she wonders what on earth's wrong with me. Tomorrow I'll go round there and give her the present I've bought and ask her to come for a bit of a walk with me.

And once we're out of the house and by ourselves, without her gran a-listening from the kitchen, I'll tell her about Polly, because when you love someone you don't have no secrets from each other, and I'll ask her to be ... well, I'll ask her if she'll be my girl.

'Brogan, you aren't singin', kiddo,' one of his erstwhile workmates said to him as the pub rocked to a spirited rendering of *Hark the Herald Angels*. 'What's up, then? Are ye too 'igh-nosed for the likes of us, now?'

'Cat's gorris tongue,' someone called out. 'Or 'e's in love; tek your pick.'

Brogan just smiled his slow, good-natured smile and sat back in his seat and thought of Sara. She was so pretty, so lively ... so very, very special! Of course she was a lady, but then wasn't his mammy a lady, too? Not rich nor important, but a lady, nevertheless. So there was no harm in him at least asking Sara ...

'Come on, son, you must be wore out,' his father said at length, getting to his feet. 'Ah, here come them Army lasses ... let's be on our way.'

'What Army lasses?' Brogan said as he and his father pushed their way through the crowds of revellers towards the open door. 'Do you not like them, Daddy?'

'They're harmless enough; they take their magazine, the *War Cry*, round the pubs and use the money for the poor,' Peader shouted above the confused babble of sounds around them. 'See them, shaking their tins?

They'll be making a Christmas dinner for them as wouldn't get one otherwise, so I'll pay me whack as we pass. Come on, lad, you're asleep on your feet and we must be up for early Mass tomorrow.'

Brogan looked at the bonnets bobbing along through the crowd of drinkers and grinned. 'Oh, *that* army! I'll put a copper or two in the tin as well if I can get near enough.'

But he couldn't reach the tin so he handed his loose change to the nearest drinker and had the satisfaction of hearing it going from hand to hand, hearing a soft, sweet voice raised in thanks as the money clattered into her tin.

'We don't want the paper, Miss,' Peader roared above the din. 'It's a contribution, that's all.'

'God bless you, friend,' came back the answer, and then they were out of the pub, the doors swinging to behind them, and under the frosty stars.

'We'll not be up too early tomorrow,' Peader remarked as he unlocked the front door and swung it wide. 'Eight o'clock Mass is early enough, I fancy. We'll go to St Mary's; it's not far.'

Brogan agreed; he would have agreed to anything which meant that he could get to Snowdrop Street sooner.

'You'll forgive me, Daddy, if I leave you, in the morning?' he said as they climbed into their beds, for Peader had borrowed a folding bed for his son's brief stay. 'Only I'd like to go round and see a friend for an hour or two. I'll be back for me dinner.'

'Fine,' Peader said. 'I'll have a crack wit' me pal Barney up the road. Or I might give a hand wit' the dinner.'

His landlady, Mrs Burt, was a friendly soul who encouraged her lodger to come into the kitchen and 'potter about', as she put it. Peader, a domestically minded man, enjoyed this very much better than a more formal lodger-landlady relationship and agreed with his son that good lodgings could make all the difference.

So, satisfied that his father would be happily occupied whilst he himself went on his visit, Brogan very soon settled down to sleep.

Next morning he awoke with a glow of anticipation such as he had not experienced since he was a child. He was going to see Sara, and this time he would tell her what was on his mind and not sit with his mouth open and no words coming out.

He went to Mass with his father and afterwards they exchanged small gifts and ate a hearty breakfast – bacon and egg, fried bread and a good deal of toast and marmalade. Mrs Burt then set Peader to cleaning sprouts, sitting on a stool in the doorway and chatting to his friend Barney, who had popped in, he said, to wish everyone the compliments of the season.

'Dinner's at one o'clock, no later,' Mrs Burt called jovially after Brogan's disappearing back, and Brogan shouted that he'd not be late and continued to stride purposefully down the road.

It was a sharp morning but the sun was out. Brogan whistled as he walked. He'd enjoyed his breakfast and he was looking forward to his dinner, but the best part of the day was almost upon him.

Sara!

He reached Snowdrop Street and felt his heartbeat increase. What would she be doing? Cooking dinner, with a smut of flour on one cheek and her hair curling in damp tendrils on her cheeks because of the heat from the fire? Or sitting before the fire with her gran, opening a present, or . . . or . . .

He had reached number three. He hesitated for a delicious second, then knocked.

A moment later he knocked again, fear replacing the anticipation in his heart. Where on earth was she? She would have gone to church by now, surely, and come back to prepare the dinner? But there was no sound in the house and when he peered through the front window the fire was either damped down or out, he could not tell which.

He was about to knock again when the front door of the next house opened and a young woman in her early twenties appeared on the doorstep.

'Mornin',' Brogan said politely, touching his cap. 'Can you be tellin' me what's happened to the ladies of this house? I've come round to wish them the compliments of the season but I've had no answer.'

'I 'eard you knock, so I thought I'd best come an' tell you they've gone out,' the girl said. 'Went off ever so early, all three of them.'

'Three?' Brogan said questioningly, his heart doing a nose-dive down into his boots. 'But I thought . . .'

'Oh, aye, but there's three of 'em livin' there now, you know. There's Mrs Prescott, Sara, who's Mrs P's granddaughter, and this Boote person.'

'Boote? Who's he?'

'Boote is Army – cor, I made a joke – an army boot,' the girl said, grinning to herself. 'Me mam said that's where they've gone, to the Barracks or whatever they calls it. I ask you, on Christmas Day – what a place to go for your dinner! Oh, that Boote . . . the two of you ain't met, then?'

'No,' Brogan muttered. 'No, we've not met.'

'Oh. Well, Sara's very thick wi' the Boote, I don't

mind tellin' you. Off they go, the two of 'em, on bikes during the week and on foot at weekends, 'eads together, laughin', talkin' all sorts. Me mam says it's nice, but I ain't so sure. We're all good Catholics in this street, we've none of us 'ad no time for the Army. Still, there you are, it's young Sara's choice, ain't it?'

'Y-yes, I suppose . . .' Brogan stammered. 'Sara's really fond of this Boote, then?'

'Oh, aye, rare fond,' the girl confirmed. 'They'll be back teatime, though, if you'd like to come round later. All three of 'em, mind.'

'Thanks,' Brogan said. He turned away. 'Thanks very much. I'll come back later, then.'

But as he made his lonely way back across the streets to Walton Road, he knew he would not be back later. There was no point. He would not go back again.

By the time mid-January arrived Sara was convinced she would never get another job which was as much fun as that of a bread-delivery girl. But she knew she must work at something, so when Miss Boote told her that there was a vacancy in the laundry, she applied.

The laundry was not a particularly pleasant place. When she went for the interview Sara had to cross the main washing room where row upon row of immense earthenware sinks were filled with steaming hot water. Women, in suds to their elbows, stood in front of the sinks, beating the washing with dolly-pegs. When they thought the sheets were clean they would hook them out of the hot water with wooden tongs, dump them on the slimy wooden draining boards whilst they drained off a bit, and then carry them over to the opposite side of the room, where the rinsing was done in different sinks.

The women in this room were mostly in their middle

years so far as Sara could judge; the younger girls were employed in the ironing room and in the packing department, where the job vacancy was. The clerk who had brought Sara across for her interview explained that here you had to be very smart because every garment, particularly the shirts, had to be folded in a special way and pinned, too, so that even the sometimes rough handling of the delivery staff would not unfold them.

'What matters is that when the customer unfolds the shirt, the collar and the dickie part are uncreased, and the cuffs, too,' the clerk said. 'Remember that when you do the test.'

'I will; did you say delivery staff?' Sara said, immediately interested. 'I've been doing delivery for the Co-op bakery. Only over Christmas, of course,' she added truthfully.

'We use vans, and boys,' the clerk said. 'But our packers is all women. He smiled at Sara. 'Packing ain't so bad, the gals seem to like it awright.'

The supervisor who conducted Sara's interview was a sour-looking spinster with sharp eyes behind tiny gold spectacles. She knew Sara wasn't like most of the girls who worked in the laundry, Sara guessed, but could not quite decide precisely why that was. So she sent her down to the packing room for a test to see whether she was what she termed 'neat-fingered' and, forewarned by the clerk, Sara made a good attempt at the folding of two shirts, two enormous sheets and a pile of handkerchiefs.

'You'll do; start Monday,' the supervisor said almost grudgingly. 'Be here by eight o'clock sharp.'

'I will,' Sara said. 'You didn't mention the salary . . .'

'The wage,' the supervisor corrected. 'It's paid weekly, on a Saturday night, and it's ten shillin' a week for the first three month, risin' to fourteen shillin' and sixpence if you give satisfaction an' remain with us.'

'I see. Thank you very much,' Sara said, thinking that whilst ten shillings a week was dreadful, fourteen and six was not to be sneezed at. She turned to leave the office, hoping against hope that she would be able to find her way back to the main gate, for the laundry was immense. It included a huge courtyard criss-crossed with rope clothes lines, for in the bad old days the clothes had been hung outside, and a modern drying room where blasts of hot air from the furnace which heated the water dried the clothes in a surprisingly short space of time.

'You'll get your uniform on Monday . . . best be here by seven-thirty, so's you're ready for work by eight,' the supervisor said, stopping her in her tracks just as she reached the door. 'Did you see the uniform?'

It was the ugliest uniform imaginable, Sara thought sadly, but there you were. What was that quotation? *Better a dinner of herbs where love is* . . . Well, in her case it was better an ugly uniform and hard work where love was than coldness and a beautiful home.

Not that she expected to find much love in the laundry! The supervisor did not look the sort of woman who enjoyed much – probably her chief enjoyment, in fact, would come from bawling out those under her. No, the love would be provided by Gran, and for friendship and a sense of purpose, there was Clarrie Boote and the Army.

'I'll send for a clerk to show you out,' the supervisor said sourly as Sara's hand began to turn the door-knob. She walked over to the door, pushed past Sara and called out to the young man who had accompanied Sara across to the offices earlier. 'Mr Brown, take this person to the main gate.'

'No *please* from the old bat, you notice,' Mr Brown said ruefully as he accompanied her. He was a young man of about Sara's own age with red hair, freckles and a decided squint for which he wore large tortoiseshell-framed glasses. 'Did she introduce herself? Thought not, that's like the old bat. She's Miss Bateman, actually . . . the old bat to you and me now, Miss. And I'm Peter Brown – Pete to me pals.'

'I'm Sara,' Sara said rather shyly. She doubted that she would have much to do with someone as important as a clerk, though. Miss Bateman had made it pretty plain that packers were the lowest of the low. 'Will I work directly under Miss Bateman, Mr Brown?'

'You'll see 'er from time to time, but she ain't in the packin' room,' Mr Brown said reassuringly. 'Miss Todd is over you . . . she's awright is Miss Todd.'

Sara worked hard at the laundry for three months, from mid-January to mid-April. She found the work tiring and exacting – at least on her delivery bicycle she had been able to sit down on the saddle as she made her way from one part of the city to another – but she soon discovered that whilst her hands were busy her mind could be anywhere. Dreaming, in fact, made the job bearable. And also the fact that, after three months, her wages would considerably increase. Sara wasn't greedy by any means, but she found it very hard to manage on what the laundry paid her.

'It's not wharr I wanted for you, queen,' her grandmother had said when she returned on Saturday night after her first week, 'but I can't deny the money's a help. What are you doin' this evenin'?'

'I'm going along to the Barracks, with Clarrie. I'm joining the Songster Brigade and we're having a rehearsal. Remember Clarrie saying that Miss Gotts was in hospital and too ill to take part in fund raising and so on any more? She's been most awfully kind to me, Gran. Clarrie and I visited her in the Stanley last night and she's given me her uniform. We're roughly the same size and she said, if I could make use of it . . .'

'Oh, flower, does that mean you're a Salvationist, now?' Mrs Prescott said, looking distressed. 'But you've always gone to church!'

'I went to church because my parents took me, and when I moved in with you I went to chapel, because that was where you went. But I'm going to the Barracks for myself,' Sara said gently. 'I've never seen the point in a religion which simply paid lip-service to fairness and goodness. The Army don't do that, Gran. They work very hard for what they believe, and they sing hard too, and laugh hard!'

'Yes, I remember. I enjoyed my Christmas Day more than I've done for years,' Mrs Prescott admitted, a smile curling her lips. 'That Major . . . he'd ha' made a cat laugh!'

'I know. I love going to the services as well as to the singing,' Sara said. 'Why don't you come along sometimes, Gran?'

'Do you know, I believe I will?' Mrs Prescott said slowly. 'What was it somebody said? *Why should the devil have all the good tunes?*' She chuckled. 'And why should the stuffy, self-satisfied upper classes, who put money into a collecting tin and think that's sufficient, get all the best congregations? Yes, I'll come along to the Barracks with you on Sunday, see what I think of a proper service.'

That had been in January. Now it was April, and Sara, who was now an extremely quick packer, had been told to call at the office on her way home, to see Miss Bateman.

'My three months is up, so I should get a pay-rise,' she said excitedly to Liz, the girl who worked next to her on the packing bench. 'I could do with a few bob more. Gran and Clarrie and I manage all right, but it's by the skin of our teeth sometimes.'

'You *should* gerrit,' Liz said rather cautiously. 'But the old bat's mean as 'ell's 'ot, chuck. If she can see a way to get out of payin' you she'll grab it, I tell you straight.'

'I'm fast, I'm tidy and I've never arrived late or left early; let her find fault if she dare,' Sara said at once. 'What's more, I've gone to marking without a single moan when we're ahead with our work in here. And no one in their senses can stand marking.'

Marking was done in a small, hot room by a team of girls with special indelible pencils and reels of tape. On sheets and towels the customers' surnames and their laundry number were marked on the actual article, but on clothing a tape would be made and then stitched in where it would not be noticed. On the tail of a shirt, the hem of a nightgown, the waistband of pyjama trousers. Sara was no seamstress and very much disliked the pernickety, fiddly business of sewing on the tapes, though she thought the writing part was rather fun.

But it was the position of the marking room which made it so unpopular. It was right up against the offices, and Miss Bateman was forever popping in and criticising one's work, one's handwriting, the positioning of the tapes . . . Sara shuddered at the thought of being within reach of Miss Bateman whenever she was sent through there.

'You shouldn't write so nice and neat. You should cultivate sweaty 'ands, like I done. She never axed me to mark but once,' Liz said, her hands continuing to smooth and fold as she talked. 'Still, it's better than bein' sent to iron shirts what've been starched, I can tell you.'

When they were short in ironing Liz was often called for and though she grumbled, she took a pride in her work. Sara laughed at her.

'Oh, you! You shouldn't iron so beautifully, then. If you'd got any sense you'd rest the iron on a shirt-tail a moment too long, or turn cuffs under instead of over.'

'Yes, well. The money's not bad,' Liz said. 'Eh, look at the clock – we'll be 'eadin' 'ome in twenty minutes.'

'Via the offices,' Sara said. 'Come with me, Liz! I'll be really upset if the old bat tries to deny me that pay-rise.'

And half an hour later, when she came out of the supervisor's office, she was as upset as she had anticipated.

'The rise? Oh yes, I can have the rise. If I move to marking full-time,' she said furiously, her eyes big and shiny with unshed tears. 'So I said I'd rather stay in packing if she pleased and she said very well, but I'd have to work another three months on my present wages. Oh, Liz, and Gran and I have talked about what we'd do with the extra money . . . I thought I'd do an evening class, learn shorthand and typing.'

'Never mind; I dunno a single gal as gorra rise after three months,' Liz said consolingly as they walked down to the gate. 'She never lets anyone gerraway wi' that three months business, it's always six.'

'Hmm. Well, one of these days I'll find something else, something which pays more money for shorter hours,' Sara said darkly. 'And then won't I just tell her what to do with her job!'

Chapter Ten

June 1932

'Are you excited? I'm the most excited I ever was,' Polly said, stroking her mammy's dark curls. It was a fine June evening and having put young Ivan, protesting vigorously, to bed, the two females of the family were wedged into the windowseat of their living room, chatting quietly and occasionally turning to stare down at the other members of the family, indulging in a game of hurley in the street below.

'I believe you've mentioned that you're excited over the "do", if you can call a celebration of Mass at the Eucharistic Congress a "do", a grush o' times already today,' Mammy said drily. 'You've even worked Ivan up, and he a babe of three! He shouted at me when I put him into his bed that it weren't fair; he was too young for to join in the game of hurley and nor he couldn't go to the Mass tomorrow, and wasn't Phoenix Park his favourite place, now?'

'I'd have been down there too, so I would, playin' hurley wit' the fellers, only I'm to stay pure for the Mass tomorrow,' Polly observed, turning to look out of the window and bringing a snort of amusement from her mammy's lips. 'What's so funny, Mammy? You can't stay pure *and* play hurley with the boys, can you?'

'I don't think your purity would be affected by a game of hurley,' Mammy said. 'But never mind, I won't have you out there now, tirin' yourself out and your big day tomorrow. Come on now, tell me the rest.'

'Well, Sister says if we've not got white veils sure and wouldn't a piece of butter muslin do the trick fine? And we're to assemble by the Wellington monument at an ungodly hour . . . only she didn't say that, Tad said that . . . and we'll all be marched to our places and all the children in the whole of Ireland will be there, you betcha!'

'Don't talk American slang,' Mammy said disapprovingly. 'Or I'll stop you going to the tuppenny rush so I will. There's a lot of rubbish shown to kids these days, I know it.'

'You don't, because you never come to the fillums,' Polly said, rubbing her head against her mother's neck like a small, affectionate cat. 'I'm quite tired; am I all ready for tomorrow, Mammy? For the biggest day so far in me whole life?'

'You've got your veil, and your white dress, white shoes, white ribbon,' Mammy said, counting the items off on her fingers. 'Did the sister say to take your dinner or a drink? If all the children in Ireland are crammed into Phoenix Park won't you need a bite and a sup?'

'Sister said not to drink too much or we'd want to go, and sure no one would think of such a thing wit' all the holy fathers around,' Polly observed. 'But we can take a little bottle if we like.'

'To go into?' Mammy said, then laughed apologetically; her daughter's outraged glance told her she had overstepped the mark. 'No, of course not, how foolish I'm bein'. The sister means you to wet your whistle with cold tea when the Mass is over.'

'That's right,' Polly said sleepily. 'Will I go to bed

now, Mammy? Only I'm after callin' for Aideen before 'tis light, tomorrow mornin'.'

'Poor babe! Yes, all right. I'll come and tuck you up.'

'I'm not a babe, I'm eight,' Polly said, climbing down from the windowseat and knuckling her eyes with both fists. 'If tomorrow's me big day, and Aideen's big day, and Tad's big day, is it the biggest day in the whole world for children everywhere?'

'Well, no, because they aren't all going to a children's Mass in Phoenix Park, to see all the papal dignitaries,' Mammy said. 'Now come along, into bed wit' you and I'll bring you a hot drink. You'll sleep better and you won't need too much drink in the mornin'.'

'All right. Mammy, I wish I could stand near Tad tomorrow. But they're puttin' the boys one side an' the girls the other, Sister says it's only right. And besides, Tad's at the National School now and I'm at the Convent, and the nuns don't think we should mix even wit' the girls at the National,' Polly said drowsily. 'I'd sooner stand wit' Tad, Mammy.'

'What about Aideen? You wouldn't let Aideen stand all alone, would you, alanna?'

'No-oo, she could stand on me other side,' Polly observed. 'I'm so excited, Mammy, that I'll never sleep a wink all night; you do know that? Everyone in my class is so excited they won't sleep a wink, not a wink!'

'Sure, you won't sleep a wink,' Mammy said soothingly. And when she came back and Polly was sound asleep she only smiled, and drank the hot drink herself. But she did wonder, as she got ready for bed, whether it was right of her to pay out money to have Polly convent-educated, when the boys all went to the National School.

But a wee girl's different, she told herself resolutely as she climbed into bed beside her sleeping daughter.

Sure and haven't I always known she was a special child, God-given, so should have extra special care taken over her? Besides, ever since Polly began to talk about her guardian angel I've known that her sister, the one Brogan told me about, was still watching over her precious one. I wouldn't like to let that little girl down. And it's fine teachin' they get at the Convent, a grand education. Polly will turn out a real little lady so she will and that's what we all want.

Dawn breaks early in June and Polly was up in time to see the first light greying the sky. Mammy woke her, speaking low, stroking her face.

'Polly, me love, you'd best get up now. Aideen's mammy will be wakin' her, and Tad'll be stirrin', and you don't want to be last, do you?'

Polly came wide awake on the instant, eyes round, feet feeling for the rug.

'Has mornin' come, then? Oh, where's me white dress? I mustn't be late, I'd never forgive meself . . . hold on . . . is me bottle of cold tea ready? Sister says cold tea is good for us. Where's me veil? I need pins . . . oh, I haven't washed . . . I haven't brushed me hair . . . me teeth . . . oh janey, I'm in a state so I am!'

'Calm down, alanna,' Mammy said, laughing. 'Just do things one at a time, like you usually do – I've called you before the boys because you've got more to do. They're wearin' their best things, sure they are, but that doesn't mean white veils an' that. Now first, wash. The fire's lit and the water's warmin' in the kettle. Then clean your teeth, then brush your hair. I'll fix the veil and put a ribbon in presently. Now stop *worryin'*, for you're in good time, you won't be late. I'm sure Aideen isn't even up yet, and as for Tad, he'll be like

Bevin and Donal, he'll leave everything to the last moment. He'll still be snorin', I daresay.'

'Oh, but it's different for boys; boys don't care,' Polly said, flapping barefoot through into the kitchen and hopping with impatience whilst her mother took the kettle off the fire, poured hot water into a bowl and stood the bowl on the side table. 'And anyway, you know what Tad's mam and dad are like.'

'I do,' her mother said, fetching a clean piece of towel from the slatted shelf beside the fire. 'He'll get himself up and no fuss, either.'

'If he comes,' Polly said rather bitterly. 'He was sayin', after school yesterday, that wit' a million children there no one 'ud notice one feller less. I told him I'd kill him and never, never marry him if he missed a chance to clear out his immortal soul, but you know Tad.'

'I daresay his immortal soul will survive uncleared,' Mammy said, smiling and bending down to give the fire a poke. 'You're a bit young to be considerin' marriage, though, alanna.' She straightened, a hand to the small of her back, then took a piece of soap off the mantel and handed it to Polly . . . 'Wash well now, behind the ears an' all remember, for wouldn't you feel bad if the holy father thought to himself, *there's spuds that child could grow behind her little lug-holes?*'

Polly, washing, giggled. 'If he wants to see where spuds could grow he'd do better on the other side of the Park, where the boys are. There!'

'What d'you mean, *there*? If you think you're clean, Polly O'Brady . . .'

'Well, you do me nails, then,' Polly said grandly, holding out a small white hand whose black-rimmed nails made her mother moan beneath her breath. 'Sure an' I don't know how me nails do it when I keep the rest of me hands spicky-clean. Mammy, I am goin' to marry Tad, one day. We've agreed.'

'Oh well, if you've agreed, there isn't a thing I can say,' her mother said placidly. She began work on Polly's nails, using a sharpened matchstick. 'You could grow spuds in the stuff I'm gettin' out from here, young lady, I tell you! What on earth have you been doin wit' yourself?'

'Playin', mostly,' Polly said. 'Hurry, Mammy, hurry, I've not got me white dress on yet nor I haven't brushed out me hair nor put me veil on . . . I'll be late, I know I will!'

Polly trailed home from Phoenix Park later that day, head in the clouds, one hand firmly grasped by Mammy, the other by Bevin, for the whole of Ireland, it seemed, had congregated in the park that day and it would have been all too easy to get separated.

The older boys had made their own way home and because of the vast numbers Polly had been unable to find Tad, but Mammy, with Ivan in her arms, had stayed as close to the crowd of children as she could get and had pounced on Polly and Bevin the moment the service was over. Now they were making their way out of the park as fast as they could, the children, at any rate, eager to get fed and watered, for a hard biscuit and a sip of cold tea had been no substitute for a proper meal.

'Did ye see God, Polly? I saw 'm,' Ivan remarked as they made their slow way across the seemingly endless grass. 'Big an' white he was, wit' gold hair like yours, Poll. He was floatin' on a cloud smilin' an' beamin' down on all the pretty lickle girls an' the smart chisellers.'

Polly sighed impatiently. 'What an eejit you are, Ivan

O'Brady! You only see God when you die an' go to heaven. If you saw somethin' now 'twas an angel so it was.'

'Oh,' said Ivan, considering this. 'Well, I seed an angel, then. Did you see 'um, Polly?'

'I seen me own guardian angel,' Polly said loftily. She did not intend to be bettered in holiness by a child of three! 'More than once I've seen her. She takes good care of me, so she does.'

'A girl angel? There ain't no such thing as a girl angel,' Bevin put in loftily. 'Angels are big, hefty fellers wit' t'umpin' great wings. You wouldn't catch a puny weak girl carryin' wings like that – she'd founder at the first flap.'

'My guardian angel doesn't have wings,' Polly said at once, ruffling up like an angry turkey cock. 'My guardian angel doesn't need wings, she's got a shawl thing . . . she spreads it out like this . . .' she held out the skirts of her white confirmation dress, ' . . . and she can go anywhere in no time at all at all. She's me friend, my angel.'

'Oh, yeah? She sounds a quare ould wan to me,' Bevin said nastily. Holiness in such enormous quantities, Polly concluded, had been a bit much for her older brother. 'What's her name, then, Poll, if you're such pals?'

'Jess,' Polly said without a second's hesitation. Her mother stopped short so suddenly that Polly, lagging behind, bumped into the backs of her legs. 'That's her name, Jess.'

'Angels aren't called Jess,' the irrepressible Bevin said jeeringly. 'Are they, Mammy? Angels are called Gabriel, or – or Saint Something, not just Jess.'

'Don't argue about such things, Bev,' Mammy said, beginning to walk forward again. 'Anyone want to pop in to the chipper on our way home? I'll stand you all one and ones, for a treat.'

And with the happy prospect of a fish and chip supper, angels were forgotten, for the moment at least.

Sara did not have the pleasure of telling Miss Bateman what to do with her job quite as soon as she would have liked, but the opportunity came at last, though not before Sara had received the promised pay-rise.

As Miss Bateman had grudgingly promised, in July Sara's money was increased to fourteen and sixpence and things became a little easier.

'We're fine now, for the summer, but when winter comes we'll be scrapin' the bottom of the barrel again,' Gran said. 'Still, you've done awful well, Sara love. There's not many as bring in fourteen and six every Friday.'

Sara agreed that she was lucky, but she didn't feel it. She felt ill-used. She had tried and tried to get another job with absolutely no success. She had started evening classes but no employer wanted a young woman of nineteen who had only experienced evening classes and shop work. They could not offer her the sort of money they would offer a beginner, kind employer after kind employer told her. When you've got some office experience under your belt . . .

Yet when her chance came she did not, at first, recognise it.

She was at the Barracks, taking a Sunday school class because Miss Boote was otherwise engaged. It was a large class and the children were on their school holidays so they were bored, weary of the bad weather – it had rained all week – and consequently difficult to handle. They were poor children from the many slums in the area, but they were by no means lacking in spirit, or indeed, in inventive devilry, and Sara had already been sworn at and had a small offender standing in the corner from whence, whenever he thought her attention was elsewhere, he would turn round for a second, tongue hanging out like a Dix's carpet, and then turn back to face the wall once more, shaking with laughter.

'Have you finished your silent reading? Good, then we'll play a game,' Sara said presently, struck by a brainwave. 'It's a sort of hide and seek, only you won't have to leave this room. I used to play it when I was your age.' She took a piece of chalk and went over to the small blackboard, then after some thought, wrote the word 'Barracks' on the board.

'See that word? Well, it says "Barracks", doesn't it? But hiding inside that eight-letter word there are others, and you must find them and tell me how many words you think there are. The winner gets to choose the next long word. Do you understand?'

They understood and looked bored. They don't want to stretch their brains, Sara thought despairingly, they want to stretch their legs and their arms – they want a *real* game. But it's raining cats and dogs out there, I can't possibly let them play real hide and seek – this will have to do.

'Good. Then everyone who wins a round gets to write the next word on the board, and gets some dolly mixtures. I'll have to buy them on my way home, but . . . no, I've a better idea. The first one of you to get five points can run a message for me, down to Demarco's, and buy me the sweeties. Now come on, how many little words can you see in "Barracks"?'

A hand went up; slowly.

'Yes, Mark?'

'I see two, Miss.'

Another hand promptly began to wave.

'Three Miss, three if you count the "s" as one!'

'All right, Albert, give us your three.'

'Bar, Miss, like they 'ave in pubs, an' rack, like a clo'es rack, an' racks, more'n one rack.'

The kids laughed. They sat up straighter, their interest caught.

'What's the longest word you know, Albert? Because you have to write a good, long word on the board now.'

'Salvation, Miss . . . I can spell it, an' all.'

'Oy, Albert, wharrabout Colonel? Can you spell that, eh?'

'He's doing Salvation . . . come along, Albert, here's the chalk.'

Albert speedily got the necessary points and was despatched for dolly mixtures, these being the smallest sweets Sara could think of and thus the easiest to divide, and the game changed, at the suggestion of the small boy who had been in the corner for telling Miss Cordwainer that he would listen if he bleedin' well felt like it and not 'cos she told him to.

'If you lerrus use the letters in a different order, we could make an awful lorra words,' he said excitedly. 'Like "Carpet", what we only got three out of, like . . . if we'd changed the *order* o' the letters we could of made tea, pea, cat, crap . . . all sorts.'

Sara looked at him suspiciously; was he being rude again? But he was beaming at her, and she saw that he had a cheeky, intelligent little face and also that he was enjoying the challenge of using his mind, of sorting out the letters in a given word to form others.

'Well done, Andrew. Anyone else want to have a go?'

They were cautious about it, but after half an hour

the room rang with shouts as the children outdid each other, even the duller children being able to offer one or two suggestions once they understood the game.

And in the middle of this, a woman whom Sara had seen in church but never spoken to walked into the room.

'Miss Boote ... oh, I beg your pardon, Miss Cordwainer, I didn't realise you were taking this class. Is everything all right?' She lowered her voice, moving nearer to Sara as she did so. 'It was the noise ... I know what these children can be like, they aren't an easy class, and I thought poor Miss Boote might be glad of a third party, so in I came ... but you all look very happy, I must say.'

'I'm sorry, Lieutenant,' Sara said, feeling her cheeks warming. 'But it isn't a game you can play quietly ... we're word-making.'

The lieutenant turned and looked at the blackboard with its scribbled words, the main one above, the smaller ones below. She looked back at Sara, brows rising.

'These children are playing at word-making? Or are you doing the work for them?'

'No, indeed,' Sara said immediately. 'Every one of the small words has been suggested and written in by a pupil. And the latest main word, 'Songster', was Biddy Callan's.'

'*Biddy*? But I didn't think she could read or write,' the lieutenant hissed. 'She's the youngest of twelve, you know, and ...'

'She may not be able to read or write, but she knew the word "Songster" and she can make little words from big ones by the sounds,' Sara explained. 'The girl sitting next to her, Annie, she helps, but Biddy does most of the work, really she does. Why don't you stay and watch for a moment?'

Lieutenant Marks stayed and the children, as children will, played up to this unexpected audience by giving of their best. One or two of the suggestions were a little near the knuckle but Sara passed over them and to her relief, though the lieutenant's eyes twinkled, she, too, pretended to notice nothing.

When another officer came in to say that Sunday school was over for the day and would the children like milk and biscuits before they left, he found the children in great form, sharing out a bag of dolly mixtures whilst Sara and the lieutenant chatted.

'I'm impressed, Miss Cordwainer,' the officer told her. 'These are difficult children, and you've kept their attention and kept them happily employed for two whole hours on a wet Sunday afternoon.'

'I've just said the same,' the lieutenant said, smiling. 'In fact I've just asked Miss Cordwainer if she would consider working with children. In a paid position, I mean.'

'And the upshot of it is,' Sara told her grandmother jubilantly when she got home that night, 'that Miss Marks has offered me a job, teaching! She runs a small school in the Walton Road area – it is fee-paying, but the Army sponsors most of the children – and she needs someone to teach the little ones, the children of five to around seven. She and her sister teach the older kids,' she added. 'Oh, Gran, what do you think?'

'It sounds very nice indeed, queen, far better than that laundry. But what 'ud they pay you, each week? I wish it didn't matter, but it does.'

'The salary is thirty-eight shillings a week,' Sara said, wide-eyed. 'It sounds too good to be true, doesn't it? But it isn't, it's what teachers are paid. And if I work hard and become qualified, I'll get more!'

'Aye, but you aren't qualified,' her grandmother

pointed out. 'What are the chances of gettin' qualifications, queen?'

'Well, I don't know. But I got my higher school certificate, or the equivalent, in Switzerland so Miss Marks is going to see what she can do. I believe there are teaching courses; if I could save up enough and go to college and pass the exams then I should be able to teach anywhere.'

Mrs Prescott had been sitting in the chair by the fire, shelling peas into an enamel colander, now she put the peas on the hearthrug and the colander on the nearest chair and held out her arms.

'Come and give your gran a big kiss,' she said. 'Oh, I'm so pleased for you, love! To leave that miserable laundry, and to gerra job where you'll be usin' your intelligence . . . it's what I've always wanted for you.'

'It's a dream come true,' Sara admitted. 'And tomorrow I'm going over to the offices to have a word with Miss Bateman!'

Time passes, time passes, Brogan told himself, sitting like a gentleman in a third-class carriage, bound for Liverpool. It's gettin' on for a year since I was last in the city and it's taken that long for me to want to go back. But it was true; time does not only pass, it heals, too. By March, Brogan had been able to admit that Sara had a perfect right to fall in love with a soldier if she so wished. By June, when his mammy's letters were full of this Eucharistic Congress and how beautiful Polly had looked in her communion veil, he had also been able to see that since he had never given Sara the faintest inkling of his own feelings, she could not possibly be expected to take him into account at all, far less consult him before getting herself a feller.

By the end of October, when the hunger marchers

were fighting the London bobbies and Ramsay Mac-Donald was 'urgently reviewing' the government's policies on unemployment, he was able to tell himself frankly that he simply could not be in love with a girl he'd met, at most, half-a-dozen times, most of the meetings being between himself, a young man, and the child she had been then.

And if, by some freak chance, he had been in love, then he had better pick himself up by the scruff of the neck and chuck himself out of love, give other girls a glance now and then.

So when Peader had said he was going back to Ireland for Christmas this year and invited Brogan to join him, Brogan decided he would, and that he'd go up to Liverpool a couple of days early. He hardly ever used the holiday to which he was entitled, why not ask for some time off now?

He did, and it was granted. Brogan's employers admired his dogged hard work, his handling of the enormous engines he drove, his even temper and the fact that, like his father, he rarely drank.

'Most railmen drink; 'tis the only relief from the tarble thirst you get from workin' in the engine cabs, and it eases the strain on your muscles when you've been luggin' great bundles an' boxes o' goods off the trucks,' one of the other men said to Brogan. 'Why not you, Brog?'

'Sure, I do drink,' Brogan had protested. 'But not the hard stuff. I'll have a glass of porter now and then ... but I'm not wedded to the drink, like some of youse.'

And this time, maybe I'll go round to Snowdrop Street and get her out of me system once and for all, Brogan told himself as the train chugged nearer and nearer to its destination. Maybe I'll greet her as a friend, meet her young man, and get her off me mind and out of me heart, for until I do, I won't look at anyone else and that's God's truth.

Because Brogan was lonely. He could understand, now, his father's quiet longing to be back in Dublin, to hold his children on his knee, to share the fireside with his wife. Me daddy's a grand man, one of the best, he told himself now. To stay away, earnin' money, when he's all that love an' affection waitin' at home! Where does he find the strength?

But Peader was strong; Brogan had always known it. Peader knew he could go home, take up his life again, maybe even get a job, though that was uncertain. But once he was home the babies would start coming again, one a year, and Deirdre would start looking like all the other tenement wives – worn out, weary, weighed under by kids they could barely support, let alone bring up the way they wanted to.

'Sure an' I love your mammy and I'd do anythin' to stop that happenin', so I would,' Peader had said heavily, when they had been discussing going home again. 'But I'm a good Catholic an' she's a good Catholic . . . if you're together the babies just come. And how many fellers have jobs, in Swift's Alley? Half a dozen? And what do they earn? Nothing, compared to us, Brog. But bringin' me family over here, now . . . well, I'd do it like a shot – will do it, once I've put enough by to get a nice little home.'

'How much more do you need, Daddy?' Brogan asked. He had been contributing, lately, to that nice little home, because he was earning good money and scarcely spending any. Of course he had always sent money home, but even so his savings were mounting.

'I reckon another two years will see me sendin' for them,' Peader said contentedly. 'Eh, but I can't wait to see their faces when we've got a good little house with a bit of garden, near to the railway but not too near, and we're all settled down in it, snug as bugs in rugs.'

Brogan worried a bit because he knew his father had never mentioned such a move to Deirdre, and guessed that his mother would take some shifting, so she would. Niall and Martin were in good jobs now, Donal was bidding fair to be the first member of the O'Brady family to go on to further education – they talked about a degree – and even Polly was shining brightly in school and had her own circle of friends.

How would they transplant? And – the big worry – what if someone recognised Polly and wanted to take her away from the O'Bradys? It would break Mammy's heart, and Daddy's . . . and mine, for that matter, because I'm desperate proud of Polly so I am, desperate proud.

She was a lovely kid. Pretty, intelligent, lively. If anyone tried to take her away from us I'd kill 'em, Brogan thought with unaccustomed violence. So what'll happen if Daddy brings the family back to Liverpool?

He remembered the other child, the little girl who had told Sara she was searching for her baby sister. What had happened to her? Brogan knew the family had been thrown out of Snowdrop Street long ago for non-payment of rent. He had heard about it from a fellow railman, how Stan Carbery had blustered and hit the kids, shouted and yelled at everyone, whilst his wife had wept and begged him not to take it out on them for indeed it was no one's fault.

And from that day to this, there had been no word of them. Had they moved to cheaper housing somewhere, had Stan got a job, become respectable? If I tell Daddy we might lose Polly if he brings them across the water, will he change his mind? Sure and that would be a terrible thing to do, with him so desperate hungry for his Deirdre and their children. Could the Carberys all be dead, wiped out in some epidemic or other? He remembered them as a large family of hungry, impoverished children. Surely such a family would make some sort of mark on the community in which it lived?

Brogan sighed and decided he would ask around. And when they were in Dublin, over Christmas, he and Daddy would sound out the family on how each member felt about crossing the water. Niall wouldn't come, nor Martin. You didn't get a job in a bank, or a good position in the offices of Guinness, and then whistle them down the wind for a parental whim. Besides, Niall had a young lady, they were saving up to get married. No, Niall and Martin wouldn't come over, und :r any circumstances.

The train was slowing down now, though. Familiar sights began to pass slowly by outside the window; Lime Street station loomed, with the platform crowded with people either meeting this train or waiting for the next.

Brogan stood up and reached for his bag, then, because he always believed in helping those less fortunate – which, in this case, meant every other person in the carriage – he reached the rest of the luggage down.

'Journey's end, ladies,' he said pleasantly to the two dried-up little spinsters who had sat opposite him since Crewe, eating mints – in a very ladylike way though – and discussing, in faint, mouselike tones, what they would do for Christmas. 'Are you goin' on from here, or is Liverpool your destination?'

'We're continuing on to Crosby, by bus,' one of the ladies said. 'If you could see a porter, young man, we would be most grateful . . . our cases are heavy.'

'Sure, I'll give someone a shout,' Brogan said easily. 'And I'll put your cases on the platform meself.' He turned to the rest of the carriage. 'Anyone else need a hand, now?'

Sara had enjoyed her first term as a teacher mightily, but she had found it tiring, though why she should do so after her months in the laundry she could not understand.

'Leaving, Cordwainer?' Miss Bateman had said unbelievingly when she had gone into the offices to give a week's notice. 'Are you not satisfied with the wages we pay you? Packing is a simple job which any neat-fingered girl could undertake. You are well-rewarded by any standard.'

'Money isn't in question, Miss Bateman,' Sara said. She was tempted to drop the title, since Miss Bateman had done so from the moment Sara's job had started, but she thought she might need a reference one day – or a handkerchief laundered, she thought wickedly. Miss Bateman would launder a handkerchief nicely, but writing a letter of reference would probably be beyond her! 'I've obtained other employment.'

Miss Bateman's mousy eyebrows rose into her hairline.

'Really? Where, may I ask? Which of our competitors would be foolish enough to take on a girl as high and mighty and discontented as yourself?'

'Of course you may ask, Miss Bateman,' Sara said gently. 'But I'm afraid I shan't be answering. You phrased your question so rudely, you see.'

Miss Bateman goggled. There was no other word for it. Her tiny eyes seemed to start from their tiny sockets and her mouth formed a large, horrified 'O' of sheer disbelief. No one, Sara was sure, had ever answered her back before, let alone accused her of rudeness.

'Good afternoon, Miss Bateman,' Sara said, seeing that the older woman was, temporarily at least, bereft of words. 'I shall leave next Friday.'

She was halfway down the corridor and heading towards the big laundry room when the office door shot open behind her.

'Miss Cordwainer!'

So my title has been reinstated, seeing as how I'm leaving and joining the world outside the laundry again, Sara thought, amused. But she turned gracefully towards the office doorway, in which Miss Bateman was now framed.

'Yes, Miss Bateman? Did you call me?'

'You'll work until Saturday noon,' Miss Bateman said crisply. 'A full week is specified.'

Sara had said nothing. There was no point. She would wait until Friday, check her wage-packet, and then decide what to do. And anyway, working another five hours wouldn't hurt her.

But now, with Christmas fast approaching and the holidays soon to start, she found that she was exhausted. She had spent the last couple of weeks making Christmas decorations with her class, buying simple ingredients and showing them how to turn peppermint oil, icing sugar and cochineal into pink sugar pigs, cutting newspaper into strips, painting them and gluing them together to make paper chains. She had even taken four members of her class out to Fazackerley on the number twenty-two tram and from thence to Simonwood, where the five of them spent a wonderful day cutting holly and mistletoe from the woods and hedgerows to decorate the classroom.

And Gran was not well at all. Her rheumatism had

got worse and worse and now her joints were so painful that she could sometimes scarcely move. So when Clarrie made her suggestion Sara seized on it with delight.

'I'm goin' home for Christmas, to me folk in the country,' she told Sara one evening when they were up at the Barracks, cutting vegetables into cubes for soup. 'Well, I say country – it's Formby, in fact, which is more seaside, I suppose. I were wonderin' . . . would you and Mrs Prescott like to come home wi' me? Mam and Da would be tickled pink, they've heard so much about you both, and provided you don't expect nothin' grand, I think you'd enjoy it. Me mam's a great cook an' she loves entertainin'. They're Army, of course,' she added. 'There's a Hall not too far from my parents' place, so we can go there for the Christmas services and so on.'

'Oh, Clarrie, it sounds wonderful,' Sara said eagerly. 'I'm awfully worried about Gran, you know. Her rheumatism seems to be getting worse so rapidly. Dr Mac says he'll take her into hospital for a few days, try to get a better idea of why this stiffness has come on so suddenly, but Gran says she won't go. She says there's nothing they can do so why don't they just let her struggle on. And aspirin helps, apparently. And she's got some awful smelly stuff she says the cab drivers used to use on their horses . . . that helps, too.'

So on Christmas Eve they set out for Formby, not on the tram but on a crowded service bus.

'It's better for all this luggage,' Clarrie said, eyeing the boxes and bundles her guests had brought with them and shoved under the seats and piled in the aisle with some dismay. 'Wharron earth have you gorrin there, the pair of you?'

'Christmas cakes, Christmas puddings, a box of fruit,

two steak and kidney pies . . .' Sara began, counting them off on her fingers and only laughing when Clarrie said mockingly: 'Coldhamcoldbeefpickledgherkins-salad . . .'

'No quotin' *The Wind in the Willows*, 'cos it were my copy you read, cleverclogs. As for the grub, we wanted to make a contribution,' Mrs Prescott said. 'God above knows how long my fingers will flex enough to make pastry and cakes, so I'm usin' me gift whiles I can.'

'Oh, keep your fingers active at all costs,' Sara begged, twinkling at her grandmother. 'If you stop cooking we'll go and live somewhere else, won't we, Clarrie? Because you're the best cook in the whole world, Gran.'

'Oh, you're safe for a bit,' Mrs Prescott assured her. 'So far it's just me knees, me shoulders and me back . . . what's left is workin' fine.'

'Then sit back and enjoy the scenery,' Sara said. 'Oh, isn't it wonderful to be going away for a holiday? Especially into the country and beside the seaside, all at the same time – I feel really adventurous!'

'Don't give us none of that – you've lived in Switzer-land, you know about travel, Miss Boote remarked. 'I wonder what me mam's got for us teas?'

'Gran, are you awake?'

Sara and her grandmother were sharing a bed in the Bootes' back room, which had been converted into a bedroom because Gran couldn't manage the extraordi-narily steep and narrow stairs. They had eaten a grand tea with potted shrimps and boiled ham, potatoes from Mr Boote's own allotment and milk from the farm down the road.

'Lovely to have it fresh, instead o' tinned,' Clarrie

said. 'Though it's easier to use tinned at the Barracks; it don't go off as fast.'

'Well, the apple pie's prime,' Mr Boote observed. 'You're a genius with pastry, Mrs Prescott, and I'm a good one to judge, for until I tasted your apple pie I'd ha' said Mrs Boote had no equal; now I'm not so sure.'

Great hilarity all round, especially from Mrs Boote, who was very like her daughter to look at, small and plump with kindly eyes.

And the evening had continued in the same vein. They had played cards, betting with matchsticks because, Mrs Boote said, the Army had seen too much of the seamy side of betting to agree with it. Then they had tea and mince pies, and Mrs Prescott assured Mrs Boote that she hadn't met her match for marvellous, light pastry.

'I'm not denyin' I'm good,' she said solemnly, 'But you're better, Mrs Boote, and I never thought I'd say that to a livin' soul.'

So now, lying in the strange bed, Sara kept her voice low.

'Gran, are you awake?'

'Just,' came the muffled reply from under the sheets. 'But 'twon't last, queen, for I'm very tired.'

'Aren't they nice, the Bootes?'

'They're grand people. She's been a good friend to us, has Clarrie. I won't feel so bad, leavin' you, with them to give an eye.'

'Leaving me?' Sara sat up in bed, cold dread flooding over her. 'What do you mean, Gran?'

'Well, queen, I'm no chicken. One of these days I'll leave you – you must have known that!'

'Oh . . . one of these days, yes, I suppose . . . but the way you said it, it sounded close, somehow,' Sara said uneasily. 'Don't scare me, Gran, by talking like that. I don't know what I'd do if you weren't waiting for me when I come home.'

'Well, I'll be around for a while yet, no doubt,' her grandmother said comfortably. 'Unless you kill me off by keepin' me awake all night, that is!'

She laughed and after a second's hesitation Sara joined in. But the seed had been sown, and Sara knew her grandmother was right. Mrs Prescott was seventy-three and no longer as strong as she had been and she had to warn her granddaughter not to expect her to live for ever.

So she's just being practical, Sara told herself, heaving the sheet up over her shoulders, and I must be practical, too. Gran's old; I mustn't set so much store by her company that I go to pieces when she dies. I've got to learn self-sufficiency, as Gran once did – as Clarrie has.

But she knew, as she felt sleep overtaking her, that it would not be easy.

She wasn't there again, of course. Brogan went round and knocked on the door as soon as he and his father had finished their supper on Christmas Eve and no one answered, though the neighbour poked her head round the door. It wasn't the same girl as last time but a younger, prettier one. She smiled at Brogan.

'Hello – they're away. Gone for Christmas. They'll be back day after Boxing Day.'

Brogan groaned. 'Oh lor, and I'm off meself in the morning, to Dublin on the boat. Isn't that just me luck, now?'

'Well, when will you be comin' back?' the girl asked curiously. 'Can you not pop round then?'

'I might,' Brogan said cautiously. 'Only . . . is things

the same? Have Sara and her gran gone away wit' her army friend?'

'That's it,' the girl said. 'Gone to stay wi' the parents, Mr and Mrs Boote, as 'ouse guests.' She sighed enviously. 'They'll 'ave a gay old time, I reckon.'

'I'll try an' come round again when I'm passin' through on me way back to Crewe,' Brogan said, trying to sound firm and resolute but merely succeeding, he thought, in sounding offended by Sara's absence. He had taken off his cap when the girl had first spoken, now he replaced it on his head. 'Season's greetings to you, Miss,' he finished.

Walking down the road, hands in pockets, head down, Brogan tried to tell himself that he should take this as a warning. Sara was obviously living in the pocket of this Boote person, he couldn't blame her, but he had best forget her.

After all, I didn't do a thing to keep meself in her mind; I didn't even write, he reminded himself. Only letters were so hard, you had to put on paper things you wouldn't mind saying, but didn't fancy seeing in black and white.

He was home at his father's lodgings before the dark depression hit him, mocking him with his total inadequacy, his stupidity, the sheer absurdity of expecting a girl like Sara to take a feller like him seriously. He sat glowering in the chair by the fire and Peader, assuming that his son, like himself, was suffering all the awful pangs of extreme homesickness and was unable to bear the thought of waking, tomorrow morning, with only the voyage on the ferry ahead of him instead of the usual jollities of Christmas Day, said they'd best be off to bed, for they'd a long day ahead of them tomorrow.

'I've a long life ahead of me, and I don't know what

I'm goin' to do wit' it,' Brogan said morosely. 'I'm sick an' tired of bein' alone, Daddy, sick an' tired.'

'Never mind, boy,' Peader said bracingly. 'By this time tomorrow we'll be in the bosom of our family – for a whole week!'

And if Brogan's smile was not as wide as it could have been, Peader was too absorbed in his own happy anticipation to notice.

Christmas in Dublin would have gone well but for the vexed question of the family crossing the water. Deirdre, when it was put to her, did not show any of the enthusiasm at the thought of being with her man again, living as a proper family once more, which Peader had confidently expected. Instead she pulled a doubtful face; sure and wasn't she Dublin born and bred? She'd never considered leaving the area, she was happy here, knew everyone, was known by everyone. She didn't want to end up living in a foreign country, not understanding the people, not knowing the customs, longing all the time for Dublin, the Liberties, even for Swift's Alley and the neighbours she had known all her life.

And Peader, who never grumbled, who had lived alone in England now for twelve years, suddenly saw red – he, who had never shouted, never thrown his weight about, actually shouted, went red in the face so that veins stood out on his forehead!

'*You* don't want to live in a foreign country? *You* won't understand the people, or know the customs? What about me, you selfish bitch? Haven't I lived there for a dozen years, sent all me money home, been heartsick for Dublin, for you, for me kids . . . and haven't I stayed there, regardless, so's you could be happy, have a decent life? Yet when I ask if you could come over the water to be with me, what do you say?' Peader put on a squeaky voice: '*Oh, Peader, but amn't I Dublin born and bred? What would I do in a foreign country, knowin' no one? How would I live, not understandin' their ways?*' He reverted to his own voice. 'In twelve years, Deirdre, I've never laid an eye or a hand on another woman, I've t'ought of you every night, every mornin'. But by God, if you won't come back wit' me, then that's goin' to change so it is!'

Polly, who had been curled up on the hearthrug, leaning against Delilah, with Lionel purring on her lap, stared with big eyes at this sudden and unexpected parental storm. Her father had used a bad word – worse, he had used it to describe her mother who was the best person in the whole world! And what had happened to their lovely Christmas contentment? It had vanished the moment Daddy started talking about them living in Liverpool so they could all be together. But now Mammy was crying and Daddy was quiet, his big hands resting on his knees, his eyes cast down.

'Mammy,' Polly ventured. 'What's Liverpool like?'

'I don't know, alanna, and I don't want to know . . .' Mammy began but this, it appeared, was too much for Daddy. He crashed out an oath and jumped to his feet.

'I'm not stayin' where I'm not wanted,' he said thickly. 'I'm for the pub – are you comin', Brogan?'

Brogan never argued with anyone and now Polly saw that he looked acutely unhappy. But then he seemed to remember something, and he stood up.

'I'll come wit' you, Daddy,' he said. 'Mammy needs time to think – and to remember, perhaps.'

It sounded threatening. Mammy thought so too, for she gave another strangled sob and held out her hands to Brogan, but he turned and left the room in his father's wake, only casting one quick, comforting glance at Polly. *It's nothin', really,* the look seemed to say. *They'll be over it in a trice, alanna, and kissin' an' huggin' by bedtime.*

It would have been nice had she believed it, but the minute the door closed behind them Mammy ran over to her, picked her off the hearthrug and gave her a fierce, rib-cracking hug.

'Sure an' you wouldn't want to go over the water to Liverpool, would you, my darlin' girl?' she said coaxingly. 'It's a cold, dark country, England, full of cold, dark people. They don't sing, nor worship, nor even speak as we do. Ah, you'd be unhappy far from your school, from Aideen . . . from Tad, for that matter. Say you'd rather stay here, wit' your mammy.'

'I'd rather stay wit' you, Mammy,' Polly whispered, but she felt a traitor even saying it. Brogan and Daddy were so good, they worked so hard, Mammy was always saying she wanted them back in Dublin again. Well, they couldn't come back, Daddy had explained it so that even Polly understood. But they could go to him. He had said a house in the country, a bit of a garden . . . a good life. Was that so terrible? Was it so bad to live in another country, when you were living with someone you loved?

But Mammy was crying again, great big tears were coursing down her cheeks and plopping on to poor Delilah, who looked up, eyes heavy with reproach. He wanted his warm and cuddly Polly back on the rug, and Lionel, stalking indignantly towards him having been tipped unceremoniously off Polly's small lap, was making him nervous. Delilah's large, tent-like ears quivered apprehensively upright as he wondered what the ginger cat might do to him, when Lionel got close enough.

'Your mammy's not a selfish . . . a selfish person, is she, Polly?' Mammy was saying between sobs. ''Tis your daddy's who's the selfish one, threatenin' to take me across the water – me, a Dublin rose, to be torn up by me roots and planted in cold Liverpool soil . . . oh, I cannot, cannot bear it!'

'Daddy won't make you go, Mammy,' Polly said. She found she was crying herself – oh, Mother of God, what a great baby she was, thank heaven Tad wasn't here, for devil a bit of sympathy would she get from him, for blubbin' like a baby just because her mammy was doing the same. 'Daddy's good an' kind, you've always said so. He sends all his money home, the dote, an' he's not a drinkin' man, either, thanks to all the saints.'

Hearing her own words quoted back at her stopped Mammy in her tracks. She sniffed, wiped her nose on the back of her hand, then began dabbing at her eyes with the linen runner which stopped the Brylcreem from the boys' heads getting on the nice chairs.

'He *is* good and kind, alanna. So why does he want to make me so unhappy?'

It was unanswerable, of course. But even as she spoke, Mammy loosened her grip slightly and Polly slid through her hands like a trout through water and landed back on the hearthrug where she immediately flung her own arms round Delilah and gave him a kiss right on the end of his wet, black nose.

'Dear Delly,' she said against his soft face. 'Shall we go a walk? It's Christmas night, we might see Santy Claus – or the banshee!'

'Oh, bugger the banshee,' Mammy shouted suddenly, as Polly got to her feet. 'You're not goin' out there alone and leavin' me here, so miserable? Ivan's been asleep this past hour and the boys aren't home yet . . . I don't want to be here alone!'

'But Delilah's got to go out for his last visit,' Polly

pointed out primly, conveniently forgetting the many times she had whined to Donal or Martin to take the dog out for her because it was cold outside and she was terribly tired. 'When he was a little puppy you said to me, you said, "Who's goin' to take him out at dead o' night for his last visit?" and I told you then I would, so I have to, of course.'

'Oh, all right, leave me then,' Mammy said wearily. 'I'm goin' to bed.'

And for the first time ever that she could remember, Polly came back to the house, fresh and tingling after a brisk run through the streets with one hand on Delilah's shaggy head, to find her mother actually in bed and to all intents and purposes, asleep.

I wonder should I jump in beside her? Polly asked herself as she changed out of her clothes into the shift she wore in bed. Only she did say I was to have the mattress in the livin' room, and I could lie it on the sofa if I'd a mind.

When she was in her shift Polly went and poured herself a drink of water and then pulled out the mattress. Her bedding was folded up on top of it and she shook it out, hoping that Daddy and Brogan would come back in before she was asleep so that one or other of them could sit by the fire and read her a story. She was perfectly capable of reading herself a story, of course, but Mammy had formed the habit of story-reading when Polly had been small and somehow the habit had continued – and Ivan loved the stories too, which was nice. The two of them sat on either side of Mammy, thumbs in mouths, and listened in perfect amity for once. And then sleep came so much quicker and easier, with lovely story-thoughts churning gently round in your brain and all your worries banished.

But the clock on the mantel ticked and tocked and

the pendulum swung hypnotically and Lionel, curled up in the crook of Polly's knees, purred so deeply and vibrantly that soon keeping awake was more than Polly could cope with. Her eyelids drooped, firelight dazzled on the lids, thoughts slowed . . . and she slept.

She was woken by soft voices; men's voices. Brogan and Daddy. She did not want them to know she was awake so she opened a crack of her eye and peered at the clock on the mantel first. It said three o'clock in the morning – she had scarcely known there was such a time! And Daddy and Brogan were sitting on either side of the fire, in the good chairs, talking.

'Daddy, I know how you miss her, I know, none better.' Brogan was saying. 'I don't know the hunger, because I'm a single feller, but I know the missin'. In me own way I miss the kids, too, specially Polly. But Daddy, would it be fair to take the littl'un back to Liverpool? There's that to consider when you're thinkin' it out, too.'

'No need.' That was Daddy's voice, dark and flat with despair, but with a slur to it that Polly had never heard before. 'Deirdre won't cross the water; mebbe I shouldn't have asked her.'

'You had every right,' Brogan said, his gentle voice almost angry. 'Every right in the world, Daddy. Mammy cannot realise, she cannot have thought, of what you've done for our family. Why, you've been after givin' them the best years of your life, and when Mammy thinks on, she'll be shamed by what she's said tonight.'

'I called her a selfish bitch,' Daddy said dully. 'When I know in me heart she's the most generous woman who ever walked this earth. Why did I do it, Brogan? Why did I set my tongue to words I'm ashamed of? It

285

wasn't the drink for I'd not touched a drop, as you well know.'

'Well, you've touched a drop now, so don't go maudlin on me,' Brogan said, with humour in his voice. 'You've a hard head on you, Daddy, for you drank enough porter to drown a better man – I never seen anything like it in all me puff. Now shall I be helpin' you into bed? Or will you jump in as you are?'

'I'll wake Deirdre,' his father said crossly. ''Tis a wife's duty to help her man to bed when he's had a few. If I'd been like other men she'd have been helpin' me to bed these many nights . . . and suitin' me when I got there, too.'

'Daddy, hold your tongue or you'll be sorry in the mornin'.' Brogan was laughing, Polly could tell. 'Suitin' you, indeed – you sound like Father O'Leary when he's got one of his hell-fire preachin' moods on him. Go on, I'll give you a hand out o' them trousers.'

'You will not!' Daddy sounded as though he'd suddenly come wide awake. 'What if the child woke? I'll go to me bed now, Brog, and 'tis time you went to yours. You'll be sharin' wit' Donal an' Ivan. Don't squash 'em in the night; I was always afeared to squash 'em when they were babbies an' slept in our bed.'

'I won't squash anyone, Daddy.' Brogan was laughing again. 'By the waters of Liffey, you'll have a head on you in the mornin', no error. Night, now.'

'Night, son,' Daddy said, and Polly heard him fumbling his way out of the room. Then she heard voices murmur for a few minutes, then silence.

After a few moments she opened her eye another crack and risked a peep. Brogan was damping down the fire. He was still grinning to himself. Perhaps it won't be so bad as it seemed, earlier, Polly thought hopefully. Grown-ups is so strange, perhaps by morning they'll have forgot they quarrelled.

Presently, the rosy glow of the fire damped, Brogan took the candle, which had guttered low in any case, and left the room. Polly could hear him moving around for a while, then she heard the bed creak, and then there was silence.

What a day this has been, Polly thought suddenly. Mammy and Daddy had a fight with words, the first ever, and Daddy had too much porter and talked in a funny way, the first ever for that, too. Then they said more about Liverpool than they ever had before . . . and we might go and live there, when Daddy's saved up enough money to buy a little house with a garden.

But that would mean leaving Tad, her thoughts continued. Sure an' I can't do that, not wit' Tad and me marryin', the way we said when we're old enough. But then she wouldn't marry until she was old . . . twenty, maybe . . . so she might as well live in England as here, until then.

But three in the morning, after all the excitements of Christmas Day, is not a good time for lying wakeful. Before she had done more than remind herself what an odd day it had been, Polly was asleep once more.

'Peader, me dear love?'

'Sorry, I was tryin' not to wake you,' Peader mumbled, dealing with his own trousers, darkness and all, for despite his brave words to his son he did not fancy his chances of getting Deirdre out of bed to undress him just because he was a mite the worse for drink. 'Go back to sleep now, I'll manage.'

'Peader, I've been lyin' here thinkin'. Never was there a better man alive than yourself, nor a more selfish, cowardly ould wan than me.'

Even with his head thick from too much porter and his soul aching from too much plain speaking, Peader chuckled. His young and pretty wife, who so deeply resented the Dublin habit of referring to the woman of the house as 'the ould wan' that she had forbidden her sons to use it, could not prevent her tongue turning traitor on her when she was deeply moved.

'Well, alanna, and I'm sorry I said what I did so I am, for I know well that it was the shock made you speak as you did. If I could come home to stay . . . but my darlin' girl, my little colleen, I'd not turn you into the chief wage-earner again, whiles I ran from ship to ship searching for work, or sweated my guts out on the railways, earnin' less in a month than I do in a week across the water.'

'No, I know you wouldn't.'

Peader, his outer clothing removed, climbed carefully into bed beside his wife. He lay down, then turned and took her in his arms, half-afraid she might pull away.

But she did not. She lay, almost purring, in his embrace and then began to say again that she was sorry, that she had not meant . . . that she would go with him to the ends of the earth if that was what he wanted.

'And sure no one'll know our Polly for any but our child,' she said breathlessly, arching her body against his. 'Ah, Peader, say you forgive me!'

'Forgive? We both spoke hastily, out of turn,' Peader said. It was all he could do to keep his hands still on her, he longed for her with such violence, such heat! 'Now we'd best sleep, alanna, for I'm goin' to have a thick head in the mornin', me son says.'

'Are you not goin' to love me?' Deirdre said in a small, coaxing voice. 'Ah, love me, Peader, show you forgive me for the wicked t'ings I said!'

Peader hesitated – and was lost.

'I forgive you, my own, my sweetheart,' he told her. He let his hands run gently over her sweet, smooth body, anticipating what was to come. 'Oh, Deirdre, I've wanted you so, longed for you so!'

'Do you think I've not spent nights cryin' because you're far away, not able to comfort me?' his wife said softly. 'Ah, Peader, 'tis no life for either the one nor the other, kept apart. You are right and I was wrong. When you're ready for me, I'll cross the water for you.'

He sighed deeply and then squeezed her hard, not heeding her laughing, breathless protest.

'You're the only woman I'll ever want, ever look twice at,' he whispered. 'Kiss me, Mrs O'Brady!'

Chapter Eleven

September 1933

Sara woke early, which was unusual because it was Saturday and Saturday, so far as she was concerned, was a real day of rest. On Sundays she went to church at the Barracks, taught Sunday school and helped with the dinner which was served to those who would otherwise not receive one. She loved Sundays because she was with her friends and doing work which she enjoyed and knew to be useful, but Saturday was the day she indulged herself. A lie-in, a trundle round the shops pushing Gran in her wheelchair, a cold meal at midday, a trip to the cinema to see the latest Hollywood epic, a good high tea with a couple of boiled eggs, or potted shrimps, or a piece of smoked haddock . . . yes, Saturdays were good days.

Sara lay where she was for a moment; what had woken her? Then she remembered. Of course! Today was moving day.

Ever since the previous Christmas, Gran had been finding it more and more difficult to manage for herself. Finally, at Easter, the doctor had told Sara that she would do well to try to move her grandmother into a small flat or a bungalow.

'Your grandmother has rheumatoid arthritis; her joints are almost immovable already, though her mind is both lively and active. She's managing quite well now, but if she could cut out the stairs her life would be far more comfortable. You've only the parlour and the kitchen downstairs in Snowdrop Street, and there is a step to negotiate to get out of the front door, so converting would be difficult, if not impossible. But get her on one floor, in a property where the wheelchair can be used indoors, and I believe she'll flourish for many years to come.'

Sara nodded. She had noticed how hard it was now for Gran to heave herself up the stairs and how exhausted she was after each fresh attempt.

'You rent the house in Snowdrop Street? Then it should be possible for you to make a move. If you could get something near the school where you teach, then you would find things easier all round.'

'I'll have a try,' Sara had promised. 'I'll ask the Army whether they know anywhere suitable.'

The Army ran what they called eventide homes for old people, but she knew without even asking that Gran would not be happy in such a place. The trouble was, the disease had attacked her whilst she was still a busy and bustling housewife. She would not be content to sit all day with other old people, who were just waiting for the next meal. And anyway, Sara did not want her grandmother to become bedbound a moment before she was forced into it.

That night, as the two of them were serving in the soup kitchen, Sara had told Clarrie what the doctor had said.

'So I'll be looking round for somewhere nearer the school,' she explained. 'Will you come with us, Clarrie? It'll be nearer for you as well, since school and your bank are quite close.'

'I'll go wherever you an' Mrs Prescott go,' Clarrie said at once. 'You oughter get somewhere without too much trouble, things being the way they are.' She jerked her head at the line of people waiting to be served. 'There's more of 'em every night,' she said quietly. There's more people out of work every day, folk goin' broke, wages being cut. Look at that queue.'

Sara nodded. She had noticed that all the Army's soup kitchens were now being attended by large numbers of people who would once have scorned to accept a bowl of free soup and a hunk of bread. The Depression was biting deep in Liverpool and many were out of work or existing on tiny wages. Sara's own salary had been cut because numbers of children attending the school had dropped sharply. Parents who could scarcely feed their families had to put their children into the state schools rather than use their pitifully small resources on even the cheapest of private education.

Clarrie, however, asked to take a cut in her salary, had faced the bank manager out and refused point-blank.

'I'm cheap any'ow,' she said firmly. 'I do the work of a feller but you don't think to pay me a feller's salary, even though I'm not livin' wi' me parents so I 'ave the same expenses as a feller. If you cut me money then I won't be able to live in lodgings, see? And me parents live too far out; it wouldn't make economic sense for me to come all the way here to work.'

The bank manager had, as Clarrie put it, 'huffed and puffed a bit', but he had not tried to reduce her salary again.

So Sara and Clarrie had set out to find a more convenient house which they could afford, and ended up well-satisfied. An Army family, living in Florence Street, found themselves in financial difficulties after the husband lost his job. He was a builder by trade however, and instead of haunting the labour exchange he set to and converted his small home into two flats.

So, hearing, on the Army grapevine, of Sara's plight, Mrs Flaherty offered to let them rent the ground-floor flat which, she assured them, would be plenty big enough and would be ready for them to move in shortly.

'Me an' Bernie will manage fine wi' the top flat,' she said eagerly. 'Oh, Miss Cordwainer, you don't know what a weight off me mind it would be to 'ave at least some money comin' in regular.'

'Well, it doesn't seem much,' Sara said doubtfully, but she, her grandmother and Clarrie felt that, if they all contributed, they would be able to manage.

'It would be a life-saver,' Mrs Flaherty said. 'And seeing as you're Army we'd be on the same footin', in a way. But come round an' tek a look, Miss Cordwainer, see what you think.'

Sara and Clarrie had gone round the same evening, and were delighted with the flat. It was well-planned and would allow them a bedroom each, and a small living kitchen. Best of all, though, when Sara explained to Mr Flaherty that her grandmother was in a wheel-chair and finding walking very difficult, he immediately said he could build a water closet on the kitchen, so that Mrs Prescott would not have to go out in the cold to spend a penny.

In due course they had taken Mrs Prescott to view the accommodation and, as Sara had anticipated, she was charmed with the flat.

'I don't want to use me wheelchair more than I need,' she said, eyes shining as she looked round the tiny kitchen. 'But I can gerrit in here, if I've a mind. I'll be able to whizz out to the shops if I want . . . no difficulty manoeuvring me wheelchair through that nice wide doorway! And the kitchen's so neat – everything to hand – that I'll be able to do me cooking, I'm sure I shall!'

'And if you don't feel up to it, Mrs Flaherty will give you a hand,' Sara said tactfully. 'It couldn't be better, really, because though I *could* come home at lunchtime, it would put Miss Marks out.'

'And there's the Victory Picture Palace, only a couple o' doors away,' Mrs Prescott said, pursuing her own train of thought. 'I could go there every afternoon, if I had a mind.'

'And if I'm needed, the school's no distance,' Sara agreed. 'Clarrie's bank is no distance, either. And the Barracks is handy, too.'

'And the Flahertys are my type of people,' Mrs Prescott added. 'We'll do all right here, chuck.'

So now it was moving-in day. Sara got out of bed and looked around her, at the room she had shared with Gran for months now, but found she had few regrets over moving to Florence Street. She had grown fond of Walton, and agreed with her grandmother that it would be good to live in such a lively part of the city.

She washed quickly at the washstand, trying not to splash, then dressed, but by the time she finished her grandmother had woken up. In fact she had swung her legs out of the bed and was trying to get her slippers on.

'Don't bother, Gran,' Sara said, kneeling down beside her. 'I like to help you to dress, you know I do, and besides, it's far too early for you to be up!'

'Oh well, if you insist,' Mrs Prescott said, letting Sara help her back into bed. I tell you, growin' old tries a body's patience, queen. Are you goin' to get me a nice cuppa?'

'I am. And then I'll give you a hand with dressing, your shoes are difficult I know, and then we'll start getting ourselves organised. Thank goodness the stuff's all in boxes and tea-chests, all we've really got to do today is to see that old Mitchell doesn't break half the china and glass whilst he's loading it on to his cart and count the tea-chests in and out. And once Mitch is away Clarrie and I will give the place a brush through and then we'll all get a taxi round to Florence Street.'

If it weren't for me you could have managed on the tram,' Mrs Prescott observed as Sara crossed the living room and headed for the back kitchen. 'Eh, it'll be strange not living in Snowdrop Street – I've been here almost fifty years, you know. Still, I'm not far from me old pals, they can come visiting if they've a mind. And it's not often I ride in a taxi . . . I'll feel like royalty!'

The move, contrary to Sara's expectations, went like clockwork and by three that afternoon they were in their new home, and very tidy it looked, with the furniture in place, the curtains up, and the brand-new linoleum laid. Sara had suggested taking the Snowdrop Street linoleum with them but Mrs Prescott had been firm.

'It's been on the floors fifty years, queen, it won't move. We'll leave it for the new people,' she said. 'We'll go down the Scottie; a couple of rolls of linoleum won't break us and it's nice to have a clean floor to start out.'

But they took the living-room carpet, old though it was, and it came up clean, without any fuss or bother.

'Buy the best and you'll not regret it,' Mrs Prescott said now, surveying the old carpet and her decent sofa and chairs. 'Looks right homely, don't it?'

The girls agreed that it did and bustled about lighting a fire, getting the tea and generally making themselves at home.

'I'm taking the *War Cry* round tonight, though,' Sara said quietly to Clarrie as they worked. 'Can you stay with Gran, Clarrie? Only I don't want to leave her alone on her first evening in a new place.'

Clarrie agreed that she would stay in, so at seven o'clock Sara put on her uniform and set off for the Barracks.

The place was bustling, as usual. Adjutant Edcott, a middle-aged lady with rather unlikely black hair, came over as soon as she saw Sara.

'Ah, Miss Cordwainer,' she said heartily. 'You and I are doing the local public houses this evening and it's your first time, isn't it? Mostly the men are pleasant to us, but one or two can use language . . . do you blush easily?'

Sara nodded, feeling her face grow hot, but Adjutant Edcott only laughed.

'I see you do,' she said, still chuckling. 'Well, well, it's a very pretty blush. My own attitude to bad language overheard in public houses is that I'm not on my own turf, so I can't object. As you know, dear, nice women don't frequent such places so the men feel they can blaspheme freely. Will that worry you?'

'I hope not,' Sara said. 'But Adjutant, you should hear some of the children at school when they don't know there's a teacher about. Their language would make your hair curl, honestly it would.'

'Well, there you are, then. You won't mind the odd naughty word. And the men are generous, particularly those who are . . . well, a little merry, should we say? Yes, it's amazing what they'll put into the collecting tin. And a good job too, because we need every penny we can get in these hard times. Shall we set out?'

'I'm ready,' Sara said, checking the seams of her

stockings by twisting round and staring down at them. 'I like to look neat when I'm out and about, don't you?'

'I do. We owe it to the Army, I always think. Very well, Cordwainer; best foot foremost now!'

Together, the two women marched along the pavement and into the first public house they reached.

'We're doing very well,' the adjutant said after an hour or so had passed. 'My dear, you're becomingly flushed, I'm sure that's why your tin is so heavy. A critic once said to me that it was immoral, taking young girls into public houses to persuade drunken sots to part with their cash, but that's not how I see it. It makes the men feel good to see a pretty girl, they find it easier to pay up, and giving to charity is good for one's immortal soul. See?'

'Considering how many people are out of work I think we've done well to get as much as we have,' Sara said later, as they crossed the road, heading for another public house. 'And people have been quite polite, too. It hasn't been too bad at all.'

She did not add that she had enjoyed herself, because it would not have been strictly true. She had not enjoyed many of the fulsome compliments she had received, nor the hot hands on hers, nor the leers, winks and muttered comments which the speakers might have assumed – wrongly – that she did not understand. And the smell of alcohol, cheap cigarettes, sweat and dirt was not too pleasant, either. But she had enjoyed the singing in one pub, the good-natured chaff in a second, the simple friendship the men showed to one another. And the fact that some of the men, particularly the older ones, showed a great respect for the Army.

'Your lot saved me grandad's life, just about,' one man said. 'He's in one of your eventide homes – happy as Larry, he is, now. Got other old'uns round him, see – and he ain't in the workhouse, which he were tarble scared of.'

He put a handful of small coins in her tin and Sara, smiling, thanked him. 'God bless you,' she said. 'That goes a long way towards helping others, like your grandad.'

But now, crossing the street, walking briskly with the heavy tin held protectively inside the shelter of her coat, Sara felt the glow of success. She had done well! This was her first try at taking round the *War Cry* and it had not been as bad as she had expected. I'll do it again, she told herself, breathing in the clean night air. It's worth a bit of hassle and embarrassment to know you've done so well.

'Queen's Arms next . . . and that's the last,' the adjutant said briskly, as they approached the big public house on the corner of Salop Street. 'They're a nice crowd in here – mostly Irish. A lot of 'em are navvies, working on the Mersey tunnel, and the rest are railmen, mostly. You want to hear 'em sing . . . eh, it can tear the heart from your breast, but don't you tell them that – they're all Catholics, and they don't sing a good, rousing hymn tune, they go more for ballads, laments, that sort o' stuff.'

'Not *Nellie Dean*?' Sara said mischievously. They had heard the song rendered in almost every pub they visited and were both heartily sick of it by now. 'I'd be grateful for anything that wasn't *Nellie Dean*, I believe.'

Adjutant Edcott was saved the necessity of replying because they reached the Queen's Arms at that point and plunged in through the open doorway.

Immediately, Sara sensed a different atmosphere to that of the Pacific Hotel, which had been their last stop. The pub was less crowded, for a start, and the atmosphere a good deal purer, for few of the assembled men were smoking. And though most men had a pint before them they were talking quietly, playing cards, laughing . . . and singing.

'It's enough to tear your heartstrings,' the adjutant beside her murmured. 'They're far from home and their songs say what they cannot. Still, we've work to do,' and she stepped forward with her sheaf of news-papers and her collecting tin. 'Evening, gentlemen, would any of you like a copy of the *War Cry*? We don't charge, but if you would like to put a contribution into the tin . . .'

Sara moved forward, smiling, thanking, and would not have noticed the large, quiet man in the corner if he had not spoken to her as his money tinkled into her tin.

'I hope you do some good wit' me money, Miss, for I'm putting most of me pennies away so I am . . . I'm hopin' to bring me family over come springtime, if I've managed to rent a decent little place by then.'

Sara glanced at him and was beginning to say she hoped he would soon find somewhere nice when she took a closer look. He was smiling up at her, an innocent, friendly smile. He had not recognised her – but why should he? She was disguised by her bonnet, but he looked no different from the way he had looked on that long-ago night when he had walked her home after her parents had abandoned her outside the church.

'Mr O'Brady? It *is* you! Don't you remember me? I'm Sara Cordwainer, you walked me home when I was out rather late one night. Your son Brogan was a friend of mine, but I've not seen him for years. Has he gone home to Ireland?'

Peader O'Brady looked at her properly for the first

time, looked at the person beneath the bonnet, not just the uniform. Then he grinned delightedly, revealing big, white teeth.

'Miss Cordwainer! Well I'm blessed! I didn't know you belonged to the Army.'

'I didn't, not when we met. But I joined up quite soon afterwards and I've never regretted it. How – how is Brogan? And yourself, of course.'

'Brogan's fine, and so am I. He's a train-driver now, for LMSR, working out of Crewe. He's done well. And what are you doing, Miss, apart from collecting money for the Army?'

'I'm a teacher in a small school,' Sara said. 'Brogan always said he'd drive the train one day – I'm very glad for him. Is he happy? Married? I suppose he could easily have children, for he must be . . . twenty-three or so by now. I'm twenty-one.'

'Sure an' Brogan's twenty-five, and devil a bit is he married.' Peader looked at her, his cheekbones reddening. 'He went round to your place last Christmas, and the Christmas before. He – he wanted a word.'

'I don't think he ever arrived,' Sara said. She frowned. 'Now wait a minute . . . last Christmas Gran and I – and Clarrie, of course – went to stay with Clarrie's parents, in Formby. But the Christmas before that – that would be 1931 – was my first Christmas with the Army. We were out all day, serving Christmas dinner to those who needed it. Oh dear, I am sorry I missed him.'

'Aye. He got real down,' Peader said. 'He did want a word.'

'I'm sorry. And now he's in Crewe, you say?'

'Aye, that's it; Crewe. But he visits me from time to time.'

'Well, next time he's in Liverpool you must tell him

to come and see me,' Sara said, suddenly gay. It would be lovely to see Brogan again, to watch the slow smile dawn in his eyes, the slow smile curve his lips. 'The only thing is –'

'Come along, Cordwainer, don't stand gossiping there,' Adjutant Edcott said bracingly. 'I've sold out – how have you done?'

'Oh, I've two left . . .' Sara smiled at the square-faced man sitting next to Peader. 'Would you like a copy of the *War Cry*, sir? We don't charge, but if you feel you can afford a contribution . . .'

The man grinned at her and stood up the better to get at his pockets.

'Sure an' you're welcome to a copper or two just for de sake of your lovely smile,' he said gallantly. 'And Seamus here will have one too, eh Seamus?'

''Tis lucky to take the last,' Seamus said, dipping into his own pocket. 'Though we'll be askin' for soup from your kitchen, Miss, when de tunnel's dug and finished.'

'Won't be long now,' someone else volunteered. 'Eh, it's been a wicked ole job – wicked. What wit' the water running down the walls an' the great rocks to be blasted out . . . eh, it's been wicked.'

'Last one gone, Adjutant,' Sara said, smiling at the men. She leaned down and spoke directly to Peader.

'Don't forget, next time Brogan comes, tell him to be sure to call.'

'I will, but Brogan said somethin' . . . is there a feller named Boote . . .?' Peader said, reddening still more. 'I wouldn't want to be after raising false hopes . . .'

'Our lodger's name is Boote – Miss Clarrie Boote,' Sara said. 'Oh, I must go, but don't forget – tell Brogan to call.'

And then they were outside the pub once more, and above them the sky fairly hummed with stars.

*

Grace saw the two Salvationists come out of the pub; she was lurking in the shadows of the Queen's Arms on Walton Road, waiting for closing time. She didn't spend as much time as she once had outside the Mile End pub, even though Kitty now lived there. The kitten had grown into a handsome cat and after a terrible scene at home, in the course of which Kitty had been lucky to escape with his life, Grace had taken him round to the Mile End pub and asked the landlady if she would keep him.

'Me da tried to kill 'im,' she explained, her voice breaking. 'They need me at 'ome, now, but me da will use Kitty to keep me in line. 'E says 'e'll strangle Kitty if I doesn't do what 'e says.'

The landlady's eyes were soft and sorry; she took the cat and told Grace she could come round whenever she liked to see Kitty, and Grace availed herself of the offer whenever she could. But because she was now big enough to be useful at home, she had begun to roam more widely, trying to keep well away from the neighbourhood of their court. And since the Mile End was a pub occasionally favoured by her father, Grace tended to hang around mostly on the Walton Road. She missed Kitty and the friendly landlady, but she liked the neighbourhood – there was a prime soup kitchen quite near, she'd had many a meal from the Army people who manned it, to say nothing of free boots, the loan of an Army blanket, and once, a lovely thick jersey to see her through a patch of bad weather.

She liked the Sally Army, but she never hung around near the Barracks or the soup kitchen for too long; she didn't want anyone to put her into the workhouse or any other institution, so she never let them know she slept rough six days out of seven. And at this time of night, she kept well out of sight. But she sighed to herself as the two women came out of the pub, smiling, talking. It would have been nice to have called out, had a word. Nice, but dangerous. But very soon now the pubs would want to close and the men would come out and she might get all manner of bits and pieces, to say nothing of coppers. She watched the bonnets bob off down the road, then went back to lean against the pub door.

And wait.

The news of her evening was too good to keep to herself. The minute Sara arrived home she told Gran that she'd met Brogan's father.

'And he said Brogan had been in Liverpool two Christmases ago and last Christmas, and he'd called in Snowdrop Street, but we were out,' she told Mrs Prescott. 'Imagine – he did call! I thought he'd forgotten all about me, or moved away, or both. Mind, he could have written, but men don't like writing much, do they?'

'Not labourers,' Mrs Prescott said, a trifle sharply, Sara thought. 'But no doubt he's a nice enough young man, in his way. Did you give the father our new address?'

'Oh goodness, I quite forgot,' Sara said, hands flying to her cheeks. 'Oh, how stupid I am, the poor fellow will go round to Snowdrop Street and think I'm deliberately keeping out of his way! Oh, Gran, what a fool I am! But I know where Mr O'Brady goes of an evening, and it's not too far from here, so I can always pop in and tell him we've moved.'

'Well, that's all right, then,' Mrs Prescott said. 'It's time you met young men other than Army ones.'

Sara bristled. 'What's wrong with Army ones?' she said. 'They're very nice.'

But inside herself, she was saying softly, *But they aren't as nice as Brogan O'Brady, that's for sure.*

It was a real pea-souper, Brogan thought, examining the range of instruments sparkling before him on the footplate of the engine and wishing that one of them was a magic eye which could see through fog. Weather like this was the very devil, because you simply could not tell where you were. Time stopped mattering, you had to slow down so much, and though you should be warned of a station's approach by the detonators on the track, you would not have been human had you not worried. Men did forget . . . and then you would go right past a station and there would be trouble from indignant passengers, hours late already, wanting their homes and their beds.

'Hold hard now, Harry.' Brogan leaned out of the cab and peered through the swirling fog. Harry Brett, his fireman, stopped shovelling coal for a moment and they both listened. Somewhere a cow lowed, the sound as mournful and pessimistic as a foghorn at sea. 'We're in flat country because we've not been through a cutting for a powerful while, and we're a way from a town, because of the cow. But that doesn't mean there isn't a station coming up. Oh well, we should know quite soon now.'

Presently they got steam up again and began to move rather faster. And of course the minute they did that the detonators went off, sending Brogan reaching for the brakes.

'Dear God in heaven, those bloody things will have me heart stopped yet,' he said, whilst Harry stopped shovelling coal for a moment to wipe his face with the rag which hung at his belt. 'This'll be Stafford, then. Thank God, we're makin' progress.'

'Home by midnight at this rate,' Harry said. He hated getting in late because it meant he would have to walk home – the buses would have stopped running and Harry lived some way from the station. 'And we're on earlies tomorrow.'

Brogan sighed. 'Aye, and I was goin' to write to me family tonight – we're scattered all over, now. There's most of 'em in Ireland, but Niall has recently gone to America, then my father's in Liverpool, there's me in Crewe . . . if we didn't write we'd lose touch.'

They crept into the station, slowed even more, stopped. The guard shouted and Brogan leaned out of his cab once more. All down the train doors were opening, people were jumping down, porters rushed about . . . they didn't look too pleased with life, Brogan noticed. Ah well, everyone hates late trains. And the newspapers would be late, too . . . they were beginning to load them, and the big brown post bags, into the luggage van. The guard came along the platform towards him, looking tired and cross.

'I'm goin' to get a butty from the refreshment room seein' as we're runnin' late,' he began. 'Do you want somethin', fellers?'

'A cup of tea and a currant bun or a cheese sandwich . . . lemonade will do if they don't have tea,' Brogan said. 'Same for you, Harry?'

'Aye, something to eat and anything to wet my throat,' Harry decided. 'I'm easy.'

'Good,' the guard said. 'If one more bugger asks me why the train's runnin' so late I swear to God I'll swing for 'im. Right. We've got six minutes here, 'cos o' the post; train·won't pick up many passengers tonight, though. Folk don't wait when we're this late.'

'If they cut down any more on the number of trains folk will have to walk,' Harry observed. 'Wish we had

305

a New Deal, like the Yanks. They know how to deal with a Depression, they're making new jobs, you know, puttin' bread into the mouths of those who lost their jobs through no fault of their own. Not like here, where it's every man for himself.'

'We don't have a Roosevelt,' the guard reminded him. 'We've only got old Ramsey Mac.'

'True. And I think the fog's thinnin' out a bit – the wind's gettin' up, that's why. Go on, Fred, or we won't have time to drink the tea before the refreshment room is shoutin' for their mugs back!'

It had been a long, hot summer without a drop of rain to green the grass or grow the potatoes. Forest fires had raged at the height of the drought and folk living in the tenement housing had longed desperately for a cool breeze, and for rain. But the kids were delighted when the weather only broke a couple of days after they returned to school.

'Sure an' it can rain all it likes now,' Tad said generously, sitting cross-legged on the O'Bradys' window-seat and watching the rain pelting down outside. 'Because it's only school it's ruinin', and I've no time for school. In another couple o' years . . .'

'You'll be out and workin', Polly chorused with him. She knew the remark off by heart and sometimes she wondered whether Tad said it so often because he was afraid. There weren't many good jobs around and Tad, with his threadbare clothes and his bedraggled person, seemed less likely than most to find one of them.

But work or no work, Tad and Polly had enjoyed the summer holidays, that was for sure. They'd fished for pinkeens in the Grand Canal, netting them out of the greenish, turgid water and into glass jam-jars which they would later use as their admission to the tuppenny rush on Saturdays. Tad was a good swimmer and showed off by diving into the water under Griffith Bridge; Polly preferred the other side, known as the Shallow, where she could dabble and paddle and dream, and sometimes practise the three strokes which was the most she could manage before her feet sunk to the muddy bottom. And since Tad still sold newspapers Polly had taken to helping him, getting almost as good at leaping aboard a traffic-stranded train and off again before it moved as her brother Brogan had once been.

Tad didn't make much money, but at least he made some, and as he assured his small helper, anything was better than going back to Mammy empty-handed.

'Because the ould feller's into everythin',' he assured her. ''Tis not his money alone that gets spent in Deegan's, but every penny he can find, these days. Mammy's earnings, mine, young Dougal's even. So I never take money home, not even a kid's eye. I take bread, sausage, spuds . . . things to eat. An' if me ould feller's on the warpath, sure an' I keep out o' the way till he's cooled down.'

So when the weather broke in the first week of the new term, Polly shrugged her shoulders, thanked the good God for a fine summer, and continued to help Tad with his various tasks.

Weekends were different, though. At weekends, after you'd sold your papers or carried sacks of spuds around or run messages for anyone who asked, your time was your own.

'We'll go after blackers,' Tad said the first Saturday as the two of them sat in the windowseat glumly watching the rain. 'Sure an' if it goes on rainin' we'll be the only ones, so we'll get a grush o' berries. The jam factory buys 'em if you get nice ones, or your mammy could make blackberry an' apple pie.'

'Where'd she get the apples, though?' Polly asked. 'Unless you buy her some.'

Tad snorted. 'Buy her some? When we can box the fox? 'Tis early days, the fellers won't be after apples yet awhile, but you an' me, we could go round to the house by the park. Sure an' the orchard there's too big for one family so it is.'

'Mammy says boxing the fox is thievery,' Polly pointed out self-righteously. 'And I don't want to do thievery.' She thought it over. 'Well, I don't want to get caught,' she amended.

'Polly, when did I ever lead you into trouble and get you caught? We'll be in and out before the folk at the big house know there's a Christian soul in the place beside themselves. Trust me!'

It was true that though Tad had led her into several hair-raising adventures, he usually managed to extract her from the same without damage, but Polly was still doubtful. And picking apples and blackberries in the rain would be nasty, chilly work.

She said as much to Tad, who looked offended at this criticism of his fine, money-making idea.

'Sure an' it'll stop rainin' any minute, alanna. Trust me!'

'Why should I? You aren't a weather prophet. And besides, even if it stops the trees will be powerful wet an' so will the blackers.'

Tad heaved a sigh and slid off the windowseat. Ivan, building bricks on the rug, turned to stare at them. 'Has it stopped?' he asked. He had been asking the same question ever since breakfast, and Polly sighed.

'No, it hasn't,' she said. 'But we're goin' out anyway, Tad and me.'

'You're takin' me!' Ivan shrieked, jumping to his feet so hastily that he spilt building bricks everywhere. 'I'm goin' out if you're goin' out!'

But at that point Polly's mother appeared, a pair of spectacles perched on the end of her nose, a letter in her hand.

'No, you aren't goin' anywhere, Ivan,' she said briskly. 'Polly an' Tad's goin' to post me letter, that's all.'

She held out the letter and Polly took it. 'Who's it to?' she asked automatically, and then, glancing at the writing on the front of the envelope: 'Oh, it's to my daddy. Did you give him a kiss from me, Mammy?'

'Probably,' Mammy said absently. 'But I had a lot to say to him; mebbe I didn't remember to send your kiss. Why don't you write one on the back of the envelope, Polleen? Then he'll be sure to see it first off.'

'I will,' Polly said joyfully. 'Where's your pen, Mammy?'

'In the kitchen; I went there for some peace and quiet, away from the young gentleman there,' Mammy said, jerking her head at Ivan, sitting amidst the ruins of his brick castle and glaring tearfully up at them. 'Now no nonsense, Ivan, your sister has a message to run and you'd only slow her down.' She winked at Polly. 'Sure an' she won't be long.'

'Watch Lionel; by the time he's washed himself from heel to toe we'll be back,' Polly said, smiling at her little brother. 'Be a good boy for Mammy now.'

Deirdre watched as Polly drew crosses on the back of the envelope and added the words *kisses from your loving Polly*, and then she watched as the two youngsters went out of the room. She listened as they clattered down the stairs, then watched again as they

309

emerged in the street below. The letter was still firmly grasped in Polly's small and probably grubby hand.

I've done a wrong thing, a wicked thing, Deirdre thought suddenly. I ought to run down the stairs, and across the yard and into the alley. I ought to stop Polly, say there's somethin' in the letter I forgot, get it back . . . throw it into the heart of the fire. That would be the right, the kind thing to do.

But it had taken her months to screw up her courage after Peader's last visit, and actually write the letter that had been forming in her head ever since last Christmas. And this morning, when she looked out of the window and saw the rain coming down like stair rods, sure and hadn't it seemed the right moment, the best opportunity she was likely to get? The kids were home to give an eye to Ivan and she could sit quietly at the kitchen table and compose the letter.

Why hadn't she written it before? Why hadn't she told him that she'd thought it over and she couldn't leave Dublin? Not wouldn't, just couldn't. Because hadn't he been away a dozen years or more and hadn't she grown used to being a woman alone? But with money coming in, a little voice reminded her mockingly. Her life was easy compared to most, she didn't even have to work, scarcely remembered the bad old days when Peader had been here, getting one day's work a fortnight perhaps, whilst she tramped out to the farmlands, dug potatoes, paid the farmer for them and wheeled them home again in her wooden box on wheels which had once belonged to a rich man's perambulator. She had wheeled them to the markets, Moore Street, Francis Street, anywhere, and sold them, with Brogan in an orange box beside her, then Niall, then Martin.

Peader had been good to her, even then. Helped all

he could, raced desperately along the docks from read to read, imploring work, putting himself out for the other men, even going out to the tips when things got desperate, to pick over the rubbish. Rooney men they called them, tip pickers, ragged and hopeless, they were down there all hours, turning over the rubbish for something they could sell. Old metal, decent rags, glass bottles – anything.

And then he had come to her and said there was work over the water. Well-paid work, too.

'They'll be diggin' a tunnel under the Mersey in a year or so,' he had said, eyes shining. 'And there's men wanted on the railways ... me pal Johnny's goin'. He says it's his last chance to get out o' debt. Well, we're not in debt, alanna, but at the rate we're goin' God alone knows how long it'll be before we have no choice. Pawning's all right, but borrowin' money ... well, that's the way to trouble.'

She had begged him not to go, not to leave her, but they'd both known that it was go or starve. She was expecting her fourth child and it had been a bad pregnancy. She'd not been able to get out to the fields for the spuds and buying in and then selling didn't make the money. Brogan was eight, he'd started in selling newspapers and Deirdre had always vowed to give her boys their childhood. No work until they were twelve, she and Peader had said. But it all went by the board when the kids were crying for food, their cheeks hollowing ...

Peader had left for England and the money had started coming immediately. Good money. He'd worked on the London Underground, tunnelling through the cold clay and never a word of complaint out of him, though he told her afterwards that there were times he was so tired and so sick from the foul air that he'd been tempted to miss a day or two, get himself right.

But he'd never done it. He'd worked grimly on until he heard of vacancies for linesmen and labourers on the railway in Liverpool, then he'd applied and got it. When Brogan was fourteen he'd sent for Brogan, too. There was work for a strong lad and since Brogan could share his lodgings a roof over his head was no difficulty.

So why can't I go to him, run his home for him and bring up his children in Liverpool, just as if it were Dublin? Deirdre asked herself. And didn't rightly know the answer. She liked her home, her neighbours, her life . . . but what was any of that compared to Peader? She loved him, always had, always would . . . but crossing the water? Living there, with the English, a people she hated and feared? Sure, Peader did it, but she wasn't a man, she was a weak woman, and she could not face it. Better that she should tell Peader now than later, when he'd got a place for them and was expecting her to arrive with all her goods and chattels.

So why did she hang out of the window, in the rain, and try to see whether she could still catch a glimpse of Polly and Tad? Why did she suddenly snatch Ivan up in her arms, fling her old waterproof round the pair of 'em, and go chasing down the stairs like a girl again? If she knew she was right, had made up her mind . . .

She knew where Polly would take the letter, because Polly was good about things like that. She'd go to the Post Office on James Street because she'd not trust a precious letter to her daddy to an ordinary post box. So if I hurry I can still catch her before she pops it into the letter box, Deirdre told herself. Kids always dawdle when they're sent on messages, it's grown-ups who are always in a hurry.

She ran, breathless, and told Ivan he was a great lump so he was and in the end had to put him on the pavement, seize his hand, and run with him through the rain, splashing in and out of puddles, avoiding the piles of rotting vegetables, old rags and other debris which littered the pavements.

'Shall we have a pie?' Ivan said breathlessly as they passed a bakery. 'I'd like a pie, so I would.'

'Not now, me darlin' boy, later, when I've caught your sister,' Deirdre panted. 'Later, I promise.'

Ivan was a good boy, though spoilt. His mammy was in a hurry, he would just have to hurry too, was his attitude. Once he complained of a pain in his side, once he fell down and was heaved summarily to his feet again. On and on they ran, mother and son, and they reached the Post Office just in time to see Polly and Tad turning away from the letter box.

'Mammy!' Polly cried. 'We've done it, we've posted your letter to Daddy!'

And she had to say, good, thank you, alanna, because she had asked the child to post it. But she must have looked desperate worried, for Tad put a hand on her arm.

'What's the matter, Mrs O'Brady?' he asked kindly. 'Did you leave somethin' out, then?'

'I did . . . and put somethin' in that I never should have,' Deirdre said distractedly. 'Oh, Tad, I never should have . . . but there, I suppose I can go home, write again.'

'We can't get it out of the box,' Polly said, looking worried. 'Oh, Mammy, you did say to post it – and it's got me kisses on the envelope so it has!'

'Never mind, it's me own fault,' Deirdre said turning away from the box. 'I'll go straight home this minute and write another letter . . . just a note, you know, wit' the things I missed out of the first letter all put in.'

Ivan was snivelling, clutching his side, so she swung him into her arms. 'Ah, come on, don't let me down now, you've been such a good boy,' she said coaxingly. 'I'll buy you a pie so I will, and we'll make our way home and have a good cup of tea.'

But when she reached home the fire had gone out and it took a while to relight. And then Ivan was cross and kept complaining that his breath hurt in his chest so it did, from hurrying. Deirdre ministered to him, relit the fire, made some tea and then sat herself down to write a second letter.

In many ways it was easier than the first, yet still she toiled over it, anxious to get it right. She'd realised how selfish her first letter had been, she'd forgotten all he'd suffered over the years, she *would* come over the water to him when he'd found them somewhere to live.

Having written the letter she put it in an envelope and looked around for a stamp. No stamps. She must have used the last one on the previous letter. Sighing, she went to her drawer and got out some pennies, then placed them, and the letter, on the small table by the door. When Polly came home, worn out, God love her, she would ask the child as a special favour to take the second letter to the post, and she'd give her and Tad a kid's eye each – a threepenny bit – for the message.

There was a piece of bacon to boil for their dinner and a great many spuds to peel, for though Niall was in America – doing very well, his letters said – the rest of the family was still at home so there were many mouths to feed. I'll make a duff for after the bacon, Deirdre told herself. A nice duff with a bit of sugar and plenty of suet . . . that will line their stomachs.

Humming to herself now the letter was written, working away at the meal, occasionally breaking off to make sure Ivan was all right, Deirdre found all her old calmness and pleasure in small things return. Idly, she wondered why she had written the damned old letter in the first place. She'd been feeling out of sorts for a month, two months, perhaps that was it? She was no longer young . . . Brogan was twenty-five so she'd been married twenty-six years, and she'd been twenty-two on her wedding day.

I'm forty-eight, an ould one indeed, Deirdre thought, chopping onions and wiping the resultant tears away with the back of her hand. Forty-eight years old and as frightened of change as a four-year-old! Worse, because a four-year-old would relish change, not understanding the complications.

But it was no use repining; the first letter was on its way, the second about to join it. Sure and with my luck he'll open the first and be terrible upset, Deirdre told herself. But then he'll open the second . . . and the sun will come out and the rain will stop and he'll be his old self again.

After some time it occurred to her that the kids should have been home by now. But kids being kids, they could have gone off on any wild goose chase. They'd be home for their tea – she knew them!

It wasn't a long walk to the big house, but you had to go down a country lane, which meant that Polly daw-dled, because she did love country lanes so she did! There were the verges, with grass up to your knees, and the hedges, rich with different varieties of trees, and there was the white dust of the road which, when it rained, turned into the smoothest, richest mud in the world. It had rained a lot today, had only stopped within the last half-hour. The kids loved to make mud balls at the canal when the dredger barge had done its work, sludging up the rich, oozy mud from the bottom of the canal and dumping it on the bank. But this mud, in Polly's expert opinion, was even better. It was white, for a start, or perhaps not quite white, but more cream. This splodge is clotted cream from the dairy and that splodge, sure it's only buttermilk, Polly dreamed, pushing the mud ahead of her with a plimsolled foot. The mud would go through the hole in the toe of the plimsoll, but who cared, especially since it would probably rain again before nightfall. Now the sky was clear, the sun had only just set, the whole world seemed to sparkle at them, but later, on their way home, Polly laid a bet with herself that it would rain again, washing the mud from her plimsolls – and feet – as well as a bath would.

'C'*mon*, Poll, get movin', girl,' Tad called impatiently from ahead. 'If you don't hurry we'll be boxin' the fox in the dark, an' you won't like that!'

'I thought we were goin' to collect blackers,' Polly said, breaking into a reluctant trot. 'You said blackers first, then apples. And it's gettin' awful late.'

'But blackers are free, we can get 'em any time. Apples is more harder. If we get the apples this afternoon, then we can get blackers tomorrer, easy.'

Polly saw the logic of this. 'All right, then,' she said uneasily. 'Only I don't want to find meself in the police station so I don't.'

'For boxing the fox? 'Course you won't. Come *on*, Polly!'

The two of them accordingly hurried along, hand in hand, with Tad instructing Polly how she was to make a bag out of her skirt, into which he could drop the fruit.

'What's wrong wit' your pockets?' Polly asked indignantly. Why should she do all the work, take all the
blame? 'You've got pockets; girls only have knickers.'

'A skirt carries more,' Tad said. 'Besides, it means
you needn't climb the trees. If you come to the foot of
the wall and stand against it, I'll drop the apples down
to you.'

It sounded all right, so Polly trudged on, but in fact
she had been right when she said it was getting late,
though it looked as though the rain had gone for the
duration. By the time they reached the russet-bricked
wall which encircled the big orchard, it was already
dusk. Stars were pricking out in the deep-blue sky
overhead and on the horizon a faint, greenish line heralded the last of the sunset.

'Give me a back,' Tad commanded as soon as they
reached the wall. ''Tis too late for goin' down on the
grass, I'll have to pick what I can from the nearest trees
and t'row them down to you. Come *on*, Poll.'

Polly hunched down and felt Tad's feet thump her
momentarily in the small of her back as he bounded
up on to the high wall. She straightened, a hand in the
small of her back and peered into the shadows cast by
the overhanging tree branches.

'You all right, Tad?' she whispered. 'Hurry, it's gettin'
darker by the minute so it is.'

'Hold out your skirt, woman,' was the only reply
she got, but she could see that Tad was feverishly
picking . . . and they were big apples, the size of a
baby's head. Cookers, then . . . they'd make a wonderful pie. Polly's mouth watered at the prospect.

Presently the first apple descended. Polly caught it
and shoved it up her knicker-leg where it felt very
large and very obvious. If someone came along, whatever would she say?

She put the point to Tad, who said, 'They're wind-falls, stupid. Anyone can pick windfalls. Here's another for you.'

He threw it gently and Polly fielded it, beginning to feel more confident now as the darkness grew steadily deeper. But she wished she'd thought to bring a bag . . . she had already exhausted the holding power of her knickers. Four large apples were the limit there, so it really would have to be the skirt.

Then she heard the noise. Footsteps, not quiet ones either, solid, tramping sort of footsteps. Someone was coming along the dusty lane!

'Tad – ' Polly began, turning towards the sound – and was hit fair and square in the middle of the forehead by apple number five.

Tad, having started to throw the apple, saw Polly turn away, tried to grab the apple back, and fell heavily off the wall as Polly went down like a ninepin, flat on her back in the long, rain-wet grass. Tad was starting to scramble to his feet, when he, too, heard the footsteps. He froze, then his hand snaked out and caught Polly's wrist, warning her not to move. The grass was long and very wet, no one would voluntarily walk in it when they could walk along the roadway. If they kept very quiet . . .

'What about here, Mick?'

A hissing, sibilant whisper and the footsteps stopped. Whisperers are usually up to no good. Thank God, Tad thought fervently, they'll be no keener to tell on us than we would be to tell on them. But they sound old . . . twenty, maybe thirty. Men, not boys. Oh, Mary, Mother of Jesus, pray for my sins . . . make them fellers go away and I'll sell some of me apples an' buy you a big candle, I promise you that so I do!

'Well ...' the answering whisper was loaded with doubt. 'We'll not get the dogs over wit'out a struggle. Dere's a little gate furder along ... 'twould be best to try dere.'

Dogs! Oh, my God, Tad thought, and began to pray in earnest.

'How much furder, Mick? Only we want to be able to see somethin'; how can we set traps if it's pitch-dark?'

'I've a 'lectric torch, you fool. Aw, c'mon, me man, 'tis not much furder.'

Tad waited for an agonising moment until the footsteps started up again, then he lifted his head. He had time to see that the whisperers were two tallish men with lurchers held on short lengths of rope, when there was a deep and ghastly groan right by his ear. Polly was going to give the game away!

The shadows turned; Tad could see them even through the dusk, and the dogs turned too, ears pricked, muzzles scenting the air.

'What was dat?'

Desperately, Tad put his hand over Polly's mouth. She groaned again, a sort of bubbling moan and then said loudly, through his desperate fingers, 'What did you do that for, you spalpeen? Me head's split in two so it is!'

It sounded awful, even Tad realised that; hollow, spooky. And the men clutched each other and then set off at a gallop up the lane, knocking into each other and cursing volubly until they were out of sight.

Tad sat up and then scrambled to his feet. He reached for Polly and dragged her, like a rag doll, to her feet, too. 'What the hell were you doin', shoutin' out like that?' he demanded wrathfully, giving her a good shake, but the minute he let go of her shoulders she

319

fell straight down again, frightening him considerably. He knelt beside her.

'Polly? We've got to get out of dis, girl, or we're dead men!'

Polly did not move. She muttered something, but she did not move at all. In the dusk he could just make out the pale oval of her face; her eyes were closed and her mouth drooped pathetically. Oh, dear God, I've kilt her stone dead, Tad thought frantically. What the devil do I do now?

When the duff was made and simmering on the fire, Deirdre took Ivan some bread and margarine with good strawberry jam on it, a big mug of milk and a few broken biscuits. He was mollified to be given a meal in his bed and graciously ate everything that was offered, including the broken biscuits which were a big treat. He counted the pieces, then tried to fit them together, then ate them anyway, crowing with delight when he found one of his pieces was the sort with hard pink icing on it . . . everyone wanted those particular biscuits, he assured his mammy, because they were lucky, so they were. And he hadn't even picked the pink 'un out himself which must make it luckier than ever. And then, to his mother's astonishment, he never even suggested getting up and having dinner when the rest of the family got home, he just snuggled down and was asleep within minutes.

Poor wee feller, he was cold after runnin' through the wet streets after his sister, Deirdre thought remorsefully. All my fault . . . but now he's settled early, so I might as well make the best of it. I'll get the spuds on to boil, then the meal will be ready when Polly and the boys arrive. I'll ask Tad in for a bite, since he's been runnin' my messages today.

Deirdre pulled the pan of spuds over the fire, then got out her mending. She lit the lamp and, presently, Martin came in, kicked off his lace-up shoes, undid his tie and his stiff shirt, and threw himself down in an easy chair.

'Mammy, I'm wore out,' he said. 'Am I first in, tonight?'

'Not for long by the sound of it,' Deirdre said as footsteps hurried up the stairs. 'This'll be Polly and Tad, I daresay.'

But when the door burst open it was Donal and Bevin, talking nineteen to the dozen. Both boys did jobs after school, Donal sold turf from door to door and Bevin delivered newspapers. He didn't sell them, as Tad and Polly did, he just delivered them, but he earned enough for picture-money, with some left over for extras. He was saving up for a bicycle, not a new one, a secondhand model, and thought he would have sufficient money by Christmas. Both boys greeted their mother with absent-minded affection.

Mammy, that's a good smell so it is and we're starvin', amn't we? Is it nearly ready?'

'It is ready. We're just waitin' on Polly and Tad.'

'I'll wash first,' Bevin said. He grabbed the kettle off the fire, spilled some water on the hearth and got shouted at for his pains.

'Cold water if you please, Bev! Don't play around, the pair of ye! Come and set the table as soon as you're clean, Donal.'

'That's Polly's job,' Donal grumbled, but it was automatic rather than meant. The boys knew Polly always pulled her weight and so they didn't mind doing the odd feminine task if she was late, or busy.

When the boys had washed and the table was laid, Deirdre began to get really worried. 'I sent them on a message . . . little devils, they must have gone straight out to play when they'd done it,' she said, trying to peer down into the street. 'Martin, go to the corner and see if you can see them. Tell them dinner's on the table.'

Martin went down the stairs and across the courtyard, then Deirdre lost sight of him. He was gone ten minutes, during which time she dished up, then Martin came clumping up the stairs once more.

'They aren't in the alley, or not that I could see,' he said positively. 'I yelled blue murder, Mammy, but there wasn't a sign of 'em. Can I have me dinner now?'

By eight o'clock Deirdre was frantic.

'Go to the police, Martin, and tell 'em we've two kids, one of them a young girl, missin' from home,' she said. 'The rest of you, search the streets. Bevin, you go round to Gardiners Lane an' see if the Donoghues know anything. I'll have to stay here with Ivan . . . hurry, boys!'

Tad got Polly, still semi-conscious, across his shoulders, staggered perhaps a hundred yards along the verge to where some thick bushes grew against the wall, and let her down with a bump. 'Now will you wake up?' he said crossly, sitting down beside her. 'Sure an' aren't girls a terrible trouble to a feller?' He bent over Polly and stared hard at her small, pale face. 'Are you sleepin', Poll?' he asked, his voice suddenly laden with uncertainty. She looked so very small and remote, lying there. 'Oh, say you aren't dead!'

Polly opened her eyes. Large and dark and bewildered, they gazed around her, then lighted on Tad's face. A small smile tilted her mouth.

'Tad! Where am I?'

'Lyin' on your bloody back in the grass whiles

I almost die of fright; we were near trod on by two fellers, near kilt and ate by their two dogs, near took up by the polis,' Tad said wildly, in a hissing whisper. 'So keep your voice down an' lets get out of here!'

'Where's here?'

'We were boxing the fox, and you got hit on the head by an apple . . .' Tad began and was interrupted.

'Did it fall off the tree?'

It was tempting to say it had, but Tad did not trust Polly's innocent, almost dreamy tone.

'No, it didn't. But it knocked you out cold. Now can you get to your feet, girl?'

'I'll try,' Polly said feebly. 'Where's the men, Tad? An' the polis?'

'Gone,' Tad said tersely. 'Upsadaisy!'

'It must be midnight . . . it must be later,' Polly said in an aggrieved tone as they rounded the corner into Swift's Alley at last. 'What's all the people doin' up at this hour?'

'It isn't that late,' Tad said reassuringly. 'Probably no more'n ten o'clock. Anyhow, we'll be home in two ticks.' They reached Polly's block and Tad peered into the dark interior, then turned away. 'See you in the mornin', Poll.'

'Oh no you don't, you aren't runnin' out on me,' Polly hissed, grabbing his arm. 'I'll be kilt, so I will, but you're goin' to be kilt as well.'

'Oh, but not twice! Me own mam an' dad . . .'

'They won't touch a hair of your head for bein' late,' Polly said scornfully, with unconscious cruelty. 'They prob'ly won't even notice. It's me that'll get the legs slapped off me. Only if you tell 'em how I were hit on the head and made unconscious . . .'

'If I tell 'em that it's me that'll get kilt, good an'

proper,' Tad said, horrified at the mere suggestion. 'The bloody apple done it, but who'll get the blame? Who always gets the blame when you're in trouble, St Polly!'

'I gets into trouble on me own account so I do,' Polly said stoutly. 'Aw, c'mon, Tad, else I'm goin' to sleep on the stairs. I dussen't go up alone.'

'Oh, all right then,' Tad growled. 'It's dark an' all . . . give me your hand.'

Clutching each other, the two of them climbed the stairs. Slow and soft, because neither wanted a scene in the open. They fumbled noiselessly across the landing and opened the door into the living room. Tad would have done it cautiously, to hear what the first words were to be in order to have a head start if tempers were roused, but Polly simply opened it and marched into the room.

Her mammy had been sitting by the window, staring out into the dark. She turned as the door opened . . . and flew across the linoleum, arms held out.

Tad would have dodged and probably ducked as well, then run for it. Polly ran, too, he had to give her that. But towards, not away. And was folded in a warm embrace whilst Mrs O'Brady, with tears pouring down her cheeks, hugged and hugged and said: 'Oh, me darlin', we've been desp'rit worried, we've been round to the polis, we've had the whole family out huntin' . . . indeed, they're all out there still, combin' the streets.'

'Shall I go an' tell 'em she's all right?' Tad said faintly. He could imagine what Martin would do to him if he did not spread the good news, and Martin and Donal always stuck together so he'd get whipped by the pair of 'em, not just by one. 'I'll not explain, I'll just say she's home an' safe.'

Tad had always liked Mrs O'Brady. Now he liked her more than ever, for she gave Polly one last hug, then came over – he tried not to wince away – and hugged him, too.

'You're a terrible pair but I knew you'd stick by me daughter, Tad,' Mrs O'Brady said, letting go of him and tousling his already tousled head. 'It halves the worry when I know you're together. Now, Tad, come back as soon as you've found the boys; I've got a hot meal waiting.'

'Sure, Mrs O'Brady,' Tad said. She was a lovely woman so she was! 'I'll be back before you know it.'

And he most certainly was, since he met the boys as soon as he emerged into the alley. Martin looked a little anxious but Donal and Bev were taking it pretty well, considering. Bev was eating a toffee apple on a stick and Donal was kicking a smooth, round pebble in front of him, giving it most of his attention. But they all three grinned at him as he began to speak.

'She's awright, fellers. I'm awfu' sorry, your mammy said you were worried, but we got back as soon as we could . . .'

He was poised for flight despite what Mrs O'Brady had said but it seemed he was not to be thumped, on this occasion at least.

'We knew you'd be all right. Picking blackers, were you? Polly said you might. Only we knew if Mammy thought her ewe lamb was roamin' country roads in the dark she'd do worse than just worry.'

That was Martin, shoving his hands into his trouser pockets and heading for home at a good pace.

'What about the polis?' Tad said nervously. The very mention of the name made his stomach turn over. The police only had to set an eye on a chiseller to read his mind, Tad knew, and his mind didn't always want a readin' by the law. 'Your mammy said she'd told the polis.'

'Never a word did we breathe to 'em,' Donal said. 'Sure an' we *knew* you'd be safe as houses, but no use tellin' Mammy. 'Search, tell the polis, get the neighbours out,' she shouted, so we made ourselves scarce.'

'I'm glad,' Tad said in heartfelt tones. 'But s'pose we had been in trouble, Don? S'pose Polly had needed help?'

'Sure and hasn't our Poll got her own guardian angel?' Bev piped up. 'She's always tellin' us about the young girl in the ragged shawl who looks after her. Who are we to stop a guardian angel doin' her work?'

'True,' Martin said. 'I don't want no guardian angel comin' at me for tryin' to take over the job! 'Sides, Tad, you're by way of bein' a bit of a guardian angel yourself. If she were in trouble, I guess you'd get her out, eh?'

'If I could,' Tad admitted, remembering the weight of Polly across his shoulders as he'd carried her inanimate form to deeper cover. 'Oh, fellers, your mammy asked me back for a meal . . . is it all right if I come?'

'Sure that's fine,' Martin said, speaking for them all. 'I wouldn't mind somethin' meself. What *were* the pair of yous up to, Tad?'

'We was boxin' the fox,' Tad admitted, getting poised to run all over again. But the boys just nodded; they'd all done it in their time. 'Then some men came along with those thin, long-nosed dogs . . . can't think o' the name . . . and we had to hide till they'd gone past.' He heaved a sigh. Truth would always out. 'Polly were at the foot o' the wall and I were on top, throwin' the apples down. Only she heard the fellers and turned her head away just as I chucked an apple, and it got her right on the noddle.'

It was a relief to hear them laugh loud enough to

drown the sound of their footsteps. Bev folded up, holding his stomach.

'You hit Polly on the head wit' an apple, and you're still standin'?' he asked incredulously. 'I wonder she didn't marmelise you!'

'She – she couldn't. She dropped like a stone, I'm tellin' ye,' Tad admitted. 'Down she went, *bam*, and down she stayed whiles the fellers went past.'

The three boys laughed again; if anything, louder.

'Sure an' we love our little sister,' Martin said at length, wiping tears of amusement from his eyes. 'But Mammy spoils her rotten; 'twon't do her any harm to be took down a peg ... she's all right now, I guess?' he added without much anxiety.

'Right as a trivet,' Tad assured him. ''Cept for a bump on her forehead.'

'Perhaps she'll have a black eye in the mornin',' Bev said hopefully. 'What'll she tell the nuns, fellers?'

But they had reached the tenement block and Martin frowned at them, stifling their mirth.

'Quiet now; Mammy will be puttin' the food on the table and if you want to eat tonight, fellers – I'm not countin' you, Bev, fillin' your face wit' toffee apples an' your sister lost – then you won't let Mammy catch you sniggerin'!'

Going up the stairs behind the older boys, Tad digested the conversation. Polly's brothers loved her, he knew that all right. They were proud of her, though they liked to cod her, make her mad with them. But they thought she was spoiled, needed taking down a peg, and they hadn't torn Tad limb from limb for clonking her on the nut with an apple. Far from it, they thought it a huge joke. Behind the broad O'Brady backs, Tad gave a little grin. Sure an' didn't he love Polly himself, and didn't he like to cod her along sometimes, too? And she was spoiled – how many kids would have run at their mammy the way she had, when she was four hours late for her tea?

But Tad didn't mind. Mrs O'Brady trusted him with Polly, and so did her brothers. And so, of course, did Polly. She followed where he led, did as he did, and let him deal with the consequences. Why, she had been frightened to go up to the O'Brady rooms without him, yet she must have known, in her heart, that her mammy would simply be glad to see her safe!

Women is definitely funny, Tad concluded as the living-room door opened and a most delicious smell wafted out. Definitely funny – but wonderful cooks!

The apples were divided – three for the Donoghues and two for the O'Bradys – and apple dumplings were made by Mrs O'Brady, lacking blackers for the time being. In fact the apples were a thing of the past when three days later, Polly, in the living room, called through to her mother working in the kitchen.

'Mammy, what's the money doing on the mantelpiece?'

'Which money?' Deirdre said, coming into the room wiping her hands on a piece of towel, for she had just finished preparing vegetables for soup. 'I don't remember putting any money on the mantel.'

'It's pennies,' Polly said. She was running her hand along the back of the mantel shelf and she held out two large coins . . . 'They were on top of . . .'

'Me letter! Oh, God love him, it's the letter I meant to send to your daddy the day you boxed the fox and come in late! Oh, alanna, that letter should have gone days ago!' Deirdre dropped the towel and ran across the room, seizing the letter and holding it, for a second, against her breast. 'What'll I do, what'll I do?'

'I'll post it for you now,' Polly said. ''Twon't take but a minute. I'll get stamps from the post office . . . I'll fetch Tad at the same time.'

'But it's days . . . oh well, let's hope your daddy understands.' Deirdre put the letter and the pennies into her daughter's hand. 'Off wit' you, then. And this time, don't be late!'

Chapter Twelve

Peader read the letter slowly, over breakfast. Then he read it again. Then he put it down by his plate and stared at it. What in God's good name was the matter with his own Deirdre? Blowing hot and cold, yes one minute, no the next. She *knew* he had started saving for somewhere nice in the neighbourhood. He'd even spoken to the boss at work, saying that grand though it was being safety man for an area like his, he wasn't getting any younger and had thought that, if a country station wanted either a safety man or a simple linesman, he might think about changing jobs.

The boss knew Peader's worth, and agreed that in the fullness of time such a change might be arranged. So whilst a move might not come for a while, come it would, and a quieter area would be better for Deirdre and the children. Not that they'd ever known a quiet area, but he felt instinctively that his wife would find it easier to transplant herself and her family if he could offer her the enticement of a village, a proper garden, birds and flowers and fresh vegetables instead of shops, stink, crowds.

But before he could even do so, she had thrown his offer back in his face. Folly, bless her, had put kisses on the envelope, but there were precious few kisses inside it! Just that she wanted to please him but couldn't, wouldn't, contemplate a move such as he had suggested.

'Bad news, Mr O'Brady?' Mrs Burt said sympathetically. 'It's a long way from home you feel at such times.'

'Yes,' Peader said. 'Well, not good news. But it's all right, I'll get me mind round to it in time.'

And then it was time to go to work, to take his carry-out and his bottle of cold tea and go and join his gang.

He thought of little else though, all through that long day. And when, in mid-afternoon, the fog began to swirl in from the Mersey, creeping up to hide first the horizon, then the water, then the docks, the rails, everything, he scarcely took it in at first.

'Paddy, you're doing the charges on the Southport line,' his boss said at three in the afternoon. Unless it clears, that is. Be back here by seven. I want them set in time for the 8.03.'

'Right,' Peader said. He was used to being addressed as Paddy by the ignorant non-Irish. 'I'll be back.'

He trudged to the bicycle shed, loosed the padlock and rode off. Somehow the ride seemed twice as long as usual due to the heaviness in his heart. Not coming! There had been no kindly 'maybe', or indulgent 'perhaps'. Just 'not coming', and he had to come to terms with it. And the fog was, if anything, thicker. He got off his bike in the end after he'd hit the kerb twice and nearly come a cropper, and pushed it, sticking close to the pavement, keeping right in the gutter . . . and even so he found himself on Tetlow Street and had to cut down Heather Street to reach his lodgings.

Mrs Burt made him a good tea but was cross when he said he had to go out again. 'Sure an' they work you like a black,' she grumbled, making him up a fresh carry-out despite his protestations. 'I know how it will be, Mr O'Brady, you'll find yourself trudging that line until all hours. Fog isn't only the seamen's curse, it's the railwaymen's, too.'

Peader laughed. 'You should hear the passengers,' he said. 'The trams stop runnin', and the buses. Taxi drivers are so busy peerin' out t'rough the windscreens or out o' the side winders that they miss your street . . . Fog's the curse of the English nation so it is.'

'Don't you get fogs in Dublin?' Mrs Burt asked curiously, handing him his hat. 'If that's true, I'll be movin' over there meself.'

Peader tried to laugh again, but the remark hurt as much as a punch in the gut. Movin' there herself, indeed! Oh God, if only Deirdre's letter had said that she'd come to him! Once, she would have, he knew it. But over the years of managing alone she had somehow grown hard, less loving. With independence, it seemed, had come indifference. His happiness, which had once been their happiness, had been paramount. Not any more.

'Are you takin' the bike, Mr O'Brady?'

'More trouble than it's worth,' Peader decided. 'I'll walk. See you later, Mrs Burt.'

He set off through the fog. He would stick to the kerb, count the turnings, and not get lost. He ought to know the way blindfold after all these years.

He arrived in good time, picked up his detonators already packed into the old haversack, and set off. As soon as he was clear of the yard itself the fog smelled different; of coal-dust of course, of damp and mildew, but also of loneliness. You're all alone out here, Peader me boy, the fog declared, clinging as diamonding dewdrops to his donkey jacket, his serge trousers, even his big heavy boots. And you'll stay that way because they don't have the gangs out in this, too dangerous, and

332

the next train's not due till eight and it'll be late. Bound to be.

There was no way of telling where you were, of course, you simply had to count your paces. The trouble was, Peader was so full of unhappiness that he could not concentrate. Twice he had to go back, all the way back, to the road bridge, which was a point that not even the fog could hide, and retrace his steps.

But he decided on the third attempt that he was probably more or less in the right spot. He would count the rails, put his detonators in position, and walk back. Then he'd have his cold tea and his bread and Maggie Ryan – not that Mrs Burt would have heard of him having only Maggie on his bread; there was cold mutton in some of the sarnies and good red cheese in others – and set off again to reset the line if the fog hadn't lifted in time for the ten fifty-eight.

He fumbled the detonators out of his haversack because his hands were cold and his mind elsewhere . . . why, why, WHY? . . . and then began to walk back towards where he knew the station to be. He hadn't gone ten yards, though, when he saw a shape ahead of him in the fog. Another safety man? Had someone ordered two of them to protect the same length of line? It did happen.

'Hello,' Peader said loudly. 'Who's dat?'

There was a pause, then the figure, which had been turned away from him, turned towards him.

'Hello? It's awright, I'm not doin' no 'arm, I'm just a-goin'.'

A girl's voice. Quite a young girl. Peader continued to walk towards her. He said in as kindly a voice as he could manage, 'You're trespassin', chuck . . . are ye lost? This is a dangerous place to be on such a night.'

'It is a bad fog,' she agreed. She coughed, a small,

tearing cough. 'It 'urts me chest . . . which way is home?'

He was close enough to see her properly now. She was small, and very pale, she looked to be nine or ten but her eyes were old, anxious. Twelve, maybe? Or perhaps thirteen?

'Come along, mavoureen, let's both of us get . . .'

He was walking towards her across the rails when he felt, against the sole of his boot, the rail vibrate. Just a gentle tickle of vibration at first but getting stronger and more definite by the minute.

'Train!' Peader shouted. 'Get off the rails, alanna . . . to your right now!'

She hesitated, staring blankly at the fog bank behind him, her eyes big and black in her small face.

'Which way's right? I can't hear no train . . . I'm searchin' for me baby sister, you see . . .'

Peader broke into a run. He ran along the track, shouting at her, and she took fright and turned from him, running along the track too, but not swerving off to right or left, simply continuing to run between the vibrating rails.

'Gorl, you'll be kilt! Off dese rails . . . don't matter which way!' Peader's voice came out as a bull's roar and the girl hesitated for just long enough. Peader's stride lengthened. He reached her, seized her small, skinny body by her little, sharp-boned shoulders, and threw her to one side, not heeding her startled cry which rose to a scream, a shriek, higher and higher . . .

Or was it the engine's scream? Or Peader's? For Peader was still not clear of the rails as the 7.03 from Southport, running late because of the fog, smote him, throwing him out of its path to crash like a rag doll on to the sleepers several feet away.

*

She ran through the night, through the fog, scarcely noticing as it parted to let her by and closed in behind her. She must get help, she must, she must! That nice man had been trying to help her, he'd thrown her clear but hadn't managed to jump clear himself. And it was just what had happened to Jess, she could remember the talk, the sighs, the short-lived intentions.

Her mam had been upset, of course, but all she'd wanted really was to show everyone they weren't as black as they'd been painted. She bent everyone's ear about her lost baby, her dead daughter, but folk round their way were judged on their actions, not on what they said. And Mam was too fond of letting the kids go their own way whilst she and her husband tore each other apart.

Grace had never known any security, not once Jess had died. And she'd been envious of the baby right from the start, because Grace had been Jess's little sister, the one Jess looked out for, until the new baby had come along.

Even now, when Grace lay down somewhere to sleep, she could lull herself off by reliving the first three or four years of her life, when Jess had loved her best. Her sister's wiry, half-starved body had given all its warmth and comfort to the little sister sharing her blanket, her scrap of bread, her cup of weak tea.

Then Moll had come along and for a while things continued as before, Jess looking out for Grace, Mam for Moll. But then Moll became a nuisance to their mam and got passed on to Jess – and Grace was out in the cold.

She had wished Jess no harm, but the same could not be said for the baby. She had longed for the baby to be dispossessed so that she could creep back into that thin blanket, lie down in Jess's arms, have at least a crumb of that concern for herself. And then Jess had been killed and the baby had vanished and she had known what true loss was. But she had loved Jess with all her heart, so she had known that somewhere, Jess would be worrying over her baby sister. And it occurred to Grace, for the first time, that if she could find Mollie then she could hug, nurture, cuddle the baby. She had lost Jess, but she might still salvage some love for herself.

So she had searched and searched. She had crept round to big, smart houses and begged from back doors and asked about babies . . . and got sent off with a flea in her ear more likely than not. She had fed her hunger on promises of Mollie's rosy-cheeked warmth, on the love the little sister would feel for the big one, once she was restored to the bosom of her family.

But Grace knew she herself was thirteen or possibly fourteen, and in the ten years which had elapsed since Jess died she had never seen hide nor hair of her little sister. She thought the baby must be dead, and she hadn't been hunting for her tonight, either, it was just an excuse for being on railway property. In fact she had been hunting for the men's carry-out. Grace knew that railway workers quite often didn't eat all their food, that sometimes they scattered it for the birds, or left it where hungry urchins might find it. Some of them fed stray dogs, some stray kids, she had heard one of the men remark, and she knew it was true.

So Grace had been scavenging in the foggy marshalling yard earlier, when the man had spied her and called out. She had let him get very near her, fascinated by the rich Irish brogue, the kindness in the dark eyes. And then the train had come, and he had been hit . . . and she must, she must get help!

She could see a light shining ahead of her, just visible

through the fog. She had a stitch now but she ran still, and came panting up to the light. It was streaming out of a small hut and when she poked her head round the open door she saw five large men, a coke-burning stove and a dog.

'Someone's been hit by the train!' Grace shouted, her voice very thin and small suddenly. 'He's up the line . . . he's hurt bad!'

The men surged to their feet. The oldest, who had a beard, said: 'Can you show us where, chuck? Can you find 'im again in the fog? Is it a railwayman, or someone else? A kid, perhaps?'

'It's a railwayman,' Grace said breathlessly. 'Folly me!'

With the men hard on her heels and the fog swirling around them, thick and yellow as phlegm, the little group set off. Don't let 'im be dead, God, Grace prayed as she did her best to retrace her steps. Oh God, don't let 'im be dead!

When the train had passed, silence crept back. The fog seemed to sigh and settle, thicker than ever, densest, perhaps, around the man's body, lying motionless beside the tracks.

The only sound was the *drip, drip* of water, falling from the overhead wires. And another sound . . . was it the patter of feet, running, running, away from the terrible figure across the sleepers? Or was it the patter of the blood which ran from the man's terrible open mouth?

Brogan knew within the hour.

'There's been an accident, Mr O'Brady,' the policeman said, standing on the doorstep, his helmet in his hand. 'You've got to get to Liverpool, pronto. It's your dad; a train hit him.'

Brogan didn't wait to ask questions, there was, in any event, no time. He went with the policeman to the station where he boarded the train and reached Liverpool an hour later. He went straight to the hospital where they had taken his father's broken body.

'You could telegraph your mother,' the nurse said kindly. 'She's not on the telephone, I suppose? Or you could telephone the nearest police station, they'd gerrin touch for you.'

'I'll telegraph,' Brogan said tightly. He straightened. 'I'd best send a telegram.'

He had been given his father's clothing and had checked through as the staff had requested, to make sure that nothing had been taken. There was a large blue and white checked handkerchief, his father's old hunter watch, stopped now, and some loose change. And .he letter.

He had read the letter because he'd not understood how his father could possibly have got in the way of the 7.03 when he knew, none better, that it was expected. Like all the men who walk the lines, Peader could have got careless, but – in fog? At night? When every bone in your body, every solitary muscle and nerve, is on the look-out for that tell-tale vibration in the rails?

After he'd read the letter he'd understood and for thirty minutes a great longing to feel his mother's slender throat between his hands had consumed him. But ... she was only a woman, she could not help her feelings, her desperate desire for her own home, her own place. Besides, to be angry, wanting revenge, was no way to help any of them. His mother would be no better a person if she carried a load of guilt to the grave. Better that she never knew his daddy had received the bloody letter, that she was simply told he'd been struck by the train whilst fixing detonators to the line, in fog.

So he went and sent his telegram – *Peader hit by train stop Please come stop Brogan* – and then returned to the hospital.

They were having their tea when the knock came at the door. Mammy was presiding over the pot with Polly beside her and the boys in their appointed places. Polly jumped up and opened the door; the boy handed over the small yellow envelope and Mammy looked up, saw him – knew. Her face whitened as though the blood had been dragged away from it and her eyes darkened. A hand flew to her throat. Whilst the boys were clamouring, Mammy snatched the envelope from Polly's fingers and tore it open. She read it at a glance, then tottered over to her chair and collapsed into it.

'Is it me daddy? What's happened, Mammy?'

Deirdre said nothing; she simply sat, staring at the telegram, until Polly took it from her and read it aloud.

'*Peader hit by train stop Please come stop Brogan.*' Polly frowned. 'Daddy's been hit . . . oh, Mammy, Mammy, is me daddy . . .'

There was silence. You could have heard a pin drop. Then Donal took the telegram from his sister's fingers and knelt down by his mother's side.

'Mammy? Does it mean Daddy's gone? And Brog doesn't say where we're to go, nor anything! I'll go down to the post office, telephone to England, see what I can find out. You wait here now – understand?'

Deirdre nodded, closed her eyes. Donal ran from the

room; they heard him clattering down the stairs, then they heard the outer door slam.

'I wish Martin was home,' Polly whispered. She sat down on the floor, close to her mother's chair, clinging to Deirdre's skirt, and after a moment her mother sat up a little straighter and took her daughter's hand in hers.

'Martin won't be long, alanna. And Donal will be back soon enough, you see.'

But it seemed a long time before the door opened again and when it did, Donal slipped back into the living room.

'Did you get t'rough to Brogan?'

'Is he . . . is he . . .'

'What happened, son?'

The questions came all at once and from more than one throat. Donal went straight to Deirdre and knelt down before her. He took her hands and spoke directly to her.

'Mammy, I got t'rough to the polis, an' they put me t'rough to someplace called the Stanley Hospital. Daddy's awful bad, but there's hope. They want you to get the next boat. Will you pack a few t'ings now, then we'll take you down to the docks for your ticket.'

Deirdre got up. Moving like a sleepwalker, she crossed the room and went out, leaving the door ajar. Polly, white as a sheet, glanced at her brothers, then followed her mother out of the room. Within seconds of them leaving there were footsteps on the stairs and Martin came into the room. He looked round.

'Where's Mammy? I was workin' late . . . what's up?'

'Daddy's hurt bad. Hit by a train,' Donal said. 'I told Mammy to pack a bag; Brogan sent a telegram, saying Mammy must go across the water.'

Martin hissed in his breath. 'What happened, for the Lord's sake? Daddy's a careful man . . .'

'It was foggy, so Daddy was laying the detonators,' Donal explained quietly. 'He couldn't have heard the train, because he stepped into its path.'

Unnoticed by any of them, their mother had come back into the room. At Donal's words she threw back her head and gave a keening wail. 'Ah, Peader, Peeeaaddder . . .'

It was uncanny, horrible, coming from their happy, humorous mother. Martin stepped forward, raised a hand and slapped his mother sharply across the cheek. The keening wail stopped as suddenly as it had begun. Deirdre put her hand to her face, incredulously, as though she expected to find blood running. Then she shook her head in a dazed fashion and took a deep, gulping breath.

'Martin, your daddy's dyin' and it's all . . .'

'He's not dead yet, Mammy,' Donal said. 'Martin and me'll take you down for to catch the boat. You've packed a bit of a bag, now?'

'I have. But . . . but I can't be goin' alone, I can't, I can't!'

'I'll go wit' you, Mammy,' Martin said. 'But I can't stay, I'd lose me job for sure. Still, once you're wit' Brogan you'll be all right, hey?'

'Aren't we all goin', then?' That was Bev, staring from face to face.

'No, indeed,' Martin said. 'Too many people are worse than too few. Donal, can you give an eye to 'em for a day or so? Make sure no one steps out of line?'

'Yes, sure I will,' Donal muttered. 'Is there nothin' else I can do indeed, Mart? Poor Daddy! What a turble t'ing.'

'Aye. No, there's nothing else, save keep 'em safe

until . . . until I can come home.' He turned as Polly came back into the room. 'Got Mammy's bag packed? Good girl.'

'Mammy's puttin' her coat on, then she'll be ready,' Polly said. 'Will I come wit' you, Martin? To take care of me mammy? She's not well, poor soul.'

'I'll take care of her,' Martin said. 'You do as Donal tells you, alanna, and keep house for Mammy. I'll be home in a day or so and Mammy'll come back as soon as she can.'

'Right,' Polly said. She was still pale. 'Martin, will ye give me daddy a kiss from me? To make it better?'

Bev started to speak, then stopped. He turned from them, his shoulders shaking. Donal got up from the table and put his arm round his brother and Martin, too, stood up.

Bev . . . come on, man, don't give way. We'll all do what we can . . . We all love, Daddy . . . come on, we'll all have a bit of a cry, then it won't seem so hard and cold.'

Deirdre came back into the room. She was wearing her black winter coat, a rather pretty rose-coloured felt hat and her black court shoes. She carried a shabby black hold-all and her cracked, black leather handbag.

'Ready, Mammy? Kisses all round, then.' The children crowded round, hugging her, kissing. 'Now you'll be prayin' for Daddy, each day, all of you?'

'Sure we will,' Polly said through her tears. 'Though if Daddy goes to Jesus he won't stay in Purgatory a moment, once Jesus knows who it is waitin' to come into Heaven. He'll have our daddy out o' there quick as you can.'

Martin caught hold of her and hugged her very tightly for a moment, then he spoke over the top of her red-gold curls.

'Sure and Daddy's mortal bad, alanna, I'd be the last to deny it, but he's not knockin' at the pearly gates yet awhile. 'Tis prayers for the livin' you must be makin', not prayers for the dead!'

'But Mammy said our daddy was dyin'.'

Deirdre's eyes filled with tears and colour flooded her cheeks. She picked Polly up and hugged her hard, then kissed the child's smooth, tear-wet cheek. ''Tis wrong I was to say such a t'ing, alanna. If we all pray very hard every day, your daddy will come home to us so he will.'

That night, after they had waved the ship off on its way to Liverpool, the boys and Polly walked back to the Liberties and when they reached Thomas Street, without a word said, they turned automatically into John's Lane Church.

It seemed odd to go into the church when there was no service on, Polly thought, but the red lamp burned on the High Altar and the blue one in the Lady Chapel and somehow the church no longer seemed strange but calm, serene. When Donal beckoned she followed him and the other boys into the Lady Chapel and Donal went and bought them a candle each. Polly knew which one was hers, it was thinner than the others and a tiny bit smaller but it was, she decided, the nicest. Donal lit the taper which was laid by the big candle and then brought the light over and the children lit their own candles, and Polly went on her knees and stared at her candle flame very hard and then began to pray.

The O'Bradys were not an exceptionally religious family. They went to Mass on a Sunday, paid their dues, bought candles, kept a shrine on the mantelpiece, holy water in a stoup by the door. But they did not ask the father before taking decisions, never visited the church mid-week, did not expect or ask for any particular favours from God.

Peader was less religious even than that. When he was home in Dublin he usually went to Mass on Sunday, but Polly guessed that he seldom attended church in Liverpool. Deirdre had once asked him about his church over there in her presence and, taken by surprise, his replies had lacked conviction.

'Sure an' you're a heathen, Peader O'Brady,' Deirdre had teased. 'Don't tell me; I know it all. A little drink here, a little drink there, and sure Sunday's over before you know it's begun, so it is.'

But now, praying as she had never prayed in her life before, staring at her candle flame, something happened which gave Polly comfort as well as conviction. Beside the candle flame and just behind it, she could just make out a vague figure, a shape. It was the girl Polly had first glimpsed on the stairs and now, when Polly looked straight at her she wasn't there, but when Polly stared at the candle and concentrated, she came, smiling, back.

She's me guardian angel, and she'll look after me daddy for me, because I know well how horrible it would be wit'out me daddy, Polly decided. And presently, when the boys scrambled to their feet, she got up and took Donal's hand and hugged it tight. Donal was sixteen, as good as a man, and he had snail trails down his face where the tears had been shed; poor Donal, he had neither her faith nor her guardian angel.

'Don, it'll be all right,' Polly whispered as they made their way home. 'Me guardian angel was in church so she was, and she smiled at me, gentle and beautiful. She's goin' to take care of our daddy, I know she is.'

And Donal, who had laughed before today and

344

codded her about her guardian angel, looked down at her and smiled and squeezed her hand.

'I'm sure she will,' he said, keeping his voice low as Polly had done. 'I'm sure she will, alanna. For a train's a turble big t'ing to be hit by. Our daddy will want all the help he can get to make him better so he will.'

Deirdre sat by the bed. Peader had tubes leading out of here and into there. He had so many cuts and abrasions on his face that she'd not recognised him at first . . . ah dear, and he so beautiful! But the spark of life still flickered, though he lay, eyes closed, face stern, far from them.

The nurse who was looking after him told Deirdre that he was a very strong man, strong as an ox, with a strong heart and good lungs.

'He'll need that strength in the weeks to come,' she had said, and Deirdre had smiled like an idiot. 'Weeks to come' meant he wasn't going to die in five minutes, which was how he looked with his grey skin and his mouth half open and his eyes sunk back into his head. 'You pray for him, Mrs O'Brady, and spend as much time as you can with him whilst his wounds heal. Who knows? He may walk out of here yet.'

That plunged Deirdre into depression again, because that made it sound as though it would need a miracle to get Peader on his feet again. But all you could do was pray and stay, pray and stay, and perhaps one day Peader would open an eye, smile, speak.

'His injuries are terrible,' the doctor had said when Deirdre had first arrived. 'It's a miracle he's here at all, Mrs O'Brady. But with every day that passes wounds heal a little bit and blood strengthens, bone knits. If we can just keep him alive . . .'

'Home each night at six, Mammy,' Brogan told her,

and though she had tried to insist that she must stay with Peader, she saw the sense of it in the end. Besides, the nurses made it plain they didn't want her all night as well as all day.

'We can do wit'out you as a patient, too, Mrs O'Brady,' Sister Lucy Flanaghan told her roundly. Lucy, being a Dublin girl herself, spoke out as one Irishwoman to another. ''Tis ill you'll make yourself, my dear.'

So Deirdre took herself off home each night to the small house in Salop Street, and slept in the bed where her Peader had slumbered for the past dozen or so years. And if his pillow was wet with her tears by midnight, sure and didn't she keep her unhappiness to herself when she went on to the ward? Cheerful she was then and optimistic, holding his poor hand, with the stitches marching across it like a railway line and stroking his cheek and telling him to get well soon, please, for hadn't she come a hell of a long way to see him, and wasn't it a poor thing that she was forced to sit by his bed and talk to herself, now?

But Peader never stirred, never moved a muscle or made so much as the tiniest sound. Nurses came in and made his poor, stiff limbs exercise, they wagged his arms and legs and turned him over, and Deirdre winced at the great, livid scars all over him and wondered, sometimes, whether he would ever be well. But then she would chide herself for her lack of faith and thank God he was still alive and on her way home would rush into the nearest church, which happened to be St Athanasius', on Chancel Street. There she would light a candle, genuflect, and then pray hard until her knees ached and her chaotic and painful thoughts gradually eased and smoothed out. Only then would she make her way back to Mrs Burt and the meal which awaited her.

'How shall I pay her?' she had asked Brogan just before he left for Crewe. A good job had to be nurtured at a time of high unemployment and Brogan dared stay away no longer. Martin, having delivered her and seen his father, had caught the next boat back to Ireland and the rest of the family. 'I've no money, son.'

'I'm paying; don't worry about it,' Brogan muttered. 'I'll leave you some money, Mammy, and send you more each week.'

Standing on the station platform, they had looked at each other, each knowing the worry that nagged them.

How long? How long would Peader lie there and how long could Deirdre stay? It was all very well to say she'd stay for ever, but the only money coming in back in Dublin was Martin's with Donal's part-time work and any pennies Polly could earn. Soon rent would be due, food would run short, school fees would be demanded for the coming term. Brogan sent what he could but he was supporting Deirdre and himself as well as the family, now. He could do no more.

'We'll manage, Mammy,' Brogan said quietly at last. 'If the worst comes to the worst sure an' aren't there the St Vincent de Paul men, or the Assistance? The kids will not starve.'

'They'd starve sooner than call in the Vincent's men,' Deirdre said. 'They humiliate you, Brogan, tell you that others manage on less. Your daddy saved us from all that. Oh, dear God, let him get well!'

'The Ward Sister's hopeful,' Brogan said. 'Mammy, here's me train, I can't stop. But I'll be back to see the pair of youse as soon as I've a day or so off. Ring the booking office at Crewe station if there's any change. They'll see I get the message.'

'I will,' Deirdre promised. 'And I'll write you each week, son, when I write to Polly and the boys.'

She waved the train off, and then returned to the Stanley, and her man.

'It's goin' to be a funny old Christmas so it is,' Polly grumbled to Tad as the two of them made their way through the Francis Street market one Saturday afternoon in early December. 'No daddy, no mammy, and no presents, either. And precious little dinner, Martin says.'

'I'll give you half what I make if you help me wit' the papers,' Tad said, but without much enthusiasm. 'We can't pick spuds because the ground's froze hard, but I suppose we could go for cabbage. They cut cabbage, don't they? You don't have to dig or nothin'.'

'Tell you what; we could get holly and mistletoe and hawk it round the big houses, the rich houses,' Polly said suddenly. 'I know most of 'em have it growin' in their gardens, but they buy it usually. Why don't we do that?'

She was sick and tired of keeping house, to tell the truth. Sick and tired! She had never realised how hard mammies worked, and finding out had put her right off marriage, and that was the truth so it was.

She just never stopped and the boys, who had been good with Mammy, weren't good with her at all. They would peel spuds at a pinch, and they brought water up and emptied the slop buckets and that was it. Everything else was Polly's job, Polly's responsibility, and she was getting heartily sick of it. And then, yesterday, Martin had started talking about Christmas dinner . . . sprouts, a bird, a pudding . . . and Polly had told them straight.

'I can't cook things like that,' she had wailed. 'And

I won't. You're a bunch of lazy moochers and if you don't help me more you'll go hungry so you will, because I won't cook so much as a spud for youse!'

'Temper, temper,' Martin said. 'Brogan told us to pull together, Polly, and he told you to mind me. Remember?'

Polly did remember, but that didn't make it any easier to bear.

'Don't care; shan't cook,' she had said succinctly. 'Nor I shan't light the fires, 'cos that last lot of turf you brought in was drippin' wet – soaked, it were. It's someone else's turn, and it'll be someone else's turn on Christmas Day, an' all.'

'We're workin' hard,' Donal said in an injured voice. 'You aren't even at school, Polly.'

Polly had volunteered to give up school until her mother returned and this, she had soon realised, was a tactical error of giant proportions. How often had she got out of an unpopular task with a cry of 'I've got to do me eckers!' But now such pretence was useless. Kids who aren't at school don't get homework, they have to listen to the excuses of others, knowing them to be excuses but powerless to do anything about it.

But now, Tad and Polly had drawn level with a fish stall, or rather with a basket-car full of fish. It smelt, but Tad pulled Polly to a halt.

'Holly an' mistletoe for Christmas! Sure an' the girl's a genius, so she is! Phoenix Park!'

'I thought we might go to the country,' Polly said uncertainly. 'We can catch a tram for quite a way, then we can walk.'

'Sure we could, but the big houses in Phoenix Park, they like holly hedges. It keeps the chisellers out, d'you see? So why not get some little, berried bits today, an' go out after mistletoe after Mass tomorrow? We could sell it for six bunches a penny . . . something like that. 'Tis all profit, after all.'

'All right, I'd do anythin' rather than housework,' Polly agreed rather bitterly. She had left the beds unmade, the porridge pan unscraped, the clothes unwashed, and she intended to keep it that way.

'Other girls raise *families* when their mammies are workin',' Martin had pointed out when she moaned at him that she was nothin' but a slave. 'Kids of seven do all the messages, bring up the babies, cook the food . . .'

''Tis a liar you are, Martin O'Brady!' Polly had yelled. 'I'm nine and I can't do all that. As for Ivan, sure and he's not a baby at all, he's a *fiend* so he is!'

The fiend, sitting on the hearthrug with a piece of paper and some stumps of pencil, looked up and grinned. He knew Polly hated him right now but he didn't much care. He got up when he felt like it and went out to play with his friends, bowling hoops down Thomas Street, chasing cats, cheeking shopkeepers. It was great sport and his mammy would never have allowed it, but Polly was just pleased to get him out of her hair now and then and seldom bothered to ask where he had been. And she fed him, so that was all right.

'So you're on, then?' Tad chuckled and rubbed his hands. 'We'll be rich by the time Christmas comes!'

'Rich and scratched to ribbons,' Polly moaned two hours later, as they wheeled their borrowed perambulator across the dusky meadows of Phoenix Park. But though her arms and hands smarted, she felt rather pleased with herself. The two of them had gone round the back of the President's house, the most important man in all Ireland, and they had hacked away with the breadknife at the holly bushes there and chucked their prickly spoil in the pram and now they were wheeling it home.

'We ought to see if the President would like to buy some to make a Christmas wreath for his door,' Tad whispered, and Polly had giggled, though she was secretly rather shocked. Fancy stealing holly off an important man and then selling it back to him!

But in fact, by the time their pram bulged with holly, they were too tired and it was too late for selling anything.

'Tomorrer we'll do the countryside an' get mistletoe,' Tad said, pushing beside her. 'After Mass, mind. I don't aim to imperil me immortal soul just for a few pennies.'

'Your immortal soul's in poor shape anyway, 'cos stealin' holly's a sin,' Polly said. She did feel rather ashamed of herself. Boxing the fox was one thing, that wasn't stealing exactly, even the police didn't call that stealing. But taking the presidential holly . . . well, that wasn't quite so straightforward.

'You can't steal holly,' Tad said impatiently, shoving away at the pram much harder than Polly was, so that they waltzed right across the sandy path and into the grass verge. 'Have a care where you're pushin', girl! No, you can't steal holly, because it's a wild tree, a woodland tree. You've sung *The Holly and the Ivy*, haven't you?'

'What's that got to do with it?' Polly asked. Her back was aching and her scratches burned like fire. Hell fire, she thought apprehensively. Oh, God love me, I didn't mean no harm, honest!

'Well, the holly and the ivy are Christmas things, and they grow wild in the woods. So you can't steal 'em. Nor mistletoe,' Tad said instructively. 'I swear to God, Poll, that I wouldn't lead you into stealin', because I promised Martin to see you was all right.

And it's fine holly, wouldn't you say? It's got a *grush* of berries. Have you seen the holly in the market? Not a berry, most of it. Oh aye, ours is good holly, we'll see our money back on that lot.'

'We didn't put any money out for it,' Polly said crossly. 'Oh, Tad, and when I get home there'll be no fire, no supper cooked, no washin' done. Oh, I want me mammy back mortal bad!'

Sara had met Peader in the Queen's Arms, so naturally, the next time she was collecting in the pub, she expected to see him, sitting in his corner seat with his friends around him. But he wasn't there. She was collecting of course, handing out the *War Cry* and rattling her tin to raise money for the Army's various charitable ventures, which meant that she could scarcely pop in next day to check that Peader hadn't merely been absent from his usual corner for the one night.

But a couple of weeks later she was in again and little Freddy Mack was there.

'I wonder, you're Irish, aren't you?' Sara said, having listened to his brogue for a few minutes. 'Do you know a fellow-countryman of yours called Peader O'Brady? I'm by way of being a – a friend of his son's, Brogan O'Brady, and I'm rather keen to get in touch.'

The small man looked at her pityingly.

'Peader O'Brady was hit by an express train, when he was laying detonators in fog,' he said. 'There's sorry I am, Miss, to be the one to tell you.'

'My God! Oh, I'm so sorry . . . you don't know what's happened to his son Brogan, do you? We were friends years ago, but I've not seen him for a long time. I'd like to send him my condolences.'

Freddy Mack shrugged.

'He's gone back to Dublin,' he said. 'He went a whiles ago; he'll be workin' over there now, taking care of his mammy and the young 'uns.'

'And – and you don't think he'll come back?' Sara said faintly. She felt as though she had stepped into a pit of darkness, which was absurd, because Brogan was only a friend after all, and she'd not seen him for a long while. 'Not at all? Not ever?'

'There's a young lady,' Freddy Mack said, wrinkling his brow. 'I can't be recallin' her name, now, but there was a young lady he spoke of from time to time. Likely he's marryin' her, Miss.'

'I see. Well, thank you, Mr Mack,' Sara said politely, through dry lips. It serves me right, she thought, never really trying to get in touch with him again, always assuming he'd turn up, cap in hand, and we'd pick up our friendship where we left off. Well, that won't happen now, Sara Cordwainer, so you'd better start wondering what you're going to do with the rest of your life! Resolutely, she moved away from Freddy Mack, her newspapers fanned out in front of her.

'Would anyone like a copy of the *War Cry*? Thank you, sir, that's very generous of you. God bless you, sir.'

And presently, when all her copies of the paper had gone, she made her way back to the Barracks with Clarrie and as they walked home through the chilly night air, she told her friend all about Peader O'Brady, and a little bit about Brogan, too. Because I've got to learn to accept it, and acceptance comes easier if you're frank about something, she told herself. I'm terribly sorry about Peader's death, but . . . oh, I'm going to miss Brogan so badly! I hated not seeing him, but at least, before, I knew, or thought I knew, that he was going to come back to me, one day.

'So finding that Peader was killed by a train is tragic, but it's a coincidence, too,' she ended thoughtfully. 'Because there was a similar tragedy years ago, it was how I came to know Peader and his son Brogan, actually. And that involved a train-death.'

'The young girl? And the baby that simply disappeared?' Clarrie said at once. 'Your gran told me that story when I first went to live with her, but I never realised your friend Brogan had anything to do with it. Did you ever ask him what he thought had happened to that baby?'

Sara nodded. 'Yes, that was the first thing I said to him, as I remember. But he couldn't tell me much, only that he was sure the baby was safe and happy, nothing else.' She paused, then took Clarrie's arm. 'I'll tell you something else, Clarrie. The first time I met Brogan I was running after a little girl who I honestly thought might be one of the Carberys. You see she came up to me as I was starting to eat a pastie I'd bought . . .'

The story was soon told and Clarrie eyed her friend thoughtfully. 'And you thought it was the sister who'd been ill and stayed at home when you met Jess and Mollie? I wonder if it really was her? It could have been just wishful thinkin', chuck.'

'I suppose,' Sara admitted cautiously. 'Anyway, Brogan was really nice to me, really kind, and we kept in touch for ages. Only then we moved away from Snowdrop Street . . . well, you know how it is.'

'I do,' Clarrie said. 'You like this feller, don't you?'

'Very much,' Sara said at once. 'Not in the way you mean, though! He's just a friend and someone I'm sad I've lost touch with. But if he's gone home, to Ireland, we'll probably never clap eyes on each other again.'

'Oh, I don't know,' Clarrie said. 'People who matter

to each other have a way of turning up. Just keep on living, and hoping, and you'd be surprised at the way God can turn things round. But to change the subject completely, chuck, are you comin' carol-singing round the wards at the Stanley on Christmas Eve? You've a pretty voice and we could do with a female soloist. You've been properly taught, what's more. Say you will!'

'Of course I will,' Sara said readily. 'It's a date then, Clarrie.'

But for the rest of the evening her mind felt sore with loss. Why hadn't she made more effort to keep in touch with Brogan? Mr Mack was undoubtedly right, if the poor chap was taking care of his entire family he would need a wife, so he'd marry some pretty little Irish colleen and never think of young Sara Cordwainer again.

And it serves me right, now I'll be a spinster all the days of my life and undoubtedly that is what I deserve, Sara told herself. I love children, but I'm a teacher, I don't have to have a family of my own. As for men . . . apart from Brogan, I've never met one I'd even consider marrying.

Not that I ever considered marrying him, either, she reminded herself hastily as she and Clarrie cycled through the quiet streets. But I did like him as a friend. Oh, if only I hadn't been so heedless, so careless! If only I'd gone straight back to the Queen's Arms, instead of waiting a whole month!

'What's on your mind, chuck?' Miss Boote said presently, as the silence between them stretched. 'You're very quiet all of a sudden.'

'I'm tired, I think,' Sara said. 'I'm really ready for my bed.'

But when she got there, it was a long while before she slept.

Chapter Thirteen

April 1934

'When one door closes another opens.' Sara had been hearing it all her life, particularly from Gran, and right now she needed to believe it, because things were not good. The job which she had valued was about to finish, through no fault of her own, and a fortnight earlier, Mrs Prescott had suffered a slight stroke. She had been cooking, and had pulled out a chair and climbed on to the seat to reach a high shelf on which were some spices they did not often use ... and the next thing Sara knew was the crash as Gran and the spices hit the kitchen floor together.

'She's one of the lucky ones,' Dr Pemberton had told her when he had examined Mrs Prescott and was having a quiet word with Sara in the kitchen. 'Look on it as a warning; if we all heed the warning and take care, she may well live out the rest of her life with no recurrence. And she's lost none of her faculties.' Dr Pemberton looked at Sara over the tops of his little gold-rimmed glasses. 'She could have been partially paralysed, she could have lost the power of speech, she could, at worst, have been little better than a cabbage. As it is, she's just very shaken and will take more care in future.'

'No trying to climb on chairs again, Gran,' Sara scolded her gently when she returned to the bedroom. 'It was my fault, but I never realised you'd try to get to the top of the cupboard with me around to reach it down for you.'

'I don't like being a nuisance,' Gran muttered. 'I feel odd . . . funny.'

'Of course you do! A fall like that isn't something to be treated lightly at your age,' Sara told her. 'But the doctor says a couple of days in bed and you'll be running around like a spring chicken again.'

'Wheeling around, you mean,' Mrs Prescott said, but she smiled at her granddaughter. 'Oh well, mustn't grumble, and I'll heed what the doctor says. I mustn't act like a ten-year-old, me bones won't stand for it.'

So now, making her way along the pavement towards the tram stop, Sara told herself that she was grateful for the warning and would take better care of Gran in future. For Gran was her rock, she could not imagine life without her. But she would have to do something quickly or she would be in no position to take care of anyone.

Miss Marks had explained to her why she was going to have to let her go at the end of term, but Sara had seen it coming. The school was a small private one, and as the Depression bit deeper so pupil numbers shrank. The last thing a man without work can do is pay school fees, however reasonable, when free schooling is available.

'With pupil numbers now so small, Miss Cordwainer, my sister and I can manage easily between us,' Miss Marks had said. 'I'm deeply sorry because you are an excellent teacher, but by saving your salary, at least our little school may continue, in a smaller way of course, to flourish.'

Sara understood completely and had taken her dismissal in good part, but that didn't mean she'd not been secretly dismayed. And now Gran's stroke had meant they were even more dependent upon the money brought in by herself and Clarrie. So without saying a word to anyone else, Sara decided to go and see her parents. After all, they might have talked about having to retrench when she first returned from Switzerland, but that hadn't stopped her mother from shopping at the most exclusive stores in Liverpool, nor her father from running an extremely expensive motor car. By now, their economies might well be over, and it would cost them very little to reinstate Gran's pension.

If it was just myself I wouldn't dream of asking, Sara told herself defiantly as she got off one tram and changed to another which would carry her the rest of the way to Aigburth Road. But Gran's different. She brought my mother up, loved her, spent money on her, and she's had a hard life. How can a Christian such as my mother professes herself to be turn round and refuse to help her own mother when she's in need?

The tram rattled on its way and when it reached the terminus at Croxteth Gate Sara got down and turned into Aigburth Road, aware, suddenly, that she felt nervous. But the die was cast, it was too late for regrets. She had never contacted her parents since the day they had left her in the house in Snowdrop Street; now circumstances had forced her to ask a favour from them, not for herself but for her grandmother. The worst they could do was refuse!

Sara walked on through the sweet and sunny afternoon; it was good to be away from the city centre, good to breathe fresh, clean air and to hear birdsong rather than the traffic's roar. She reached the house in its large grounds and stopped for a moment, looking rather apprehensively between the gateposts. The house, at any rate, seemed unchanged. The windows sparkled with cleanliness, the gravel was raked and weed-free. It was not the home of people who were having to count their pennies, Sara concluded, setting off along the curving drive, her shoes crunching on the thick gravel. If she stood on tiptoe she could just see the glasshouses where the gardener had once grown so many rare and delicious things. There, too, glass sparkled and she could see, through it, the healthy green of plants. There was no doubt about it, the place looked just the same, there were no signs of a shortage of money . . . she would really have to make the attempt.

She reached the front door and pulled the bell. She heard it jangle and realised that her heart was beating uncommonly loudly, almost loudly enough to compete with the bell in fact. Still, it was too late to retreat. She must go ahead, having undertaken the journey.

She had already decided to say nothing about losing her own job, though. She neither wanted nor needed help from either of her parents, not after the way they had treated her. I can cope, she told herself, standing on the doorstep. But Gran – she's a different kettle of fish. She's been quite ill, and she's reached an age when she should be looked after; I'll tell Mother that if she's difficult.

She heard the tread of someone approaching the door. It opened.

'Miss Sara!'

'Hello, Williams,' Sara said, smiling at the young man. Williams had been employed by her parents for years; some things, apparently, did not change. 'Is Mrs Cordwainer in?'

'Well, no, Miss. She and the master moved out the best part of a year ago. They went to Preston, I believe.' He looked at her curiously. 'They didn't tell you?'

'No. But I've neither seen nor heard from them since

I left,' Sara said quietly. 'Do you have their address, Williams?'

'No, Miss. But Mrs Arbuthnot might have. I'll go and ask her.'

'Wait, Williams! Who's Mrs Arbuthnot?'

Williams, who had turned away, turned back.

'Why, the Arbuthnots live here now, Miss. They took the staff over when they bought the house. They're very nice people, Miss, and I do believe the mistress does have an address for your parents.' He stood aside and waved her to go past him. 'Wait in the study, Miss, while I find out.'

But Sara shook her head.

'It's all right, Williams, I'll wait here. It's a lovely day, I prefer to be in the air. If you could just ask Mrs Arbuthnot to write the address on a piece of paper . . . and Williams, can you just say a friend wants it? I'd rather she didn't know it was me.'

'Of course, Miss,' Williams said at once. 'I shan't be a moment.'

He was back quickly, a sheet of blue writing paper in his hand. 'Here we are, Miss Sara . . . I trust you'll find it helpful, Mrs Arbuthnot's written down the telephone number, too.'

'That's wonderful,' Sara said gratefully, taking the paper. 'To tell you the truth, Williams, it's Nanny Prescott. I'm living with her now, and she's been ill, so I thought perhaps my mother should know.'

Williams looked concerned. 'I'm sorry to hear that, Miss. And if there's anything we could do, Miss . . . the staff, I mean . . . we were all very fond of Mrs Prescott.'

'Thank you, Williams. It's a kind offer, but we'll manage. Good day to you.'

Walking back to the tram with her hands shoved into her coat pockets and her collar turned up, Sara reflected that she was not really sorry she had not seen either of her parents. I was probably panicking too soon, she told herself. I've been very lucky with jobs in the past. First I got the job in Barringtons and when my mother spoiled that for me I found the laundry work, and then I got the teaching job . . . I'll be all right, I'm sure of it.

Yet despite the failure of her errand she realised, as she climbed aboard the tram, that she felt happier than she had done for days. The truth was she had decided to see her parents once more against her better judgement. Now, having tried and failed, she felt fully justified in not trying again. And since she'd not told anyone she was visiting Aigburth Road she would not have any explanations to make, either.

She had intended to go straight back to Florence Street, but she thought she might pop into Clarrie's bank before seeing Gran again. Clarrie had said she'd put the word about that Sara was looking for a job and you never knew, she might have heard of something suitable already. It would be best to check, Sara decided, before getting the tram back into the city centre after lunch to start on the office bureaux.

So when she climbed down off the tram on Walton Road, Sara went straight to the bank. She went past the long counter with the clerks sitting behind the grilles and knocked on the door to the offices. After a short pause a girl opened it.

'Can I help . . .' she began, and then, recognising Sara: 'Oh, hello, Miss Cordwainer; do you want to see Miss Boote?'

'Yes, please,' Sara said gratefully. 'Can I come through?'

The girl led her through to the small office where Clarrie sat with three other secretaries. Clarrie finished rattling away on her typewriter and then stood up and came over to her friend.

'How did your visit go?' Clarrie asked and for a moment Sara wondered how she had found out about her trip to Aigburth Road. Then she remembered that she had told Clarrie she was going to see whether there were any jobs on offer in the office bureaux.

'I've not been round the bureaux yet, to tell the truth. So rather than going into the city centre first, I've come here to see if you've heard of anything. You said you'd ask around amongst the Army . . . did you have any luck?'

Clarrie looked smug. 'Maybe. Miss Marks had a word with Major Ellis and there *is* a job, though from what I understand it isn't a permanent job, but it might tide you over. The major says it will probably last for six months or so. I know you'd rather have permanent work but the trouble is, everyone's cutting down. So I won't say any more, I'll leave the major to tell you what's on offer. He said he'd see you this evening, at the soup kitchen.'

'I hope it's something I can do,' Sara said. 'Because the rent bill and the fuel bill and the food bill all turn up with great regularity, needing to be settled. I suppose I could have a try for shop work, but I've been out of it for rather a long while. Still . . .'

'Cheer up,' Clarrie said bracingly. 'I think it's work you might enjoy . . . but I did give my word not to talk about it until it's been put to you. You haven't told Mrs Prescott your job's finished, I take it?'

'No point in worrying her,' Sara said. 'She would worry, too, though she'd never let us know it. No, as you say, something will turn up.'

Walking along Walton Road in the direction of their

flat however, Sara found herself wondering what on earth the job could be? The Army did employ people in large numbers, but she had not heard, on the grapevine, of a vacancy for a particular job, nor did she think that anyone had retired, or moved on, in the area. How will I wait until this evening to find out what it's all about? she asked herself, hurrying along the pavement. She had intended visiting the office bureaux in the city centre but with the possibility of a job connected with the Army, would not such a visit be a waste of time? She had just decided to suggest to her grandmother that they should go for a walk in Stanley Park and leave the bureaux until next day, when someone hailed her.

'Miss Cordwainer! *Just* the person I wanted to see!'

It was Major Ellis. He was a tall, commanding-looking man with a big white moustache, wavy white hair and very bright blue eyes. He approached Sara at a smart pace, then stopped and took both her hands in his.

'Such excitement, Miss Cordwainer! Have you got a minute? Would you like a cup of coffee, or tea, or – or a bun or something?'

'It's awfully kind of you, Major,' Sara said. 'I gather you wanted to speak to me about the possibility of some work? Only Clarrie wouldn't tell me anything, save that you wanted to talk to me. But she said there was no hurry; you'd see me this evening, at the soup kitchen.'

'Yes, but since we've bumped into one another, what's wrong with right now?' the major said. 'And – you aren't hurrying off anywhere? – only if you've a moment I think we really should talk.' He looked impatiently up and down the road. 'Ah, Andrews' Café – the very place.' He took her arm. 'Come with me,

Miss Cordwainer – Andrews' does delicious coffee and marvellous cakes!'

'Do tell me what this is all about, Major,' Sara begged as they hurried along the pavement. The major was clearly so anxious to get to the café that he was almost running and she, perforce, was almost running too since he had her elbow in a firm grip. 'And do slow down, people will think you're kidnapping me!'

'So I shall, so I shall,' the major said, mystifying Sara even more. '*Such* news, Sara – just wait until I tell you!'

And at last, seated in Andrews' Café with a pot of coffee and a plate of cream cakes before them, Sara discovered what it was all about.

'Some time ago we had a bequest, Miss Cordwainer,' the major said impressively. 'A good, kind woman who wanted to do her bit for those less fortunate left us a mansion! Yes, a mansion, in the Woolton area of the city. She suggested in her will that it became either a children's home or an eventide home, but we were able to do nothing until all the legal difficulties had been untangled.

'Well, it has taken time, but we are now free to go ahead, and we've decided – in fact the feeling was unanimous – that we should open the place as a home for children. It's ideal for them, it has wonderful grounds and is surrounded by countryside . . . ideal for kiddies. And there has been so much hardship amongst the young because of this Depression! We've done what we could, but we've not been able to put a roof over young heads. But now . . .' he rubbed his hands, beaming all over his face, ' . . . but now, Miss Cordwainer, our opportunity has arisen and we shall seize it with both hands! Work on the new premises will start in a week or so.'

'That's marvellous, Major,' Sara said warmly. She

took a bite out of her cake. 'Very good news. But – forgive me – I fail to see why you wanted to tell me!'

'Why, because we're going to need workers, Miss Cordwainer, hard workers! And at the meeting last night Miss Marks told us that she had been forced to ask for your resignation, which means, of course, that just at the present moment, you are not gainfully employed. Unless . . .' he raised his eyebrows quizzically, ' . . . unless you've already obtained another position?'

'Not yet, Major. Jobs are hard to find,' Sara said regretfully. Because it was the school holidays, no one had really noticed her being out of work, but she was, of course.

'Aha!' the major said triumphantly. 'Then would you consider working for the Army for six months or so? As you know, we have trained officers for the majority of our work, men and women who've been through the staff college, but this is a little different. The thing is, we need someone to oversee the changes and alterations which must be put in hand before we can open the house for destitute children. We want a person with practical experience of building matters and also someone who has been working with children and can advise on what will suit them best. A simple example is water closets – Miss Marks pointed out that for very young children a lower – er – position is more – er – '

'I understand,' Sara said quickly, smiling to herself. 'But I know nothing about construction work, I'm afraid. Isn't there someone who could do both, so to speak?'

'Oh, didn't I explain? Young Alderwood will oversee the builders, but he doesn't feel in any way qualified to give advice on the *planning* of a home for young people. And once the house is altered and we open up,

366

we would hope, Miss Cordwainer, that you might come on the staff of the home as someone to help with the children, to make them feel wanted, cherished. Miss Marks says you have a very nice way with young people, so who better than yourself for such a task?'

'Well, Major, it s-sounds marvellous, but . . .' Sara stammered, almost overcome. A job in a million – and one she would delight in! She liked Robert Alderwood too, though he was fifty if he was a day, but she supposed that to the major, a man in his late seventies, fifty *was* young. And she would be helping the very children she had long felt guiltiest over, children like the Carberys, who lived in miserable penury, victims of society rather than members of it. 'If you think I could do the job . . .'

'I'm sure you could. As you know, we pay a fair salary to our employees though we cannot, of course, afford to throw our money about. I realise you have to support your grandmother, however . . .'

The sum he named seemed fair to Sara. She smiled at him.

'That would be fine, Major. When would I start?'

'Well, we thought next Monday, if that was all right. Now, any other questions?'

'Yes, one. Would I be expected to live on the premises whilst the alterations were in hand? Only as you know, my grandmother is crippled with arthritis and is in a wheelchair. Furthermore she has recently suffered a slight stroke. She could not possibly manage without my help.'

'At first, the house will probably be uninhabitable, but once the work is finished you might be expected to live in, though it may not be necessary,' the major said. 'Later we'll have a full-time matron, who will undoubtedly live in. At this stage, I'm not sure about the rest of the staff – but shall we cross that bridge when we come to it? Anything else?'

'No, I can't think of anything . . . oh, when can I see the house?'

'Tomorrow morning, at nine o'clock. We're all going to meet there, the Committee, yourself, young Alderwood and the head of the building firm which we hope will do the alterations. Is that all right? Can you join us at nine o'clock sharp?'

'Oh, *yes*,' Sara said at once, already looking forward to her first glimpse of this mansion. 'Certainly I can. I'll be there.'

'Good, good.' The major rose to his feet and Sara followed suit. 'Now I must get on, I've a great deal to do.'

Sara and her companion left the café, and outside, the major shook her hand.

'Until tomorrow, Miss Cordwainer,' he said. He sketched a salute and was several yards away when Sara suddenly remembered something.

'Major . . . wait! What's this mansion called?'

The major turned back, smiling, slapping his brow.

'I'll forget my own head next,' he said jovially. 'Of course, I haven't told you, have I? It's on Beaconsfield Road, Miss Cordwainer, and it's called Strawberry Field.'

Grace often wondered about the feller who had saved her life that night, but she didn't think he could be alive, still. Which meant he was with Jess. Wish I'd had a chance to talk to him, she thought as she roamed the streets, searching for food. I could have asked him to tell Jess all sorts – that the baby never was found, just for a start. That I'm still alive and makin' me way awright, as well. And that I think of her often – all the time, just about.

But that was daft thinking, because everyone knew you couldn't get messages across to them that had passed on. It just weren't possible. And the big man would have had other things than her sister on his mind as he approached the pearly gates. At least Grace imagined he would, though she knew herself to be ignorant about such matters. How could she be anything else? She had not attended school after she was seven or so; you had to have boots and decent clothes for school. She didn't go to church much, either, for the same reason. The priest tutted when he saw small boys with their little bums sticking out of their kecks and small girls with no knickers under brief, ragged skirts, and sent them home with instructions to their parents to see that they were properly clothed in future. And that, of course, made her da angry. It were bad enough round their place in the ordinary way, but when her da was angry it quickly became not only unbearable but dangerous.

So Grace and the other Carbery young had simply slithered out of the educational and religious net and had not particularly worried over their lack. Grace had loved school, the quiet orderliness of it, the intriguing lessons, but she knew better than to annoy her da.

Almost two years ago, he'd killed their mam. Oh, he'd never swing for it like he deserved, Grace knew that, but he'd killed her, nevertheless. A drunken argument, a fist in the face at the top of the stairs . . . Grace had heard her mam hittin' every step, just about, as she crashed down 'em. The scuffers were called – not by us, Grace thought, ashamed, but then they would have had to face their da after – and a doctor came with 'em. The doctor said Mrs Carbery had broken her neck in a fall and Mr Carbery, sobered by the mere sight of his wife with her head on at right-angles, said they'd been comin' back after a night on the ale and she'd slipped on a piece of orange peel at the top of the flight. When all the fuss was over and they'd taken Mam off to the hospital mortuary he'd threatened the kids with the beating of their life and instant strangulation if any of them ever breathed a peep about what had really happened.

But there was no point. Mam had never protected them from her bullying, baby-beating husband, had stood by and watched them being battered with an impassive face, so there had been no love lost. Grace knew that none of the kids felt any affection for the woman who had given birth to them and ignored them ever after. It would have been nice to have seen their father taken away by the law, but the truth was, they dreaded the workhouse. Da made sure they dreaded it – he said the workhouse had made him what he was today, and told them terrifying stories of unbelievable cruelties. And when he wasn't scaring the wits out of them he bullied them, screamed and shouted at them, took the food they brought in and any money they were unwise enough to have about their persons, and generally mistreated them, with the inevitable result.

They went. One by one, silently, a child would slip out of the door in the morning and not slip back in at night. At first the child would be gone a few days, but then it slid into weeks, months. And Stan Carbery bellowed that he'd kill 'em if he ever laid hands on 'em and bore down even harder on the ones that were left. Then he brought a fancy woman back and Grace, who had stuck it longest, slung her hook as well.

They became street children, dodging the scuffers and kindly but interfering adults, running like the wind the moment anyone in a uniform appeared on the street, begging, stealing, living from hand to mouth. They slept in the parks, in any public place left unlocked, under steps, in areas. If the wind was in the right direction Grace often scraped together a pile of cardboard boxes and newspapers and slept in a sheltered jigger.

There were eight of them when their mam died. The only other girl beside Grace, Addy, had left home a good deal earlier and after their mam's death Grace guessed she'd moved right away from the Pool. She'd had a feller . . . she'd had several fellers. She'd be with one of them, Grace supposed, and wished she could have gone with the older girl.

Then their da decided he could do with fewer kids and put the four youngest into the Father Berry Orphan Asylum, where doubtless they were a good deal better off than those still at home. Grace sometimes wondered why he hadn't got rid of them all to the orphanage, but imagined she and her three brothers were probably too old to be taken in. You four can work so you're workhouse fodder, their father had said gloatingly, when any one of them looked especially like rebelling. And he made them work for him, Grace toiling in their dirty rooms, the boys selling papers, nicking fruit, going messages. They never saw the money they earned, of course, and very soon realised that their only chance of staying alive was to escape, get out and stay out. And now, of the four who had deserted their father and kept out of institutions, Grace saw only her older brother Sid from time to time, and the truth was she didn't like him much. He was growing too like their father – a bullying lout of a lad quicker with a cuff than a kiss.

She avoided the second brother, too. Solly was smaller, not so aggressive, but he was a sharp, secretive kid. He did well on the streets, Grace was certain. He had joined a gang of hooligans who battened on anyone weaker than themselves, and Grace kept out of their way.

She hadn't seen Alf for a long time, probably more than a year. He was next to her in age, a sickly, whining boy. Grace thought he was probably either in hospital or dead. But there was nothing she could do about it; she had no means of finding out about Alf and, in any case, could not have helped him. It was all she could do to keep herself alive – and out of her father's way.

He wanted her back. She was a useful slave, a punch-bag, someone to send on messages and then to beat up if something went wrong. She feared him from the bottom of her heart and never went near the noisome court where he and his latest lady-friend drank and screamed at one another... and probably fought, Grace thought, knowing her father.

So no wonder she remembered with affection and gentleness the man who had saved her life at the expense of his own! She could still remember the look on his face, the feel of the hands which had seized and flung her to safety. She knew his name, too, because when she'd led the men back one of them had exclaimed: 'Dear God in Heaven, it's Peader O'Brady! He's dead, for sure.'

She'd run away then, unable to bear the guilt. She had as good as killed him – the scuffers would be after her, she'd been trespassing on railway property, she'd be in awful trouble, imprisoned, flogged ... sent to the workhouse.

But the days passed, and the weeks, and nothing happened. If people stared at her in the street it was because of the state she was in. Unwashed, ragged, half-starved, cold even in warm weather, she was not a pretty sight. But a scavenging child must keep on the move or it will be taken into custody, and Grace dreaded that. She had no idea what the scuffers or the priests or the teachers did to kids who lived on the streets, who begged and stole, but it would be something unpleasant, she knew that all right. In her whole life, nothing that had happened to Grace Carbery had led her to expect fair treatment at the hands of adults. The only love she had ever received had been from her sister Jess . . . and Jess had died so long ago that Grace could scarcely remember her face, save that its expression had been sweet.

So now Grace had a new hero. Peader O'Brady, who had cared so much for a girl he did not even know that he had risked – lost – his life to save her. Grace had carried a heavy basket of shopping all the way from the Great Homer Street market to Wilbraham Street, a considerable distance, and the threepenny joe thus earned had been spent on a candle, which she had lit for Peader O'Brady. Grace knew nothing of purgatory, sin, the life hereafter; how could she? No one had ever taught her. But she knew folk lit candles when someone they loved died, or when they were grateful for something, and she loved Peader O'Brady, and was grateful for what he had done for her. Lighting a candle with money which would otherwise have been spent on food seemed a small enough price to pay. It never occurred to Grace for one moment that the people who came in and out of the church, telling beads, genuflecting, putting their money in the box and lighting up their candles, had none of them paid, penny for penny, anywhere near as much as she.

Because Grace Carbery, who had so little, had willingly given her all for that candle.

*

Brogan sat by the bed and held his daddy's hand and talked soothingly into his daddy's ear. Mrs Burt had let him have the small front bedroom so he could be near his mammy and he spent every hour that he was not working sitting by his father and talking to him.

Summer was upon them now, with its long, light evenings and warmer days. And Brogan had moved back to Liverpool. First as a fireman and only recently as a driver, he had learned the road between Crewe and Rugby, and then he had done his time on the road between Crewe and Liverpool until he knew every inch of the track, every light, every signal, every bump in the rails, indeed. And now, when he needed so desperately to be back in Liverpool, the Powers that Be on the LMSR line had put him to learning the Liverpool to Southport road, which meant, of course, that the move back to living, once more, in Liverpool was a natural one. It just showed that prayer worked, Brogan's mammy said triumphantly, when he told her he'd be staying in Liverpool now. She'd lit candles and prayed for her son's support and presence, and she had got it.

And now, by Peader's bed, his son continued his monologue.

'So then, Daddy, I walked along by the pier head and breathed in the good salt air of the sea, and thought about Dublin. Daddy, you know Mammy's here wit' you, longin' for you to be better? Well, it means the kids is by themselves so they are, and you know Polly's only a spalpeen, a baby almost. When you're better, Mammy will take you home . . . oh, Daddy, can you not hear a word I say?'

'Talk to him,' the doctor had said. 'His body has healed but his mind's wheeling out there in limbo somewhere, waiting for something, or someone, to call him back. So talk, argue, laugh, cry, but keep doing it, and one day, he'll respond.'

Brogan picked up his father's hand, once so huge and gnarled, now so thin and white and pathetic somehow. He squeezed it.

'Daddy, I'm worried over Polly so I am! Can ye not hear me? She's only a little girl and she's tryin' her best to keep the family together whiles Mammy and I . . .' For a second Brogan's voice failed him; his father's eyelids had flickered and a slight frown had gathered on his pale brow! 'Daddy! Can ye hear me, Daddy?'

'A little gorl . . .' the words were whispered so faintly that Brogan could barely catch them. 'A little gorl . . .'

He had spoken and his words had made sense, for hadn't Brogan been talking about Polly and his worries concerning her only seconds before?

'That's right, Daddy, she's just a little girl,' he said excitedly. 'Can you take a drink now? There's a glass of barley water by your bed . . .'

'A little gorl . . .' the whisper faded to nothing but even as Brogan watched, he saw his father's lips frame the three words again.

A passing nurse found herself grabbed and hustled over to Peader's bed by his handsome young son who did not even seem to know he was handsome – nor to take any notice of even the prettiest and most forthcoming nurse.

'Sister, Sister, he spoke, me daddy spoke! I was talkin' about me little sister, and me daddy said *A little girl*! Honest to God, Sister, he spoke!'

'Talk about your sister some more, Mr O'Brady,' the nurse said, almost as excited as he. Peader had been gradually regaining his physical strength for weeks now. His wounds had healed up well, but his mind had refused to recognise any stimuli which had been offered. If only they could interest him, bring him back!

But though Brogan continued to talk to his father until the nurses on the night-shift turned him out, not another word passed his lips.

Everyone knew, soon enough, that Peader had spoken. Deirdre spent hours in church, on her knees, thanking God – and then demanding a repeat performance when she herself was present. She was a little hurt that Peader had responded to talk of Polly and not of herself but what did it really matter, after all? What mattered was that he had spoken, was on the road to recovery.

'Bring Polly in,' the doctor said next day when the incident was related to him. 'He's clearly very fond of the little girl; she must visit him, talk to him.'

'She's in Dublin . . . but I could go back, bring her over,' Brogan said excitedly. 'Oh, Mammy, we should have thought – Daddy always responded well to Polly.'

But there was no need, because that very same night, Peader spoke again. Deirdre and Brogan were by his bed, getting ready to say goodnight to him because the night-shift wanted them out. Deirdre bent over, kissed him on the brow and then, on impulse, recited a bit of a poem she sometimes said to the children.

> *Matthew, Mark, Luke and John,*
> *The bed be blest that I lie on,*
> *Four angels to my bed,*
> *Four angels round my head,*
> *One to watch and one to pray*
> *And two to bear my soul away.*

Deirdre was turning away from the bed, Brogan was taking her elbow, when Peader moved his head restlessly on the pillow, and spoke, his voice slow and rusty from disuse.

'That little gorl – is she an angel?' Peader said.

Meanwhile, things had reached a parlous state in the O'Brady place in Dublin. Mammy wrote regularly, Brogan intermittently, but the children hardly ever wrote back. Polly had decided that work must be evenly divided and drove poor Ivan into screaming fits by sitting him down with a bowl of spuds and telling him to 'scrub the dirt off that lot or I'll not let you play out for a week, young feller'.

The rooms were dirty, untidy, unwelcoming. Polly did more than her share but it seemed to Donal and Bevin that she spent an awful lot of time making them do household tasks which, they felt, were unsuited to the superior sex. And then the priest came round.

'How are ye managing?' he said jovially, entering the living room without knocking, the priests naturally having little respect for a handful of kids, Polly thought to herself, glancing hastily round the room. 'Oh, Mother of Jesus!'

Polly knew what had called forth the exclamation – but he didn't know how hard it was to manage when you were only just ten and hadn't ever been taught housekeeping skills. And then for a moment she saw the room through a stranger's eyes and was ashamed. Dust everywhere, food lying about waiting to be eaten, dirty clothing scuffed into corners, clean clothing in rumpled, unironed heaps. And the hens.

Mammy would never have stood for the hens, but then she didn't have Polly's problems, and Tad had given her the hens, anyway. She had never asked where he'd got them because she suspected she might not like the answer . . . but she liked the hens. They got on well with Lionel the ginger tom-cat, with the tortoise-shell stray which Polly had lately acquired, and with Delilah the dog, though Delilah got angry when he found the hens pecking away at his half-chewed bones. And Lionel teased them sometimes by hiding on top of the dining table and then leaping on to a passing feathered back, which Tad said – and he, as the donor of the hens, should know – did not help egg production.

The eggs were lovely, though. You couldn't go into the country to collect eggs, but you could go and collect corn, and with the corn plus any old bits of rotting fruit or vegetables which the stallholders in Francis Street threw out at the end of the day, you fed the hens.

'Poultry, my child?' That was the priest, his voice faint with disbelief. 'In your mammy's good parlour?' his voice rose, gained a little strength. 'Oh, God save you, that one's drinkin' out of the holy water stoup so it is!'

'That's not the holy . . . oh, well, someone's stood it on the floor by mistake,' Polly muttered, red to her ears. 'Honest to God, father, they have a nice tin bowl for their water . . . the bloody dog must of kicked it under a chair.'

'Wha-aat?' roared Father Feeney, his voice coming back alarmingly suddenly. 'What did ye say, child?'

Polly, who never swore and had simply repeated what Martin had called Delilah when he had caught the dog thoughtfully chewing the stiff white collar to his best shirt, reddened still further, or at least she supposed she had because she felt as though she were on fire so she did.

'Oh! Sorry, Father . . . the naughty dog, I meant. The naughty dog must of kicked it under the chair.'

'Kicked what?' Father Feeney said. 'What the divil

are you talkin' about, child? What I'm sayin' is you've turned your mammy's lovely home into a madhouse! Dogs, cats, hens and dirt. It won't do, Polly, indeed it won't.'

'I know it won't, Father,' Polly said – and did the best thing she could have done. She bolted across the room and landed fair and square in Father Feeney's waistcoat, or where his waistcoat would have been had he been a man and not a priest. 'Oh, Father, it's so awful here wit'out me mammy!'

Polly, a regular attender at Sunday school, a buyer of candles and the owner of one of the sweetest, purest voices ever to be raised in John's Lane Church, knew herself to be one of Father Feeney's favourites, otherwise she would never have dared. Priests, the boys frequently complained, could hit harder than teachers or policemen, so they could. But Father Feeney, after the initial staggering back, put his arms round Polly's narrow shoulders and gave her a comforting squeeze.

'Sure and it's none of it your fault, alanna,' he said roundly. ''Tis the lads, wit'out a doubt. But 'tis a woman's hand that's lackin' here. I'll send someone round.'

A fortnight earlier Polly's heart might have sunk at the thought of adult interference, but not any more. All she wanted was another woman to come and take the responsibility off her shoulders. She gave a consenting mutter and hugged Father Feeney harder, causing him to sit down rather abruptly on the arm of the sofa. But he patted her soothingly, told Ivan to get off his bum and put the holy water stoup back where it belonged, out of that evil hen's reach, and then stood back, putting Polly gently away from him.

'Don't worry, girleen, we'll soon have this place

straight,' he told her. 'I'll send someone up at once. Is your mammy sending you money?'

'Brogan sends as much as he can,' Polly said, starting to try to shush the hens back into the kitchen. In a way it was a pity the priest had called; she and Tad had talked about acquiring a pig, but though pigs looked very sweet when they were small, she could imagine that one of the big ones could do a deal of damage in Mammy's nice parlour and besides, it might not like the cats and Delilah. 'Will I give the person you send money then, Father? Only we don't have much to spare . . . I'm not at school any more, which is a saving . . .'

'Not at school, alanna?' Father Feeney's voice had gone high again. Ah, God, I've give meself away, Polly thought. Priests an' teachers always stick together, don't they so? He'll tell me what's wrong wit' the National School so he will; he'll say what's to pay there?

'What's wrong wit' the National School?' the priest said, echoing Polly's thoughts. 'There's no money to pay there.'

'It's the time; I can't spare the time when I've all the housework an' the cookin' an' the messages to do,' Polly said plaintively, trying to ignore the glance which the priest sent around the room. Ivan, sitting on the floor scrubbing potatoes in a bowl of filthy water, said loudly: 'I do the messages, Poll – you make me.'

Polly waited until the priest had turned to stare at a peculiarly arrogant hen as it strutted in from the kitchen and then she aimed a kick at Ivan which landed rather neatly on his small bottom. Ivan yelled, then scrambled to his feet to kick back just as the priest said in an outraged voice: 'It's a cockerel!'

'What, that hen?' Polly said. 'What's a cockerel, Father?'

'It's a male hen, alanna. It – it's the daddy to the little yellow chicks. What in God's good name are ye doin' wit' a cockerel up here?'

'Tad said they'd make little chicks if we waited a while,' Polly said in a satisfied tone. You could trust Tad, she thought, he was almost always right. 'Oh, so that's the daddy, is it?' She examined the cockerel closely, but apart from the scarlet ribbon-thing on his head and the dangly red bobbles on each side of his beak he looked just like the other hens to her. 'So that's why he doesn't lay eggs, is it?' she added. 'He's the daddy, so the others are the mammies, and they're the ones that lay the eggs. Do I have it right, Father?'

'You do,' Father Feency said in a strangled sort of voice. He put a hand into his collar and pulled it away from his neck as though it were too tight for him. 'Glory be to God, it's an education, this place.' He turned and opened the door on to the landing, then turned back. 'Polly, you'll be in school tomorrow, either at the Convent or the National School; is that clear?'

Polly had always known it was too good to last and besides, what with Brogan's money, Martin's earnings and the hens, they weren't too badly off financially. Summer was almost upon them and she and Tad had various plans for the summer. They included cockling at Booterstown, taking the pram out into the country and digging spuds (after dark, Tad had said evilly), working at fruit picking and rabbiting.

'Rabbit is grand so it is,' Tad had said. 'You'll love rabbit.'

Polly had agreed that she would, and it was not until she realised that they were talking at cross-purposes

– she of hutches, he of pots – that she vetoed that suggestion. And Tad had agreed, presumably because the thought of Polly lovingly rearing rabbits to eat the hens' corn was more than he could bear.

'You're nutty about animals so you are,' he grumbled, but made no further attempt to persuade her and suggested, instead, that they might dig worms for the hens. But Polly, thinking this was unsporting to say the least, said worms gave her the creeps so they did, so that one had been shelved, too.

'Polly!' the priest said warningly, now. 'Did ye hear what I said now? School on Monday; understand?'

'Yes, Father,' Polly said obediently. There were, after all, only another few weeks to the end of term. 'I'll be glad to go back so I will.'

After the priest had gone, however, she and Ivan began to try to tidy up.

'I don't like hen's shit,' Ivan whined, trying feebly to get it off the linoleum. 'It's sticky and stinky.'

'Shut up and scrub,' Polly ordered. Then, relenting: 'If you get it off, Ivan me little love, sure an' I'll give you an egg to your tea – two eggs.'

'An' bread an' Maggie Ryan?' Ivan said, scrubbing away. 'An' chewed apple?'

'It's *stewed* apple,' Polly said reprovingly. 'Do try and talk proper, me boy. Yes, you shall have two eggs, bread an' margarine, and stewed apple. Only you've got to get the lino clean first.'

She then set to herself, wondering rather apprehensively who the father would send, but presently there was a knock on the door and a gentle, very young voice said, 'Can I come in, now? The father sent me.'

'Come in an' welcome,' Polly said. 'Oh, Miren, 'tis glad I am to see you! I was wonderin' who Father

Feeney would send . . . don't be cross, but it's got a bit messy so it has.'

'Whoever knew me cross?' Miren said. 'Good Lord, hens! I *t'ought* I heard some funny sounds here, as I went past.'

Miren lived on the floor above and was a poor unfortunate, but everyone liked her and pitied her, too. She had come to Dublin as a housemaid and had become pregnant as had many another before her. Sacked and forbidden to go home, she had given birth to her baby and handed it over for adoption, and then she had done the only thing she knew, for no one wanted her, now, as a housemaid.

'Damaged goods they call the girls they've ruined, the so-called gentry do,' Mammy had said once, referring to the poor girls who shared a couple of rooms on the floor above their own. 'And many of those poor innocents have been murdered in their beds by men who take their pleasure and then won't pay for it.'

'Innocents?' the neighbour to whom the remark had been addressed said in a bemused tone. 'Sure an' that's not the right word I'm thinkin', Deirdre.'

'It is so,' Deirdre had asserted. 'Innocent they were when they came to this town despite what life has done to them and innocent they'll die, for they've no malice or evil in their souls.'

But now Miren was looking round the room and tutting gently so Polly put both arms round the older girl's waist and hugged her hard.

'I'm sorry, Miren, about the mess, but I'm only ten and . . .'

'Don't worry, little one,' Miren said. 'Help me and we'll have it clear and bright in two shakes of a . . . oh, my God, what's that doin' here?'

'He's a man-hen,' Polly said rather proudly. 'He's

383

goin' to help the other hens, the woman-hens, to make little yellow chicks; Father Feeney says so.'

'Oh, does he?' Miren said. She was laughing. 'Cockerels peck, or have you already found that out, alanna?'

'He doesn't peck me, I'm his friend. I give him corn an' cabbage an' turnip,' Polly said. 'Besides, I like him. My friend Tad gave me them.'

'Glory be! How many have you?'

'Seven hens and one man-hen,' Polly said. 'What did you say he was called?'

'A cockerel, alanna. Eh, it's like old times to see hens scrattin', but it's not the place for them, you know. Hens needs outside, they needs to peck an' croodle an' pick at fresh grass, worms . . .' Polly shuddered, ' . . . leaves, all sorts. You could get the boys to make you a run an' keep 'em in the courtyard.'

'No, indeed,' Polly said. 'They'd be stole an' ate. You know what folk are. Besides, they're happy in here really they are, Miren. They peck an' pick at the dirt between the floorboards in the kitchen, an' they eat their corn . . . they sit by the fire of an evenin', just like the cats, blinkin' at the flames. And the eggs is good . . . once we beat 'em in milk an' made a custard – it was the nicest thing!'

'Oh well, I'm a country girl meself,' Merin said philosophically. 'But what'll you do when they're old, past layin', child?'

'Get more, an' retire these,' Polly said. She turned to the nearest hen, which was thoughtfully tugging at a loose thread on the rag rug, doubtless under the impression that it had found a worm at last. 'You won't be ate, I promise,' she informed its indifferent back.

'That's cleared that up, then,' Miren said. 'And now, alanna, let's get on wit' our tidyin'!'

Chapter Fourteen

August–October 1934

The day the doctors officially agreed that Peader was out of danger, more, that he was going to get well, Deirdre lit an altar-full of candles and thanked God, his Holy Mother and all the saints. She stayed on her knees for an hour, thanking the whole of the heavenly host, just about, she even threw in a special little prayer of thanks to Polly's guardian angel, for sure and hadn't the angel done her work well? Deirdre had needed to concentrate wholly on her man, and though she had worried a little when Polly told her that Miren was now coming in daily to 'help out', the truth was that beside the crippling anxiety of a sick husband, every other worry paled into insignificance. But that particular worry was over, now, for the doctors, nurses and support staff were delighted with Peader's progress.

'He'll not work as a safety man again, but there's nothing to stop him doing a clerical job,' the doctor told Deirdre a couple of weeks before she took her husband home. 'And the railway has agreed that they'll find him something – a country station, probably, with a small ticket office which needs manning. Or a level crossing, because you'd have a little cottage, a garden . . . now that's a job you could help him with, my dear.'

A level crossing! From that moment on, Deirdre was all smiles. Her worries disappeared like frost in June at the mere prospect of a little cottage and a garden. She knew, now, that her strange attitude to Peader's suggestion of a move had been partly fear of the unknown and partly the change of life. The doctor, when consulted, had told her that the change of life was something with which she would learn to cope, that he could give her some pills, but that she probably would not need them now she knew the cause of her bad temper and depression. And because she loved Peader deeply, always had and always would, and wanted to be with him, she knew that she would be able to tackle this old change of life, to take it in her stride. She would conquer the bad temper and depression, not allow either to rule her. And, armed with this resolution, she found that her attacks of unhappiness and misery had all but disappeared. Love, and nearness, had won. She would cling to Peader wherever he was, whatever he did, and they would be all right.

She had acknowledged, both to herself and to Peader, that the letter had been dreadful, a terrible mistake. She had shown him the other letter, which had arrived soon after his accident, explained how she had regretted the first one as soon as it was in the box, begged his forgiveness. And Peader had smiled his faint smile and said what was there to forgive? She was here, wasn't she? She loved him, didn't she? Well, then!

And he was a hero. The fellers who had gone out and brought him back after the train had hit him hadn't told the whole story when they thought Peader was going to die; the little girl might have been in trouble and there would have been no point. But when they realised that he was going to recover, Trucker Jones blabbed it all over.

'Peader's a bleedin' 'ero,' he told everyone who

would listen. 'Fellers say 'e didn't 'ear the train in the fog – as though an old railwayman like Peader wouldn't 'ave 'ad 'is ears akimbo, strainin' to 'ear, let alone that 'e'd 'ave *felt* 'er approachin', same as we all do! No, it seems 'e saw this little girl, see, comin' towards him across the lines. 'E yelled 'er to gerrout the way but she didn't gerrit, went on a-comin'. So bein' the sort o' feller 'e was 'e ran towards 'er, grabbed 'er, threw 'er to safety . . . and left it too late to save 'imself.'

'Where's the little girl? Who was she?' folk asked, but neither Trucker nor his mates could tell them. The men all agreed she was young, light-haired, ragged, with a bit of a shawl round her shoulders and cracked boots several sizes too large on her feet. She had come out of the fog, screamed to them that there had been an accident, led them to the spot whilst telling them breathlessly what had happened . . . and disappeared.

The newspapers got hold of it, of course. It wasn't only the *Echo* which gave the 'mystery girl', as they were soon calling her, banner headlines. The nationals did, too. And when the Dublin papers realised Peader was a local they, too, published the story – with suitable embellishments, naturally.

Deirdre wrote to Polly that she and the boys should be terrible proud of their daddy and Polly wrote back that they were, so. And then Deirdre realised that Peader was actually worrying about that little girl.

'But, me darlin', you saved her life, everyone knows that,' she said gently, walking beside him in the grounds of the convalescent home to which he had been sent. 'You can't doubt that . . . and what else could you have done?'

Peader sighed. 'I'd have fed her,' he said, in the new slow, careful voice which had come to him after the accident. 'I'd feed 'em all, if I could, all the little gorls an' the chisellers an' the babes in arms who don't get enough to eat.'

Deirdre squeezed his arm. 'So would I, me darlin', so would I,' she agreed. 'And when the little girl comes forward, we'll see her right.' She smiled up into his face, her eyes unshadowed now. 'Brogan's coming to visit you this evening; you'll like that!'

Peader loved strolling with Brogan in the grounds of the convalescent home. He knew, now, that he was going to be offered a level crossing with a little house attached, that he would man the crossing, open and close the gates . . . it sounded idyllic. And there was a garden. Peader knew nothing about gardening but wasn't Brogan the expert there? Since he'd been in the convalescent home, furthermore, Peader had done a lot of talking to the gardeners and felt he was beginning to learn. He found he couldn't wait to get his hands on that garden . . . oh, the cabbage he would grow there, the magnificent crops of potatoes, the fine carrots and onions!

So naturally he was ready and waiting that evening, standing by the side door through which his son usually came. He would be out in a few days, going home to Dublin for a while. There, he would arrange for their possessions to be shipped to Liverpool. They would say goodbye to their friends and neighbours, walk out of the house in Swift's Alley, and journey back to England to take up his new job.

But he was worried about Polly. To bring her back here . . . was it asking for trouble? He knew what Polly meant to Deirdre and to the rest of them as well. He would never forgive himself if, by bringing her back, they lost her.

But it wasn't likely, was it? Deirdre knew about Polly's past, that her mother had not loved her children, that her father was a brute and a bully. She knew about Jess, too, and how, after Jess's death, Peader and Brogan had decided that bringing the baby back to Ireland was the only safe course. She had never questioned it – why should she? She knew her men, knew they wouldn't have lied to her.

And weren't we right? Peader reminded himself stoutly now. Decent food, fresh air and lots of love had turned his little girl into a beauty – if she'd been left in Liverpool, to drag herself up as best she could, Peader was sure she would look very different, now.

And he wanted to ask Brogan about the girl who had been pushed to safety from under the wheels of the train. For one confused moment, when he'd come round in hospital and heard Deirdre reciting the poem about angels which his children loved, he had thought that perhaps the girl on the tracks had been an angel. But he knew it wasn't so, of course. He could still feel the thin shoulders of her against the calloused palms of his hands, still feel the slight weight of her. And she wasn't a ghost, either, even though she seemed to have disappeared so completely. She was just another little stray cat of a child, unloved, uncherished, searching for the means to continue what passed for her life.

Brogan would find her, though, if anyone could. Brogan was kind, generous-spirited; a broth of a boy in fact. He shouldered burdens with never a frown, undertook anything asked of him, seldom argued, never complained. So if he, Peader, explained how important it was to him to find that scrawny little girl, asked Brogan to keep an eye out when he was any-where near the marshalling yards, then there was a good chance his boy would come across her in the fullness of time.

Because once they were back from Ireland, the rest of the family wouldn't be seeing much of the city of Liverpool again. It would be straight out on to the Wirral, to their new home, and they would find out how country living suited them.

Peader gave a big, contented grin, he couldn't help himself. Just the thought of having all that loveliness around him brought his wonderful luck to mind and made him smile. Of course he would not be unscathed; he would walk with a stick for the rest of his life, feel pain from some of his wounds, never be able to do really heavy work. But what did that matter, when all was said and done? He could man his crossing, open and close his gate ... and dig his garden, plant and hoe, weed and sow. What more could a man ask?

Brogan left the convalescent home that evening in a thoughtful frame of mind. That young girl – wasn't it an odd coincidence, now, that there had been two extremely dangerous accidents on the rails just there, both involving a young girl? When Jess Carbery had been killed there had been no one near enough to save her, but this time, his daddy had acted fast and the child had escaped unscathed.

Was she a Carbery? She couldn't possibly be, the family seemed to have disappeared. And it was hard, now, to remember exactly what Jess had talked about that evening in the draughty little shed so long ago. But she had mentioned another sister, a child, then, of three or four. Had she used her name? But that he truly could not remember, and in any event, since he had no idea what the child was called whose life had been saved by his daddy, remembering would do very little good.

And even if she was a Carbery, did it really matter, make any difference? His daddy had been shocked and distressed by the skinny waif wandering the railway and had wanted to help her no matter what her name was. So do I, Brogan told himself quickly. I want to help her, too. But if she is the missing Carbery daughter, wouldn't that be grand, now? The fellers say Jess haunts the track, searching for her little sister, but if she's in Heaven then she knows full well that the sister we've rechristened Polly is safer, and happier, with us than she ever could have been with her own family.

But if Jess was searching for the other sister and not Polly at all, it would make a sort of sense. She would be anxious about Grace, the child she'd left at home on that snowy Christmas Day. Now look at that, Brogan told himself, when you don't try sure and doesn't the name pop into your head as though it had never been forgot? Of course she was Grace, I remember now.

He had walked out of the convalescent home grounds and now he set off along the quiet and dusty roadway, meaning to head for civilisation and a tram stop, but it was such a nice evening that he thought he'd walk, instead. He reached the top of Beaconsfield Road, hesitated, then turned down it. He could pick up a tram on the main road, but the gardens and houses down here were marvellous, he often went this way after he'd left his father. And it was a perfect late summer evening, with sweet gusts of perfume blowing to him on the breeze and the birds singing their hearts out as the sun sank in the sky.

Brogan walked slowly, looking long and keenly into each garden as he passed. The convalescent home had once been a manor house of some description and the grounds were tended with care, but some of these houses had gardens almost unbelievable in their beauty. Brogan lingered more than ever, gazing at smooth lawns, flower-beds rich with roses, wisteria clambering over grey stone or russet brick, and of course at the wonders he could only guess at because they were imprisoned behind the glittering walls of glasshouses or conservatories.

But presently, about halfway down the hill – for Beaconsfield Road was on a steepish hill – he came to a house which was not surrounded by an impeccable garden. It was overgrown; fancy that! There was a tennis lawn with grass almost knee-high, weed-choked flower-beds and a gravel frontage which was not only weedy, it was also covered with piles of bricks, a concrete mixer, a great many long planks of wood and assorted tools connected with the building trade.

It's being rebuilt, or altered, at any rate, Brogan thought to himself, stopping to stare. It's going to be something different – I wonder what? And I wonder whether they'd be glad of a chap to help with the garden, in the evenings and on his days off? He missed his Crewe plot and Mrs Burt, kind though she was, could not conjure a garden out of thin air for him to help her with. She had a smelly little back yard where the only things which flourished were bits of old bicycles and a couple of washing lines. Allotments, though they did exist in the city, were all full and were passed on, Brogan gathered, from father to son. So if these people really could do with help, Brogan was the feller for them.

Pity he didn't know their name, though. But as he was about to pass regretfully on, he glanced at the big stone gateposts. *Strawberry Field* the legend on the gatepost ran. Brogan nodded to himself and committed it to memory, then walked on, a little faster now. Tomorrow he would begin to put out feelers to find the little girl his father felt he had lost. He would speak to the gangs who worked the marshalling yard because, like Peader, he suspected that the kid probably hung around there, hoping for scraps of some sort, using the sheds for shelter. And if that failed he could go round the schools when he had a couple of hours off, see whether he could find out from teachers or pupils if the 'mystery girl' was known to them. And then he could try churches, priests, parks and places of entertainment beloved of kids – the Saturday rush for example.

I'll find her in the end, Brogan told himself. I'll start tomorrow.

By the time September came round, Sara was beginning to see light out at the new children's home. She was a small cog in a fairly big wheel, but *how* she enjoyed herself! She had not realised how much she had taken in, without realising it, about the running of a large house and larger garden, and now, at last, such knowledge came in useful.

'Leave the garden surrounding the house itself until last,' she advised. 'Because whilst the alterations are going on it will only get trampled flat anyway. For now, let's put all our efforts into getting the house right – and into keeping the vegetable garden and the greenhouses producing. That way, we'll have a reasonable amount of fresh fruit and vegetables when the children come in.'

She was learning a lot, too – more than she taught, definitely. She learned how to plan rooms in which children can happily spend their days and nights, to make nurseries for very young children, bedrooms for others, playrooms, classrooms, sitting rooms – in fact she began to learn how to plan a house in which children and adults may live happily together.

She was still not living in, which was a blessing in a way, since her grandmother was becoming increasingly frail, even Sara's prejudiced eye could see it. Mrs Prescott enjoyed living in Florence Street and found it easy to get to the shops, but she went out less and less and relied more and more on Sara and Clarrie. However, she had become a cinema enthusiast and once a week a neighbour wheeled her round to the Victoria Picture Palace where she sampled everything they had on offer – comedies, horror, thrillers, cowboy and Indian films.

'You should come wi' me from time to time, queen,' she told her granddaughter. 'For one thing it takes you out of yourself, and for another, it entertains you. What's wrong wi' that, eh?'

Sara said politely that she was sure there was nothing wrong with that, and continued to spend her evenings planning, reading, or preparing for the coming day, apart from when she was on soup kitchen duty, or taking the *War Cry* round the pubs, of course. Because she was so absorbed in her work, indeed, even her Saturdays, once an oasis of rest and pleasure, became simply another day in which to plot and plan.

'We could do so many things, if we'd a mind,' Mrs Prescott said persuasively one fine evening in August when the breeze was mild and the air coming through the window sweet. 'There's the theatre, art galleries, all sorts. If you had more spare time, queen, we could get about a bit. And there's Sat'day night dances . . . you could wheel me in perched on me chair and I could watch all the gallivanting. My, I'd enjoy that.'

She had sounded wistful but Sara, though she would

have loved to take her grandmother about a bit, was firm.

'The Strawb needs me right now,' she said, with a sigh. 'Later, when it's up and running, I'll be able to relax a bit more, enjoy myself. But right now, Gran, I dare not let up, really. Will you forgive me for being so boring?'

'No, I shan't,' Mrs Prescott said, then chuckled and leaned across the table which divided them, taking Sara's hands in hers. 'My dear girl, you're a tower of strength . . . it's just that I don't want to see you growing into an old maid, looking after me for the rest of your life. I want you to get about more, meet people.'

'All work and no play makes Jack a dull boy,' Clarrie said, and later that same week she announced, after supper, that she was going to the cinema whether Sara liked it or not.

'Come with me, Sara. Mrs Prescott's right, a bit of an outing would do you good. Besides, it'll be much more fun if there's two of us eatin' peanuts and chuckin' the shells about in the sixpenny seats! I'd enjoy meself far better if you came along, honest I would. It's not as if there was anything wrong with the cinema; the Army approves!'

But Sara, though she laughed, still shook her head.

'Can't. I'm going along with the brigadier tomorrow to look at little desks. And I'm trying to produce a drawing of the ideal locker for a child's dormitory. What's on at the Vic, anyway?'

'I'm not going to the Vic, I'm going to the Astoria,' Clarrie told her. 'They're showin' Shirley Temple in *Little Miss Marker*. Do come, queen.'

'We-ell, I really ought to finish this drawing,' Sara said. 'Only I do love to watch the child stars. It's the teacher in me coming out, I suppose.' She laid down her paperwork and smiled at her friend. Oh, all right, you've persuaded me. I'll come.' She turned to her grandmother. 'Why don't you come as well, Gran? You said you wanted more exciting outings.'

'Well, I'm glad you're not turnin' into some boring little Goody-two-shoes,' Gran said unkindly from her seat by the window. 'But I've seen it – so I won't trouble you this evening. But if you're comin' past the fried fish shop when it's over, I'd like a penn'orth of chips, please! And if you'll pass over my knitting and turn the wireless on, I'll have another scarf finished by the time you get back!'

It was a good film, and Sara really enjoyed it. Coming past Platts fried fish shop on their way home, she remembered her grandmother's request and tugged Clarrie's arm.

'Gran wanted a penn'orth of chips, Clarrie. I wouldn't mind some myself, and a bit of fish. I wonder if they've got any haddock? Gran's fond of that.'

'I prefer cod,' Clarrie said. 'Oh, come on, let's treat ourselves. Fish an' chips all round, eh? And if we get indigestion, that's hard luck. It's our evenin' off, queen!'

So, armed with three portions of fish and chips wrapped in newspaper, they went back to the flat, letting themselves in through the back door straight into the tiny scullery and calling to Gran that they would be bringing her tea through just as soon as they'd got the food on to the plates.

'I like 'em best in the newspaper,' Clarrie said as she unwrapped. 'But I've gorra pretend to be a lady now and then. Good for Mrs P, the kettle's still hot. I'll just warm the pot . . . you take the grub through.'

Sara piled the food on a tray and carried it into the living room.

'Tan tara! A penn'orth of chips, Gran, *and* some fish, because we've decided to treat ourselves to a . . . Gran?'

Mrs Prescott was sitting in her chair by the window, but she had lolled over sideways at what looked like a very uncomfortable angle. She had obviously fallen asleep, for her knitting was on the floor at her feet and the wireless played on unregarded.

'Gran, we've bought fish and chips,' Sara said softly. She stood the tray down and went over to her grandmother's side. 'Well, fancy falling asleep when . . . oh, my God!'

'What's up?' Clarrie said, appearing in the doorway. 'Don't you want . . . oh, Sara, is she ill? I'll get the doctor at once . . . I'll run down the road to the telephone box . . .'

Sara stroked her grandmother's wispy grey hair back from her forehead and straightened her in the chair. Then she closed her fingers round her grandmother's wrist. Finally, she turned to Clarrie.

'Yes, do get the doctor,' she said quietly. 'But I think it's too late, Clarrie. I think she's already gone.'

'It's great you're comin' home wit' us, Brog,' Peader said as the ship drew nearer to Ireland's shore. 'Your mammy's very good, but she's got a lot on her mind. She'll stay wit' me, make sure I get down the gangplank an' so on, if you'll see to the cases.'

'I will, Daddy,' Brogan said equably. 'Is it excited you are to be seein' your native land after you've been so ill?'

'I'm more excited at the thought of the kids,' Peader admitted. 'They've been great, none could be better. I want to tell 'em so meself, Brog.'

'They have done well, especially Polly,' Brogan agreed. 'I don't suppose the boys did much in the house, knowing them, though I'm sure they carted coal, wood, water, that sort of thing. Poor Polly, she's only a baby, really.'

'She's ten years old and that's no baby,' Deirdre said rather sharply. She had been standing a short way away, gazing silently at the approaching coastline, but now she moved nearer them. 'But sure she's done well so she has. The father wrote, you know. A bit guarded, he was, but he seemed pleased wit' our girl.'

'And how'll they take the news that we're all movin'?' Brogan asked. 'Will they be pleased, d'you t'ink, Mammy?'

'Polly will be just thrilled,' Deirdre said happily. 'Because she's mad about animals so she is and the thought of livin' in the countryside and bein' able to have as many cats and dogs as she wants . . . that'll win her over if nothin' else does.'

'I *know* they're comin' home tomorrow, an' I *am* glad, sure I am, but I still don't want to send me hens away,' Polly said stubbornly. 'What's wrong wit' them, Miren? I'll keep 'em in the kitchen just for a day or so, if you like.'

'Polly, the bleedin' poultry must go,' Martin said severely from his seat by the fire. 'We've let you and them alone now for weeks – well, the eggs was worth a bit o' muck on the lino – but our mammy will go mad wit' you so she will. And you don't want that, do you, so she won't see them, is that clear? You can't keep hens in the house, that's what she'll say, and you'll spoil an' ruin her homecoming so you will.'

'I won't, so,' Polly said defiantly. 'Mammy's sensible; she'll love me hens.'

'She won't, because she isn't going to see them,' Martin repeated. 'Don't you defy me, alanna, or it's to bed you'll go straight away, and you'll not even see your hens when we let you up again.'

Polly's eyes rounded. Martin was as easy-going as Brogan and a good deal lazier; she'd had no trouble with him until this very moment, and she didn't like it one bit. Why, if he persisted, it would be he who ran the household and not her! But she did concede, having thought it over, that he had a point. Mammy might not be too thrilled to find her home overrun with hens.

'All right then,' she said sulkily after a moment. 'Say I send 'em away for a bit – where am I to send 'em? I won't let anyone lay a finger on 'em if they're thinkin' of roast fowl, Martin, 'cos they're me friends so they are.'

'Give them to someone in a ground-floor room, who's got a bit of space outside,' Martin said tactfully. Bevin, not nearly so tactful, said: 'Give them to old Halligan – no, sell them to him. He'd make good use of 'em.'

Mr Halligan was a butcher. Polly screamed.

'Don't you say that name where me hens can hear,' she shrieked. 'I'm warnin' ye, Bevin O'Brady, that I'll swing for you if you touch a feather of their heads.'

'No, no, he's only coddin' you,' Martin said, chuckling. 'What about Tad? There's plenty of space in Gardiners Lane for hens . . . doesn't he have a few of his own, come to think? You could let him take care of your hens, alanna, until Mammy and Daddy are settled again.'

'Tad's daddy might eat 'em,' Polly said with quivering lip. 'He kilt one of Tad's birds one day when he found her perched on his clean boots so he did. I won't have me birds kilt by that . . . that . . .'

'We'll have to tell Tad's daddy that they're ours,' Bevin said. He was doing his eckers sitting cross-legged on the hearthrug and now he threw down his book and smiled kindly up at his sister. 'I was coddin' you, alanna, and I'm sorry. I'll help you take 'em round to Tad, if you like. We'll go in an' see Mr Donoghue an' tell him they're our hens . . . we'll tell him we're payin' rent for 'em, then he won't dare to kill so much as a feather of 'em.'

'Well, all right,' Polly said at last, having tried – and failed – to think of a better solution. She didn't trust Tad's daddy, but she did trust Tad. He never let her down, no doubt if she explained the seriousness of the situation he would stand by her again.

So they put the hens in pillowcases and carried their squawking burdens down the stairs, across the courtyard, along Swift's Alley and into Francis Street, where some ribald remarks followed them from interested stallholders, and finally into Gardiners Lane. As luck would have it, Tad was mucking around in one of the ruined houses and called them over.

'Hello Poll, Bev,' he said cheerfully. 'What you got there, eh?'

'Me hens,' Polly said heavily. 'The ones you gave me, Tad. Martin says we can't have 'em in the rooms when Mammy and Daddy come home tomorrow. Can you keep 'em for us if we pay rent?'

'How much?' Tad said with all his usual bluntness. 'And will the rent include corn?'

'We'll give ye a tanner a week,' Polly said briskly, her interest aroused. A tanner sounded like a lot of money, but feeding the hens, Polly knew, was no sinecure, and Tad might not find it easy to beg scraps the way she did.

'A tanner! Make it a bob and we're in business.'

'Ninepence,' Polly offered, enjoying the huckstering now. 'Ninepence and not a penny more, Mr Donoghue.'

Tad laughed. 'Done!' he said. 'And you must help gather the corn, Poll, or it won't be fair.'

The arrival of Mammy, Daddy and Brogan, long anticipated, was every bit as good as Polly could have wished. Daddy's face had a long scar across one cheek, all purple and wrinkled still, and another across his forehead, thin and angry-looking. His hair had gone snowy white, but Polly thought it suited him, and he walked with a stick and slowly, at that, and he took his time getting in and out of chairs, and it had taken him a long, long while to mount the stairs, but other than that he was just the same. Her dearest daddy, with his slow speech, his slow smile, and his quick kindnesses.

Polly had done her best, aided by Miren, and thought that all traces of her feathered friends had been removed. To be sure, the first thing Mammy noticed was the crack in the big mirror, the second thing that the ornaments on the mantel were either gone or chipped. Polly, forewarned that she must not mention the hens at first, murmured that she'd been careless, she was sorry, and wished she had told the truth when Brogan took her aside later and asked her for the pawn tickets.

'For you surely had to take 'em down there,' he murmured, smiling at her. 'But you couldn't tell Mammy.'

'No, they are broke, truly,' Polly admitted in hushed tones. She lowered her voice still further. ''Twas me hens, only don't say a word to Mammy. At first they flew, 'cos their wings wasn't clipped. But Miren said Mammy mustn't know, you see, so I had to tell a fib.'

'It's possible she may guess, alanna,' Brogan said cautiously. 'There's corn in between the floorboards in the kitchen; I noticed it meself so I did. But she won't worry, because . . .'

He broke off and Polly, assuming that he thought they were about to be interrupted, returned to the kitchen, where she was making a meal for the family with quite a lot of help from Deirdre despite Polly constantly telling her, in a very motherly way, to 'go and sit yourself down, Mammy, an' have a nice crack wit' your sons!'

Teatime came. They were all round the table, even Martin having returned from his work, when Daddy broke the news. He sat back in his chair, took a sip of tea, cleared his throat and addressed them.

'You can see I'm well again, but not so spry. In fact the bosses have changed me job, because a safety man needs his full strength, and a deal of agility, too.' He laughed, but no one else even smiled. The accident was too close for that. 'Yes, well. So they've given me a crossing gate. It's in beautiful countryside. There's a cottage with a good garden, and we'll be able to grow a good deal of our own food, and we can keep hens . . .' Polly's ears pricked up, ' . . . pigs, all sorts. So what d'you think?'

'It sounds grand, Daddy,' Bevin said, grinning. 'Wait'll I tell the fellers!'

'Polly?' Peader spoke enquiringly, but he was smiling already.

'Oh, Daddy . . . hens and pigs! I'll look after 'em, I know all about hens.' She turned to her brother. 'Can I tell 'em now, Brogan?'

'Go ahead,' Brogan said. 'Mammy thought you'd be pleased.'

'I've been keepin' hens,' Polly disclosed. 'Only they

made me take 'em round to the ruins, where Tad keeps his. They said you'd not like hens in your parlour, Mammy.'

Deirdre nodded her head slowly. 'Me ornaments – and the corn between the floorboards,' she said ruefully. 'They were right, alanna. But hens in their proper place now, that's another thing altogether so it is.'

'You kept hens here, in our good rooms?' Peader said incredulously, 'Whatever next, alanna? And don't say pigs, because . . .'

'She wanted to have a pig,' Ivan said, placidly cramming half a round of bread and margarine into his mouth. 'But she was afraid it would eat the dog and the cats when it got big.'

'I never did . . . I only said . . .' Polly squeaked, very confused. She turned to her mother. 'Oh, Mammy, it's just . . . and anyway, we're goin' to live in the country! Oh, I'm so, *so* happy!'

And indeed, as soon as tea was over she begged leave to go round and tell Tad that his rent for the hens would not be coming in for long.

'We'll be away in a couple of weeks,' her father had said. 'We won't take the linoleum, but everything else will have to be packed.'

So off Polly trotted on the familiar round. Out of Swift's Alley, along Francis Street . . . and there was Tad, with a dirty old sack, grubbing in the gutters for damaged vegetables for the hens!

'Tad! Oh, Tad, you'll never guess what me daddy's telled us!' Polly gabbled, clutching his sleeve. 'He can't be a safety man no more, 'cos he was hurt bad so he was, but he's goin' to be a railway crossing man instead, wit' a cottage, an' a garden, an' pigs an' hens . . .' She stopped short. 'Tad? Aren't you pleased, now? You can come each day an' see the pigs, if you like.'

'Where?'

'What d'you mean, where? Where can you see the pigs? In their sty, when we've made them one.'

'No, Poll,' Tad said patiently. 'Where's this crossin'?'

'Oh, I see, but what does *where* matter? It'll be on the Howth Road, I bet . . . oh, I *hope* it's there, 'cos of the sea.'

'Ask your daddy,' Tad said in a very peculiar voice. If he hadn't been a chiseller, Polly would have thought he was upset, trying to hold back tears. 'I'll come back wit' you now an' you can ask him right away.'

'Sure I will,' Polly said stoutly, but for the first time, a niggling doubt crossed her mind. Why should the LMS give her daddy a crossing to take care of on a Southern Ireland line? She knew all about the LMS because Daddy and Brogan talked about it. But . . . but they wouldn't give him a line in *England*, surely, and him Irish through and through? She scowled at Tad but he wasn't looking at her. He was staring at his feet, bare and dust-coloured, as they padded along the pavement.

They reached the O'Bradys' door and Polly shoved it open and tugged Tad inside. Scarcely through the door she said loudly, 'Daddy, where's your crossin'? *Say* it isn't in England, *say* it isn't!'

Peader had been dozing in a chair by the fire whilst Deirdre cleared away the tea things and his daughter's abrupt entrance into the room had disturbed a rather pleasant dream. Now, he rubbed his eyes, then yawned fiercely. Deirdre must be washing up in the kitchen; he could hear the clatter as she brought the crocks out of the soapy water and stood them on the bit of a draining board he had made for her himself on his last visit home. She was singing a tune beneath her breath and sounded very happy. Peader sat up straight and tried to answer Polly's question.

'What? Me crossin', d'you mean? It's on the Wirral, alanna, that's a very pleasant part of the country, very pleasant indeed. You'll love it so you will.'

'It's in England, that Wirral, isn't it, Mr O'Brady?' Tad said in a hollow voice. 'You're takin' me pal to England!'

And before anyone could so much as say a word Tad had whipped round and could be heard thundering down the stairs.

'Oh dear,' Peader said inadequately. 'What's worryin' Tad then, alanna?'

Polly ignored the question. 'Daddy?' she said slowly. 'Daddy, Tad's not right, is he?'

'Me darlin', I t'ought you knew, t'ought you'd guess,' Peader said, all his happiness gone and guilt swamping him. He'd not thought of this one, not thought of the kids havin' to leave their pals! 'Of course it's in England, but that's . . .'

'Oh, Tad, Tad!' Polly burst into tears and before Peader could move she was out of the room and clattering down the stairs in Tad's wake.

Peader had got to his feet and was halfway across to the door when Deirdre popped her head into the room.

'I heard that,' she said reassuringly. 'Don't be in a worry, me darlin', 'twas bound to occur. She'll come round when we say Tad must come an' stay wit' us from time to time.'

'But a boy can't pop across the water just like that,' Peader said heavily. 'Oh, why didn't I *think*? She's heartbroken, so she is.'

'I know he won't come to stay, an' so do you, but 'tis a comfort for the child,' Deirdre said. 'She'll accept it better and by the time she realises he's not come over she'll have a dozen new friends an' a whole new life so she will. She's only ten, that's no age, and in England she'll have a better chance than she would here, didn't you say?'

'I did. There's factories, shops . . . yes, I'm sure she'll get work when she's old enough,' Peader said, returning to his chair. 'You're a good woman, Deirdre. When the young one comes back we'll comfort her wit' promises.'

'That's it,' Deirdre agreed. 'Now you sit and rest awhile; close your eyes.'

'Go back to sleep, you mean, like an ould feller,' Peader said, wryly, but he leaned back in the chair and closed his eyes.

It was a long while, however, before he could sleep.

Polly had stood in the stern of the ship and watched Ireland disappear, and now she was standing in the bows and watching Liverpool approach. It was huge so it was – and there were some grand and beautiful buildings. But although the sun was shining a pall of smoke hung over the city, greyish yellow smoke, and the voices which came to her ears both from the shore and from many of the sailors were harsh, with turns of phrase which were new to her.

Brogan was standing beside her and now he put an arm about her shoulders. 'Don't scowl so, Polly,' he said. 'Liverpool's a fine city, but you won't be stayin' there long. You'll be off to me daddy's new crossing in a matter of days. Now you'll like that, won't you?'

'I shall not,' Polly said firmly. 'I want to be wit' Tad so I do. I *like* the Liberties, an' Dublin, an' me school, an' me pals.' She shivered and pointed ahead of her, to where the big buildings were getting ever closer. 'What's *that*?'

'It's the Liver building. Them's the Liver birds, sittin' on them little tower things. English sailors who've travelled from all over the world know that when they can see the Liver birds, they're nearly home.'

Polly sniffed. Then she rubbed her eyes and sagged against Brogan's comforting arm.

'It's no use, is it, Brog? I can be as horrible as I like, but I'm still only ten years old. They won't let me go home, will they?'

'No, alanna, they won't let you go home,' Brogan said quietly. 'Not yet, not till you're a good deal older. But 'tis the same for all of us. Daddy and me, we have to stay to earn our livin', whether we will or no. The boys will have to stay too, until they're old enough to try for work over the water, that is. So you're in good company. We've all got to earn a crust, eh?'

'Martin and Donal stayed in Dublin. Why couldn't I stay wit' them?' Polly said, but she spoke without much conviction. She knows, poor kid, that what's done is done, Brogan thought, and felt, for a fleeting second, the helplessness of a child, carried hither and thither by the wishes of an adult world which she cannot really understand.

'You can't stay wit' Martin because he'll be workin' hard, wit' no time to take care of a little sister,' Brogan pointed out. 'Polly, love, you'll be happy in your new home, I promise you. Aren't your hens in the hold this minute, an' Delly, an' both cats? And won't you have new pets, more hens, pigs? And the whole of the lovely countryside to play in, what's more.'

'But not Tad,' Polly reminded him. 'Never Tad.'

'You must write often, two or three times a week,'

Brogan said. 'You must tell him every little thing that happens, and then, when you do meet again, it'll be as if you'd never been apart.'

'I will, so,' Polly said, cheering up a little. 'Daddy said yesterday I might be able to have a little horse of me own one day.'

Poor Daddy, Brogan thought, desperate to make up to this odd little daughter of his for taking her away from her playmate. Indeed, though he used the term 'playmate', he thought that she had behaved as though she and Tad had loved one another! And wit' her ten years old and the lad no more than twelve, that wasn't likely.

Was it?

Her grandmother's death changed Sara; she had always worked hard but now she seemed to have very little interest in what went on outside Strawberry Field. She and Mr Alderwood were determined to get everything right, and at last the day came when the major pronounced himself satisfied and brought the new matron along to inspect things. That lady pronounced herself delighted with everything and suggested that they should have an Open Day, at which friends, relatives and local dignitaries might see for themselves what a pleasant place the Strawberry Field Children's Home had become.

'Well, Clarrie, we'll be opening the place up in no time at all now, so the brigadier has decided to have an Open Day,' Sara said when she got back to the flat that night. She and Clarrie had kept the place on, though without Mrs Prescott's small pension – and warm presence – their ability to continue to pay the rent and stay there would probably not last. Besides, Sara had been offered a live-in post at the home and thought she would take it. 'You will come, won't you? All sorts of local dignitaries will be coming, and a great many high-ranking Salvationists of course. And when the Open Day is over we're going to have a little tea party – that is, the friends and relatives of everyone who's helped to make Strawberry Field what it is today – and you can all tell us what you think.'

'I just wish Mrs Prescott could have seen it,' Clarrie said with a sigh. 'But there, I expect she can in her way – she'll be rare proud of you, queen. And you must accept the job, you know. I'll find someone else to share here. And thanks for invitin' me to the Open Day – I'll do you credit, chuck. I'll go down to Zena's, get me hair set, and I'll wear me new suit – or should it be uniform?'

'The suit, I think,' Sara said. 'There are going to be an awful lot of uniforms about! And – and thanks, Clarrie.'

'What for? For comin' to a free do, where'll I gerra cuppa tea?'

'No, silly. For telling me to go ahead and take the job, which I'm longing to do. For making me feel it's all right to – well, to leave you in the lurch, in a way.'

Clarrie tutted. The two girls were in the living kitchen, both knitting away though with different measures of success; Clarrie had been taught to knit as a child, Sara had never mastered it.

'Well, a poor sort of friend I'd think meself if I didn't tell you to take the job, the way things are. And as for leavin' me in the lurch, you're doin' no such thing. I tell you, folk will be fallin' over theirselves to take a share of a place like this 'un. Now who's goin' to put the kettle on, you or me? 'Cos I'm dyin' for a nice cuppa.'

It was all very well to feel confident that the house was now fit for occupancy when you compared it with how it had looked six months ago, but when the Open Day dawned, Sara discovered that she was actually nervous. People who had never been up the drive before, let alone in at the big front door, were going to be staring, peering into cupboards, possibly even criticising. She went from room to room, tidying, straightening, trying to see it through the eyes of a stranger, but in the end she simply went into the big front hall and waited. It was too late for changing her mind, too late for adjustments, even. She must simply smile and accept whatever the visitors said.

It helped that she wasn't the only one who was nervous. The brigadier, who would be running the home, was nervous too. She tidied her study, went and changed the pink and white checked cloths in the dining room for blue and white, then changed them back again. She ran a finger along the banisters and couldn't find any dust, then she hurried into the kitchens to check that arrangements for the staff tea party were complete.

'Relax, Brigadier,' Sara said at last. 'I thought I was nervous, but you're so much worse that you've made me feel quite calm.'

'You won't have to explain to the Lord Mayor if he finds fault,' the brigadier said. 'Oh, is that them now? Lor, whose idea *was* this, anyway?'

'Yours, and a very good idea it was, too,' Mr Alderwood said, winking at Sara. 'Just stop fussing, Matron . . . I do believe I hear a car!'

It was only the major, but as he opened the door Clarrie appeared behind him, mounted on her bicycle. She got off, leaned the machine carefully against the house wall, and then came in, smiling broadly.

'Ah, Miss Boote,' the brigadier said, coming forward. 'Isn't this exciting? Would you like to come in and see what we've done on the ground floor, whilst we wait for the official party?'

'I'm early; but better early than late,' Clarrie said. 'Yes, I'd love to see what you've all been up to . . . ain't it a lovely big garden, though? I've never seen one so big, it's more like a blinkin' park!'

'But we can't start until the Lord Mayor arrives,' Sara hissed, only to be told the brigadier knew that but thought she would enjoy showing someone round who didn't make her nervous.

'Don't worry, the major and I will call the brigadier back the minute the official cars arrive,' Mr Alderwood said as Sara began to fuss. 'It's better that she has something to do other than worry whether everything's perfect. You go with her, my dear, we'll hold the fort here.'

The kitchens were wonderful, Clarrie said with all her usual enthusiasm. Large and airy, with beautiful modern cooking stoves, sinks at the right height so that those who worked at them would not be perpetually stooping and views of the garden from the large windows.

'My mam would love it,' Clarrie said, clearly setting the Boote seal of approval on the Children's Home.

The rest of the ground floor lived up to the kitchens, what was more. The dining room was very large, but it seemed cosy because it was designed with family life rather than institutions in mind. Small tables for four, six or eight were scattered around the room, there was a polished wood floor, rugs, pretty lampshades, ornaments on the mantel . . .

'It's homely, that's what it is,' Clarrie announced.

And the living rooms were pleasant, the playrooms well planned with furniture to fit children from two or three to fourteen or so, though they seemed a little bare with neither children nor toys yet in occupation. 'And them grounds, Brigadier – it's a paradise for kids.'

'We've not started on the gardens, yet,' the brigadier said rather evasively. They had disagreed over the gardens. She wanted velvet lawns, flower-beds, trees. There was already an orchard and a very good vegetable garden, though the orchard was full of elderly apple trees and the vegetable plot was just full of weeds. But Sara and Mr Alderwood thought that a beautiful, orderly garden would make the kids feel uncomfortable. They wanted it left as it was except for the front which, they agreed, would have to be made respectable as soon as possible.

'Well, you'll want to do some hedge-trimmin' an' lawn-cuttin', no doubt,' Clarrie agreed. 'But the rest . . . well, kids all want places they can climb trees an' swing on gates an' dig an' plant for theirselves. So why not leave it wildish, like?'

'It has been suggested,' the brigadier admitted. 'So you think it's a paradise for kids as it stands, eh, Miss Boote?'

'I do,' Clarrie said decidedly. 'Let the kids 'ave a say, Matron. Let 'em get their hands dirty, diggin' an' plantin'. There's nothin' kids like more.'

And indeed by the time the official party arrived all the brigadier's nerves had vanished under Miss Boote's soothing comments and she was able to show her distinguished visitors round and give them a running commentary on the work which had been done without a blush. She even told the party that the gardens would not be cleared and made beautiful; that was work the children themselves might undertake and plan.

Sara, following the party, winked at Clarrie. She was elated, walking on air. It was clear that these important, influential people approved of what had been done – better, they liked it. When the brigadier said they would be having their first destitute children in at the beginning of the month they offered help, money to be spent on clothing, food, playthings.

And finally the official party cut the length of ribbon which had been tied across the foot of the stairs and declared that the Strawberry Field Children's Home was open for business.

'Now all we want is the kids,' Sara said quietly to Mr Alderwood. 'This has been grand, but it's not what we're here for. We're here for the kids.'

Brogan was glad when the crossing was over; Polly hadn't enjoyed it, she'd been too busy staring back at Ireland and longing for Tad, and he had felt ridiculously guilty, as though he'd done wrong to take her to Ireland in the first place if he was then going to turn round and bring her back here again.

But he busied himself getting all their gear ashore and then to the tram stop, for the family were to stay tonight in a cheap hotel just off the Walton Road, and he would go back to his lodging with Mrs Burt, and then, tomorrow, he would go with his family to his daddy's new post – the level crossing with the cottage and the large garden.

He had thought getting them off the ship was bad enough, but getting them aboard the tram was worse. The conductor of the first tram to arrive refused even to consider having the crated hens aboard, and he didn't like the cat basket much, either, though he only sniffed when Delilah, ears flattened, eyes staring anxiously, was lugged aboard.

'I'll get a taxi to fetch the hens to Salop Street,' Brogan said. 'It won't tek me but a minute.' He climbed down off the tram-step, wondering what he'd done to deserve all this. Why the hell did they have to *bring* the bloody hens, he was thinking to himself. Hens were hens, Polly could have let Tad keep these; Brogan would have bought her some more when they were settled in, honest to God he would.

He lugged the hens, in their crate, over to the taxi rank. The first driver said he didn't carry freight and suggested, jeeringly, that Brogan should carry them on his head, as doubtless he carried them when trotting over his ancestral bog.

Brogan smiled at him and turned away, but his fist must have been thinking of something different, for instead of following his body it whammed the driver of the first taxi right on the nose, causing him to give a howl of mingled pain and rage. Brogan gave him a surprised glance and turned to the second driver. The second driver, oddly enough, was much more polite. He said that he, too, never carried freight and though he would like to oblige . . .

'I'd take 'em if I was you, pal,' Brogan said. 'Because I'm a big feller, tryin' to do right by me family, an' they're wantin' these hens so they are.'

The second driver, looking thoughtfully at his pal's scarlet and swollen nose, decided that he would oblige just this once. Brogan loaded the hens into the cab, called Bevin to come off the tram and travel in the cab with the hens, and gave his young brother some money.

'The driver's a grand feller so he is,' he told Bevin. 'He'll help you unload 'em, carry 'em to the door for you, very like. When you arrive give the door a knock

414

an' when Mrs Burt comes, explain we'll not be long. Sure you'll be all right?'

Bevin said he would be grand, just grand, so Brogan rejoined the rest of his family aboard the tram, whose conductor was beginning to say he wouldn't wait any longer, not if it was for the King himself.

'Isn't this fun, Polly?' Deirdre said as Brogan sat wearily down by them and the tram jerked into motion. 'Did ye see the overhead railway when Brogan pointed it out? What about a train chuff-chuffin' along in the air, then? What about that, eh?'

'I – I don't know,' Polly said. She was staring all round her, and there was something in her attitude which worried Brogan. She didn't look like a totally confused stranger, she looked more like – like someone who half-recognises a place and doesn't want to do so. But that was impossible; Polly had been a babe in arms when she left the city, she'd been no more than nine months old!

'Sure an' of course you know,' Deirdre said bracingly. 'You like it ... it's fun, isn't it? Ivan thinks it's fun, don't you, little feller?'

Ivan, bouncing in his seat, said yes, it was fun so it was, but Polly just sat, staring. Delilah gave a little moan and leaned against her legs. He didn't like the motion of the tram and several times made swallowing, gulping movements of his throat but to Brogan's immense relief, the dog didn't actually throw up. Perhaps we'll get back before anything else happens, he thought hopefully. Ah God, what are those bloody cats doin' now in the name of all that's wonderful?

The cat basket was rocking as the inmates apparently hurled themselves at each other, caterwauling loud enough to make the other passengers on the tram turn and stare. Peader grinned and made soothing noises in the direction of the wildly rocking basket but the conductor, who must have known a thing or two about cats, gave the wicker a good kick as he passed it. Shocked, Lionel and Samson stopped attacking each other and silence descended.

'Even the cats don't like all this,' Polly muttered, glaring darkly at the conductor's oblivious back. 'Even the cats t'ink we've run mad so they do. And poor Delly . . . oh Delilah, don't be sick, there's a good feller!'

Delilah swallowed, shivered, and then moved to lean against Peader's knee. He cast his eyes up at Peader with a pitiful expression; let's get off, he seemed to be saying, before I chuck me liver and lights on to the deck!

Brogan leaned across the dog. He took hold of Polly's hand and began to play with her fingers.

'Round an' round the garden, like a teddy bear . . .'

Polly had sunk back into her reverie but the childish game brought her mind back to the present. 'Stop that, you big Brogan, 'tis not a baby I am,' she said crossly, snatching her hand away. 'Oh . . . oh . . . where's *that*?'

'Nowhere in particular,' Brogan said, following her gaze. 'Oh, the market, you mean? We're goin' along Great Homer Street, there's always stalls an' that.'

'It looks a little bit like Francis Street,' Polly said wistfully. 'I wonder what Tad's doin' now? He's missin' me already. I can tell.'

Brogan sighed. 'Of course he is, alanna,' he said gently. 'But you're a big girl now, you just said so. You're here, wit' Mammy, Daddy, me, your brothers and all your animals . . . so stop lookin' backwards and look forwards, instead.'

Polly sighed but her hand gentled the dog's silky head and her eyes fell on the cat basket with affection. Brogan could see he'd made his point.

'I'll try, Brog,' she said resignedly. 'I really will try.'

Mrs Burt had a grand tea waiting for them and by the time they had left their bags at the Belvedere Guest House they were all in urgent need of tea.

'Those bloody hens,' Bevin said, 'One of 'em, the one wit' the red tassles on its head, squeezed t'rough the slats of the crate an' pecked the taxi driver on the back of the neck. He was *wild* so he was. He said words Mammy would have smacked his head for – words Brogan would have biffed him on the nose for!'

'Words you've never heard in all your born puff, I suppose,' Brogan said sarcastically. 'And who said you could swear at the hens, anyway?'

'I didn't swear at them, it was . . .'

'You said bloody hens,' Ivan said placidly. They were washing up for tea in Brogan's room and now Ivan began to slick his hair down with water. 'If Mammy was here she'd wash your mouth out so she would.'

'Oh, I see what you mean. But she'd do better to wash the taxi driver's mouth out. Honest to God, Brog, the language the feller used . . .'

'Wash your hands, never mind your mouth,' Brogan said. 'The hens is here now, so no point in moaning. Tomorrow we'll be takin' them to the country, where hens belong.'

'In a taxi cab?' Bevin said suspiciously. 'Or on a tram? Because I tell you, Brogan, you may be me big brother but I'll not travel wit' them hens again . . . not by meself I won't. They're Polly's birds, let her cart them around.'

'You liked the eggs,' Ivan said. Brogan regarded his little brother with new respect. You had to hand it to Ivan, he wasn't yet five but he didn't miss a trick. 'You can't have eggs wit'out hens, Bev.'

'I'm not sayin' all hens is bad, I'm not even sayin' hens isn't all right in their place, what I'm sayin' is . . .'

'Shut up, the pair of ye!' Brogan roared, suddenly losing his temper. 'I've heard enough of the bloody hens, d'you hear me? The subject's *closed*.'

He led his brothers down the stairs to the parlour where high tea awaited them, and grinned to himself when he heard Ivan whisper to Bevin: 'Did ye hear what Brogan said, Bev? He swore just like that taxi driver so he did!'

In the parlour, Peader, Deirdre and Polly waited for them whilst Mrs Burt presided over the pot.

'Tea for you all? Tea, boys?' she enquired affably. 'Help yourself to the loaf now . . . I've soused some herrin', there's a dish of baked potatoes, and Peader's goin' to carve some mutton for anyone who fancies a slice. Now . . . who's hungry?'

Polly ate her tea in a daze. It was very strange, one minute she hated this place so badly that she could have screamed, the next she felt a weird, tugging sort of affection for it. But she had never been here in her life before, she'd only heard tell of it from Daddy and Brogan, so why on earth did she feel this way?

She liked Mrs Burt, though. Mrs Burt had said Delilah was the handsomest dog she'd ever met and the cats were charming. She had shaken hands with Delilah and given the cats a saucer of milk. And what Mrs Burt called high tea was delicious, one of the nicest meals Polly had ever tasted. But food wasn't everything, and even the nicest food couldn't make up for being away from Tad.

'You'll make other friends,' Daddy had said, which just went to prove that grown-ups did not understand. Of *course* she would make other friends, she had had a *grush* of other friends in Dublin, always had had. But other friends weren't Tad. There could only be one Tad in her life.

So Polly ate her tea rather silently, then walked back to the guest house with Mammy, Daddy and her brothers. Delilah was staying with Brogan and so were the cats. The hens, still in their crate, were staying in the back yard, under the washing lines. Only people were allowed in guest houses, Mammy had explained, and Polly had tried hard to understand and be sensible.

She was sleeping with Mammy and Daddy too, in a tiny pull-out bed which was stowed away, during the day, under their big bed. The little bed was great fun, the nicest thing about the room which, otherwise, was pretty ordinary, though enormously large and extremely bare to one accustomed to the crowded, close-knit life of a Dublin tenement.

'You'd best go to bed now, alanna,' Mammy said about an hour after they'd finished their high tea. 'We've a full day tomorrow so we have, and you'll be wantin' all your energy to help wit' the move.'

'All right,' Polly said obediently. 'I am tired.'

She was tired, too. The only thing was, tired or not, she simply could not sleep. She lay in bed, staring at the ceiling, her mind filled with the most curious thoughts, until her parents came up to bed. And then she shut her eyes tight and pretended as hard as she could that she was asleep because if they knew she was awake they would only worry. And of course she listened to the conversation as her parents prepared for bed.

'Sure and she's fast off,' Mammy murmured quite soon after they entered the room. 'Poor little soul, she's wore out . . . what a day, Peader!'

'Aye, what wit' the cats, the dog, the hens...' he chuckled. 'Still, tomorrow we'll be in the country.'

He sounded infinitely content but Polly felt a pang of real distress. Tomorrow they would be in the country; so what was wrong with that? The country was nice, she knew because she and Tad had visited the country ... oh, Tad, Tad, whatever will I do wit'out you and your lovin' ways?

'I shan't be sorry.' That was Mammy. 'The child was – was *odd*, didn't you think, when we were travellin' here, in the tram?'

'Odd? No, me love, she was just tired, puzzled and cross wit' me for bringin' you all here.'

'No, it's not that. It's being parted from Tad. But it was the way she stared around, Peader, as though she expected to recognise something ... it worried me.'

'Why on earth? This is all new to her, alanna, a great city wit' stately buildings ... it's all new, no wonder she stares.'

'No.' Mammy's voice was so low Polly had to strain to hear it. 'No, Peader, it's not new. She was here before – remember? Holy Mother, I'll be glad to leave this city behind so I will.'

'Deirdre, the child was a babe in arms, she'll not remember anything from that time. Dear God above, I hope wit' all my heart she remembers nothin', for what could she remember but hardship, hunger, and love-lessness?'

'The other one loved her.' Mammy's voice was lower, if anything. 'The other child worshipped her; you said it yourself, Peader.'

'Yes. But the other's gone from here. And I'm tellin' you, a babe that young could remember nothin' what-soever of what happened, once, long ago.' The bedsprings creaked as Peader climbed between the sheets. 'Now stop your worryin', woman, and come to bed.'

Polly lay quiet and still in her own little bed, not daring to move, hardly daring to breathe. What did it all *mean*? Why should Mammy say that she, Polly, had been here before, when she knew, none better, that Polly had been born, bred and brought up in the Liberties? And why had Daddy said she would remember nothing but hardship, hunger and lovelessness? And who, in heaven's name, was the other child?

Polly lay and pondered and wondered, and watched the moon's slow progress across the sky through a gap in the curtains. And when the night was at its darkest she got out of her little bed, picked up her clothes from the chair by the window, and stole to the door.

The door was locked. The key was big and took some turning, but Polly turned it. She slid silently out of the room and outside in the dark corridor, she dressed herself by touch. She struggled into her clothing, pulled on her woollen stockings, her stout little lace-up shoes. She even put on her coat with the round navy buttons and her small, pudding-basin hat.

It was cold in the corridor, and frightening, too. As she fumbled with her fastenings, tried to tidy her hair with her hands, straightened the woollen stockings, her head ached from lack of sleep and from the mystery which she had sensed surrounding both herself and this city. Because in one way Mammy was right. She *had* felt a weird feeling of remembering rather than merely seeing as they had got off the ship at the Pierhead and made their way to the tram stop. And though she'd said that the market had reminded her of Francis Street, she was not at all sure she had really meant that. She had meant that it reminded her of – of somewhere she had once known.

However, fully dressed, she stole along the corridor, down the stairs, and after a struggle with another big key, out of the front door. She wished Delilah were with her, but Delly was staying at Mrs Burt's house with Brogan. Knowing her dog, she guessed that by now Delly would be hogging the lion's share of Brogan's bed and snoring loud enough to wake the dead. And if he had been at the guest house there was no saying he wouldn't have jumped and barked and roused the whole house, including her parents, who would not, she knew, approve of her actions. So she decided to be grateful that Delilah was far away and let herself quietly out of the front door.

Standing on the pavement, she considered. Did she mean to run off, to stow away aboard the next boat bound for Dublin? But she knew better than to try. A child can run away, protest, escape, but it will always be brought back in disgrace in the end. To return to Dublin would be an adventure, but if she did go back and move in with Martin and Donal, what sort of life would that be? They wouldn't want her but if she insisted they'd probably let her stay. She would have to work as she'd worked whilst Peader had been ill and she didn't fancy that, no sir! She would go back to Tad one day, when she was big, and they would get married, but until then it might be best to stay with Mammy and Daddy and her dear animals.

So what was she doing out in this great, strange city, with the stars still pricking at the dark, velvet blue of the night sky, and the lighter line on the eastern horizon all that was to show, yet, of the new day?

She didn't know, to tell the truth. But having got out, she did not intend to go back to the Belvedere Guest House yet. I'll explore, have a good look round, Polly thought to herself, and immediately realised that this was just what she needed to do. At some time, in some way, she had known this city. She had felt she knew it, but listening to Mammy and Daddy, she had realised she really did know it. She had been here before . . . how, why or where was what, she decided, she had escaped from the guest house to find out.

Which way, though? Which way? Polly stood in the middle of the pavement and spun round, spun and spun until she was giddy. Then, when she scarcely knew which way up she was, she set off, reeling along the pavement like a drunk. Luck would guide her, help her, sustain her. And in a few hours, perhaps, if she was very lucky before her parents were up, she would understand just what she had been doing in the city once, long, long ago.

Chapter Fifteen

Polly trotted along the pavement, under the hissing gas lamps. She could not have said that she knew where she was going, but she let her feet take her and that seemed to work quite well, because before day had anywhere near dawned, she was on a road which she felt was familiar to her. It was wide and though there were no trams about at this hour, there were tram-lines. A main road, then. She stood on the kerb, waiting, wondering, then crossed the road and turned into a narrow street which, she saw when she looked up at the name plate on the end house, was called Snowdrop Street.

Halfway down it she slowed, stopped. All the houses were identical, terraced houses with wooden front doors and bay windows yet Polly had the oddest feeling that she knew what was behind those primly closed front doors. Or one of them, at any rate. A parlour, with ragged curtains, a kitchen behind that . . . a girl stood in the kitchen, humming, stirring a pot. A half-naked baby played on a floor so dirty that it looked like hard-packed earth. In fact the place was dirtier than any house Polly had ever seen, save perhaps the Donoghue's home.

Polly closed her eyes, then opened them again. She only got that disturbing mental picture when she looked at one particular house, yet the house looked solid, reliable, not at all the sort of place where raggedy curtains and dirt reigned supreme. It isn't like that now, Polly finally concluded, but it must have been like that once. Long, long ago, when I was a baby. If I heard Mammy and Daddy right, that is. Unless I'm goin' off me head, of course, which seems likeliest.

She stood for some while, staring up at the house in the grey dawn light. Nothing stirred behind its respectable, dark-blue curtains, not a sound issued through its respectable, brown-painted door. Whatever it had once meant to her, if it had meant anything, it was all part of the past.

Moving like a sleepwalker now, Polly walked on. She stood on the corner of Snowdrop Street and there was another big, wide street – it was Commercial Road this time. A lorry rumbled past; doesn't he know it's the middle of the night and he should be in his bed so he should, Polly wondered rather crossly. She didn't mind a cat, stalking, yellow-eyed, along a house-wall, nor a dog trotting by, pressing close to the house-fronts ... but lorries meant people and people could spell danger.

But the lorry made her look across the road to see what was over there, and she realised that there was a long, long view ... no houses, in other words. Despite the fact that it was still dark she could, she thought, smell the sea ... there were docks over the road, she was sure of it, and she liked docks. And nearer, glistening in the pale, unearthly before-dawn dark, she could just make out what looked like miles of railway lines – a marshalling yard? She remembered, suddenly, that Brogan had once mentioned that he lived near streets called after spring flowers ... Snowdrop Street, of course, she had just traversed it!

Immediately, her attention was caught and held. Brogan worked for the railway, so did Daddy – was that why she had come here, then? Because at some time, long, long ago, Brogan and Daddy had . . . had brought her here? It didn't seem quite right, but it would have to do for now.

Polly crossed the road, dodging more tram-lines. She pressed her nose to a large gap in the fence and wondered at the sheer complexity of what lay beyond. It must be the hugest mass of railway lines in the world, she thought, all laid out like steel spaghetti, curving and joining, parting and rejoining. And there were sheds and shelters and big warehouses and little cabins and . . .

In Polly's mind, a picture was forming. She was in a small hut with an earth floor, there was a stove burning brightly, illuminating the smiling faces of the men who surrounded her . . . and then, when she looked around, she saw her angel! Was this why she had come down here, to the marshalling yards? Did her angel, for some reason, want her here?

The fencing which was between the road and the rails had been put up years ago to keep prowlers, children, stray dogs, off the tracks. Polly walked over to it. It would be quite simple just to wriggle through there, to go and find that hut . . .

She was small and neatly made, though her little red coat with its black velvet collar was a bulky garment. But she got through, anyway. She felt brave, adventurous . . . she wished devoutly, however, that Tad had been with her. Somehow, he took all the responsibility for their doings upon himself so that she could enjoy without guilt their various ploys. But he wasn't here, and anyway, she was, she felt, being guided. It was undoubtedly her guardian angel again, leading her to find . . .

Polly paused again. Leading her to find what? The hut, presumably, and the firelight, the men with smiling faces. Ah, then she would know just what her mammy and daddy had meant last night – because, in some mysterious way, she was more conscious of her angel's presence here than she had ever been.

Back in Dublin the kids in her class had learned a poem by some English feller called Alfred Lord Tennyson. It had a good old rhythm for shouting and declaiming and Polly and Tad rather liked it. But this was a quiet and secret place, a place where she was quite probably not allowed to be. So Polly stole forward, taking advantage of every patch of shadow, whilst whispering the words of the poem to bolster her up and give her courage.

> *Cannon to right of them*
> *Cannon to left of them*
> *Cannon in front of them*
> *Volleyed and thundered.*

She might have got the words wrong, it might not be appropriate, it might even seem stupid when you considered the silence which surrounded her, but Polly thought it helped. It conjured up Tad, going ahead of her, a hand behind him ready to grasp hers if she felt afraid. It conjured up confidence, courage.

She had not truly known which of the small huts she was heading for, but when she was hesitating something seemed to prompt her. *That way, that way!* She turned her head and thought she saw a slim shadow flickering between two particular huts. *That way, that way!* She was afraid and chilly and yet she knew, in a strange way, that she was in no danger. Am I sleeping, she thought suddenly, am I still in my bed? If so, there's nothing to be afraid of . . . come on, Polly . . . this way!

She headed for the shed which seemed, for some reason, likeliest, still keeping in deep shadow whenever she could, darting across great patches of silver moonlight and into black shade once more. The pre-dawn chill nipped at her, the colourless world of the night was suddenly unfriendly, threatening. But then she slid in through the doorway, and it was like stepping into a different world.

The first thing she noticed was the warmth, the smell of food and people, a homely, lived-in sort of smell. The second was that the hut was empty save for a couple of rough wooden benches, a coke burner and a blanket thrown down against one wall. Polly stole forward. It was nice in here, warm and hearteningly normal after being out for so long in the greys and silvers and blacks of the pre-dawn light. Furthermore the night had seemed threatening, it had made her aware that she was trespassing, but here in the hut Polly felt instantly at home. She sat unselfconsciously down on the floor in front of the coke burner and warmed her hands at the faint red glow. She looked around again and noticed, under the nearest bench, a number of tin mugs and plates and a canvas bag. The railway gangs come here to eat their carry-out, Polly thought triumphantly. Brogan and Daddy probably came here once; perhaps Brogan comes here still. I knew I should come here . . . Brogan will walk in presently, give me a cuddle and make me go home to me own bed. But first he'll tell me why I came here so he will.

Polly warmed her hands, then she reached for the blanket and wrapped it round herself. How cosy it was! If she wasn't careful she'd fall asleep so she would and then how Brogan would tease her when he found her!

She sat up straighter, then leaned against the bench.

It would not do any harm to close her eyes for ten minutes . . .

Polly woke when she heard an irritable voice shouting somewhere near at hand. It was a man's voice, irate, threatening.

'Gerrout of it, you thievin' little cat! Go on . . . if I catches you I'll teach you to come sneakin' round our shelters . . . go on, clear orf!'

There was a clatter and a cry. Polly sat up. Long experience of living with a family of brothers had made her familiar with the sounds. Someone was shouting at a child and throwing stones to get rid of that child. The clatter had been a sizeable stone hitting a rail – and probably bouncing off and then hitting the child.

Automatically, still more than half asleep, Polly reached out for Tad, and found herself grabbing empty air. Immediately her heart started to thump like a trip-hammer. Oh, Mary, Mother of Jesus, Tad wasn't here, she was trespassing on railway property all by her lonesome and someone, someone large and fierce and terrible, was just outside the hut, no doubt waiting to thump anyone handy who happened to be smaller than himself!

Polly tried to stand up but the blanket hampered her and she fell, skinning her knees on the hard floor. The pain, however, brought her to her senses. She stood with care, threw the blanket down more or less where she had found it, and sidled over to the door, peering out through the gap, for it was not completely shut.

It was still very dark but no moon or stars shone now; a drizzling rain was falling from the dark clouds overhead and the wet gleamed on the complex pattern of the rails and sleepers, on the huts and warehouses and engine sheds . . . and on a small group of men, one of whom was still poised in the classic throwing action – arm bent back, body angled, a stone held threateningly. And well away now, running across the rails with incredible fleetness, was a thin figure in a long, draggly skirt. Clearly a female figure.

'Go on, gerrout of it or I'll break every bone in your bleedin' body!'

The man broke into a lumbering run. Polly knew a bully when she saw one and she was so indignant that she came out of the shed at a run, shouting as she did so.

'Hey, leave her alone, will ye? A feller your size, chasin' a wee young wan . . . pick on someone your own size, you big moocher!'

The man swung round with a roar . . . and Polly was off, running like greased lightning. This is quite like old times, she told herself, skipping across the rails, heading at speed for the gap in the fence. Many's the time I've been keepin' nix for Tad whilst he did something evil, and ended up runnin' for me life. But the shouting man was between her and the hole in the fence, she would have to go a bit further along. Polly ran hard, bending low, and somewhere to her right she was conscious of the other figure . . . but then the fence loomed and she ran alongside it for a bit, searching for a gap . . . found one, was through it in one wiggle and dashing across the road, horribly aware that her pursuer had emerged on to the pavement behind her, was screaming after her . . .

She ignored him, doubling down the little roads and alleys until all sounds of pursuit had died, until at last she felt safe to stop and catch her breath.

Phew, Polly thought to herself, that was close! And then she looked around her, deciding which way . . .

She was in totally foreign territory. She had never

seen this road before, and when, presently, she began to try to retrace her steps, she realised that she had absolutely no idea where she was – worse, she had no idea where the guest house was. Worse still, she could not for the life of her remember the name of it, or the name of the street on which it was situated.

It was still dark, the houses were still curtained, not a soul stirred. Polly stood like a statue for a moment in the middle of the pavement whilst the rain fell, chill, on her. And then she put her hands over her face and began to cry.

When a voice spoke quite near her ear Polly jumped and almost ran again, but she was worn out and besides, the voice was gentle. So she put her hands down from her face and looked around her.

The speaker proved to be a young girl, thin, light-haired, wearing a draggly skirt much torn at the hem, and a cloak-thing around her shoulders. She was smiling down at Polly with the gentlest, sweetest expression on her face. Polly gasped. It was her guardian angel, she would have known that face anywhere!

'Wha's the marrer, chuck?' her angel said gently. 'By 'eck, but you can run. You're well away, though – we both are – so why's you cryin'?'

None of this made much sense to Polly, save for the last question. She gave a big gulp and then wiped her tears away with the heels of both hands. Then she took a deep breath and smiled at her companion.

'I'm lost,' she said baldly. 'I'm stayin' in a guest house but I d-don't remember what it's called nor where it is. And me mammy an' me daddy'll be in a takin' if they wake up an' I'm not in me bed!'

Her angel considered this. 'Why are you in a guest 'ouse?' she enquired after a moment's thought. 'And whar are you doin' 'ere? You're from Ireland, by the sound of it.'

'Me daddy's a railwayman; we're goin' to live at a level crossin' on the Wirral,' Polly explained. 'Me brother Brogan lives here, too, so he does.'

'Where does your brother Brogan live?'

Polly beamed. So it was that simple – but of course she didn't have the brains of her angel, or she'd have thought of it for herself.

'Brogan lives on Salop Road, off the Walton Road,' she said triumphantly. 'D'you know where that is?'

''Course. Come on, I'll walk with you.' The angel tucked her hands into her pockets and then fell companionably into step with Polly. 'You'll be 'ome before you knows it, chuck.'

Fortunately, Brogan was awake when the knocker sounded. He waited a moment, then rolled out of bed and headed for the stairs. His landlady would sleep through the last trump, she only woke when the alarm clock had been shrilling away for five minutes. So he pulled his trousers on and padded down the stairs, with Delilah close at his heels, and tugged the front door open.

'Yes? My God, Polly!'

'Oh, Brogan, 'tis glad I am to see you,' his small sister gabbled, clutching his hand whilst Delilah frisked around his little mistress, licking any bit of her he could reach. 'You'll never guess what's happened – I've met me angel!' She glanced behind her, but not as though she expected to see anyone. 'She's gone, I knew she wouldn't stay, but she found me when I was ever so lost, an' she brought me right to your door! Wasn't she good, Brog?'

'Yes, indeed,' Brogan said. 'And you've been bad . . . d'you know what time it is, alanna?'

'No.' Polly's eyes opened very wide. 'Sure an' how should I know the time, Brogan, an' me wit'out a watch? Is it early?'

'It's terrible early,' Brogan said, not mincing words. 'And what's all this talk of angels, Polly? Here, get indoors and get that coat off, you're soaked to the skin! I don't suppose Mammy and Daddy know where you are, eh?'

'Well, no-oo, but if you'll tell me how to get back there, Brogan, I can be into me bed an' snorin' before they know a thing! You see, I listened to Mammy an' Daddy talkin' last night when they came to bed, an' they talked about me, Brog, so they did! They said I'd been in Liverpool before an' they were right . . . I *knew* places, Brog, so I did, just as if – as if I'd lived there meself! So I had to find out, you see.'

Brogan pushed his small sister through the house and into the back kitchen where the fire, though damped down, soon burned up brightly after a prod or two with the poker.

'Let's be havin' that coat off you,' he said. 'And the hat, and them foolish shoes . . . oh Polly, your stockin's is drenched through so they are.'

Polly sat down in the chair nearest the fire, kicked off her shoes and peeled off her stockings. Then she ran a hand through her wet and tousled curls. 'Oh Brog, I'm glad to see you! But I think you ought to take me back to Mammy at once, or she'll worry sick so she will.'

'Get dry first,' Brogan said. He took the roller towel off the back of the door and threw it over to her. 'Go on, rub your hair hard. Well, you spalpeen, what in heaven's name am I goin' to do wit' you? Runnin' away, talkin' a lot of rubbish, tryin' to blame your angel for your behaviour . . .'

'I'm *not* tryin' to blame me angel,' Polly said immediately, her cheeks going pink. 'It wasn't her fault at all at all. She brought me back, Brogan, she helped me. Only she didn't know where the guest house was, so she brung me here.'

Brogan had been putting the kettle over the flame; now he looked thoughtfully at Polly. For the first time it occurred to him that bad though his little sister frequently was, she had never, so far as he knew, been a liar. If she thought she had seen an angel then who was he to disbelieve her? And what was more, he remembered Mammy saying that she believed Jess was Polly's guardian angel. So if someone really had got Polly out of a scrape . . . well, it could have been the living and not the dead sister – Grace, not Jess.

The kettle boiled and Brogan wet the pot, made the tea, poured a cup and stirred in two generous spoons of sugar.

'There you are; drink it up,' he said, handing Polly a cup. 'And tell me about this angel of yours, alanna.'

Polly told the story quickly and well. Clearly, she was totally convinced of the angelic nature of her rescuer. But it sounded, to Brogan, as though two naughty young girls had been trespassing on railway property, two girls had run away from the bad-tempered and bullying gang boss, and then one of the girls had found the other crying in the street and had brought her home. He put this point to Polly who thought about it and then admitted, reluctantly, that her angel had borne a fleeting resemblance to the girl the feller had thrown stones at, but only insofar as they were both thin and raggedy.

'Because I've seen me angel before, in Dublin, so I have,' she reminded her brother. 'If it wasn't me angel who rescued me but a real live girl, then how come I seed her in Dublin, on our stairs?'

Brogan had to admit this baffled him. Indeed, he said no more on the subject until Polly was warm, dry and had a cup of tea and a round of bread and jam inside her. Then he got his waterproof down off its hook and told Polly he was going to take her home on the back of his bicycle, snug under his waterproof.

'You'll be back in bed in no time, if you're lucky,' he told her. 'No need to worry Mammy and Daddy with your adventuring.'

He was watching Polly's face as he spoke and saw relief light her small face.

'Oh thank you, Brogan,' she said fervently. 'I wouldn't want to worry Mammy and Daddy and the boys, indeed I would not. So if you'll say nothing, me dearest brother, then I'll keep the secret too, I'll not say a word.'

'Well, good,' Brogan said heartily. 'And now you know you really were in Liverpool once, when you were just a baby, is that enough for you?'

Polly nodded. 'I don't want to know any more, I just wanted to know if I was right so I did,' she declared. 'It isn't important, is it, Brog?'

'No, it's not important. You were here as a wee one for a short time, that's all there is to it. Look, Poll, are you ready to go back to the guest house now? Because the night's wearin' on and it'll be morning before you know it.'

'Yes, I'm ready,' Polly said quickly, nodding her head until her curls bounced. 'I won't ask Mammy or Daddy any more questions and I won't try to get back to Ireland, either, not if you think me angel wouldn't like it. I'm lucky to have me family, and to be Polly O'Brady, even if I *was* in Liverpool once, when I was very small. It's strange, isn't it, that I don't want to know anything else? But I don't, I just want to live in this Wirral wit' me dog an' the cats an' me family, and I'll be happy as the day is long so I shall!'

'Well, that's grand,' Brogan said reassuringly. 'Now if I put me waterproof round me shoulders and you come underneath it . . .'

He lifted Polly on to the seat of his bicycle and wheeled it out of the house and across the pavement. Delilah whined hopefully but was left in the house whilst Brogan cycled slowly down the road, standing up on the pedals all the way from Salop Street to the Belvedere Guest House. And once there, he saw Polly indoors and then turned his bicycle round. But not in the direction of Salop Street. As soon as he was sure that Polly was safely out of the way he headed for the marshalling yard.

It was Grace, he told himself exultantly, pedalling as fast as he could now. That poor child is living rough around the yard, and now that I know it I can find her and see that she's looked after. And Jess, me love, he added, addressing the figure that had haunted his dreams for so long, Jess, me love, you'll be able to rest in peace at last.

As Polly slid inside the guest house she did grow rather anxious, but luck – or her guardian angel – was with her. No one stirred in the house, no door opened, no inquisitive nose poked out, anxious to discover who was around so early. Polly knew her missing coat would be bound to bring forth adverse comments later, when her parents and brother woke, but she hoped to be able to get round that. Brogan was going to try to bring her back the dry garments when he came to collect them, and that, she thought, would be time enough. Mammy would be in a good old state anyway, trying to get everyone ready for the next stage of their journey. Polly thought it might be quite possible to get into the coat and hat before anyone realised that they had spent a good deal of the night under Brogan's roof.

So she went upstairs, took off all her clothes except for her shift, and opened the door to the bedroom which had been allocated to her and to her parents. She put her head round it. Mammy and Daddy slumbered still, Daddy was actually snoring.

Polly had a bad moment as she climbed into bed, though; Daddy stopped snoring, gave a huge, deep sigh and leaned up on his elbow.

'You all right, alanna?' he said softly. 'It's terrible early still.'

'I just needed to go, Daddy,' Polly said primly, but with a bumping heart. She thanked her stars she had already laid her clothing on the chair before her father stirred.

'Well, back to sleep wit' you,' her father said, lying down again. 'We've a full day later, Polleen, so sleep while you can.'

Brogan didn't find anyone in the marshalling yard, but he did not let it depress him. For the first time, he felt sure Grace Carbery was still alive, because Polly's description of the girl who had brought her home was how he would have described Jess, eight or nine years ago. He knew that Polly believed in her guardian angel, and that Mammy thought the angel was there, guarding her beloved daughter, but Brogan did not think a guardian angel would flee across the rails, shout with pain when struck by a stone, and later come and take care of his little sister, talking all the while in a scouse accent which Polly had reconstructed pretty faithfully. No, Polly had come across Grace Carbery, which meant that sooner or later he, Brogan, would find her as well.

So when he'd searched the yard he returned to Salop Street, glanced at the clock, saw he was not due to get up for a couple of hours, and climbed back into bed And very soon, slept.

Brogan was dreaming. He dreamed that he was chasing Polly across miles and miles of countryside, she flitting over bog and round briar whilst he got stuck in the mud and constantly held up. He knew it was terribly important to catch her, that it might make the difference between life and death, but he didn't know why, so he ran and ran and his mouth dried out and he got terribly thirsty and terribly hot and he could hear his own panting breath . . .

The dream changed, as dreams will. Now he was pursuing Polly across miles and miles of railway track, stretching into the middle distance. There were no trains coming, yet he knew that there were engines in the vicinity, and not far distant, either. And she was only a little girl, she could not jump from rail to rail as he did, she was scrambling over the rails, then running on the hardcore between them, and he could tell by the way she ran that the hardcore hurt her feet, was slowing her down.

But at least it meant it should be easier for him to catch her up. So he put a spurt on . . . and felt, through the rails, the vibration of an approaching train.

Brogan went faster. With the breath sobbing in his throat he hurled himself across the rails . . . he was only a matter of feet behind Polly now, he would make it, he knew he would! He reached out, caught hold of her . . . and felt the hot breath of the mighty engine on the back of his neck, the screech of steam, the weight of it . . .

And it wasn't Polly. The girl he was holding wasn't Polly at all, it was another girl. He was going to die for a girl he didn't even know! Suddenly she turned in his grasp and it was Grace, he knew her at once. He had to save her, to throw her out of the train's path and get out himself . . .

Brogan woke. He was lying in his bed with Polly's dog sprawled across his chest, breathing hot breath into his face and whining plaintively, whilst any movement he tried to make was frustrated by the entangling, sweat-soaked sheets.

'Delly!' Brogan said, relieved beyond belief to find that he'd been dreaming. 'Get on the floor, will you, where dogs belong.'

He sat up, tipping the dog off his chest. What a nightmare! It must have been caused partly by the fact that he'd spent a good deal of the night either dealing with his little sister or searching for Grace, and Delilah's weight on him and the dog's hot breath in his face could not have helped. It was early, too, but Brogan didn't fancy going back to sleep, not if dreams like that lay in wait, so he swung his feet out of bed. He looked out of his bedroom window and the rain had gone, to be replaced by a milk-blue sky and frail, autumn sunshine. I'll dress and take the bloody dog for a walk, Brogan thought resignedly as Delilah, sensing an ally, began to caper. After all, it's not a bad morning and a walk will cool me off and calm me down.

Dressed, Brogan strolled down the stairs, out of the front door and along Salop Street. It was very early still, but there were people about. Men bound for an early start, newspaper delivery boys, girls travelling a long way to start work. Delilah, with a piece of rope round his neck, behaved quite well, unless you took exception to having to stop every six paces whilst he cocked a leg against the nearest stationary object.

'What are you *doing*?' Brogan demanded after half a mile had been traversed in this fashion. 'Markin' our trail, like they do in fairy stories? Because if so, I know me way home perfectly well so I do and since I'm not lettin' you off this rope you've no need to worry yourself.'

Delilah cocked a wise and knowing eye, but continued to try to lift his leg every six paces until Brogan got fed up and simply towed the dog along. Then Delilah trotted beside him without complaint, showing a lively interest in his surroundings but no longer bothering to mark.

I wonder if he ought to be off the rope for a bit, though? Brogan thought to himself as they walked. I don't remember Polly having him on a rope in Dublin. He just wandered along behind her. He looked at Delilah, who looked back with such limpid innocence that Brogan nearly let him off the rope then and there, only commonsense prevailed. It wouldn't hurt the dog to have a rope round his neck for half an hour, for the Lord's sake! And if it was grass Delilah was after, sure and wasn't Stanley Park just a stone's throw away? I'll go there and mebbe let him off for a few minutes if there's no one much about, Brogan decided. He can have a bit of a run and do what he has to do, then we'll go home for breakfast.

Brogan liked the park, with its bandstand, little shelters, glasshouses and, of course, its boating lake. A dog could have a run there without fear of the traffic ... he could not bear to consider how he would behave should Delilah be hurt whilst in his charge. Polly would marmalise him, just for a start.

So Brogan and the dog walked to Stanley Park, which was quiet and pleasant in the very early sunshine. And Brogan let go the rope and Delilah behaved in an exemplary fashion, just sniffing round and running on the grass but coming back at once when Brogan called.

Until he saw something across the road, in Anfield Cemetery, and set off like a greyhound to investigate.

Brogan followed, of course. The pair of them tore across Priory Road and into the cemetery. It's a cat, Brogan thought. Oh, dear God, if Delly catches it an' hurts it what'll I do?

But then he remembered Lionel and Samson. It seemed unlikely that Delilah, who lived cheek by jowl with two members of the cat family, should suddenly turn round and chase one. Few canines knew better how sharp are a cat's claws, or how difficult they are to untangle from one's soft and unprotected nose.

But still, who knew? It might have been a rabbit, living on all the lovely grass in Stanley Park and in the cemetery. So Brogan ran and shouted and Delilah just ran . . . until their path was barred by a sturdy woman with a bunch of chrysanthemums in one hand.

'Look out!' Brogan roared, and grabbed the rope, which fortunately was stronger than it looked. Delilah skidded to a halt and yelped as the rope cut into his brawny neck, but Brogan almost had the woman off her feet, his shoulder catching hers and spinning her round, to crash quite hard on to the gravel path.

'Are you all right, missus? Be God, I'm awful sorry so I am,' Brogan gasped, lifting the woman gently to her feet. ''Twas the dog, divil take him! He's a lollopin' great fiend, so he is . . . are you hurt, now?'

The woman snorted, then smiled at Brogan.

'It takes more than a thump from a mad dog to kill me dead, young man,' she said. 'Tek me flowers for a minute, whiles I see if me leg's broke.'

'Broke? Oh, God love you, it can't be broke . . .' Brogan began, but the woman waggled her foot a couple of times and then pointed at the ankle.

'I were jokin', but be the look of it it's sprained. See that colour? And though I'm the last one to urge a young feller such as yourself to admire me legs, they don't usually 'ave one ankle twice the size of t'other.'

Brogan looked and indeed the ankle seemed to be swelling before his very eyes. Even through the woman's sensible stocking he could see the bruise coming out, purple and black and painful-looking. He swallowed uncomfortably. What a thing to do, and he was supposed to be taking Polly's coat round to the guest house as soon as he could. But this woman would not be able to get far under her own steam, one glance at the ankle convinced him of that.

'I can see you're right, missus. Will ye let me take you round to the Stanley Hospital? For you'll not be able to put weight on that ankle.' He cleared his throat self-consciously. 'I've a bicycle . . . if you'd not mind me wheeling you across the park then I'll go home and fetch it.'

The woman had tried her weight on the foot and had lost colour as a result. She leaned against the nearest object, which happened to be a gravestone, and tried to smile again, but it was a shaky effort.

'I'm sorry, I'm feelin' a bit strange . . . if I could sit down . . .'

Brogan let go Delilah's rope and assisted the woman to the nearest grave-kerb. She sank down on it and took a deep breath.

'Well! It's quite painful, but I'll be all right here whilst you fetches your bike. I wonder if you could put these flowers on that grave for me? There is a vase, it oughter have plenty of water in after the rain we had last night. It's the angel and the weepin' willow tree . . . that one.'

She pointed to the monument. Brogan took the chrysanthemums and went over to the vase. He took out the old, wilted flowers and put the fresh ones into the vase, then turned . . . to find Delilah, sniffing at the angel's feet in a way which immediately alerted him to the dog's intentions.

'Delilah . . . don't you dare do that now, or I'll crucify you so I will!'

Delilah, leg poised, thought better of it. He lowered the leg and cast Brogan a long, reproachful look. The woman sitting on the kerb laughed, though it was a rather short, wheezy sort of laugh.

'Ah, dogs don't 'ave no respect, chuck,' she told Brogan. 'Me paternal grandfather, Elias Boote, was a merchant prince, or thought 'e was, which accounts for the monument. To tell you the truth I bring the flowers to please me mam. Left to meself I'd sooner give the old skinflint a piece of me mind . . . or your dog could do it for me.'

Very relieved, Brogan picked up the rope once more and turned back to his victim. 'There, now, he kept himself to himself when I shouted, thank the good God,' he said piously. 'So we've saved your grandfather's angel from a wettin', that's for sure. If you'll wait here for five minutes, Miss Boote, I'll fetch me bicycle and we'll have you in the Stanley Casualty Department in a trice so we will.'

'And the dog? Will you take 'im or leave 'im wi' me, Mr . . . I'm afraid I don't know your name.'

'Me name's O'Brady, and I'll be takin' the dog,'

Brogan said grimly. 'I'll leave him wit' me landlady just while I get you to the Stanley. She'll not mind that.'

'Very good, Mr O'Brady,' Miss Boote said. She leaned back against the gravestone. 'A bit of a rest won't hurt me, so don't break your neck rushin' back.'

'I won't,' Brogan promised. 'Come on, Delly, let's see you run now!'

Brogan was back with his bicycle in no time at all, and lifted his second passenger in a couple of hours on to the saddle with great care and tenderness.

'Sure an' if you can balance there, you'll be safe in the Stanley in less than thirty minutes,' he promised her. 'What a day this has been already . . . oh, is there anyone waitin' on you who should be told you're at the hospital?'

'Only a friend who works at the Strawberry Field Children's Home,' Miss Boote said. 'I'll telephone her from the hospital, explain what's happened. She'll come down when she can . . . but they won't keep me in, not for a sprained ankle.'

'Strawberry Field,' Brogan said thoughtfully. Where had he heard that name before? 'That's a familiar sort of name.'

'It's a big old house out on Beaconsfield Road,' Miss Boote told him. 'It's only recently been converted into a home for destitute children – me friend's a worker there.'

'I know it. Huge grounds, but they've been allowed to go wild,' Brogan said triumphantly after a moment. ''Tis a keen gardener I am, and I thought, at one time, I might offer me services to get the place tidied up. But what wit' one thing an' another I've never got round to it. And now, wit' winter all but upon us . . .'

'They'd be that pleased if you did, Mr O'Brady,' Miss

Boote said earnestly. 'It was left to the Army, you see – the Salvation Army – in the old lady's will. They've put a mint o' money into it already . . . any help would be grand. Even in winter there's work to be done, or so they say. I believe me dad says heavy diggin's best done when there's frost to break up the soil.'

'That's true; and does the Strawberry Field home only take Salvationist children?' Brogan asked presently, turning his bicycle, complete with passenger, neatly on to Stanley Road. 'Are they full?'

Miss Boote snorted on a laugh. 'Children are children, when they're destitute they don't know if they're Catholic, Protestant or heathen, all they know is they're hungry, weary, cold and unloved. Strawberry Field is for any child – and it's only been open a matter of weeks so it's not full be a long chalk. Why d'you ask, Mr O'Brady?'

'Oh . . . I know a child, I've seen her wanderin' the streets so I have. I'm a single feller, livin' in lodgings, but I'd like to see the child settled somewhere.'

'Well, tell her about the Strawb,' Miss Boote said decidedly. 'She'll be welcome there. Me friend was a teacher and she's very good wi' kids. Yes, Mr O'Brady, if you find your little wanderer, send her along. Or bring her yourself for that matter. Then you could tek a look at the garden at the same time.'

'I'll do that,' Brogan said. 'Here we are, Miss Boote – the Stanley Hospital. They'll have you right in a trice, never you fret!'

Sara heard with some dismay about her friend's unfortunate collision with a young Irishman and his dog in the cemetery, but though Miss Boote was obviously shaken by the experience, she sounded quite capable and cheerful when she rang Sara that evening from a public call box on Walton Road.

'I'm goin' to ask you a favour, queen,' she said earnestly. 'Could you do my stint with the *War Cry* for a week or so? I wouldn't ask but I know you're still quiet out at the home, and I'll not be doin' much walkin' for a while, wi' this ankle. You've got your own bicycle still, I know, otherwise you could borry mine.'

'I'd be pleased to give a hand,' Sara said at once. Truth to tell, now that the excitement of getting the home ready for occupation had worn off, she often felt herself to be useless, at a loose end. The onset of winter hadn't helped, of course; the short damp days and long, chilly evenings were enough to depress anyone. Matron told her that she would look back nostalgically on these first few weeks once they were up and running but right now, Sara had too much time on her hands, too much time to think.

She could not forget that when she had decided to take a night off, behave like a normal girl again and go to the cinema with Clarrie Boote, her grandmother had died. Nor that Mrs Prescott had longed for more of her granddaughter's company. If I'd been at home, she kept telling herself, I'd have spotted the signs, fetched the doctor, got her into hospital . . . she might be alive today. If I'd taken her about more, pushed her wheelchair up to the dances she wanted to attend . . . if I'd not been so selfish . . . Why, if I'd not decided to buy fish and chips all round, waited in the queue, I might have got back in time to revive her.

A part of her mind knew that this was foolish, that it could have happened at any time; when she was working, when she was taking the *War Cry* round the pubs, which could scarcely be considered light entertainment, when she was shopping . . . anything. Naturally she regretted not spending more time on the older woman, but she was sensible enough to know that her grandmother could not be brought back to life by vain regrets. But the knowledge did not stop her moping.

And she had not succeeded in finding either Grace or Mollie. She had kept her eyes open and asked around but there was no trace of the Carbery family; they might have disappeared off the face of the earth. Like Brogan had. Oh, she knew he'd really only disappeared back to Ireland, but she missed him badly, thought about him often. He had made her feel young and carefree, pretty even. She had known when she was in his company that she was valued. Though there were several very nice young men anxious to take his place, she could find none of them even slightly attractive. When young Mr Briscoe had asked her to go to a dance she had gone . . . and seen Brogan's dark hair and eyes every time she caught Mr Briscoe's sad, spaniel gaze.

So in a way, taking the *War Cry* round was a good idea; it would take her out of herself. And Matron was very understanding.

'You go, my dear,' she said earnestly. 'You've grown pale and thin of late, you're working too hard and worrying too much. You've not even been working in the soup kitchen as you used, and though I know it's a long way to go, I'd rather you were active, cheerful. You'll be much better for the children if you're more involved in the ordinary life of the Liverpool poor.' She smiled at her colleague. 'You might even find us some customers,' she added. 'Our two little inmates would welcome additions to the fold.'

Sara bicycled down to the Barracks, explained that her

friend was temporarily out of commission and picked up Clarrie's newspapers. Then she left her bicycle round the back of the hall, where it would be safe from thieves. Since the Army girls always went into pubs in pairs she was happy to see that she would be working with Miss Chadwick, who was a slum officer during the day but sometimes came and sold newspapers in the evening.

Miss Chadwick was a brisk, efficient young woman in her mid-twenties and she and Sara had always got on well.

'Good evening, Miss Cordwainer, good to see you again,' she said as soon as she set eyes on Sara. 'Of course I see you on Sundays . . . but not for long, just for the morning service. Are you busy, out at the Strawb?'

'Not really. That's the trouble,' Sara admitted. 'Half the time we're just polishing furniture and lighting fires in the rooms to keep them aired. It all seems . . . oh, I don't know, I suppose it makes me feel as if all our labour was for nothing.'

'It takes time,' Miss Chadwick said soothingly. 'Surely Matron's told you that?'

'Yes, she has, of course. But somehow, I expected we'd be full in a week. There are so many unfortunate children . . .'

'Yes, but a good few of them, having escaped from their parents, simply want to keep clear of all authority, all adults,' Miss Chadwick pointed out placidly. 'But they'll gradually come in, fill the place. Then you'll look back on these early weeks as a halcyon period when you had time to think! Now, which pub shall we try first?'

'The Queen's Arms?' Sara suggested. She still had a fondness for that particular pub since it had been

Peader O'Brady's local once. She remembered meeting Brogan's father there one winter evening. They had talked about his son . . . she could still remember the pleasure the chance meeting had given her, the hope.

But it wouldn't have been the same now, anyway, she reminded herself as Miss Chadwick said no, not tonight. Tonight, it seemed, they were going further afield . . . to the pubs on Commercial Road.

'We'll start at the Eagle and go on to the Union, then we'll cross over and do the Great Mersey, the Evelyn, the Midland and the Sandhills, I think,' Miss Chadwick decided. 'It's a cold night, so at least we'll keep warm inside the pubs, and we should do well – I find people buy more willingly coming up to Christmas.'

So off they set, with their bonnets pulled on at a determined angle and every hair smoothed out of sight, their stocking seams straight, their shoes polished. They might be visiting rough areas, where the coin which tinkled most frequently into their collecting tins would be a ha'penny, but that did not mean they should not be spruce, tidy, polite.

It paid off, too. Folk treated the Army lasses with respect because the Army lasses respected them, and they bought the *War Cry* because they knew the Army did a great deal for people like them. So Sara and Miss Chadwick walked briskly along the frosty pavements, with their metal-tipped heels striking sparks as they marched, heading for their first call.

There was a brawl outside the Great Mersey when they reached it, however, so Miss Chadwick decreed that they should continue on to the Evelyn, and return when things had calmed down somewhat. Sara agreed; they were having a good evening, the money which tinkled into her tin was mounting up and the pile of newspapers in her arms was shrinking in a very satisfactory manner. What was more, folk were so friendly – she had forgotten that in the six or seven months she'd not been handling the *War Cry*.

But although all the Irishmen – and railwaymen – they met made her think of Brogan she did not recognise any of them and besides, what was the point of asking for news of him? She knew he was in Ireland, so why make herself unhappy by hearing someone reiterate the fact?

And presently, with full tins and only a couple of newspapers apiece left, Miss Chadwick suggested that they return to their headquarters.

'For we've both left our bicycles at the Barracks and you've a long way to go, my dear Miss Cordwainer,' she said. 'It's several miles out to Woolton; it was good of you to come into the city to help me out.'

Sara said, politely, that it was a pleasure but added that she supposed they really ought to go back to the Great Mersey, because it was a generous pub with a generous landlady. 'We'll get rid of the last of our papers there,' she said positively. 'Mrs Boyce will see we do so.'

'Well, if you don't mind a late bicycle ride . . .' Miss Chadwick said. 'Come along, then, best foot foremost!'

Grace was hovering near the pub, waiting as she did most nights, for closing time. She was quite pleased with life right now. She came to the pub out of habit and because the landlady still fed her, but it wasn't cold enough yet to be offered shelter and besides, she had a good place up beside a bakery. The bakers came in early, at around three o'clock in the morning, and from the moment they started work warmth and a delicious smell of bread began to drift through the narrow windows above Grace's head. One of the best things about her retreat was its narrowness; only a child, and a skinny child at that, could crawl along the narrow passage-like entrance between the wall of the next building and the bakery itself. So tucked up in her blanket and lying on a thick pad of old newspapers, Grace felt both secure and comfortable.

But now, still waiting outside the pub for closing time, Grace saw the Army lasses coming and hid, because she did not know them. The girls went into the pub and Grace stole back to huddle close to the bright lights. She never went in, of course; kids didn't go into public houses, but she enjoyed being in the vicinity of warmth, laughter, happiness.

After a while, she grew careless. She leaned against the wall, then slid down beside it. She could feel the lovely warmth of the pub from here, it was soothing, it made her sleepy . . .

She woke when someone said: 'Are you all right, my love?'

She looked up and a beautiful, concerned face was only inches from her own. A dark bonnet framed the face – it was one of the Army lasses, she'd been caught!

Somehow, she managed to get to her feet and move back, gabbling something, saying she was sorry, she'd just dropped asleep . . .

'You don't have to apologise, dear,' the beautiful girl said. 'But you aren't very old . . . isn't it time you were at home in bed? Or are you waiting for your father – is he in the pub?'

'I 'ope to God 'e's not,' Grace said fervently, forgetting herself for a moment. 'I 'ope to God 'e's a long way from 'ere.'

'Where's your mother, then? Do you live near here?'

She was so pretty, so concerned, but . . . *danger,*

danger, Grace's mind said. *She'll take you away, put you in the work'ouse – tell 'er something, anything, but gerraway before she teks you in!*

'Me mam? Oh, at 'ome, I daresay,' Grace said. She moved back a little further. 'You're right, Miss, she's be a-waitin' for me. I'd best be gerrin' off 'ome.'

She half turned, but she didn't really want to leave. Presently the drinkers would go off home and Mrs Boyce would come out, show her Kitty, now a great strong animal with a coat so thick and soft that, come winter, Grace would envy him, and then bring Grace out some food. They would chat a little, Grace keeping a bit of distance between them, as though she were a wild animal and Mrs Boyce a zoo-keeper, and then Grace would say goodnight and return to her bakery.

'Don't let me drive you away, dear,' the Army lass said. Her voice was gentle, persuasive. 'You've a perfect right to stay here as long as you want. But look . . . can you read?'

'A bit,' Grace said. She wasn't going to admit that she could not remember how to read at all, having seldom attended school.

'Very well, then. I'm going to write my name and address down on a bit of paper,' the Army lass said. 'And I'll give it to you. If you ever need a roof over your head, or any sort of help, you can always come to me. D'you think you can read a name and address?'

'Dunno,' Grace said. 'It's awright, I'm awright, I don't need nothin' . . . I don't need nobody!'

The Army lass sighed; she sounded discouraged. 'Well, if you don't need any help . . . but suppose you met someone who *did* need help? Then you could pass my name and address on, couldn't you? Not everyone is independent, you see. Not everyone has good parents, either.'

Grace was frightened and wary of anyone who addressed her directly, but she was inherently kind. She had heard the distress in the girl's voice when she had more or less thrown her offer back in her face and was ashamed of herself. It would not, after all, hurt her to take the piece of paper. She came forward and took the page the girl was offering and tucked it into one of her disgraceful pockets.

'Thanks, Miss,' she said. 'I'll keep it by me.'

And then, feeling that she had done more than her duty, she turned and made off into the night.

'What did you do that for, Miss Cordwainer?' Miss Chadwick asked curiously as they made their way home through the streets, humming now with men leaving the pubs as they closed. 'I daresay her father *was* in the Great Mersey for all she denied it. And her mother was quite likely laid out insensible, clutching a gin bottle, in some dreadful slum room somewhere. Children of such parents often find it politic to stay away from home for a night or two.'

'I know,' Sara said. 'But if she was ever in need . . .'

'You're very right, I'd not thought of it quite like that,' Miss Chadwick said, nodding. 'You gave her the Strawberry Field address?'

'I did. After all, we've a great many places still to fill . . .'

Miss Chadwick chuckled. 'Touting for business, eh, Miss Cordwainer? Well, I think you've done a kind and sensible thing, let us hope your little waif turns up on your doorstep – if she's really in need. And now we'd best hurry back to the Barracks and fetch our bicycles.'

'I wonder if she really can read?' Sara said as the two of them reached the Barracks, reclaimed their bicycles, and began to cycle down Walton Road. 'She said *a bit*, which could mean anything.'

'I doubt it,' Miss Chadwick said. 'But never mind, dear, you've done your best.'

Sara sighed and cycled on. She had no idea why she had suddenly wanted to give her name and address to the ragged child outside the pub, but she was glad she had done it. Even if the kid couldn't read, she would know someone who could. And presently, what with the cold and the moonlight and the distance she had to travel, Sara stopped conjecturing and put her heart and soul into her pedalling.

Grace crawled up to her bakery bedroom and lay down on the newspapers, then pulled the blanket up round her and sniffed, in great contentment, the smell of new bread which came floating out of the bakery's half-open window.

What an odd sort of day it had been! First she'd found that pretty, nicely dressed little girl a-bawlin' her eyes out in the middle of the road, shortly after she herself had been chased across the marshalling yard by a bullying beast of a foreman. She'd felt really sorry for the kid, lost and alone in a big city like Liverpool. So she'd offered her help and taken her home.

And this evening the Army lass had tried to do her a good turn. She'd been suspicious, but she should have realised that no one belonging to the Army would have hurt her. Why, didn't they give her soup and bread from their kitchens, supply her from time to time with a nice bit of blanket, new shoes, stockings, even? She never kept these nice things long, either they were stolen from her by street kids with more brawn or more cunning, or she had to pop 'em at the pawn-shop. Well, not the soup or the bread, of course, she downed them as soon as they were offered, but the clothes and shoes . . . nice though they were, eating was nicer.

Mrs Boyce had given her a chunk of cheese and some bread tonight. She had eaten most of it – you couldn't go off to sleep with bread and cheese about your person or you'd wake up and find yourself being investigated by stray cats or rats. Now, Grace drew out of the pocket of her dirty jacket the last bit of bread and just as she was about to eat it, noticed the piece of paper fluttering to the floor.

Sighing, she bent and picked it up, spread it out, looked at it.

There was writing on it. Well, she supposed it was writing, at any rate. It was all sort of *joined*, though, so even if she could have managed the letters, she doubted that she could ever have read the words.

Not that it mattered. She supposed the Army lass had meant she could get soup, or a pair of new shoes, if she went to her. She thought that was about all the Army could do for you.

She thought about throwing the paper away, then changed her mind and tucked it into her pocket. Might as well keep it, you never knew.

The bread was still uneaten and Grace realised she really wasn't particularly hungry so she pushed it under her makeshift newspaper pillow, heaved her blanket up over her shoulders and curled up on the newspapers; very soon she slept.

She woke because something was rustling. She opened her eyes and saw a lean grey body only inches from her face – it was a rat, investigating the bread under her pillow. Grace gave a squeak and tried to grab at the rat, meaning to throw it away from her, but unfortunately the rat, cornered by her body, gave a horrid squeal, launched itself at her, and fastened its teeth in her cheek.

It was all over in a minute. Grace grabbed the rat and pulled. The rat, probably already terrified, let go of her cheek and wriggled out of her grip, running in a horrid, slithery sort of way towards the hole in the wall which led, she assumed, into the cellars of the bakery, its long, scaly tail disappearing last.

Grace sat up. Her head was throbbing and she knew, with real dismay, that she would never want to sleep here again. Not if rats were going to attack her. She had always known there were rats on the streets, they shared her scavenging life, but she had never before been attacked by one and was astonished at her own disgust and despair. It was a horrible, horrible thing, and her face really hurt. She put her fingers to her cheek and they came away wet with blood. She could feel the tear marks where the rat had tried to hang on like a little bulldog before finally releasing her.

Presently she got up, shook herself, sorted out her bedding and crawled to the end of her retreat. She picked up her blanket, which she usually left behind for the next night, feeling worse than she had when her father had first made it imperative that she left her home. She glanced back, once, at her cosy nook, then straightened up. Best get to a tap – there were taps on the street in various places – and clean up a bit, get rid of the blood for a start. Folk didn't like a child with a bloody face, they feared it was a sign of disease and either chucked a stone to keep you off or called the scuffers.

Twenty minutes later, washed, with her hair damp and slicked down, Grace made her way to the mar-shalling yards. There was a good shed there where she could decide what best to do now that the bakery was lost to her.

She reached the shed and sat down on her blanket and thought. Twice, she got out the piece of paper and perused it thoughtfully. Mrs Boyce could read, she could take it along there . . . or she could go to the Barracks, see if they knew the Army lass. But the trouble was her face hurt and her head was throbbing and she didn't really feel like doing too much. She really felt like catching up on the sleep she had lost last night. Presently she lay down. She might as well get some rest whilst she could. She slept.

The taxi driver never even saw where she came from. One moment Commercial Road was clear and he was driving at a steady pace along it, the next there was this creature staggering in front of him. A skinny bit of a girl she was, with a raw, suppurating wound in one cheek and nothing but rags on her back.

'I didn't touch 'er, officer,' he told the policeman who appeared almost as magically as the girl had done. Trust a scuffer, the driver thought sourly, to appear when he was least wanted. 'She sorta stumbled out into the roadway an' fell over . . . she's gorra fever on 'er, be the looks.'

'Hmm. Been hidin' out in the marshallin' yard, I daresay,' the policeman said. 'Catch a holt of 'er feet, we'll get 'er out of the roadway for a start.'

She weighed nothing, you had to say that for her, the taxi driver thought, picking up her shoulders and lifting too high, then steadying her. They carried her to the side of the road but when the driver would have laid her on the pavement the policeman shook his head.

'No, we can't leave 'er on the roadway, like a sack

o' spuds. Put 'er in the back of your taxi; I'll thank you to take the pair of us up to the Stanley, get 'er sorted.'

But in the taxi, she came round. The driver saw her eyelids flicker, then lift. She frowned, struggled to sit up, then collapsed back on to the seat.

'What's goin' on?' she asked weakly. 'Where am I? Where's you takin' me? I ain't done nothin' wrong . . . I jest want to go 'ome.'

The scuffer was good with her, you had to say that, even the taxi driver admitted it, and he was fond of neither scuffers nor stray kids.

'It's awright, queen,' the policeman said placidly. 'You come over queer, like, in the roadway. I was goin' to tek you along to the 'ospital, but if you'll tell me where you live I'll get this feller to run you home.'

The girl hesitated, then plunged a hand into her pocket and produced a sheet of blue paper. She handed it to the scuffer, then stared – almost glared – at him.

'That's it, that's me address,' she said. 'Can you take me there?'

'Miss Sara Cordwainer . . . is that you, queen?' the policeman said. 'Strawberry Field Children's Home, Beaconsfield Road . . . and then there's a telephone number. Ah, I *see*.'

The taxi driver saw, too. She'd run off from some children's home and hidden up in the shed on the marshalling yard. Probably in trouble at the place . . . though he'd heard good things about the Strawb as he went about his business. It was run by the Sally Army, and he had time for them. It was a real good place for kids to be from all accounts. But before he could comment aloud the policeman leaned forward and spoke.

'Did you 'ear that, cabby? The Strawberry Field Children's Home, on Beaconsfield Road, pronto!'

The taxi driver turned in his seat, stunned.

'*Beaconsfield Road?* Are you mad, constable? That's miles out . . . I ain't made o' money, you know! Wharrabout me fare? I've gorra livin' to make, you know!'

'We'll talk about your fare later,' the policeman said soothingly. 'Just do it if you please, cabby. Strawberry Field, as soon as you like!'

Sara was making a frieze for the nursery when the knock came at the door. She and Matron were both in the staff room, working away, because Christmas was coming and they wanted to be ready. Matron was embroidering hankies with great care and dedication and Sara's frieze was to be a selection of teddy bears, golliwogs and other toys, to be drawn, painted and cut out.

'Drat, I wonder who that is?' Matron said, her needle poised for a moment. 'Are you very busy, Sara, because if so . . .'

The home was not yet fully staffed, which meant that Sara and Matron were doing most of the work. Sara, who had just finished drawing a particularly cuddly bunny rabbit, jumped to her feet.

'I'll go. It'll be that man to see about the chimney in the dining room.'

She hurried to the door, and flung it open. A policeman stood on the doorstep and beside him stood a small girl. Sara frowned. The child looked vaguely familiar; an ex-pupil, perhaps? Or a neighbour? But the child was pulling a face at her, an urgent, entreating sort of face, and the policeman was speaking.

'Afternoon, Miss. We found this young person collapsed in the street – she says she lives here.'

'That's right,' Sara said, thinking rapidly. Where on *earth* had she seen the child before? 'Yes, that's right . . . come inside, dear, and wait there, I want a word with you.' She turned back to the policeman. 'She's not in any sort of trouble, I trust?'

'None in the world, Miss,' the policeman said gallantly. 'A good child ... though the clothes she's wearin' don't look much like the sorta thing ...'

'They aren't. We haven't kitted her out yet,' Sara said. 'Oh, of course!'

She had remembered the child outside the pub, the name and address scribbled on a sheet of cheap blue writing paper. Well, well, the poor little thing! When faced with authority and a demand for her address she had immediately thought of Sara. A clear case of man's extremity being God's opportunity, Sara supposed.

'Of course what, Miss?'

'Oh! Of course she must have slipped away from a – a group of children being taken shopping,' Sara said wildly. 'Thank you, officer, for bringing her back home. Do we owe you anything?'

The policeman touched his helmet and turned away. 'No Miss, nothing at all. Any time, Miss. You do good work here, everyone knows it, I'm glad to be of help.'

As soon as the policeman had climbed back into the taxi, Sara turned back into the hall. Her unexpected guest stood at bay by the stairs, looking frightened out of her wits ... and somehow defiant, too. The wound on her face looked livid against the extreme pallor of her skin, Sara thought, eyeing the dirt which was liberally smeared over the child's face. The other night she had scarcely noticed the child's condition, but now she realised she had never seen anyone quite so dirty, nor so battered. Poor kid, she had been in the wars! Sara walked towards her, a hand held out.

'My dear child, I'm so very glad you came to me when you felt you needed a friend. If you'll come through into the kitchen I'll get you something to eat and drink. There's plenty of milk and some really delicious scones . . . but we'll take a look in the pantry, shall we, see what you fancy?'

The girl looked rather wildly round, then stared up into Sara's face. After a moment the doubt which had filled her eyes seemed to clear and she said in a low, rather hoarse voice, 'Awright. I – I like milk, I does.'

As Sara and her charge passed the staff room door on the way to the kitchen Matron emerged. She smiled placidly at them both.

'Ah, another inmate, I see. I don't imagine that this young lady came from one of the other homes, so I suppose it was our friends the police? Can you manage, Miss Cordwainer? Anything I can do?'

'Yes, a policeman brought her,' Sara said. She realised that Matron had guessed the child had not come from another home by the state of her. Their other inmates had come from reception centres where they had been cleaned up before being sent on to the Strawb. 'We'll manage, thanks Matron.' She turned to the child once more. 'Here's the kitchen, dear . . . bless me, I never asked you your name!'

'Matty,' the child said without a second's hesitation. 'Matty Brown.'

'Nice to meet you, Matty,' Sara said. She smiled and held out her hand and after a long moment, the child took it in a scratched and filthy paw. 'I'm Miss Cordwainer, I'm Matron's assistant here. And now let's fetch milk and scones and see how you feel after you've had a meal.'

Sara took it very gently, wooing the child, talking about the other children who lived at the home but who were going round the Walker Art Gallery this afternoon, and when the child had eaten as much as Sara thought she ought, she took her upstairs to the pleasant bedroom with six beds, only two of which were claimed so far.

'Would you like a bed by the window?' she asked. 'Or would you prefer to sleep on the other side, which is perhaps a bit warmer?'

'Winder,' Matty muttered. 'Only – only I told a lie to that scuffer. I only come 'ere 'cos I 'ad your address in me pocket. I di'n't want 'im to take me to the work'ouse, that was why.'

'Well, dear, I'm glad you came to me, by however circuitous a route,' Sara said cheerfully, walking towards the long cupboard at the end of the room. 'There are quite a lot of clothes in here, I'm sure we'll find something to fit you. What about these?' She took down a blue woollen skirt and cardigan, a white blouse and some white woolly vests and knickers. 'They look as if they'd fit – shall we try them?'

'But I aren't . . . I don't . . . this ain't my 'ome,' the girl said desperately. 'I can't take them clothes – it ain't like food.'

'No, I agree clothes aren't much like food, but this is a children's home, Matty. We want to help children and – forgive me – you look as if you could do with some help. So won't you give us a chance? See how you like us, how you fit in?'

The child's eyes filled with tears and she turned her head away, scrubbing at them surreptitiously with both hands. Then she turned back.

'Awright, I'll try them clothes,' she said gruffly. 'If – if you're sure.'

'Good.' Sara gathered up the nice new clothes then headed out of the room again, knowing without having to check that the child was close on her heels. 'Then I think perhaps a bath, with something nice and freshening in the water . . . what d'you say to that? Only you

462

wouldn't want to put clean clothes on a dirty body, would you?'

To judge from her expression Matty had no objection to such behaviour herself, but she agreed, obediently, that it would not do and the two of them went into the bathroom. It was large and rather old-fashioned, but the big tub looked comfortable and there were clean towels over a clothes rail in one corner.

'Would you like to take your things off?' Sarah asked. 'A bath's better for getting you clean all over, a wash is a bit hit and miss, wouldn't you say?'

'I'd sooner wash,' Matty said. 'Just me 'ands an' face.'

'I think a bath would be best, love. Because if you're going to be putting on lovely clean new clothes . . .'

Matty, it seemed, had never washed all over and did not fancy starting now. But when Sara ran warm water into the bath, splashed disinfectant and got out a bar of carbolic soap, Matty, with a shudder, began to undress.

She got her jacket off easily, and threw it across the cork-topped bathroom stool, but the filthy shift beneath seemed almost glued to her skin. Sara tried to get it off and realised that it wouldn't come. Dirt and dried blood had welded the garment to the child's body . . . and her hair was definitely verminous.

'Look, your – your shift could do with a wash,' Sara said finally. 'I think if you hop into the water . . .'

She picked Grace up, appalled by the lightness of the little body in her arms, and dumped her, shift and all, in the bath. Then, whilst Grace was still gasping from the shock, Sara held her torso gently beneath the water until the shift could be pulled painlessly from the child's grey, bruised flesh.

'Hair too, dear,' Sara said, reaching for the jug which

stood handy. 'I'll just wet it, then work up a nice lather . . .'

Matty was very good, all things considered. Sara had heard stories from Army officers of how children would fight to protect themselves from a bath, how they howled and shrieked when they felt soap stinging wounds and eyes, but Matty did all she could to help, even rubbing away at her blackened knees with a soapy flannel and letting Sara pour the jug of water repeatedly over her filthy, matted hair.

But at last the job was done. Matty stepped out of the water clean, with every bite, scratch, bruise and abrasion now clearly etched on her pale skin and her little hip bones standing out from her almost concave stomach. Sara, helping her to dry herself, asked her what the marks were, though she could guess. The child glanced down at the red bumps and the scratches and bruises, then shrugged indifferently.

'Dunno. Bed-bugs, fleas . . . some are from fights, old ones, some's where me dad battered me. Oh, and a rat bit me cheek.'

Sara shuddered, she could not help herself.

'It'll have to have some antiseptic on it, dear, or it may go bad. It's festering already. In fact you've got several nasty wounds. But we can soon set them to rights; I expect you'll not mind if the stuff I put on stings a bit.'

Sara fetched antiseptic, cleaned and dressed the wounds, then took Matty, now paler than ever, back into the bedroom. She gave her the clothing she had already selected, as well as some long black stockings and a pair of lace-up shoes which proved to be a bit too big.

'But it's better than too small,' Sara said cheerfully. 'Shall I plait your hair, Matty? It'll be lovely smooth

464

hair one of these days, such a pretty light-brown colour, too. But for now perhaps it's best tied back. I've got a nice piece of scarlet ribbon somewhere . . .'

She found the ribbon, tied the child's hair back, and then gestured to the pathetic little pile of rags which Matty had brought through from the bathroom.

'What shall I do with your old clothes, love? Only you've got all this nice, new stuff, you won't need your other things, will you? We'll keep them if you wish, of course, but if not, perhaps we might throw them away?'

Matty looked doubtful. One did not cast aside perfectly good clothes, her expression said. But then she looked round the room, at the flowered wallpaper, the pretty curtains, the beds with their white coverlets.

'That's my bed, izzit?'

'Yes, that's your bed.'

'An' these are me clothes, eh? No one else won't take 'em off me?'

'They're yours for as long as they fit you, and when you grow bigger, you'll be given new clothes.'

Matty gave the pile of rags a disdainful flick with her toe. It said a lot, Sara thought.

'Chuck 'em out,' Matty said. 'Oh . . . wait on; there's suffin' . . .' She delved into the pocket of the torn old jacket she had worn and produced a small, round object. It was greyish-white, soft and fluffy. 'That's all I want to keep,' she said rather shyly. 'Them were me sister's. It's the only thing of 'ers I've got, see?'

'What is it?' Sara asked idly. 'Is it a ball? It's a bit dirty, isn't it?'

'Yes, it's filthy,' the child agreed. 'But it's not a ball.' She pulled at the object, which became two. 'See?'

Sara held her hand out wonderingly and took both small objects in the palm of her hand. She looked at the once-white angora gloves for a long, long moment. Then she looked up.

'Grace,' she said quietly. 'Oh, my dear, you're not Matty Brown, you're Grace Carbery – and these are the little gloves I gave to Jess!'

Miss Boote had been right; the hospital strapped up her ankle, lent her some crutches, and sent her off home. Brogan, who had had to move his family out to their new home later that day, visited her there as soon as he got back. Miss Boote lived in a neat ground-floor flat in Florence Street, just up the road from his own lodgings in Salop Street.

'How are you feelin' now, Miss Boote?' he asked her when she came to the door in answer to his knock. 'I've been thinkin' about you for two days, worryin' in case the ankle got worse. But you look fine an' fit, so you do.'

'Do come in, Mr O'Brady, and thanks for the compliment,' Miss Boote said, ushering him into her living kitchen. 'Sorry it's a bit untidy, but four of us share the place and sometimes we could do with more space round us. Did you manage your move all right?'

Brogan had told her, whilst they waited in casualty, about his family's move out of the city, and now he grinned reminiscently, remembering that awful day, the complications caused by Polly's behaviour and the way her livestock had behaved.

'We managed very well in the end, if you don't count the cockerel gettin' loose and scarin' the livin' daylights out of the guard on the train, and Delly bein' sick as . . . as a dog. Heaven knows what he'd ate but it must have been an unsavoury meal. And Lionel takin' a dislike to the cat basket and tryin' to claw his way out of it. When I got back to the city I had to start work again of course, me holiday bein' up, but if all holidays are as exhaustin' as that one, I'll be more relaxed in the cab of me engine.'

Miss Boote laughed. She went over to a small gas stove and lit it, then pulled the kettle over the flame.

'You do cheer me up, Mr O'Brady! Sit down, I'll make us a nice cup of tea.'

And presently, with the tea-tray before her, she began to ask Brogan about himself and what he intended to do with the rest of his life.

'Because you mentioned giving a hand in the garden out at Strawberry Field,' she said. 'I've not said too much, in case you felt you'd better things to do with your time – after all, for all I knew you might have decided to stay with your family – but I did say I knew someone who liked gardening and I was told to send you along whenever you had a moment to spare.'

'Well, now that I've me family settled, I've a moment to spare,' Brogan decided. 'I'll go along there now so I will. I'll go back home and fetch me bike . . . I don't use the tram much – and I can be there in half an hour.' He drained his teacup and then stood up. 'Thanks, Miss Boote – you say I cheered you up – you don't know how much better I feel. First I know you're comin' on nicely so you are, and next I've the prospect of gettin' me hands on some gardenin' again!'

Miss Boote beamed. She stood up as well and accompanied him to the door.

'And you're going to do a good turn,' she said exuberantly. 'There's nothin' like doin' a good turn to cheer a person up. And you never know, Mr O'Brady – sometimes when you do something for someone else it's you that actually benefit.'

'Uh?' Brogan said, rather bemused.

Miss Boote laughed again. 'I didn't put it very well,

did I? What I meant was that doing good sometimes brings unexpected rewards.'

'Oh, I see,' Brogan said. 'Well, I'll be off if you don't mind, Miss Boote. It's a nice day for once, I might get some diggin' done this afternoon!'

When she had seen her visitor off, Miss Boote returned to her favourite chair and carefully put her injured ankle up on a small footstool. Then she reached for her book, but though she turned the pages at intervals she did not read a word. Her mind was far away, with Sara at Strawberry Field. She had deliberately reminded Mr O'Brady of his offer to do some gardening because she had a feeling that he might be that friend of Sara's who had gone back to Ireland to take care of his family. She could be wrong, of course, she acknowledged that. Or Sara might be no longer interested in her old friend. Nevertheless, there was a good chance, Miss Boote thought, that she had actually done something to bring two very nice people together.

I've never seen meself as a matchmaker, Miss Boote told herself at last, getting up from her chair and limping over to the kettle to make more tea. But even if I'm not successful, even if it isn't the same feller, there's no harm in gettin' a gardener for free!

Chapter Sixteen

Brogan got off his bicycle at soon as he reached the Strawberry Field drive and pushed it the rest of the way up to the front door. Then he swerved round to the side of the house, because a would-be gardener would scarcely approach the front door in so brazen a manner. Besides, it gave him a chance for a good look around.

The garden was in a state all right, he told himself, eyeing the beds, many of them trampled flat by builders and decorators, some simply winter-bare, but all lacking the clean, tilled look of a well-kept garden. There were roses in need of pruning, shrubs and bushes in need of cutting back, lawns positively begging for draining, cleaning, nurturing. Yes, Strawberry Field could do with someone, and he very much hoped it could be him. I'd start off with a series of bonfires, he told himself, looking disparagingly at the paths, almost hidden beneath a carpet of fallen leaves, hedges straggling across them, a paved patio mossy and puddled where it was not mounded up with dead leaves. Yes, I'd start with bonfires, then I'd go on by doing some good, old-fashioned double-digging. And then I'd get a few cartloads of farmyard muck and spread it all around . . . the place would begin to benefit by the spring.

He reached the back door. He could hear muted sounds from beyond it so he knocked politely, then stood back and waited.

*

'Oh dear, every time I put pen to paper someone either rings up or comes to the door,' Sara grumbled, putting her pen down and jumping to her feet. 'I'd only just seen the children off for their cinema trip, thankful for at least two hours' peace and quiet, when Mr Reid arrived, asking about the new geyser for the staff bathroom. Still, if this is the gardener Miss Boote asked to call, he can't come soon enough. Oh, Matron, I do wonder how I'll cope when all the children arrive, considering I'm finding three such hard work!'

'When the place is full there'll be someone else to answer the door,' the matron said placidly. The two women were in the staff sitting room, Sara trying to catch up with her paperwork and the matron knitting for Christmas. So far she had made each of their three resident children a scarlet woolly jumper, a pom-pom hat and a pair of brightly coloured mittens. Sara, entrusted with the scarves, had barely got halfway up – or down – the first. 'Off you go, Miss Cordwainer. And since you're so busy I'll do a bit of your knitting, shall I? I seem to have finished mine.'

'Oh, I *would* be grateful,' Sara said, pausing for a moment. 'I'm afraid I'm not a very good knitter. Gran did try to teach me, but she gave up because I kept producing a different number of stitches, though goodness knows how. I really don't understand it at all, to tell you the truth.'

'That's clear,' the matron said, surveying the uneven piece of knitting which dangled from Sara's needles. 'Are those holes part of the pattern, then?'

'Umm . . . I'm not sure. I'll just . . .'

Sara hurried from the room, glad to escape the difficult task. Matron, who clearly took knitting quite complex patterns in her stride, seemed to expect her assistant to be similarly gifted, which wasn't helping either. I'm good at other things, Sara told herself defensively now, crossing the hallway with a quick, impatient step. I do the books and amuse the children, do quite a lot of the cooking when Cook is on her day off or otherwise engaged, I teach Sunday school . . .

She reached the back door and flung it open.

'Good aftern . . .' Sara stopped short. 'Brogan! Oh, Brogan!'

She had told herself he was only a friend, but she did not treat him like one. She simply flew across the short distance which separated them and hugged him. And Brogan hugged her back, hugged her hard, and began kissing any bit of her that he could reach, which was entirely unexpected and entirely lovely, so far as Sara was concerned. Locked in each other's arms, they both knew the sheer bliss of reunion, and Sara felt tears form in her eyes and begin to trickle down her cheeks because *this* was where she wanted to be, *this* was where she belonged! She had thought a life of caring for children was all she could possibly desire, now she knew she was wrong. More than anything else, she wanted to be with Brogan. It was, in the end, that simple.

Brogan's face was shining. He hadn't said a word so far, but finally he held her away from him, his eyes fixed lovingly on her face.

'Sara? Dear God above, I've missed you so bad! But I'd given you up, after they told me you'd got a feller, an Army feller.'

'An *Army* feller? Who on earth told you that? I've never had a feller at all, if you want to know the truth. Oh, and Brogan, I'm so sorry about your father's death; what a terrible thing to happen.'

'Indeed,' Brogan said solemnly. 'Me father was hit by a train, it near kilt him so it did, but he recovered.

Now he's fit an' well, and livin' on the Wirral, mindin' a crossin' for the LMS. Boote, your feller's name was, accordin' to your neighbour, in Snowdrop Street.' He grinned suddenly. 'God love you, Sara, it wouldn't be Miss Boote she was meanin', would it? The young woman me sister's dog knocked over?'

'That's right, or I think it is ... certainly Clarrie was knocked down in Anfield Cemetery by a dog ... Oh, Brogan, was *that* why you never came calling? Because you thought Miss Boote was my – my intended? She was our lodger, that's all! And Peader's fit and well, you say? That's wonderful news, Brog. A little feller in the Queen's Arms told me you'd gone back to Ireland to look after your family because your father had died. He said he thought you'd be getting married over there. Honestly, what a fool I was not to check up!'

'We've been a pair of fools, both believin' whatever we were told about the other,' Brogan said. 'And what d'you think you've done to me, hidin' yourself away like this? Ah God, an' the last time we met sure an' wasn't I a tongue-tied idiot! But you were so grand, so special ... I had no words to tell you the things I wanted you to know ... ah, Sara, why in God's name didn't I just hug you?'

'I don't know,' Sara said. She knew her own eyes were shining, she could feel the tears building. 'Brogan ... this is madness! Last time we met we almost quarrelled ... We've believed all sorts of silly things about the other one ... oh, Brog, I've missed you!'

'Not so bad as I've missed you,' Brogan said tenderly. 'But why the uniform?'

Sara looked down at herself as though she didn't know what he was talking about, then laughed.

'Oh, that. I'm a Salvationist, Brog, the same as my

friend Clarrie is. Didn't you know that Strawberry Field is a Salvation Army children's home? I joined the Army a while back, when Clarrie took me up to the Barracks and showed me the sort of work they did. I knew that if I joined them I'd be able to help the people who needed it most, especially children – it gave me a purpose in life. So I'm working here now, as an assistant to the matron.'

Brogan frowned. 'You're a Salvationist, then? I never guessed, never t'ought... you said you'd met the Carbs for the first time outside a church, you see. Not that it matters, one way or t'other, alanna.' But then he began to smile. 'So we've both been livin' here, believin' the other to be out of reach! And there was me, searchin' for the Carbery young wan, and never thinkin' to ask about yourself!'

'And there was me...' Sara broke off. 'We had a new child in recently, Brog; someone you know. Grace, her name is. Grace Carbery. The baby never put in an appearance, Grace spent years searching for her, but at least we know Grace herself is safe, now.'

'What about the parents?' Brogan asked. 'The mother died fallin' on the stairs, I read that somewhere. But what's become of the father? I take it he's not in full cry after gettin' Grace back again?'

Sara shook her head.

'No, we found out that he was killed in a drunken brawl outside the Great Mersey public house on Commercial Road a month or two back. The Army was able to trace him, once Grace admitted who she really was. She was so relieved... she cried with joy, which sounds terrible, but the things he'd done to her... he was a wicked man and the best thing he could do for his kids was to die, believe me.'

'I believe you,' Brogan said fervently. 'Look, my

darlin' girl, can you come out wit' me for a while? Because we've a deal of talkin' to do, and I can't talk freely before anyone but you. And Sara, I'm not lettin' you out of me sight again until we've had this talk, so you'd best agree to it or I'll be makin' up me bed on your doorstep so I shall.'

'I'll come with you, but first you'd best come in and meet Matron and have a word about the garden,' Sara said. 'Oh, Brog, I can't tell you how relieved I was when I realised we'd found young Grace. Nor – nor how wonderful it is to see you again.'

'Ditto,' Brogan said briefly. 'I hope you'll still think it's nice to know me when I tell you . . . what I've got to tell you. But first, let's be meetin' this matron of yours.'

They took themselves off to Calderstones Park in the end. It was a cold afternoon, but the refreshment rooms were open, so the two of them chose a table in the window, ordered tea and cakes and proceeded to tell each other everything which had happened to them, both lately and long ago.

Sara, watching Brogan's face as he studied the menu, wondered how she had managed without him for so long. He was downright beautiful, with his thick, black hair which shone like coal, his expressive dark-brown eyes, and the slow smile which warmed those eyes, lit that strong, intelligent face. She knew, now, that she loved him, had probably loved him right from the start. But she did not know whether he loved her or simply liked her as a friend.

But this time I'll find out, she vowed, as they took their places on opposite sides of the small window-table. I'll find out . . . and if it's the right answer, I'm not going to pretend. I'm going to tell him I want to be with him for always, no matter how forward and bad it seems.

When their tea arrived Sara poured and Brogan insisted that she choose her cake first. Then he smiled at her, his eyes alight with affection.

'Who's goin' to start? Ladies first, I'm thinkin'.'

So Sara started, with the story of the child calling herself Matty Brown who had arrived on the doorstep at Strawberry Field. She gave Brogan a blow-by-blow account right up to the moment when Grace had brought the little grey fluffy ball out of her pocket, and Sara had recognised the gloves as the ones she herself had given to Jess on that snowy Christmas morning long ago.

It was tempting to leave it at that, to forget the other, darker side, but having decided to make a clean breast of it Sara took the plunge.

'I think the truth was, Brogan, that because my parents were indifferent to me I felt a real kinship for those other girls whose parents were indifferent, too. The Carberys, I mean. I know the circumstances were not the same, but at the root of it, the Carbery girls and myself all knew what it was to be unloved.

'So Jess touched me in a way which is probably a bit difficult to understand. It – it wasn't just the poverty, you see, it went deeper than that. But I could do so little; only give her what I had myself, which was the shilling and the white angora gloves, and of course what I gave her hadn't helped at all, not really. Indeed, for a while I actually felt I'd almost caused her death.

'My grandmother – and you – talked me out of a good deal of the guilt, but I did know how lucky I was. I had Gran, for a start, and she truly loved me. And though my parents didn't love me, they gave me things the Carbery kids would have given their eye-teeth for – food, clothing, education, self-confidence – compared to the kids from the slums, I was rich! So I decided to find the Carbery girls, who were having to fend for themselves now, and help them in any way I could.

'But it wasn't easy. I only visited Gran in the school holidays, and by the time the spring term was over and I went back to Snowdrop Street, the Carbs had been kicked out for not paying their rent and seemed to have disappeared.

'And then of course I was sent away to school in Switzerland and when I came back the first time I showed any sympathy for the poor, my parents disowned me. So back I came to Snowdrop Street, to earn my own living, help my grandmother . . . and try to find Grace and Mollie.

'Then Clarrie took me to the Barracks for the first time, and it was a revelation. There were people actually *doing* the things I'd thought about, talked about. They were working for the poor in a way I'd never imagined. They didn't just collect money, or say things should be different, they worked their fingers to the bone making sure that things *were* different. If a woman was too ill to come to the soup kitchen, the Army went to her. If a child was beaten and abused, the police brought the child to one of the Army shelters and the kid was cleaned up, taken to hospital if necessary, and found somewhere safe to sleep at nights. Old people who'd lost their homes, men who'd lost their jobs, lost hope, were all picked up, dusted down, and set on the path to recovery. I can't tell you, Brog, all the Army does because I don't know myself, yet. But I suppose in a way I wanted a share of all that shining faith, all that generosity. I admired them more than words can say and I saw that to become one of them, to work as they did, was not just a good way of helping people like the Carbs, it was the best way of helping, full stop. The Army net spreads wide, you see. Even if I, personally, wasn't able to help Grace and Mollie, others might well be doing so, and I was helping *them*.' She stopped talking, putting both hands to her hot cheeks. 'Oh, Brogan, do I sound an awful little prig? My mother called me a prig once. But I must try to explain what the Army did for me, and why I value it so!'

'I understand, alanna,' Brogan said quietly. 'And you aren't the only one to admire the Army, even though I don't share their faith. And now that you've Grace under your wing, is the guilt dead? What more could you have done, indeed?'

'I still wonder about Mollie,' Sara confessed. 'She was such a pretty child. I'd hate to think of her growing pale and indifferent, slouching around the street, begging . . . But what about you, Brogan? I remember the very first time we met you said you carried your burden of guilt, too.'

'I think I stopped feeling guilty when my mammy looked at the baby I'd got tucked under me donkey jacket, and fell in love wit' her,' Brogan said thoughtfully. 'Because I knew I was doin' what young Jess wanted. And now, every time I set eyes on our young'un . . .'

'*You* took her? Brogan O'Brady, don't say you've known where Mollie was all these years and never breathed a word to me? Oh, and I've worried myself sick, sometimes, at what I'd done.'

'Once she was wit' me mammy it wasn't my secret, you see,' Brogan said humbly. 'If it had been my secret, Sara love, you'd have known first go off so you would. But you were only a child yourself then; I couldn't risk you tellin' someone. Polly's whole life was at stake.'

'Polly? Don't you mean . . .' Sara stopped short with a gasp. 'Your little sister! She's ten years old, the only girl . . . Oh, Brogan, and whenever you've talked about her I've thought what a natural, happy child she seemed. You were right; it wasn't your secret to give away. But thank you, thank you, for telling me now!'

'I feel better for tellin' you, so I do,' Brogan assured her. 'You aren't the only one who's felt bad about those young wans. And you do understand, alanna, that I'd have told you if I could? Because – because I was fond of you from the first, so I was, and there was nothing I'd have liked better than to take the worry over the baby's whereabouts from your shoulders. But it wasn't possible, me darlin' girl.'

Brogan leaned across the little table and took both her hands in his. Then he turned them palm upwards and kissed them, starting at the wrists and moving across her palms and down to the tips of her fingers. Sara's heart did an enormous double-thump and then settled to a rapid, noisy rhythm. He loved her – didn't he? She realised she had no idea how young men behaved when they were in love, nor how young women behaved, come to that. The Army had taught her a great deal, but there were still some things she simply had to learn for herself.

'Brog? When you kissed my hands like that I felt very peculiar,' Sara whispered bashfully. 'It – it's an exciting sort of feeling. Is it wrong to feel – to feel that I'd like you to – to go on kissing me?'

'No, it's not wrong, darlin',' Brogan said. 'Sure an' isn't it how I've wanted and waited for you to feel this past decade? Look, we've sorted out what's happened to Grace and Polly, now d'you t'ink we might sort ourselves out, too? Because it's you I'm wantin' to spend the rest of me life wit', Sara Cordwainer. I know there's difficulties . . .'

'I don't see any,' Sara murmured. She could feel her cheeks begin to flame at the mere thought of what she was about to say. 'Because that's how I feel too, Brogan.'

'Oh, my love!' Brogan leaned forward ardently . . . and tipped the milk jug over. Sara jumped to her feet, perhaps a little relieved that the excitement and tension of the last few moments had so abruptly dissipated, and fetched a cloth. Laughing, she mopped up the milk, then went and fetched more. He had proposed to her – hadn't he? Was it a proposal when a man told a girl that he wanted to spend the rest of his life with her? She suspected that it was and her heart beat faster at the thought. To be with Brogan for always, as man and wife! It was what she wanted most out of life, she realised, though she had never even put it into thoughts, let alone words.

'So what are these difficulties?' Sara said presently, when order had been restored and they both had a fresh cup of tea before them. To her, the path stretched ahead, rose-strewn, sunny. 'Are you a married man, Brogan O'Brady, with a dozen kids hidden away somewhere?'

He laughed, shaking his head. 'No, indeed. But I'm a Catholic, darlin' Sara, and you're an Army lass. Liverpool may not be as bad as Dublin for mixed marriages . . .'

'It is,' Sara said. 'Oh, why didn't I *think*? But love . . . love can't be ordered and paid for, can it, Brog? You can't help who you fall in love with.'

'No, indeed, and our love's already stood the test of time so it has. Well, we'll see. I'm goin' back to the crossing cottage at the weekend, I'll see what's said when I tell them I'm marryin' the best, prettiest, most lovin' girl in the whole of Liverpool. But they'll expect such a one to be a good Cat'olic girl and raise a good Cat'olic family, and to be honest, alanna, it never crossed me mind, until you opened the door to me earlier, that you weren't a good Cat'olic girl!'

'I never was, even as a child,' Sara admitted. 'I was Church of England, Brog, before I joined the Army. And you really think your parents will disapprove? That they won't like me, because I'm a Salvationist? Not even when you point out the good we do, the work . . .'

'We won't judge them,' Brogan said. 'Wait and see. But if the worst comes to the worst, alanna, there's always America.'

'America? But why, Brog?'

'Because my brother Niall went there a while back and so I've been readin' up about the country, the prospect there. I'm an engine driver as you know, but because I'm young still there's no question, in England or Ireland, of me havin' an express, or doin' the more important lines, for another twenty years at least. I'll be doddlin' up and down branch lines or drivin' goods trains for years so I will. But if I go to the States, wit' the experience I've already had and me exam results, Niall says I'd be driving the transcontinental loco-motives wit'in a year or two, but quite early on I'd be taking out the freights. Imagine it, Sara – to be a hogger on a freight train, travelling the high iron between Marshall and Dallas, and me not yet t'irty!'

'Imagine,' breathed Sara, who did not even know what he was talking about. 'And if . . . if two people of different religions were to marry in America, Brogan, would they be ostracised, made to feel guilty?'

'No, alanna. No one would give a tinker's cuss, so long as they didn't frighten the horses!'

And then Brogan leaned across the table and gathered Sara into his arms. Crockery crashed, milk jugs spilt, cakes became crumbs. But Sara, finding herself in the one place she most wanted to be, was indifferent.

'Oh, Brogan, we'll be so happy just to be together,' she murmured against his mouth. 'Can we go and see your parents *soon*?'

'Very soon. But . . . you've no regrets, alanna? What about Grace? Strawberry Field? Your friends?'

'Grace is happy, though I'd feel bad to leave her,' Sara admitted, sitting back in her seat once more. 'But we may not need to go to the States, not if your parents take to me. Then I wouldn't have to leave the Strawb, would I?'

'My parents will love you! But you know there'll be disapproval . . . mixed marriages are frowned on; even the Salvationists would prefer you to marry within the Army, I daresay. Because I'd want me children brought up in the faith so I would. If you'd agree?'

'I'd like my children to have the freedom to choose,' Sara said after a moment. 'Would that be unfair, Brog? After all, religion's an important thing, it's not like saying "I support Liverpool, or Everton," it's a way of life. Serving God is serving God, whether you do it as a Catholic or a Salvationist. Choice is important.'

'I agree. But we'll leave that problem until after we're married,' Brogan said. 'Only I doubt that Salvationists would want you workin' on at the Strawb if you were married to a Catholic.'

'Oh? And they wouldn't want a Catholic for a gardener, I suppose?'

Brogan laughed and threw up his hands in the immortal gesture of surrender. 'Pax, pax! You're right and I'm wrong, me darlin'. And when the babies come along it isn't workin' at the Strawb you'd be anyway. You'd be taking care of me and them!'

'That sounds wonderful,' Sara murmured. 'But what about Grace? She's tremendously happy at the Strawb, but there's no doubt her sister is having a more – more normal sort of life with your family out at the level-crossing cottage.'

'Me family will want to meet her, no doubt,' Brogan said cautiously. 'But I'm not plannin' on tellin' either Grace or Polly what happened all those years ago, if that's what you were thinkin'. What I did was illegal even if 'twas for the best, I'd be t'rown in prison, very like, if it came out. And they're only kids, the young Carbs. I wouldn't be puttin' the responsibility of knowin' such t'ings on their shoulders.'

'True,' Sara agreed. 'All right, suppose we offered to have Grace to live with us, Brogan? Would you like that?'

'Look, sweetheart, stop anticipatin'. Let's take it one step at a time, shall we? And the first step is for me to go down to the cottage and break the news that we're engaged to be wed. Then I'll take you to meet them and we'll go on from there. Agreed?'

'No! If we're engaged to be wed the first thing to do is buy me a ring,' Sara said. 'Just a little, cheap one, you know, but a real engagement ring.'

Brogan got up from the table and, as Sara rose too, kissed her quickly on the side of her mouth. 'You're right; we'll take a tram into the city centre tomorrow morning, first thing,' he said buoyantly. 'You're a girl who gets her priorities right, Miss Cordwainer, I can tell that!'

Brogan walked up from the station to the crossing

cottage, a heavy bag full of small Christmas gifts slung over his shoulder. The cottage was on the telephone, and Deirdre had rung him a couple of times, once to ask if he could do some shopping for them.

'Wit' only ten days to go before the holiday we're havin' our work cut out to get the place straight,' she had shouted into the mouthpiece. 'You're in the city, me boy, so if I read you a list out, could you do me messages and bring 'em wit' you, next time you come?'

'I could and I will, Mammy,' Brogan assured her. 'But the telephone's a wonderful invention, it carries your voice to me by the electric – you don't have to bellow like that, you know.'

'Who's bellowin'?' Deirdre said, still at full volume. ''Twon't take no heed of a whisper, that I *do* know. Did ye hear me?'

'I heard,' Brogan said patiently. 'I'll do your messages then, Mammy, and see you in a week, so I will.'

And now he was walking up the lane, the hedges winter-bare but bright with berries, the grass of the verge dry and white after the long summer. Over the gates he passed, Brogan could see the clean line of plough, a field of winter cabbage growing well, pasture dotted with cattle or sheep. Trees overhung the lane, trees which, in summer, would cast a delightful shade, though now they, like the hedges, were bare of leaves, and when the lane deepened, running between high banks, Brogan could see by the foliage that when spring came there would be wild strawberries here, and violets, primroses.

'It's just like heaven,' Polly had written to him only last week. 'I love it best in the world, so I do. But I wish Tad were here too.'

And the crossing cottage was nice as well. Long and low, with the bedroom ceilings slanted, the windows set in the warm red tiles so that the house looked as though it was perpetually raising its eyebrows, it crouched midway between the track and the lane, its whitewashed walls cool to the touch in summer, warm in winter. There was an airy living room which overlooked the railway line so the family could watch the trains as they thundered past, and a large kitchen overlooking the garden where the cats strolled elegantly or sneaked on their bellies after the birds, and the borders, even at this time of year, were gay with late roses, chrysanthemums, and autumn crocus.

Brogan hitched his bag a bit higher on his shoulder and strode on. His family were happy and settled already, the boys and Polly enjoying the village school, his parents almost unable to believe the rural peace by which they were surrounded. To be sure, Deirdre had complained at first that she could not sleep at nights for the trains, whilst Peader, sheepishly, had said that the long silences between trains kept him awake. But it hadn't lasted. They had grown accustomed; indeed, Peader now said that if a train was late he was likely to wake because it hadn't gone through, though the roar of its normal progress disturbed him not at all.

There were only two trains through between the hours of ten at night and six the next morning, and now that they were settled, Deirdre had offered to do them every other night so that Peader could sleep straight through.

'But I like to wake and see to me gate,' her husband had assured her. ''Tis a pleasure to me, alanna, and no pain. And I'm fast asleep five minutes after she's gone through, you know that.'

The hens had settled as well as the rest of the family, and Delilah was in his element. Though not the meekest or most biddable of dogs, he was well content with the large garden in which he could wander, and the nearby meadows where cows grazed and willows overhung the small streams. There was a river, too. The boys went fishing with their homemade rods and Polly spent hours hanging over the water with a flour-bag on a split cane and came home with pinkeens galore, though the local children told her they were stickleback, and assured her that she would find more exciting things in the streams than that when spring came.

Brogan came alongside the cottage garden, or rather the orchard. He looked through the hedge at the old trees standing in the long, whitened grass, and thought that he and Peader really ought to start off some new stock. And then as he drew level with the vegetable patch he saw his father. Peader wore old corduroys and a much-patched shirt. His head was bare and despite the cold, his shirt was rolled up above the elbows. He was digging over a patch of ground which had not been cultivated for years but he must have heard Brogan's footsteps for he straightened, a hand in the small of his back, and turned, then gave a broad, welcoming smile.

'Brogan! Good to see you, son.'

'Good to see you, Daddy,' Brogan said, putting down his haversack for a moment. Grinning, they shook hands over the hedge, then Brogan hefted his bag once more and set off again, Peader keeping pace with him on the other side of the hedge. 'I've done all Mammy's messages, and a couple for you, as well. And I've some news for you; I hope you'll t'ink it good.'

'Sure we shall, boy,' Peader said heartily. He held open the gate, gesturing Brogan inside. 'Your mammy's got the kettle on and some oat cakes warmin'. Let's go in for a bit, it's time I had a break.'

Brogan had known, in his heart, that it was not going to be a picnic, telling his family about Sara. But he had not been prepared for the downright antagonism. Peader and the boys hadn't been so bad, but his Mammy! She had wept and wailed and said he'd go to hell so he would for marryin' an Army lass, no matter how good, sweet or high-principled.

'Sure an' even the child here would know better than to consort wit' such people,' Deirdre had said at one point, putting a protective hand on Polly's curly head. 'Doesn't she go to a school now which is *crawling* wit' Proddies, but does she bring 'em home or tell me she's goin' to wed one of 'em? Of course not; she's got more sense!'

Polly looked hunted; Brogan guessed that the religion of her schoolmates simply had not, until this moment, entered her head. Poor little creature, he thought compassionately, what a fuss about nothing, when you had to bring a child of ten into it!

'But, Mammy, Sara's a lovely person . . .' Brogan began, only to be overridden. Lovely people, it appeared, were very fine if they stayed on their own side of the fence. If they trespassed, then they were no longer lovely people. A lovely Proddy, his mother assured him, was incapable of falling in love wit' a decent Catholic boy. And, she added with a glare, a lovely Catholic boy would never demean himself by even considerin' marriage to a Protestant, let alone a Salvationist.

'But they're in love, Deirdre,' Peader pointed out, when his wife had paused momentarily in her lamentations. 'Love's not somethin' you can switch on or off like a tap, you know. D'you t'ink I'd have walked away from you if you'd been an Army lass – or a heathen Chinee, for that matter?'

'But you didn't mix wit' those sort of people,' Deirdre reminded him truthfully. 'Our boy's been mixin' wit' the wrong sort, that's the trouble. I tell you, decent Catholic boys don't even t'ink of Proddy girls in that sort of way. Why, a decent Catholic lad would as soon marry a cow in the meadow as a Proddy! If we'd been back in Dublin, now . . .'

'Oh, if, if! Don't ever condemn love, alanna. I'm tellin' you, if you'd had a ring t'rough your nose and worshipped a totem pole, I'd still have wed ye!'

'The more fool you, Peader O'Brady,' Deirdre had muttered darkly. 'I'd sooner dance at the weddin' of a cat wit' a mouse than a decent Catholic boy wit' a Proddy.'

Brogan, still annoyed at the suggestion that Sara was as marriageable as a cow, cast his mother a dark look and she scowled back at him, muttered something about scheming hussies in black stockings who were no better than they ought to be, and stamped out of the living room and back to her kitchen sink, leaving Peader and Brogan to stare helplessly at each other.

Polly, sitting on the windowsill ostensibly watching for the 16.05, turned and stared at them with big, puzzled eyes.

'Daddy, what's *wrong* wit' Proddies? I didn't know me school was crawlin' wit' them at all at all.'

'Oh hell,' Peader said helplessly. He never swore. 'Oh hell, alanna, don't you let such talk take root. There's nothin' wrong wit' Proddies, nothin' at all. Mammy didn't mean it, it's just . . . Brogan's her eldest boy now, and she doesn't want to lose him.'

'But she wouldn't lose you, would she, Brog?' Polly said eagerly. 'The Proddy wouldn't take you away from us, would she? She'd come here as well – I'd like that.'

'Well, don't tell Mammy,' Brogan growled. 'If she

t'ought I'd influenced you to think well of a Salvationist sure me head would be on a spike on the crossin' gate, instead of on me shoulders. I was goin' to bring Sara to meet you next weekend . . .'

'Better not,' Peader advised. 'Leave it a week or two. Come over wit' her in the New Year. Your mammy won't be rude . . .'

'Oh, no, she'll just tell Sara she's as marriageable as a cow and a scheming hussy in black stockings,' Brogan said bitterly. 'How can I bring me innocent girl here, Daddy, when there's talk like that?'

'I'll make sure Deirdre's polite and welcoming,' Peader said grimly. 'Polly, go out an' play!'

'It's cold out,' Polly whined. 'I'm waitin' on the 16.05, the driver's me friend, he waves!'

'He's a Proddy, you'd better not wave back,' Brogan said, just as his mother re-entered the room. She coloured hotly, but ignored the remark, holding out her hand to Polly.

'Come into the kitchen, alanna. I'm bakin' scones, you can put a few extra currants in, make them wit' laughin' faces.'

'I don't want to,' Polly muttered. 'Mammy, I *like* the kids at school, I didn't know they were Proddies.'

'No, well, 'tis a small village, alanna, we can't choose . . .' Deirdre began, only to be interrupted.

Peader jumped to his feet, his face turning scarlet and veins beginning to bulge on his forehead. He slammed both fists down on the small table, and shouted at his wife.

'I won't have you turnin' the child into a mass of blind prejudice so I won't! Now tell us all you spoke out of turn and when the New Year comes we'll meet Brogan's young lady and judge for ourselves. D'you understand me, Deirdre O'Brady?'

Deirdre, looking stunned, muttered that she supposed it would be all right if that was his attitude and held out an appealing hand to Polly, who continued to shake her head.

'Go wit' your mammy, Polleen,' Peader said quietly. 'And in ten minutes or so we'll all have a nice cup of tay and one of those scones she was talkin' about. And the first weekend after the New Year, Brogan shall bring Miss Cordwainer to visit us. I'm the master in me own house and I say who's welcome here!'

Brogan had to tell Sara, of course. He went round to the Strawb and waited until she had put the children to bed and finished work for the day. Then he announced that he was going to do some digging and would be grateful for her company. Sara accordingly put on her thick grey worsted coat and her red tam o'shanter and went and stood beside him whilst he double-dug the vegetable patch.

'Well?' she asked impatiently after a few moments. 'What did they say? Was it bad, Brog?'

'It was,' Brogan said, not mincing matters. 'Me daddy was fair; he always is. Me mammy wasn't. But we expected it, didn't we?'

'Ye-es,' Sara said doubtfully. 'Then what are we to do, Brog? You don't want to marry in the face of your mother's objections, I suppose, and I can understand it because your mother's always been good to you. Honestly, if you . . .'

'I'm to take you round to the cottage in the New Year,' Brogan said. 'We'll sort it all out then. When Mammy sees you . . .'

But even to his own ears his words did not have that air of confidence which he wanted to convey.

'Shall we take Grace, as well?' Sara suggested presently. Brogan could see her self-confidence had taken a nasty knock and stopped digging for a moment to reach across and give her hand a squeeze. 'No, it's all right, you did say it might be difficult. It's just that because I'm so happy I can't see how anything like two different religions could possibly matter. If we do as we said – turn and turn about – what's wrong with that? Only you'll have to take them to Mass and Confession, because I – well, I'm a Salvationist when all's said and done.'

'We don't have any children yet, me darlin',' Brogan reminded her with a smile. 'So that's a matter between us, for the future. And we won't take Grace when we go to the crossing cottage, not the first time. I've a feelin' we'll have our work cut out to make me family see reason wit'out addin' Grace to the party.'

Because Grace liked to garden, she spent a lot of time with Brogan, sweeping leaves, tidying hedges, making bonfires, and with every day her self-confidence – and her naughtiness – grew. Brogan applauded this, but did not fancy having to cope with it at the crossing cottage.

'I thought she might take their minds off me, that's all,' Sara said meekly. 'What'll I wear? Not uniform?'

'Definitely not uniform,' Brogan said quickly. His mammy would go mad if she saw how very beautiful Sara's legs looked in the despised black stockings, or how becomingly the bonnet framed her lovely face! 'Somethin' warm, alanna, because – because we'll maybe take a walk after dinner. And somethin' pretty, because I'm proud of you.'

'Oh, Brogan,' Sara said. 'Oh, Brogan, I do love you!'

Sara had known meeting Brogan's family would be

an ordeal, but in fact it was worse than her wildest imaginings. First, they walked into the cottage to meet a positive barrage of eyes. Not just Deirdre, Peader, Polly, Bevin and Ivan, but Donal, too, because he had come over for a job interview and was spending a day with his family at the same time.

Then, having been introduced all round, Sara was invited, by Deirdre, to take a moment to tidy up, which meant going upstairs with her hostess and trying to make light conversation with someone, whilst combing her hair and hanging up her coat, who simply said nothing but let her eyes roam insultingly over her.

Finally, of course, Sara had been stung into speech.

'Mrs O'Brady, I know you can't be too pleased that your son has brought a Salvationist home . . .' she began, to be swiftly interrupted.

'Pleased? Is it pleased I should be that me eldest, dearest son has broke me heart wit' his selfishness and gone against family tradition? But there, Miss Cordwainer, he's a handsome feller, I'll grant you that, and likely to earn good money by and by. I shouldn't be after blamin' you for seizin' the chance of him.'

Sara opened her mouth, closed it, opened it again, then turned on her heel and made for the stairs. She was hot with rage – according to her hostess she was, in addition to being a Proddy, a fortune hunter as well! But down in the living room, she decided on a plan of action. From being tongue-tied and diffident, she became, once more, Miss Cordwainer of Aigburth Road. She talked amusingly about her work, the children in her care, the soup kitchens of the inner city. She showed a great interest in Peader's garden and insisted that he take her round it. She went up to the boys' room and admired the view, their pictures, the stories they told her. She did not have to woo Polly, who was frankly delighted to find that Brogan's young lady thought her dog a fine fellow, her cats beautiful, her hens useful and her rabbits sweet. She deferred constantly to Deirdre, tried to help her with the meal, admired her possessions and said the cottage was the prettiest house she had ever visited. Deirdre sniffed, snubbed her, turned the conversation, but she could not have complained about Sara's manners.

And by the time Brogan was helping Sara into her coat so that they would be in good time for their train, she knew she had won. They liked her! Well, everyone except Deirdre, and her mother-in-law, Sara thought sadly, was a lost cause. But the others would come to the wedding, though it would have to be a register office ceremony. They would wish her happy, even though they also wished her Catholic. It was the most she could hope for.

Christmas at Strawberry Field had been the happiest so far in Grace's entire life. She had loved every minute of it, from the excitement of Christmas Eve to the wonderful moment, on Christmas morning, when they had been taken to the Barracks to see the crib, and to join the rest of the congregation in praising God and singing their hearts out. And there was Christmas dinner – so much wonderful food – and present-giving round the tree, then Christmas tea – more wonderful food – and finally, stories round the fire before bed. The only disappointment, in fact, had been that Brogan was spending Christmas with his family.

Soon after Grace arrived at the Strawb, Peader had come into the city specially to see her, and it had been an emotional moment. Grace had stammered a few words of thanks, had muttered that it was her fault that he'd almost been killed . . . and Peader had enveloped her in a bear-hug, told her that the boot was on the other foot – if she'd not run like the very dickens he'd have been long dead, so he would – and invited her to visit him and his family at the crossing cottage, just as soon as it could be arranged.

Grace was absolutely delighted to find that she loved Peader just as much as she loved Brogan. 'They're goin' to ax me to stay,' she told Sara, beaming. 'They've gorra gel, you know, norra lot younger'n me – Polly she's called. If we gets on . . . well, it'll be nice, eh? Wish we was there now, Sara.'

Sara agreed, and admitted she missed Brogan too, which made Grace cast her a rather thoughtful look. She understood that she was a child and Sara was a young woman, so of course Sara spent more time with Brogan than she did, but she did hope Sara was not going to get ideas about Brogan. The Irishman was Grace's ideal and she had every intention of marrying him just as soon as she was old enough. But of course she had not told Brogan this, not yet. His surprise and delight she took for granted, but she wanted to be beautiful for him and that meant putting on more weight, brushing her hair – and teeth – with horrible and boring regularity, and taking baths.

Grace was not particularly keen on baths. Being in the warm water was nice enough, but she was secretly afraid of slipping beneath the surface and drowning, and she did hate getting out and having to rub herself dry. But Sara told her that young men like young ladies to be extremely clean, so Grace, gritting her teeth, bathed.

Not that Sara was right all the time. Grace knew a great many men who had married thoroughly dirty women – her father was one – and seemed to find clean ones daunting, not attractive at all. She said as much to Sara one evening when Sara had come back from a day out rather subdued. They were in the bathroom and Sara was getting earth out from under Grace's nails with a small object called an orange stick. Grace was complaining that she'd not have a fingerend left to bless herself with if Sara kept on digging like that and they were both laughing when Sara finished Grace's right hand – she had already done the left one – and stood back.

'There! Lovely nails, nice clean hair, and your skin's all pink and white now, after all this washing! And whatever you may say the nicest men all value cleanliness next to godliness ... it isn't just a biblical thing, love, it's actually true. And since you are becoming such a very pretty girl, I want to ask a favour of you.'

'Ask away, queen,' Grace said loftily. 'I'd do jest about anythin' for you, Sara, after all you done for me.'

'Well, I'm getting married, dear, and I'd love you to be a bridesmaid. It won't be a white wedding, it's going to take place in a register office because as you know I'm a Salvationist and Brogan's a Catholic, but ...'

'Brogan? Wharrever does it matter if Brogan's a Catholic or a Sally Ann?' Grace asked. 'He ain't bein' a bridesmaid too, I suppose?'

She meant it jokingly; she knew fellers weren't bridesmaids. Sara smiled, but it was perfunctorily.

'Oh, Grace, you know very well he isn't going to be a bridesmaid! He's the bridegroom, of course.'

There was a horrid silence. Grace, unable to believe her ears, tried to tell herself that a bridegroom was probably a male attendant to the feller Sara was marrying, but an awful suspicion had entered her mind.

'Bridegroom? Brogan? You do mean *our* Brogan, Sara? Brogan O'Brady?'

'That's it. We're getting married in a few weeks. I'm afraid his family aren't terribly pleased because ... '

'No!' Grace was so indignant that her voice came out as a squeak. 'No! I don't believe it!'

She meant she didn't – couldn't – believe that Brogan, *her* Brogan, had actually asked Sara to marry him. Oh, she knew they were *engaged*, whatever that might imply, but being married was different. Being married was for life, and she wanted to marry Brogan herself, they were well-suited, anyone could see that! But Sara immediately got hold of the wrong end of the stick.

'It's true. His family aren't very pleased because they want him to marry a Catholic. But we don't think it matters, Brogan and I, so ... '

Grace was dressed in her nightgown. Now she jammed her slippers on to her feet and flapped towards the door. 'I didn't mean ... I meant I won't be a bleedin' bridesmaid,' she called back over her shoulder. Her voice, to her horror, was distinctly wobbly. 'If 'e's so bleedin' stupid ... after all, it must ha' been clear ... why the *devil* couldn't 'e 'ave waited ... Well, I'm *not* goin' to be a bleedin' bridesmaid, no matter what you say!'

And she tore out of the bathroom, slamming the door so hard behind her that it echoed like a cannon shot.

Sara, thoroughly upset, ran out of the bathroom and, after a second's hesitation, into Grace's bedroom. It appeared to be empty, so she hurried down the stairs and into the kitchen. No Grace. Sara was about to try another room when the back door opened and Brogan, in his stockinged feet, came gingerly into the room.

'I've done the marrow bed ... ' he was beginning,

when he saw Sara's face. He crossed the kitchen in a couple of strides and took her in his arms. 'What's the matter, me love? Who's upset you?'

'Oh, Brog, I asked Grace to be my bridesmaid and she said no, and rushed out of the room,' Sara wailed, clutching him. 'I don't know what I've done wrong I'm sure; she's always seemed to like me, but . . .'

'I'll have a word,' Brogan said grimly. 'How can she upset you so, alanna, and you askin' her to stand by you on your weddin' day! Where's she gone?'

'I don't know,' Sara said, clinging on. 'Don't go after her, she's done nothing wrong, it's just . . . I really don't understand!'

'Nor me. Did she say anything else?' Brogan asked. 'Or did she just say *no* and leave the room?'

'She swore a bit, and said why couldn't he have waited, I think,' Sara said, having given the matter some thought. 'I don't know what she meant by that, but . . .'

'Oh dear,' Brogan said helplessly. 'Oh dear . . . I think I may know. I'd best have a word, love. Can you fetch her out – and then leave us for a few minutes?'

'Of course,' Sara said. She dried her eyes, blew her nose, then left the kitchen, to return presently with a defiant but red-eyed Grace, who marched into the room and sat herself down on the table edge, saying as she did so: 'She says you want a word wi' me, Brogan. I were 'avin' a quiet moment to meself, but she come and dug me out.'

'She was under her bed,' Sara said. 'Hiding! Really, Grace, I don't know what I've done, but . . .'

'I'm goin' to sort that out,' Brogan said soothingly. 'You go and finish your work, Miss Cordwainer, whilst Grace and I have a bit of a crack.' He waited until Sara had left the room, then turned to Grace, perching on the edge of the kitchen table and looking, even to Brogan's unaccustomed eyes, extremely defiant. 'Now, Grace, Miss Cordwainer told you she and I plan to marry quite soon, and she asked you to be her bridesmaid. I understand you turned us down.'

'Us? Well, yes, but you di'n't ask me, did you?' Grace said belligerently. 'You never even told me you was gettin' wed! You could of telled me!'

'Yes, I could. I'm sorry, Grace, if I hurt your feelings, but you see Sara and I have known each other for years, and you and I are quite new acquaintances, wouldn't you say?'

'I'd say friends,' Grace muttered, very red about the gills.

'All right, we're quite new friends, then. Isn't that so? Sara and I have known each other for ten years, you see.'

'I daresay,' Grace said. Her lip, to Brogan's alarm, first jutted and then trembled. 'But, Brogan, you're me best, me very best pal! I thought mebbe, one day . . .'

So I was right, Brogan thought, dismayed. The poor kid's gone and got a crush on me so she has. Now what am I to do?

'Sure an' you're me best pal too, Grace,' he said, playing for time. 'But when I first met Sara she was your age . . . about twelve. I've waited ten years . . .'

He let his voice trail into silence. Grace studied her hands, the scone dough, the floor at her feet. But when she did speak, her voice was gentle.

'Waitin's hard, ain't it, Brogan? Is that what you're tryin' to say? If you did . . . if you did wait, you'd be real old – is that it?'

Crossing his fingers for the half-lie, Brogan nodded. 'That's it, Grace. A feller can't wait for ever. And besides, in ten years' time you'll mebbe have met a nice young feller . . .'

'No I shan't,' Grace said. But she didn't sound fierce any more, just forlorn. 'I won't ever meet anyone like you, Brog.'

'No, you'll meet someone better,' Brogan assured her. 'Grace, will you please, please, be our bridesmaid? You'd make us both very happy, so you would.'

'Will I 'ave to wear flowers in me 'air?' Grace said suspiciously. 'I don't want the other kids mockin' me.'

'You'll wear whatever you're comfortable in,' Brogan assured her. 'Sara's goin' to buy you somethin' really nice – a dress, shoes, the lot. Look, alanna, I'm goin' to let you into a really big secret, something that not even Sara knows yet. Do you promise you won't tell?'

'I promise,' Grace said eagerly. Already her woes were lessening at the prospect of new clothes; now there was a secret, too.

'After we're wed, Sara an' me may be goin' to America to live. There's a better life there for a train driver, or so I've been told. And because you're goin' to be our bridesmaid we'd like you to come an' visit us there, in a year or so, when you're old enough for the journey.'

'America!' Before his eyes the small, pale face lit up, the grey eyes glowed. 'Oh, Brogan, will you write to me? I can save the stamps . . . you can tell me all sorts about wharrit's like over there. Ooh, think of the fillum stars you'll meet!'

The crisis was over, peace was restored. Brogan, promising to write to Grace as often as he possibly could, was thankful to have got over heavy ground so lightly.

And presently, when it was time for Brogan to leave and Sara walked him down to the gate, he was able to put an arm round her, give her a squeeze, and explain what had been the matter.

''Tis an odd thing when a child of twelve or thirteen thinks she's in love wit' a feller so it is,' he said. 'But I think she's over it, now.'

'What's odd about it?' Sara demanded, standing on tiptoe to kiss his cheek. 'I was a child of twelve or so when I first met you, and I fell in love then. Didn't you realise it, Brogan? Ah, what a modest soul you are!'

'I know,' Brogan said. 'I've a delightful nature so I have. And now I'd better love you and leave you, alanna, or I'll miss me tram.'

Chapter Seventeen

'But why won't you come, Mammy? You've always loved a wedding so you have and Sara's goin' to look a picture, Brogan says so. And the boys are comin', all the people from the Strawb... you'll miss out, Mammy!'

Polly's voice was pleading, but loud. She was standing before her mirror putting the finishing touches to her new dark-green coat and matching hat and Deirdre was in her own room across the landing. It was necessary to shout or the two could not have heard one another, and Polly felt that it was important to keep begging her mother to accompany them right up to the last moment. Peader had given up days ago and it had caused a rift between the two of them but Polly was sure that, given the chance, her mother would change her mind.

Polly had been looking forward to this wedding ever since Brogan had told them that it was to take place in early March and though she was not to be bridesmaid after all – Mammy had forbidden it – she was going to give the bride a lucky horseshoe before the happy couple got into the cab which would take them down to the docks. And this had meant a new coat and hat, new shoes and a great deal of fuss and excitement.

But from her mother's bedroom there came a low reply to Polly's shout. 'I'm not comin' to see me boy tied to a Proddy,' Deirdre said, with more than a trace of tears in her voice. 'Your daddy said I needn't, if I didn't want to, and I don't want to, so I'm not comin', and there's an end to it.'

Polly sighed. 'You're spoilin' our day, Mammy,' she said truthfully. 'It won't be the same wit'out you. Please, please come to the weddin'. If you don't, Brogan will be heartbroken so he will.'

This time, there was a snort.

'Oh, yes? Well, 'tis heartbroken his mammy is, I'm tellin' you. Darin' to tell me I was cruel to spoil that Proddy madam's big day . . . I only wish I might!'

Polly sighed again, gave a last glance in the mirror, and headed for the stairs. 'All right, Mammy,' she said kindly. 'You stay at home and be miserable. Daddy says I may hold his arm like a grown-up lady, and at the hooley afterwards I'm to have a sip of wine and a big piece of weddin' cake.'

Silence.

'Ivan's wearin' his white carnation already,' Polly went on as she descended the stairs. 'He looks a proper little man, Mammy. Oh . . . you won't forget to feed Delly and the cats? And me hens, me rabbits . . . best check on the eggs, because the speckled hen kicks them out of the nest if you aren't careful.' Polly reached the hall where the rest of the family waited. They were to catch an early train into the city centre. She raised her voice. 'Bye, Mammy. Have a nice day, now!'

Silence.

'Never mind, alanna,' Peader said, seeing his little daughter's face fall as her mother failed to so much as come to the head of the stairs to wave them off. 'We're goin' to have a grand day so we are. My goodness, don't you look a sight for sore eyes?'

'She's not so dusty,' Ivan said. He was very conscious of his new suit and the huge buttonhole which tickled against his chin. 'Aw, c'mon, Poll, don't keep lookin' over your shoulder! We've a good walk to get to the station, remember.'

Sara was crying. Now that it had come to it, she was realising how much she'd miss the Strawb, the other staff, the children. And though she longed to be Brogan's wife, she hadn't really thought that they would have to go off to the United States of America as soon as the knot was tied. But things were difficult, she acknowledged that. Folk were so tight-lipped, so disapproving of their union, as though the fact that Sara was a Salvationist and Brogan a Catholic should have made their love – and their marriage – unthinkable.

'Sara, me love, we'd be very uncomfortable livin' in the centre of Liverpool, wit' such strong disapproval all around us, to say nothin' of bricks t'rough the winders an kids shoutin' in the street,' Brogan had said when he had told her they would be having their honeymoon aboard a transatlantic liner bound for the port of New York. 'I took you home once, and Mammy wasn't kind to you. And when the babies come, what d'you t'ink folk will say then, eh? We're best out of it.'

'But what'll we live on, until we find work?' Sara had said, stalling desperately. 'Can't we just try it here first, Brog?'

'We'll live on my wages as an engineer,' Brogan said, trying not to sound proud with a total lack of success. 'I've got a job to go to, alanna. I had me certificates copied in a fair hand and I listed all me experience, got some good references, and I sent the whole lot off to Niall. He got me a job wit' a railroad company, starting two weeks after we land. So what about that, eh?'

She had had to say it was wonderful, that he was

wonderful, and it *was*. But America was a long way away and she was giving up her career, her home . . .

'The Army's waiting for you across the water,' the brigadier said comfortingly when Sara tried to explain how she felt. 'You can go on with your career over there if you wish to do so, or you can simply continue to worship with your fellow Salvationists. My poor child, you won't be lonely or left out, not if you go to the nearest citadel and tell them you're an Army lass.'

But it was a big step, and one that Sara was reluctant to take whilst Brogan and his mother were still at odds with one another. So yesterday she had telephoned to the crossing cottage and spoken to Peader.

'We're going so far away, Mr O'Brady,' she had said. 'Can't you persuade your wife to come along, just to bid us goodbye? Brogan can't believe she'll let him down when she's been such a wonderful mother to him.'

But Peader had told her that he'd been forced to agree that Deirdre should stay at home.

'Better that than spoilin' your weddin' wit' a long face,' he'd said heavily. 'I'm disappointed in Mrs O'Brady, I am indeed. But the rest of us will be there to wish you well.'

So be thankful for small mercies and stop behaving like a spoilt baby, Sara scolded herself, carefully wiping her tears away on a small linen handkerchief. Grace will be here any moment and I don't want to show her a long face. She really would tell me off, since I'm the happiest, luckiest person on earth today!

And presently Grace came knocking on the door, resplendent in a smart pink coat with a black velvet collar, a lovely furry muff and patent leather strap shoes. Sara, eyeing her appreciatively, thought her a far cry from the draggly, raggedy orphan-child who, only months before, had been begging outside the Great Mersey public house.

'You look lovely, Miss Cordwainer,' Grace said shyly, coming fully into the room. 'Wharrabout me, eh? Awright, am I?'

'You're a picture, Grace,' Sara said warmly. 'Is it time to go down yet?'

'I reckon. The brig called out the car's 'ere, anyroad.'

'Right.' Sara took one last, long look at herself in her mirror. She saw a slender, pale young woman in a cream-coloured dress with a leaf-green coat over it. Her hair was piled on top of her head in a coronet of dark curls and she was carrying a bouquet of spring flowers. 'Off we go then, Grace!'

Polly found the wedding service disappointing, but then Daddy had warned her it wouldn't be like a proper church wedding. Still, it didn't take long, that was one advantage, and afterwards they went back to the Strawb for a bit of a hooley and then it was into the cars and down to the docks. Polly had watched Grace being a bridesmaid enviously and as soon as the ceremony was over the two girls got together and started chattering for all the world, Peader said, as though they'd known each other for ever.

'You must come and stay wit' us at our cottage out in the country, alanna,' he said to Grace. 'Our Polleen would like that, wouldn't you, Poll? And then you can talk until the cows come home.'

Polly said she would like that and Grace, her whole face brightening, said it would be prime. 'I ain't never been in the country, norrin the 'ole of me life,' she told Polly. 'But I reckon I'll like it more'n any old city. I could 'elp Mr O'Brady in your garden – I'm a dab 'and at gardenin' thanks to Brogan.'

And when the party made its way down to the docks the two girls stood together, both with hands plunged into their coat pockets so that they could bombard the bride and groom with confetti as they arrived to board the ship. Polly was wildly excited but she knew tears were not far distant, and she saw that Grace was similarly affected. Oh, I suppose she loves Miss Cordwainer – Sara – like I love Brogan, Polly thought to herself. And poor Grace must hate the thought of her going off, perhaps for ever, to another country, like I hate Brogan leaving. It was all very well for her daddy to say Polly could go and visit him there, but that was what they said about Tad and it hadn't happened; she doubted that it ever would.

And then the bride and groom arrived, and the confetti was thrown and there were huggings and kissings and quite a lot of crying. And then Brogan, with his arm round Sara, led her up the gangplank and on to the ship and the O'Bradys stood and waved and waved and Polly felt tears begin to slide down her cheeks and saw, beside her, that Grace was crying too.

Deirdre had told Peader that she would take care of his crossing for him, so she was rather indignant when a tall young man with very pale skin and bright ginger hair turned up about half an hour after the party had left and informed her that he was her husband's stand-in.

'I'm to stay until the weddin' party gets home,' he said. 'Mr O'Brady said there would be a dinner standin' by the oven waitin' to be popped inside, an' I've gorra list of all the trains. So any time you like to leave, Mrs O'Brady . . .'

I couldn't stay, after that, Deirdre told herself, changing hastily into her best coat and hat and putting on her smartest shoes. I might as well just walk down to the village, I might do a bit of shopping, wait and meet the train . . .

Lime Street station is an enormous, echoing place when you're by yourself, but by now, Deirdre had acknowledged that she would go down to the docks. She would make sure no one saw her, but she would watch Brogan and that stuck-up little madam going off on the liner. And later she'd find Peader and the others and perhaps, because she had journeyed this far, Peader would stop being tight-lipped over her behaviour.

Because I'm right, I know I am, Deirdre told herself, emerging from Lime Street and gazing across at St George's Plain. 'Tis a wrong thing for a Catholic to marry someone who isn't, and they can't say different. Why, even the Army folk must be disappointed that the girl hasn't found herself a feller in their ranks.

Having crossed the busy roadway, Deirdre found herself by the statue of a huge black horse with an old-fashioned-looking woman on its back. Close to the statue taxi cabs stood waiting for fares and on impulse, Deirdre jumped into the nearest. The driver slid back the glass pane which separated them and asked her where she wanted to go. His accent, to Deirdre's pleasure, was warmly Irish.

'Me son's off to America this afternoon, I'm not sure . . .' she began, but apparently this was enough.

'The docks, right? Sure and I'll take you as near as I can get you, missus.' He drove for a short way through the bustling streets, then half-turned to say conversationally, 'Your son'll be on the SS *Europa*, I daresay? We'll 'ave to make it snappy, she sails on the tide.'

Sara got out of the taxi and crossed the dock to the

gangplank which she would presently ascend, then turned to the wedding party, who, unencumbered by luggage, had arrived at the quayside first. She kissed her brand-new father-in-law, her brothers-in-law and her pretty little sister-in-law and told them she would write often. Then she hugged Grace and thanked her for being such an excellent bridesmaid, and thanked Clarrie for giving her away – lacking a relative wishing to do the job she had appealed to Clarrie and her friend had obliged. Then she shook hands with the other staff members who had come to see her off, and took Brogan's hand. There was a great bustle aboard the ship which, she assumed, meant that they should be aboard so with a final round of goodbyes she and Brogan began to ascend the gangplank. Halfway up Sara had an urge to change her mind to return to the quayside, but Brogan, apparently guessing how she felt, slid a strong arm about her waist, his calm, loving presence reassuring her that she was doing the right thing.

They reached the deck.

'I told the family not to come aboard, I said parting once was bad enough,' Brogan whispered in her ear. 'Daddy's goin' to get them all back to the Strawb, where Matron's goin' to give them a supper before they get their train. We'll go below presently and take a look at our cabin, but not until we've waved them off.'

The two of them stood by the rail and waved until their family and friends had all gone, then Brogan turned to her. He smiled and squeezed her hand.

'Come on, let's find the cabin.'

It was a nice cabin, an outside one, which meant that they could look down on to the quay, far below. Brogan took off his heavy coat and hung it in the tiny wardrobe, then put a cautious hand on the bed.

'Nice and soft,' he said. 'We're all right there!'

Sara knew she should have laughed, made some joking reply, but she felt silly, unsure. Deep in the bowels of the ship the engines were rumbling, and the huge craft was beginning to sway slightly. It would not be long now before they sailed, she supposed, and felt vulnerable, uneasily aware that her whole life had now changed. She was in Brogan's charge and he was in hers. Oh, dear God, let us make a success of this strange thing called marriage, she prayed confusedly as she took off her coat and hat. She hung them up, then wandered over to the mirror. Standing before it, she smoothed her hair with shaking hands, then began to fiddle with the string of beads round her throat. Trying to keep her voice steady she said as brightly as she could: 'Are we about to sail, Brog? Should we go on deck?'

'I thought you might prefer a quiet . . .' Brogan began, then nodded, with so much loving understanding in his eyes that Sara could have wept all over again, except that she was determined to do no such thing. 'Yes, why not? Come on then, Mrs O'Brady!'

They left the cabin, climbed the companionway and crossed the crowded deck. They managed to find a spot by the rail and Brogan put his arm around her as though it belonged there. His head was so close to hers that she could feel his breath on her cheek, stirring her hair.

'All right, sweetheart? Are you goin' to give the old Liver birds a wave, then, to say goodbye? Any moment now the gangplank will be wound in and they'll cast off and – ' He broke off. 'Mary Mother of Jesus . . . what's goin' on?'

Someone was running up the gangplank, they could see it bouncing from where they stood. There were shouts from the deck – the sailors had been hurrying about, clearly intending to cast off – but the figure continued to come doggedly on.

'Someone nearly missed the boat,' Sara said, trying to make a joke of it. 'Oh, Brogan, it looks like . . .'

'Mammy!' Brogan said. He seized Sara exuberantly round the waist and almost carried her towards where his mother was arguing animatedly with the seamen at the top of the gangplank. 'She's come after all so she has!'

They reached the gangplank breathless, beaming. Deirdre took one look at them and then suddenly she was in Brogan's arms, reaching out a hand, pulling Sara, too, into her embrace.

'I'm sorry I didn't make the weddin',' Deirdre panted. 'I – I just wanted to say goodbye and to wish you happy!' And before either Sara or Brogan could say a word she had reached up and kissed her daughter-in-law heartily on the cheek. 'Now be good to me son,' she instructed, her voice tear-filled but determined. 'Sure an' you'll make him a broth of a wife so you will!'

'Madam, are you a passenger on this ship?' The officer who had spoken took Deirdre's arm in a firm grip. 'You really must go, visitors were asked to leave some while ago, we're about to set sail, you know.'

'It's all right, officer, I'll go quietly now I've said goodbye to me son and his new wife,' Deirdre said soothingly. She turned back to Sara and gave her, for the first time ever, a clear-eyed glance and a gentle, affectionate smile. 'Take care of him, me dear girl,' she said softly. 'And may God bless you both.'

When they could see no land, when the bounding ocean lay all around them, Brogan and Sara returned to their cabin and walked straight into each other's arms. For a moment they just hugged, wordlessly, tightly, then Brogan held her back from him and kissed her brow, her eyelids, her tear-wet cheeks.

'Darlin' Sara, 'tis a big step we're takin', but we're takin' it together and it's an adventure, so it is. All right?'

Sara smiled at him. 'All right, Brog,' she said. 'I can't think of anyone I'd rather have beside me on an adventure, either. Shall we find the dining room and get ourselves some dinner?'

Brogan sat down on the bed and pulled her down beside him. Then, very gently, he began to kiss the side of her neck, her face, her small, rosy ear. 'Sara?' he murmured. 'Are you sure you're wantin' your dinner now?'

Sara sighed tremulously. 'Well, I daresay I could wait for a bit, if you aren't too hungry,' she said.

Outside the cabin the sun sank in the west and the seabirds hawked and called. On deck the lights came on, passengers made their way to the dining room, to the bars and lounges. But in their small cabin, holding each other close, Brogan and Sara were oblivious. Dinner was forgotten, Liverpool might have happened in another life, America was just a dream. Brogan O'Brady and his new wife were learning to love one another.

Epilogue

It was two days since the wedding and life in the crossing cottage was returning to normal after all the excitement. And in the little bedroom overlooking the railway line, Polly lay on her tummy and, with considerable pauses for thought, wrote a letter.

Dear Tad,

Well, it was a wonderful wedding so it was and the hooley after was grand, too. I met a girl called Grace, she was nice, and all the other people were nice as well. We went and waved to Brogan and Sara and Mammy wasn't there then, but she went after. I've already told you about me animals and how happy we all are. Only I would rather be back in the Liberties, with you. I go to a nice school in a nice village and I have found some nice friends. Mammy says they're Proddies but they are all right, you'd like 'em. Only they are none of them as nice as you. There isn't a church too near so we can't go every Sunday which is great, but when I do go it is just like home in there and I think about you. You would like it here, honest to God you would, Tad. There is so much countryside, you have no idea, it stretches for miles and miles. I can pick blackers every day if I like and paddle in the brook which is just like the canal only not so big and a lot wigglier. My teacher is pretty, she says I read and write good for my age, she says I might go to the grammar school if I work hard.

Polly paused, sucking the end of her pencil. The trouble was, the only words she had were words which Tad, in his wisdom, would probably think soppy. But there you were. She would have to say them, it was the whole reason she was writing.

Mammy and Daddy like it here and so do the boys. It is fun to open and close the gate so's the cars and lorries and tractors can get by. The farm hands call me 'Ginger' and tease me but they bring me fruit and sweets so I don't mind. I could box the fox every day if I wanted but I don't, because we have apple trees and a pear tree and two plum trees of our own – think of that, Tad!

Polly paused again and gave her pencil another chew. She had written to Tad three times already and hadn't had a single reply. She had better threaten him a little. *This is me third letter to you, Tad, where is yours to me?* she enquired laboriously. He wouldn't like it, but you needed a reply now and then else you got discouraged and gave up. *I can't write for ever when I don't know if you're getting the letters. And Tad, please don't forget we're going to get married when we're big. Because* . . . Could she say it? Could she risk either his wrath or his mirth? But she knew she would have to, because Brogan had told her how he'd nearly lost his Sara through being afraid to speak out, and she did not intend to lose Tad, not she! . . . *Because I love you, Tad Donoghue,* she wrote at last, then rolled over on to her back and read the letter through, word by word, right down to the very end where she had bared her soul, her heart . . . ah, if that bloody Tad Donoghue laughed . . . didn't reply . . .

She signed off. *Please write back quick. Your loving Polly O'Brady.* Then she got off her bed and went over to the windowseat. If she looked far into the distance and let her eyes go all unfocussed she could imagine she was looking right across the country, across the sea . . . yes, there it was, way, way in the distance.

Dublin. The Liberties. Tad Donoghue.

You could go a long way for someone you loved, Polly mused, turning away from the window. Look at Brogan now, going all the way to the United States of America so that he and his Sara could be together without fighting and argument. So if she was serious about Tad, and she was, she would go back for him. Or possibly he would come over here for her. It didn't much matter, so long as they ended up together.

Polly crossed the bedroom and went out on to the small landing. Spring was coming and outside a sweet breeze blew in through the tiny open window which looked out over miles and miles of rolling countryside, to the hills of Wales beyond. Polly glanced down the stairwell; if she wanted to go for a run with Delilah before tea was served she would have to get a move on.

With the letter in her hand she began to descend the stairs and when she reached the bottom she closed both eyes and prayed. Let Tad get my letter, and let him write back, she begged. And then she addressed herself to her guardian angel. If you love me, could you just fly off to Dublin for a bit, an' keep an eye on Tad Donoghue for me? He's a naughty chiseller, but his heart's in the right place so it is, and I'm none too sure he's got an angel of his own. But I've got so much, me mammy, me daddy, me friends and me home. So please, Angel, wherever you are, give a t'ought to Tad.

Polly opened her eyes and just for an instant, in the darkness of the downstairs hallway, she thought she saw someone . . . something. Faint as mist, gentle as the spring breeze, her guardian angel smiled on Polly O'Brady.

THE MERSEY GIRLS

Katie Flynn

Spring 1913, and seventeen-year-old Evie Murphy is leaving her native Ireland for the city of Liverpool with her baby daughter Linnet – but leaving Linnet's frail twin, Lucy, behind.

But there are mixed fortunes ahead for Evie, and while Lucy grows up in the beautiful Irish countryside, Linnet is all too often forced to throw herself on the mercy of the enormous, impoverished Sullivan family. Life in a slum court during the thirties is far from easy – but when tragedy strikes it becomes the only existence possible for Linnet. Destitute, she disappears into the Liverpool slums like a teardrop in an ocean.

Lucy, meanwhile, urgently needs her sister by her side. But she has little idea, when she leaves the farm and sets off to look for Linnet, how their meeting will change their lives for ever . . .

RAINBOW'S END

Katie Flynn

Liverpool, 1904. When Ada Docherty gives birth to twins in her tiny house in Evangelist Court, she has no choice but to make Ellen, her eldest daughter, bring them up, for she must work to feed seven hungry mouths.

But in Dublin, Maggie McVeigh's lot is even harder, for she sleeps on straw in a tumbledown tenement. When a local woman, Mrs Nolan, needs someone to look after her sons, Maggie takes on the job and finds security and comfort – and love, too, with the eldest boy, Liam.

With the outbreak of war, life changes dramatically. Ellen, newly in love, follows her young man to France – but does he share her feelings? A tragedy sends Liam off to the trenches, whilst at home wartime shortages and a constant stream of bad news affect both families. But a surprise awaits them . . .

Let yourself be swept away by this warm and delightful story of two families struggling through poverty and hardship to reach their Rainbow's End.

LIVERPOOL TAFFY

Katie Flynn

Life is hard in 1930s Liverpool, and Biddy O'Shaughnessy is left destitute when her widowed mother dies. She finds herself forced to work all hours, seven days a week, for Ma Kettle, owner of the local sweet shop. Soon she can take no more and she does the unthinkable and runs away. But luck appears to be on her side. Sharing a flat with Ellen, an old schoolchum who has a special 'friend' paying the rent, keeps the wolf from the door. Then fate conspires against them and Biddy finds herself homeless once more, living rough on the mean streets of Liverpool with no one to turn to.

When she applies for the post of maid with the Gallagher family, Biddy starts to feel she might at last be able to lead a normal life. It is a feeling that is strengthened when she meets Dai, a young Welshman working the trawlers. But Nellie Gallagher, despite appearances, has a secret that will change all their lives . . .

ROSE OF TRALEE

Katie Flynn

The year is 1925, and in Liverpool Jack Ryder, a tramdriver, and his wife Lily are bringing up their only child, Rose, to be as decent and hardworking as themselves. But Lily's sister Daisy and her daughter Mona live very differently. Daisy is a lazy slut, and Mona no better than she ought to be, and Jack discourages any friendship between Rose and her cousin.

Over in Dublin, Eileen O'Neill has to bring up her children alone, since her husband Sean is working in England. Colm is a good son to her and takes care of his little sister Caitlin in addition to working hard at any job he can get. However, when Colm is sacked, Sean insists that his son goes with him to England because work is starting on the Mersey tunnel and labourers are needed.

When tragedy strikes Rose's family, they are forced to take in boarders, including Mona. And it is to the Ryders's boarding house in St Domingo Vale that Colm and his father come when they arrive in Liverpool. . .

OTHER BESTSELLING TITLES AVAILABLE

☐ Liverpool Lass	Katie Flynn	£5.99
☐ The Girl From Penny Lane	Katie Flynn	£5.99
☐ Liverpool Taffy	Katie Flynn	£5.99
☐ The Mersey Girls	Katie Flynn	£5.99
☐ Rainbow's End	Katie Flynn	£5.99
☐ Rose of Tralee	Katie Flynn	£5.99
☐ Family Feeling	Judith Saxton	£5.99
☐ This Royal Breed	Judith Saxton	£5.99
☐ The Glory	Judith Saxton	£5.99
☐ No Silver Spoon	Katie Flynn	£5.99
☐ Polly's Angel	Katie Flynn	£5.99

ALL ARROW BOOKS ARE AVAILABLE THROUGH MAIL ORDER OR FROM YOUR LOCAL BOOKSHOP.

PAYMENT MAY BE MADE USING ACCESS, VISA, MASTER-CARD, DINERS CLUB, SWITCH AND AMEX, OR CHEQUE, EUROCHEQUE AND POSTAL ORDER (STERLING ONLY).

EXPIRY DATE .... SWITCH ISSUE NO.

SIGNATURE ....

PLEASE ALLOW £2.50 FOR POST AND PACKING FOR THE FIRST BOOK AND £1.00 PER BOOK THEREAFTER.

ORDER TOTAL: £.................................. (INCLUDING P&P)

ALL ORDERS TO:
ARROW BOOKS, BOOKS BY POST, TBS LIMITED, THE BOOK SERVICE, COLCHESTER ROAD, FRATING GREEN, COLCHESTER, ESSEX, CO7 7 DW, UK.

TELEPHONE: (01206) 256 000
FAX: (01206) 255 914

NAME ....

ADDRESS...

....

Please allow 28 days for delivery. Please tick box if you do not wish to receive any additional information. ☐
Prices and availability subject to change without notice.